UNJUST

Brooke Holmes, J.D.

Content Warning:
This book contains sensitive content regarding a sexual assault that may be upsetting to some readers.

ISBN 13: 978-1-63489-630-6

Library of Congress Catalog Number has been applied for.
Printed in the United States of America
First Printing: 2022

27 26 25 24 23 5 4 3 2 1

Cover design by Emily Mahon
Interior design by Jen Rich

Wise Ink Creative Publishing
807 Broadway St. NE
Suite 46
Minneapolis, MN 55413

To my family and friends who have supported and believed in me throughout this process.

TK table of contents

CHAPTER ONE

Maxwell Williams sat in his chair at the counsel table wearing his thrift store suit jacket and matching black pants that Jason Michelson had lent him. He sat in the middle chair with Jason on one side. The chair on the other side was empty, as Rachel Nix was finishing her closing statement to the jury. Maxwell was trying his best not to let his anxiety show. A bead of sweat slowly dripped down his face. It was May 20, 2022, and it had just started to get warmer outside in the Minnesota spring. The Hennepin County Courthouse had not turned on the air conditioning yet, and that, mixed with the nervousness that Maxwell was feeling, had him sweating.

He had been here before, back in 1982. Maxwell was sitting in the courtroom next to his attorney Mr. Duncan. The courtroom looked the same then as it did now—two counsel tables, one with him and his attorney and the other with the county attorney and his staff. The judge was seated up at the bench, which was a dark brown mahogany that gave off a scary vibe. The jurors were seated in the jury box, fourteen of them. Not a single Black person sat on the jury at his first trial, despite his attorney's efforts. In reality, there was no chance of that happening. Maxwell Williams, a black man, was accused of killing his white girlfriend, who came from a prominent family. He should have known there was no way a jury was going to find him not guilty.

He was still unable to comprehend how he had gotten to this

point. Maxwell loved Amelia, and the fact that he was on trial for her murder was unimaginable. He kept asking himself throughout the trial how he had gotten here. His hands were shaking uncontrollably, so his attorney had told him to place them in his lap under the table. He could not give the jury a reason to believe that he was guilty. Despite his attorney's best efforts, the first jury had found him guilty. That is why he was back in court.

He had listened to the closing arguments from the State, then Mr. Duncan, giving the defense's closing argument. The State then had the opportunity to give a response to the defense's closing. They got the last word. That never seemed fair to Maxwell. It was his life on the line. Why did they get to go last? He had asked Mr. Duncan about that in his first trial, and he told Maxwell it was because the State had the burden of proof. The State had to prove that Maxwell was guilty of the charges beyond a reasonable doubt. Maxwell didn't quite understand what that meant, but it had sounded like a hard thing to do.

Unfortunately, in the first trial, it proved not to be that hard. The jurors had found him guilty in October of 1982 of burglarizing, sexually assaulting, and killing his girlfriend, Amelia Jackson. He had sat through the whole trial in 1982, and he wasn't convinced that the State had proven the case. He just didn't believe the evidence was there. Why would he have killed Amelia? What was his motive or whatever you called it? The simple answer is that there wasn't one. Maxwell never wanted anything to happen to Amelia. He loved her and had planned on marrying her.

Maxwell could have been biased, though, because he knew he didn't commit the crimes. He had been home the day Amelia died. He had ordered food an hour or so before she was killed. The delivery man saw him at his apartment. How could a jury believe that he then went over to his girlfriend's house and attacked her? It didn't make sense. Looking back, he always wondered if he had lost because of his attorney. He had a public defender at the time because he was just a broke college student. There was no way that he could have afforded an attorney to defend him in a trial, let alone a murder trial. Maxwell had not realized the gravity of the situation as he sat in the dreary courtroom that day in 1982 when the jury read the verdict. Sitting in his prison cell over the last forty years, Maxwell often wondered if things would have been different if he could have afforded an attorney. He had gone through all of the what ifs a hundred times. It didn't do him any good.

Most of the first trial had been a blur and Maxwell did not understand all of what was happening. It was so surreal as he was asked to stand and the court reporter stated: "In the matter of *State of Minnesota v. Maxwell James Williams*, Count I, burglary in the first degree, we, the jury, find the defendant guilty."

Maxwell had felt the air leaving his body. During the jury's deliberations, his public defender had explained that if they came back with a guilty verdict on the burglary, they would likely find him guilty across the board. There were cries around him in the courtroom. They came from his family, who was sitting in the gallery behind him. His mom, dad, two brothers, and sister had all come to support him. They sat through every second of that first trial. There were also relieved cries from Amelia's family sitting behind the State's counsel table.

The court reporter continued, "Count II, sexual assault in the first degree, we, the jury, find the defendant guilty." With each guilty verdict Maxwell felt more numb. "Count III, murder in the first degree, we, the jury, find the defendant guilty." Maxwell's soul felt like it was leaving his body as the jury read the final verdict in his trial. Even then, he did not realize the gravity of what was happening. He was going to prison, for a very long time. He wouldn't be sentenced for another two months, so he sat in the Hennepin County Jail until his sentencing. After the sentencing, he went to prison, where he had been day in and day out since that time, knowing that he was in prison for a crime he didn't commit.

It wasn't until 2021, when Rachel Nix from the Exoneration Project reached out to him and let him know that they were taking on his case, that he had felt alive again. It was the first time in almost forty years that he had hope that he was not going to spend the rest of his life behind bars. He had people who believed he was innocent and were on his side and going to fight for him. He *needed* them to fight for him until he could get to a place where he could fight for himself again.

Rachel had come to visit him in prison. Maxwell remembered her walking in with her dark green suit on. He thought to himself how confident she looked, and he instantly felt like he could trust that his case was in good hands. The two of them talked and talked for what seemed like hours, which it really was. Rachel had spent almost three hours with him at that first meeting, going over every inch of the case. She answered all of his questions that she could and spent the time explaining the aspects of the trial that he had never understood the first time through. After Rachel left the prison that day, Maxwell felt the first inkling of hope. She had been blunt with him and explained that winning the appeal wasn't a sure thing by any means, and that if they won the appeal, the new trial would be an even bigger hurdle. He understood all of that, but someone believed him, and that was a huge win itself in Maxwell's eyes.

That had been more than a year ago, and now they sat in the Hennepin County Courthouse waiting for closing arguments to finish. By the time they had gotten to trial, Maxwell went into it with high hopes that the jury would get it right this time. He was playing back the first trial in his head as Rachel finished up her closing argument.

He had heard her run through the closing a few times before, so he knew she was finishing up when he heard her say, "It is simple. The State has not gotten anywhere close to proving their burden.

They have not proven beyond a reasonable doubt that Maxwell Williams committed the crimes he is accused of. They cannot prove it, because he did not do it." She emphasized each of those words: He . . . did . . . not . . . do . . . it. Some of the jurors seemed to nod in agreement.

"Maxwell Williams is here today asking that you find him not guilty of the charges against him, and set him free from this nightmare he has been living these past forty years. Correct the wrong decision that the jury made forty years ago. Give Maxwell Williams his life back. We owe him that much." Rachel stopped for a dramatic pause to let that last part sink in, seeming to make eye contact with each juror individually. "Thank you," she said as she walked back to her seat and sat back down next to Maxwell. Jason put a hand on Maxwell's arm in a supportive manner, and Rachel put her hand on his. This was not only a signal to the jury that they fully supported Maxwell, but also a sign to him that they were all in this together.

Jeff Malone, the prosecutor, stood up and walked over to the lectern. "Ms. Nix has a way with words," he said. "Don't let her romance you. Just because she says we have not met our burden and that Maxwell Williams is not guilty doesn't make it true. You have all been sitting here throughout the trial. You have each heard the evidence against him. Maxwell Williams did this. The evidence proves that beyond a reasonable doubt. Don't let your emotions get in the way and feel sorry for Mr. Williams because he spent the last forty years in prison. He deserved to be in prison and he deserves to stay there." As he said the word "deserved," his voice dripped with contempt. The prosecutor seemed to have a hatred for Maxwell Williams, and he wanted to convince the jurors to have that same hatred. He continued, "The defendant broke into Amelia Jackson's home that afternoon. He held her down and raped her. She was lying there scared, confused, wondering how someone who supposedly loved her could be doing these things to her.

"If assaulting her weren't enough, the defendant ended Amelia's life that day. He grabbed a knife from her own kitchen and stabbed her. He stabbed her over and over again until her body was lifeless. Can you imagine what was going through Amelia's head the first time he stabbed her? Did she know she was going to die that day? Was she thinking about what she could have done differently? Was she thinking about, or calling out for, her mom or her dad? We will never know.

"Amelia Jackson died a horrific death that day in her apartment. While we may not know what her exact thoughts were while she took her last breath, we do know that she had to have been terrified. He did that." Jeff pointed to Maxwell. "Maxwell Williams did that. There is no doubt about that. We, the State, ask that you find him guilty of the charges against him. Thank you."

Jeff walked back to his seat at the other table and sat down. He had an accomplished look on his face. Maxwell's anxiety began to rise. His emotions were like a rollercoaster. That closing was good. Way better than the prosecutor's in the first case. This guy had sounded so good, he almost had Maxwell convinced he committed the crimes. He began to shake his knee up and down, a nervous tic that had begun when he was in middle school and his test anxiety started. Jason put his hand under the table and on Maxwell's knee to calm him. They had talked about this; he should try to stay calm and collected in front of the jury. They didn't want the jurors to see Maxwell sweat or have any nerves—nothing that would signify that he was guilty. He had to exude confidence that his conscience was clear, and he was innocent. That was easier said than done.

Maxwell took a deep and slow breath, trying to calm down. They had given it their all and put forth the best defense possible. Of course, there were a few hiccups along the way, but Rachel assured him that was normal. It was out of their hands now and in the jury's hands. The judge spent what seemed like two hours going over the jury instructions and verdict forms. Maxwell knew from experience that this wasn't even the worst part. The worst part was the waiting while the jury deliberated.

In the first trial, the jury had been out for almost seven hours before they came back with their guilty verdicts. During those seven hours, Maxwell was fairly confident that the jury had seen the truth. Boy, was he wrong. He thought back to what he had done while he waited the first time. Not realizing the gravity of it all, he had spent his last hours as a free man doing things that had no meaning. They were so meaningless that he couldn't even remember exactly what he did.

He did spend some time with his family, which was good, but it wasn't quality time. He should have spent those last hours talking, hugging, and crying with them. They deserved it. If he had known that would have been the last time that he could have physical contact with them, he would have hugged them a little longer and a little tighter. Instead, his young, overly confident self figured he would be going home with them that night.

"Are there any questions?" the judge asked the jurors. Maxwell realized that he had been zoned out and in his own thoughts. When nobody raised any hands and there was a general consensus of heads shaking no, the judge dismissed them from the courtroom to start deliberations. Everyone stood as they left the room.

"It's 3:47 p.m.," Rachel said, stating the official start time of deliberations, after the judge dismissed them as well. There were no other cases scheduled in this courtroom, so the three of them left all of their stuff there. They walked out to a conference room right outside the courtroom and sat down. "How are you feeling?" Rachel asked Maxwell.

"His closing was really good," Maxwell said with concern in his voice. "Don't get me wrong, Rachel, you did amazing. I'm just worried because that was the last thing the jurors heard before going back there. He did way better than the first prosecutor, and they found me guilty then."

"That's true," Jason admitted, a lingering note of concern in his voice as well. Rachel shot him a look that said he wasn't helping. "But remember, the jury didn't have all the facts back then. The prosecutor didn't turn them over the first time. They had the deck stacked against you. I am feeling optimistic," Jason said, though he wasn't sure he believed that himself. The truth was that he was worried. Rachel had done amazingly well, but so had Jeff Malone. The trial had gone anything but smoothly.

It was done now, and they had all done the best they could. Now all they could do was wait. The three of them sat in the small conference room exchanging small talk nervously, each of them momentarily glancing at their watch, phone, or the clock on the wall every few minutes to see how much time had passed. Minutes felt like hours. About an hour into deliberations, Jason went and grabbed his laptop and said he might as well get some work done while they waited.

Rachel decided to work on some things too, and Maxwell had brought a book with him from the prison to read during the wait. Suddenly there was a knock at the door. Everyone seemed to simultaneously hold their breath. Jason looked at the time on his laptop: 6:24 p.m. There was no way they were back with a verdict already, he thought to himself. Rachel waved the bailiff in.

"The judge wants everyone back in the courtroom," he said.

"Is there a verdict?" Rachel asked, her voice shaky and uncertain. The silence for those few seconds felt like it dragged on.

The bailiff answered, "No. They are still deliberating. I think the judge is going to send everyone home for the night."

"Everyone, except for me," Maxwell said. He looked around and said, "Sorry. I didn't mean to say that out loud." He lowered his head in shame. He would not get to leave like everyone else. The only way he was leaving the courthouse or jail was if the jury came back with "not guilty" verdicts across the board. The judge had denied their motions for bail while waiting for the retrial to happen. Maxwell was stuck in jail until the jury made their decision, and then possibly heading back to prison. He pushed those thoughts aside.

Jason and Rachel packed up their things, and Maxwell grabbed his book. They walked out of the conference room and waited as the bailiff unlocked the courtroom door. He held the door open for them as they walked in and sat back down on their side. They sat in silence for five minutes while they waited for Jeff to arrive. He came in looking flushed, as if he had just run to get back. He looked over at them and must have felt the need for an explanation. "I had gone home to help put the kids to bed. Had to quickly get dressed again and get back here."

Jason and Rachel just nodded their understanding—even though neither had kids, so they really didn't understand. Maxwell sat silently, looking forward, not wanting to make eye contact with Jeff. He'd had the chance not to pursue the charges against Maxwell again after Rachel and Jason pointed out the missteps the first prosecutor made. He did not relent, though, and went forward full force. Maxwell had avoided eye contact with him for the duration of the proceedings. Now he couldn't help but look at him and wonder why he couldn't admit that the State made a mistake back then. Why had he put everyone through this again?

The judge came back ten minutes later and called the jurors back in. He explained to everyone that the jury had informed the bailiff that they still had a lot of deliberating to do. The judge decided it was a good time to break for the night. He gave the standard orders not to talk about the case with anyone or do any research on it. Then he told the jury to report back at 8 a.m. sharp the next morning to continue their deliberations.

The jurors were excused, and the judge held everyone in the

courtroom a little longer, allowing the jurors time to gather their belongings and leave before letting anyone else go. Attorneys cannot have any contact with jurors outside of the courtroom until after they render a verdict. Any communication before then, no matter how small, is considered an ethical violation. Once he was convinced he had given the jurors enough time to get in their cars and leave, the judge dismissed everyone and left the courtroom.

Jason and Rachel talked with Maxwell and gave him encouraging words before he was taken back to the jail. They packed up their things and left the courthouse, walking out to their cars. There was an eerie silence between them. Neither one seemed to feel like starting a conversation, despite how close they had gotten during their work together on this case. They went home separately and tried to sleep, anxiously anticipating another day of waiting.

The jury ended up making Maxwell and the attorneys wait almost three full days. The three of them were waiting in that same conference room, eating some Subway sandwiches for lunch, when the bailiff came and knocked on the door a little before 2:30 p.m. They figured the judge was just going to send them all home again a little early for the night, as he had the night before. Jason opened the door for the bailiff.

"The jury is back," the bailiff informed them with little to no enthusiasm. There was a collective deep breath among Jason, Rachel, and Maxwell. They had grown tired of the constant anticipating and had moved on to the point of being okay with the wait. That meant there was more time that Maxwell could spend outside of a cell.

There are many superstitions about how long juries are out and what that means their verdict is going to be. Rachel had explained those theories to Jason when Maxwell wasn't around. She didn't want him overthinking the length of deliberations too much. This was the longest a jury had ever been out on one of her cases, which according to the superstitions meant they were going to return a guilty verdict. Rachel had been thinking about this ever since the first full day of deliberations had come to an end. Because of that, she wanted Maxwell to get as much time away from prison as possible. Waiting at the courthouse eating takeout was better than being in a cell and eating prison food. Most places are better than a prison cell.

Jason had tried to play devil's advocate when Rachel first brought up this concern, pointing out that in the first trial the jury had only deliberated seven hours before coming back with guilty verdicts. Rachel still didn't seem convinced. Despite her growing concerns, she stayed as calm and confident as she could when she was around Maxwell. If he was going to be sent back to prison, she wanted to try to keep his time here as positive as possible.

The three of them looked at each other and got their bearings. They went through the routine of cleaning up everything they had with them and walked back to the courtroom. The bailiff unlocked the door and held it open for them so they could walk in and sit at the defense table for the last time. The table was no longer covered with trial binders and notepads. It was empty. The attorneys had finished clearing it off during day two of waiting. They sat down at the table and Rachel took out a clean new notepad and a pen, her hand shaking slightly. Maxwell noticed, and his anxiety shot back up. His leg was shaking uncontrollably now. Jason did not reach down and stop it this time. Instead, he was tapping his fingers on the table as he sat idle, waiting. It was so quiet in the courtroom that they could hear the clock on the wall behind the bench ticking ominously.

Jeff and another individual walked into the courtroom about five minutes later. Jason leaned over to Rachel. "Who is that?"

It seemed like it took a minute for the question to register, then Rachel finally turned to look at who Jason was asking about. "That's the head prosecutor for Hennepin County. He must have been around and heard there was a verdict. He comes sometimes to watch," she explained, a noticeable tremble in her voice. She had stopped every few words trying to shake it, but that just made it worse.

A few more minutes passed, and the bailiff called for everyone to rise. They all stood, and the judge walked in, his black robe flowing behind him, his eyes looking tired. The fatigue of a multiple-day trial and days waiting for the jury appeared to be taking the same toll on him as it did on the attorneys and Maxwell. He sat down and said, "Please be seated." Once everyone had sat back down, he continued. "It sounds like we have a verdict. Court reporter, are you ready?" He looked to his left. She nodded back at him. The judge looked to the bailiff. "Okay. Call the jury back in."

Everyone instinctively stood, and the jurors piled back in to find the seats that they had become accustomed to over the past week, few of them making eye contact with Jason, Rachel, or Maxwell. The three searched the jurors' faces for any indication of what their decision was. There were no noticeable looks or signs that would show what was about to happen. They finished coming in and sitting down in the jury box.

"Please be seated," the judge ordered, and everyone sat. "Members of the jury, do you have a verdict?" There was a unanimous nodding of the jurors' heads.

"Who is the foreperson?" the judge asked, and an older woman raised her hand. Crap, Jason thought. That was one of the jurors they had thought was against them during the trial. She had seemed to be listening carefully to and nodding along with the State's witnesses, seemingly indicating she believed them. Jason thought it was a bad sign that she was the foreperson.

"Will you please hand the bailiff your verdict form?"

She handed the form to him, and the bailiff brought it over to the judge. The judge read it, and his face showed no reaction. He looked at the jurors. "Is this a unanimous verdict?"

The foreperson answered, "Yes, Your Honor." The other jurors all nodded their heads yes. The judge handed the verdict form to the court reporter. "Will you please read the verdicts, madam court reporter?"

The court reporter cleared her throat. "In the matter of *State of Minnesota v. Maxwell James Williams*, Count I, burglary in the first degree, we, the jury, find the defendant . . ."

CHAPTER TWO

One Year Earlier

Jason Michelson was driving his 2020 Honda Civic through the streets of Minneapolis Tuesday at 5:30 a.m. He had left the office just seven hours earlier, after pulling another 120-hour week there the week prior. Jason worked at one of the biggest law firms in Minneapolis, Goldstein Brandt Miller and Fredrickson, as a fourth-year associate in the commercial law section. As a twenty-nine-year-old bachelor who had graduated top of his class from Mitchell Hamline School of Law four years earlier, he had his choice of law firms and areas of specialization.

Originally, before starting law school, Jason had thought he wanted to practice criminal law. His interest in criminal law was why he'd joined law school in the first place. However, Jason quickly learned, after shadowing a prosecutor for a couple days, that he did not want to go that route. There were too many rules and hierarchies in place that would restrain him from being able to practice law the way he wanted to. In addition to that, prosecutors didn't make much money. Not that it was all about the money to Jason, but he had grown up in a home that wasn't wealthy. He hoped that by going to law school, he could help his mom and siblings financially if they needed it.

Criminal defense attorneys at private firms could make good money, but Jason wasn't sure if he could morally represent criminals who were clearly guilty of heinous crimes. Once he had decided that criminal law was not a great fit for him, he was Googling "highest-paid attorneys" and seeing where that took him. It was pretty consistent across the board that commercial law attorneys made among the highest salaries per year—along with personal injury attorneys, but Jason never saw himself as an ambulance chaser. After he did that research, he started to take a few commercial law courses at school, and he fell in love. The last year or so of law school was dedicated to taking courses that would help him in a commercial law position.

Prior to taking the bar exam, Jason had interviewed at three of the biggest firms in Minneapolis, along with firms in Washington, D.C., Seattle, and Boston. Even though the out-of-state firms were very prestigious and would have made a nice change of scenery, Jason was born and raised in Minnesota and all of his family lived there. His mom had always told him that he wasn't allowed to leave Minnesota. He wanted to believe it was a joke, but there always seemed to be some seriousness to it. Even though he was twenty-five years old at the time and could make his own decisions about his life, his mom's voice was always in the back of his mind urging him to stay. In the end, he realized that he couldn't be that far from his family, even if he didn't get to see them very often anymore with his workload. Just knowing that they were all a quick half-hour ride away gave Jason a sense of comfort that he would have lost if he had taken one of the jobs outside of Minnesota.

When Jason was taking his interview with Goldstein Brandt Miller and Fredrickson, he already had his heart set on another firm, Phillipson Tieson Caldwell and Brinks. He had completed all three sessions of interviews with them, including the firm tour. He was at the point of signing the offer letter acknowledging his acceptance when he got a call from the managing partner at Goldstein Brandt Miller and Fredrickson, Zachary Brandt, saying that they wanted to move forward with an interview. Mr. Brandt told him that they had been right in the middle of a major trial when the associate interviews were supposed to be taking place, so they had missed the deadline to send out the interview invitations. When Mr. Brandt realized what had happened, he had had his paralegal look through the 150 applications that he was assigned, and she had narrowed it down to fifty. Mr. Brandt had looked through those fifty and decided to move forward with ten interviews for a new associate to work under him. Jason Michelson was one of those ten, and Mr. Brandt called to let him know that because of their oversight, they were skipping all of the introductory interviews and going straight to the final interviews to pick the best candidate for the job. He asked Jason to come in the next day to meet the team and see if Goldstein Brandt Miller and Fredrickson was the firm he would call home.

Jason was very surprised and impressed that the managing partner himself not only wanted to interview him to be his associate but had called himself to set up the meeting. As the call was coming to an end, Jason was looking at the almost signed offer letter from Phillipson Tieson Caldwell and Brinks, pondering what to do. The offer letter was good for another ten days, and it would still be there after the meeting tomorrow. What would it hurt for Jason to go and see what Mr. Brandt had to offer?

Mr. Brandt finished up what he was saying, cleared his throat, and said, "Well, Jason, what do you think? Will you come in and meet with me tomorrow?"

Jason, making a final determination, answered, "Thank you, Mr. Brandt, I would love to come in and meet with you tomorrow." *Love to.* Why had he said that? This was the managing partner of one of the biggest law firms in Minneapolis, and he just told him that he would "love to come in and meet with him." After hearing that, Mr. Brandt would probably rescind the offer. Jason closed his eyes in frustration at how dumb he must have sounded.

To his surprise, Mr. Brandt said, "Perfect. How about you come over at 9 a.m. tomorrow? Make sure you bring your parking ticket for validation. The costs of those ramps are like armed robbery." He chuckled at his attempt at humor.

Jason let out a fake laugh and said, "Nine a.m. sounds great. I will see you then, Mr. Brandt."

The two hung up, and Jason pushed the offer letter to the side and grabbed his laptop. Time to do a little more research on Goldstein Brandt Miller and Fredrickson so that he was ready for the meeting. It was customary in law firm interviews for the interviewee to go online and learn everything they could about the firm through their website and the partners' LinkedIn accounts. Jason found it gave him the edge on other applicants to look at the partners' other social media too, so he could get a full picture of who they were in and out of the office.

After about an hour and a half, Jason found out that Zachary Brandt was a married father of three girls, nineteen, sixteen, and fourteen; he had a house in Florida that they went to once a month each summer; he was an avid Vikings fan; and he drove a 2020 Mercedes-Benz AMG GT.

In addition to what he learned about Zachary Brandt, Jason found information on his three senior partners, six junior partners, and he discovered the names of the seventeen associates working under him. He was confident that he had done enough research to get by at the meeting the next day, so he went to the fridge, grabbed a beer, and went to sit on his couch to watch some TV.

Jason lived in a studio apartment in downtown Minneapolis. It was one big room, with a small bathroom attached, a stove and microwave up against one of the walls, and just enough space for both his twin-size bed and a small couch. It was all that he needed at the time, and honestly all that he could afford, costing him $1,700 in rent a month, a small fortune he paid throughout law school using a mix of his student loans and the meager pay from his jobs. He finished his beer while he watched the Minnesota Twins lose in extra innings to the New York Yankees. He looked at the clock on the stove and saw it was almost 11 p.m. He decided to get to bed so he would be well rested for his meeting the next day.

Jason slept great, and his phone alarm woke him up at 6 a.m. with the sound of Jimi Hendrix's "Purple Haze". He threw on his tennis shoes, grabbed his earbuds, and walked out his door to go for his morning run. He locked the apartment door and ran down the four flights of stairs and out to the street. As he ran his typical five-mile route that morning, Jason was beginning to get excited about his meeting. He was still very impressed that the managing partner himself had called to set it up and that they were skipping the hassle of initial bullshit interviews. Jason didn't understand why they did it, but there were usually at least three interviews before anyone got an offer at a big firm.

The first introductory interview was with someone in the HR department. Then, if that person liked you, you made it to a second interview with a mix of junior and senior partners in your area of practice. After that, you would maybe get a little face time with the partner you would be working for, and then a tour around the office and admittance to a firm event where they showed you how great it was to work there. What they didn't tell you was that these firm events only happened once a year for the exact purpose of convincing people to sell their souls to the firm. In reality, all of those attorneys worked so many hours each week that there was no way for firm events to happen more than once a year. Everyone knew this, but it was still fun to schmooze for a little while and see if you could handle the assholes at the firm on a daily basis.

Jason got back from his run, jumped in the shower, and forty-five minutes later he was driving to the meeting at Goldstein Brandt Miller and Fredrickson, his excitement still seeming to rise. He wore his only suit jacket that he had bought at a secondhand store and had his mom sew new buttons onto. He was not sure why he was suddenly so intrigued with this meeting and the firm, when just fifteen hours earlier he was about to send in his acceptance to an offer from elsewhere.

Jason drove into the parking ramp at 8:30 a.m. and looked for a parking spot. Jason's dad, a military man, had always taught him that if you are fifteen minutes early you are late. That was drilled into his head at a very young age. If Jason was less than fifteen minutes early, his anxiety began to become unbearable. Even though his dad had been dead for years, this was one of the things that always stuck with him. He would often think of his dad whenever he arrived at places early and had some extra time to sit in his car and think before going in.

Jason pulled into a parking spot at 8:34 a.m. and put his parking ticket in his pocket so that he wouldn't forget to get it stamped for validation by the receptionist at the firm. He would likely be there at least an hour, and that meant parking would be $25 and his monthly budget would take a hit. Yes, Jason would be making the big firm bucks in a few short months, but for now, he was still on a broke law student's budget. He reviewed his notes that he had written down the night before, grabbed his official Mitchell Hamline notepad, and went to the elevators to go to the receptionist's desk. He ended up arriving at the front desk at precisely 8:45 a.m., fifteen minutes early on the dot. He smiled, thinking of his dad.

The receptionist had Jason sit in the waiting room and he looked around the office, taking in all of the art and furniture around the waiting area. Most firms hired interior designers to pick out their furnishings and art in the waiting areas to maximize the impression of prestige and professionalism. Goldstein Brandt Miller and Fredrickson's waiting room had impressive décor and art that looked like it cost way too much money. Behind the receptionist was a big conference room with all-glass windows and doors. In the center of it was a big oak table that could seat at least twenty people. Jason gave it a nine out of ten on the first impression scale.

At 9 a.m. on the dot, Mr. Brandt came out to greet Jason. Usually a paralegal, associate, or other staff member would come greet the interviewee, not the managing partner himself. This was another point that Goldstein Brandt Miller and Fredrickson had gained for themselves. Jason continued to be impressed. Mr. Brandt welcomed him to the firm and made some small talk as he showed him around the main floor. Mr. Brandt informed him that the firm owned twenty-two of the building's floors and each floor had its own conference room, similar to the one with the glass windows and big conference table that this floor had.

After they had walked around the main floor, Mr. Brandt showed Jason the commercial-size kitchen that had a rotation of chefs on duty seventeen hours a day. Next, he showed him the Starbucks on the fifth floor that was for firm members, clients, and guests only. Then he brought Jason to the thirteenth floor, where the firm had a full in-office gym equipped with all of the most recent state-of-the-art equipment. All of this—the kitchen, Starbucks, and gym—was free of charge to members of the firm.

None of the other firms had amenities like these, and Jason was impressed. This was like something you would see in movies and on TV shows about high-end law firms. He had never seen anything like it in real life.

After showing Jason all of the amazing amenities that the firm offered, Mr. Brandt took him to the fourteenth floor of the Goldstein Brandt Miller and Fredrickson offices, which was the seventy-fourth floor of the building. Jason was introduced to seven of the associates he had looked up the night before, three of the junior partners, and one of the senior partners. Only half of them seemed like the know-it-all douchebags that Jason wanted to avoid. That was pretty good odds for a law firm of this size, and to be fair, Jason had only met them for a few short minutes. They might end up not being so bad.

The last stop on the tour was an empty office the size of Jason's apartment. Jason thought about it and realized that he had met most of the other associates in offices of similar size. This was new to him. Most law firms had their new associates in a bullpen-style setup, with cubicles partitioned off by those ugly gray movable walls. Did the associates here actually have their own offices? That was unheard of for anyone of less than junior partner status.

Mr. Brandt turned on the lights and said, "Well, Jason, this would be your office." He looked over to take in Jason's reaction and seemed to get some satisfaction from the awe that must have shown on his face. "We have an interior design firm on retainer that will work with you to pick out all of your furniture, art, and anything else that you want in here. You would start working with her right after you sign on, so we can make sure everything is set up for you on your first day."

Jason was taking it all in, wondering if Goldstein Brandt Miller and Fredrickson was too good to be true. He turned in a circle and looked around his potential office. Mr. Brandt spoke again. "Listen, Jason, I am supposed to meet with the other nine interviewees over the next two days, but let's be honest. You were my first choice. I have asked around and know you have offers at some of the other big firms in town. I want to offer you the associate position right now and not waste my time with the other candidates. What are your thoughts?"

The look on Jason's face must have gone from awe to shock as he stammered, looking for the words. No other law firm process had been this fast. Most of the time, after that third interview, it took a week or two for an official offer letter to come. Then they gave you two weeks to consider the terms of the offer before deciding. Mr.

Brandt was making Jason an offer on the spot after just an hour-and-a-half meeting with him. He didn't know what to say. He didn't know what the salary was, what the billable hour requirement was, or any of the firm's rules and obligations.

Sensing the hesitation, Mr. Brandt cut in again. "Look, I know this is atypical of the normal process, but I want you to be my new associate, Jason. You have an outstanding resume, and you seem like you will fit in well. I will have my assistant print off the official offer letter for you to take with you. I will push back the rest of my interviews and give you the night to think about it. Can you get me a decision by 8 a.m. tomorrow?"

Jason found the words, still taking in the whirlwind of everything going on, and said, "Yes, that should be enough time. I am very impressed with you and the firm."

Zachary Brandt smiled, looking pleased with Jason's response. "Good. I am glad you like the place. As you know, you would be spending many hours a week here. We try to make it as comfortable as possible for our employees, and compensate them handsomely for their work. If you work hard for us, you will be rewarded accordingly."

Mr. Brandt checked his watch and then walked Jason back to the elevator, using his keycard to open the doors. "Why don't you head back down to the lobby and wait for my assistant to bring down the offer letter. Like I said, Jason, I really want you to work for me, and I hope you are as excited about us as we are about you." The elevator door opened, and Jason stepped in, hitting the button to go back to the lobby. "I look forward to hearing from you tomorrow morning, 8 a.m." Mr. Brandt reiterated; it was more like a question.

Jason nodded and responded, "Thank you very much, Mr. Brandt. You will hear from me tomorrow morning by 8 a.m."

The doors closed, and the elevator started to go back down to the lobby. Jason hadn't even seen the offer letter yet, but he had a feeling in his gut that he knew Goldstein Brandt Miller and Fredricks had just taken over the top spot in his mind. He wasn't usually one to make rash decisions based on his emotions. He was the type of person who made pro-and-con lists for everything and contemplated them for a few days, going back and forth in his mind, before making a final decision. Something about this was different. The whole process of the meeting, the amenities, the people he met, it was all different and better. But there was still that little nagging feeling in the back of his head that there was some kind of catch.

The elevator doors opened, and he walked back into the main lobby. He smiled at the receptionist, who looked at him with a wide smile. "It's pretty impressive, isn't it?" she asked. "I came from a firm in New York to work here, and this blows them out of the water. It seems too good to be true, but it isn't. They deliver on all their promises."

It was like she was reading Jason's mind and addressing his concerns. She started again. "Well, Mr. Brandt must really like you. I got a note that his head assistant is putting together the offer letter to bring down to you before you leave." All Jason could do was nod. The receptionist smiled at him and went back to answering the phones.

Ten minutes later, a petite blonde-haired woman walked up to Jason.

"Mr. Michelson?" He nodded and she handed him an official-looking envelope full of papers. She smiled and said, "We look forward to hearing from you by 8 a.m. tomorrow. I am sure I will be seeing a lot of you soon." She winked, turned, and walked away. Jason couldn't help but watch her in her tight black dress, her six-inch heels clicking with each step.

Jason said a final thanks to the receptionist and walked over to the elevator to get back to his car. He got on and rode it down to the parking ramp. He got into his car and began to open the envelope to read the offer letter, not able to wait until he got home. He ran his hand through the seal to open the top of the envelope, and pulled out a stack of papers. The first one was a letter on the official Goldstein Brandt Miller and Fredrickson letterhead. On the top in all caps, it read OFFER LETTER FOR JASON MICHELSON. Jason began reading, and his jaw dropped as he got to the salary section. Their offer was $20,000 over the highest offer from any other firm he was considering. He kept reading. The benefits, the billable hour requirement, and the other rules all seemed to be like the other firms'.

Jason finished reading the offer letter and looked through the other documents. They had included all of the new-hire paperwork: the tax forms, health insurance forms, information to put on the firm's directory, and his emergency contact info. Jason usually would have thought putting all of the new-hire paperwork in with the offer letter was presumptuous, but for some reason he didn't feel that way now. He was still in shock, but soon realized that his mind was made up. Jason Michelson would be the newest associate at Goldstein Brandt Miller and Fredrickson, working for managing partner Zachary Brandt.

Jason put the packet on his passenger seat and buckled up, already mentally rewriting the letter to Phillipson Tieson Caldwell and Brinks, regretfully declining their offer. As he put his car in reverse, he realized that he had forgotten to get his parking ticket validated by the receptionist. He stopped and put the car back in park, then looked at the passenger seat, considering his next move. His mind was made up—he was going to accept the offer, so why put it off any longer? He grabbed the packet of papers, shut off his car, and went back to the elevator to head back up.

Jason got off the elevator and walked to the reception desk. The receptionist looked up and smiled at him. "Back so soon?" she asked playfully.

Jason handed her the parking ticket. "I forgot to get this validated. Sorry about that."

She took the ticket from him and stamped it, then handed it back to Jason, who stood there lingering. She looked at him questioningly. "Was there something else?"

Jason smiled. "Is Mr. Brandt available? I would like to talk to him about accepting this offer."

The receptionist's smile widened as she picked up the phone. "Let me call his assistant and see if they can have you come back up."

Jason spent the next six hours filling out his new-hire paperwork, meeting more partners at the firm, eating a catered-in lunch, and working with IT to get his login information and computers set up. He ended the day talking with the interior designer, going over what he wanted to do in his new office—the office that was the same size as the studio apartment that he had been living in for the last three years through law school. This all had to be a dream, he thought to himself.

As he got back in his car that evening, the clock on his dash read 5:15 p.m. Jason realized that the smile had not left his face since he had officially said it out loud, that he was accepting the offer. The receptionist, who he found out was named Elizabeth, was right. It did seem too good to be true. But at that point, Jason didn't care. He was ready to start this new chapter of his life and the career that he had dreamt of for years.

He got home that night and sat down on the couch with another beer from the fridge. Looking around his little apartment, he laughed, thinking back to his new office that was the same size. He called his mom to give her the good news, and also texted a few of his law school friends to brag a little about his amazing new law firm. Jason went to bed that night looking forward to July 1, 2018, his start date as the new associate of Goldstein Brandt Miller and Fredrickson.

CHAPTER THREE

Jason pulled into his parking spot at 5:45 a.m. and rode up to the main floor lobby of Goldstein Brandt Miller and Fredrickson. He got off the main elevator, and walked over to the firm's elevator, opening it with his keycard, which was permanently attached to his hip. He rode it up to the fourteenth floor and walked into his fully furnished office. It had his bookshelf full of law books, his desk and cabinets full of case files, and his desktop open to the ninety-seven emails that had come in since he left there a little over seven hours earlier. He sat down and started going through them.

Around 7 a.m., Amy Reinstad, Jason's assistant, came in with his second cup of coffee for the day. Jason had been approved to hire his own assistant a year prior, when he was billing hours higher than any other associate on his floor. He interviewed twelve people and knew right away that Amy was the right person for the job. Since making the decision to work at Goldstein Brandt Miller and Fredrickson, Jason was more decisive and no longer had to make pro-and-con lists for absolutely everything. He offered Amy the job on the spot, just as Zachary Brandt had done with him.

Since that day, Amy had been the best assistant Jason could ask for and really was like his right-hand woman. It was almost like they had one joint brain. Jason would need something drafted or filed, and by the time he would get around to telling Amy to do it, she would come in and tell him it was already done. Jason quickly learned that this wasn't by coincidence. Amy would sometimes listen in on Jason's calls and would often check his to-do list on his desktop. Jason found it weird and intrusive at first, but once he realized how efficient it made the two of them, he no longer cared. The confidentiality rules that were so strict for lawyers applied to their staff too, and Amy had signed confidentiality agreements when she was hired. There was no harm in her listening in and knowing things in real time. It really did prove to be beneficial in the grand scheme of things.

Jason normally started his day before 6 a.m. and left around 8 or 9 p.m. He worked seven days a week most of the time. His firm gave him three weeks of paid vacation, but Jason had never taken more than three of those days off. His cousin had gotten married two years ago, a destination wedding in the Dominican Republic. Jason really didn't want to take any time off—he was very busy that weekend with a lot to get done for work.

Ultimately, his mom convinced him that he needed the break, and he relented and went. Despite using a day of vacation for the three days he missed, Jason worked at the airport, on the plane, and most of the time he was in the Dominican Republic. He just had the pleasure of working poolside instead of in his high-rise office in Minneapolis. Thinking back on it, it was a nice change of scenery to work poolside. Maybe he would consider taking another working vacation again soon.

Amy was only expected to be in the office fifty hours a week, but she was in from 7 a.m. until at least 6 p.m. most weeks, Monday through Friday. She would frequently also come in on Saturdays to get additional work done with Jason. She never worked Sundays, though. She was a devout Catholic and was a firm believer that Sunday was the day of rest, so she made it a rule that she would not work Sundays under any circumstances. Jason was fine with that. Amy already went above and beyond and worked harder than any other assistant, in his opinion. He could be biased, though, on that. Amy often gave Jason shit about working on Sundays and said that he should also take that day off. She would go on and on about how he was a young, attractive, successful man and that he needed to take a day off to have a life before he became a burnt-out, cranky old man.

Jason always listened to what Amy told him, but he brushed it off. There was too much to get done to take a day off each week. Plus, what would he do on Sundays? He hadn't had a girlfriend since his 1L year of law school, and that had not ended well. She got mad when he picked up a job as a law clerk at a firm after his 1L year in addition to taking a few summer classes. She said Jason never had time for her anymore. He had thought she would understand since she was in law school too and should be going through the same things as he was and having the same hectic schedule. She decided not to take any summer classes, though, and went to the Hamptons with her parents instead of finding a job.

The fact that her parents had a place in the Hamptons should have been Jason's first clue that things wouldn't work out. Jason could hold his own pretty well in a crowd of rich, privileged people, but unlike many of his classmates he didn't come from a wealthy home. His dad was an Army veteran who worked at a mechanic's shop, and his mom was a schoolteacher who taught ninth-grade English. Jason had three siblings and had always worn hand-me-downs from his older brother Kyle.

He focused on getting good grades and getting a scholarship to college. Jason was a pretty good hockey player in high school. "Pretty good" was being modest. He was good enough to get a full scholarship to Minnesota State University, Mankato, to play as a forward for the Mavericks. Unfortunately, he tore his anterior cruciate ligament (ACL) his sophomore year of college, and his doctors wouldn't clear him to play after that. He lost his scholarship and had to get a few jobs in addition to a lot of federal loans to get through the rest of undergrad.

Jason knew that, while he was good at hockey, he wasn't good enough for it to go anywhere after college. He had realized in high school that he wanted to go to law school. One of his favorite shows growing up had been *Law & Order: Special Victims Unit*. He would sit for hours after he was done with homework, or after work at night, watching reruns of the show. Jason was always good at figuring out who the criminal was and solving the crimes along with the detectives. His love for the law grew from there, as he began a job cleaning for a small law firm in his hometown of Stillwater. He started cleaning the building twice a week once he turned fourteen. You didn't have to be sixteen to do that job, and Jason figured any extra money would help.

He would get there around 4:30 in the afternoon on Tuesdays and Fridays to clean the offices. Jason started to get to know some of the lawyers there, and they would sometimes talk with him about their cases. That led to Jason coming in on Thursdays to shadow, sit down and talk with the attorneys, read through cases, and brief them for the attorneys. And he would ask them general questions that he had.

His freshman year of high school, Jason started working at the law office, and he continued working there until he started college. Jason stayed in touch with most of the lawyers over the years, and they always told him that he had a standing job offer once he graduated law school. Jason appreciated that and would have loved to work with some of those same attorneys who mentored him early on, but they only practiced in criminal law, family law, and personal injury, none of which Jason saw himself doing, despite his early love for *Law & Order: SVU*. By the end of his time in law school, he had the grades and experience to work at a big law firm, making more money in six months than both his parents could make in a year. He felt like he owed it to himself and his family to use his talents to take the better-paying job so that he could help them out.

Jason still lived in the studio apartment he had lived in throughout law school. He didn't see the point in getting a new place. Realistically, he wasn't there to do much other than eat an occasional dinner and sleep. He didn't need to have some fancy big apartment that would just sit empty all of the time.

Jason would occasionally go out on dates with women, but he would always come up with an excuse not to go back to his place. Even though he had no problem living in the studio apartment, he was a little embarrassed bringing dates back home there. How would it look for this big Minneapolis lawyer to be living in this dingy apartment?

Jason wasn't sure why he cared. He didn't plan on dating any of these women past the third date. That was usually about when women got fed up with his work schedule and realized the life of dating a lawyer wasn't all that it was cracked up to be. Sure, they made good money, but they were never around to spend any of it. Usually by the third date, Jason had rescheduled at least two of the three meetings because of emergencies that came up at work. He would forget to return their calls or would leave their texts unread. Jason was never really focused on women and dating. He knew that he wanted to be a successful attorney, and he had dedicated his life to that.

Jason Michelson was the definition of a workaholic, and that is what he preferred. He was still young; he had time for dating and settling down once he made partner at the firm. Once he hit the five-year mark, he would qualify for junior partnership, and Zachary Brandt had already been making comments about that happening. Jason would worry about everything else after that.

Amy, on the other hand, did things in the opposite order to Jason. She got married right out of college, where she got a legal administration degree. Her husband, David, proposed after her graduation ceremony. They got married six months later and had their first daughter, Megan, ten months after that. They went on to have five kids total, and Amy was a stay-at-home mom until they all reached school age. She had worked for a small law firm prior to having Megan, but when she tried to go back after maternity leave, she realized that it wasn't the right time. Amy and David decided that it was better if she stayed home with the kids to save on daycare costs and raise them in a traditional way. They were lucky that David's job afforded them the ability to do that. Jason's family couldn't make that work when he was growing up.

When their youngest son Matthew was starting the second grade, David got hurt at work and had to take some time off. There was a lapse in time between his injury and the time that workers' compensation paid him when the family was living off their savings. During that time, they decided that Amy needed to go back to work. She had loved staying home and taking care of her kids, but she was excited to get back into the professional world. She had enjoyed getting her legal administrative degree and her work prior to having Megan. Her family needed her to get back into the workforce, and she was ready to have something for herself outside of her kids. Amy was ready to take over the financial burden for the family.

As she started applying, it soon became clear that her long lapse in employment put her at a disadvantage. She began getting many rejection letters without even having the opportunity to interview. She had received about fifteen rejections and was starting to get discouraged, when she went on Indeed.com one night and came across a listing for a legal assistant at Goldstein Brandt Miller and Fredrickson. She had heard of the firm and looked up their website. She saw the position was for an attorney named Jason Michelson. She read his bio on the website. The qualifications listed for the job required a lot more experience than she had, but something told her to apply anyway. Amy sent in her application around 4 p.m. the next day and was surprised to get an email at 7:45 p.m. from Jason Michelson himself, inviting her in for an interview.

When Amy showed up for the interview, she thought it went really well. Toward the end of the official interview, she said, "I have to ask. I didn't have many of the qualifications that the job listing required. Why did you have me come in for an interview?"

To which Jason responded, "My mom had my older brother young and never got to use her degree before starting a family. It was really hard for her to find a job in her field. Nobody wanted to give her a chance, even though I know she would have been the hardest worker anyone could hire." He paused, and then went on, "I am probably not supposed to say stuff like this, but I saw your gap in employment and assumed it was due to having a family. I thought about my mom and how if someone would have just given her a chance early on, she could have been great." Jason paused again and looked away from Amy, not making eye contact. He continued, "I wanted to see if I could give you that chance." Amy was speechless.

The interview went on for another hour as Jason asked Amy about her family and she showed him pictures of her kids. She was amazed that a powerful twenty-something attorney took the time to really listen to her and learn about her family. The two of them clicked and Jason offered her the job on the spot, with the salary being much more than Amy could have ever imagined. She started the day after that and had been working her ass off for Jason every day since, proving that he was right to take a chance on her. The pair ended up being one of the most productive associate-assistant teams in the firm.

CHAPTER FOUR

Amy stood and waited after setting down Jason's coffee as he finished up the email he was sending. He looked up at her and smiled. "Good morning, Amy. How was your night with the kids?" Jason knew her son Luke had had a band concert the night before. Amy had needed to leave earlier than normal to make it to the school in time.

"It was as you would expect. A bunch of fifth graders trying to play instruments, loud and clumsy," she laughed.

Jason laughed. "I will have to come to the next one."

Amy looked at him and raised an eyebrow. "Oh yeah?" she said, her voice surprised. She went on, "Maybe you can bring a date with you."

Jason rolled his eyes. "Here we go again. You know your job description doesn't include assisting in my love life."

Amy smiled. "Well, you know I am just trying to help. You won't be young and handsome forever." She winked and took a seat at the chair opposite his desk and got out her pen and paper. "So, what's on the agenda for today?" They went through their to-do list for the day. Jason had a few meetings and phone calls, and the rest of the day would be spent on a big merger for one of his clients. Those things would all start at 8 a.m., so Jason had to try and get through the remaining twenty-five emails before then.

Jason got that look on his face like he had to get back to it. Amy knew the face well, so she gathered her things and got up to leave.

"You know where to find me," she said as she left his office to go to her desk, which was positioned right outside of his office door. This was a modification that the firm added when Jason hired Amy. As she was leaving, Jason brought his attention back to his emails.

He was finishing up on his final response when the "new email" notification flashed across the bottom of his screen. Jason sighed to himself. Not even a minute of reprieve after finishing all those emails before having more to deal with. It was okay, this is what he was used to. He looked at the clock; he had four minutes before his first call at 8 a.m. Jason clicked back to the screen that showed his unread emails and noticed it was an email from Zachary Brandt and it had an "importance" tag on it. On Outlook Email, the email service used by Goldstein Brandt Miller and Fredrickson, there was a way an email could be sent with high importance, or what Jason called an importance tag. The email title read "READ ASAP Changes to Firm-Wide Pro Bono Policy."

Pro bono is the term used to describe when an attorney takes a case for no fee. The attorney knows that they will not receive compensation via a retainer fee, contingency fee agreement, or by any other means. These are the cases that attorneys take on to use their skills to "make a difference in the world," a way for attorneys to give back to the people who need their services but cannot afford to pay them. The Minnesota Bar Association gives out recognition to attorneys who report at least fifty pro bono hours per year. Providing these services was always pushed in law school and by the Bar as a way for attorneys to "give back to the little guy." Or at least that's how it was perceived by Jason.

Jason opened the email and realized that it had multiple attachments, and the body of the email itself was a few pages long. He did not have enough time to go through all of that before his first call. He decided to leave it for now and read over everything when he had a small break between meetings and calls. Jason looked at his calendar for the number to call his client and picked up the phone to make the call.

Phone call after phone call, meeting after meeting, then Jason finally had a break in his day to sit back down at his desk. He looked at the time on his desktop: 1:45 p.m. Wow! The day was flying by, he thought. He looked at his emails and saw he had 172 new messages to look through. He had an hour break before his next call and he hadn't eaten yet, so he decided to go to the kitchen and get some food while he kept working. Jason always had working lunches, whether it be lunch meetings, eating during a Zoom call, or eating while he responded to emails, reviewed documents, and so on. He couldn't think of the last time he had just sat down and eaten a meal without working or thinking about work. Just another part of big-firm law.

Jason got back to his desk with his lunch, a gyro with fries, and clicked back into his emails. As he started to eat, he remembered that "importance tag" email from Zachary Brandt. He scrolled down and found the email and began reading. The email itself was a recap of the current pro bono requirement that the firm had adopted, the fifty hours recommended by the Bar Association. It recapped what that requirement entailed, why the firm originally adopted that requirement, the importance of giving back, blah blah blah. Jason skimmed through that part, as he had read it before. At the end of the email, it stated: "Please read the attachments, which lay out the new pro bono requirements and policies. After you finish reading those attachments, please read and sign the pro bono agreement form and return it to me no later than next Monday."

Jason opened the attachment and skimmed it to find that the required pro bono hours for the firm's attorneys had gone up to one hundred hours per year. He rolled his eyes and let out an audible sigh. There weren't enough hours in the day to complete an additional fifty hours of pro bono work. Jason got that it was important and a big part of being an attorney to give back, but how could they expect him to keep billing his high number of hours and dedicate that additional time to pro bono cases?

He took another bite of his gyro and spilled some tzatziki sauce on himself. "Shit!" He grabbed the napkin and tried to get it off before it left a stain. It was too late, there was already a cloudy stain on his shirt. Jason sighed and rolled his eyes again—today was just not his day. He picked up his phone and paged Amy. "Hey Amy. I just spilled my lunch. Can you please grab me one of my extra shirts from the closet?"

"Sure thing, boss, heading there now." The firm had a big closet on each floor where staff could keep extra outfit changes for occasions like this, or if they pulled an all-nighter at the office. Jason had five other shirts, two suit jackets, and three pairs of pants in the office closet for such occasions. Let's just say this wasn't the first time Jason had spilled food on himself. Nor would it be the last. Now that he thought about it, this wasn't even the first time this month he had spilled his lunch on himself. He made a mental note to be more careful eating. Getting his clothes dry cleaned was not cheap.

Three minutes later, Amy came into his office with the new shirt, a freshly pressed white button-up. "Thanks, Amy."

She looked at his dirty shirt and laughed. "Second time this month, huh? You better be more careful."

Jason stood up and took off his suit jacket and started to unbutton his shirt. He was clearly too comfortable around Amy. He looked up and she blushed, causing Jason to stop. "Oh, sorry," he said; he waited until she left before he finished changing. Then he called out for her again to come back in. She came back into the office and Jason opened the new pro bono agreement on his desktop. She sat down in the chair across from him.

"Did you get copied on this new pro bono bullshit?" he asked.

She nodded. "Well, can you put my signature on the agreement and send it back to Zachary Brandt for me?"

Amy responded, "Yes, I can do that. Did you read through it all, though?"

"I read the highlights. Why?"

"It said that the new hour requirement is in effect immediately and that all attorneys are required to do the full hundred hours by the end of the calendar year."

"What?" Jason exclaimed. "How can they expect us to do that? It's already halfway through the year. I haven't even started my initial fifty hours."

Amy waited a second before responding so Jason could take a breath to calm down. He sometimes needed that moment before he could listen again to what she was telling him. "I know. I heard some of the other attorneys complaining about the same thing earlier. It sounds like some of them already talked to Mr. Brandt about it, and he doesn't care how impossible it seems—he expects it to be done."

"But how does he expect that to happen? There aren't enough hours in a day for me to get my billable work done, let alone this pro bono crap."

"I don't know, Jason, but it doesn't look like Mr. Brandt is going to give in on this. What do you want to do?"

Jason thought for a minute, and Amy could see his wheels turning. It seemed like there was no point in arguing about it or worrying about it. Jason had to get started on his hours, and fast. He didn't have time to do a bunch of different cases that would add up to the full hundred hours. He needed something that he could get working on quickly, that wouldn't include learning new cases and dealing with new people over and over again.

Jason finally reached a conclusion and said, "Well, I guess there is nothing we can do but find me ways to get those hours. Can you put together a list of ways that I can complete my hours that don't include working with too many different clients? I get that I likely won't be able to do all hundred hours for one client by the end of the year, but the fewer clients, the better. I can't be worrying about client management on these cases."

Amy nodded. "I am on it. I will have a list to you before I leave for the day. Do you want to go over it together before I go?"

"Yes, that sounds good. It looks like my last call is at 5:30 today. We can go through it after that, if that works for you?" Jason asked.

Amy was always surprised that Jason was so concerned about her schedule and whether things worked for her. Her job was to work for him and do things that would make his job easier. She loved that he always checked if it was good for her too, instead of just dictating what was going to happen, like a lot of the other attorneys at the firm. The senior partner with the office next to Jason could always be heard barking orders at his assistant, and she was expected to drop whatever she was doing to go to him. His assistant always complained to Amy about how the attorney treated her. Amy thanked God every day that she had Jason as her boss and that he ever gave her a chance.

"That works perfectly for me," she responded. "I will have the list ready to go and we can choose what you want to do. Then I can contact those places to get you set up before I go home for the night." With that, Amy got up and went back to her desk.

Jason breathed a sigh of relief. He knew Amy would be able to narrow it down and they would get it taken care of. He was so lucky to have her in his corner. He did not know what he would do without her. Jason took another bite of his fries and then threw the rest of the food in the garbage. His food never stayed warm long enough for him to finish it all, and he couldn't bring himself to eat it once it was cold. He went back to responding to his emails before his next meeting.

❖

Jason finished his last call at 6:15 p.m. and had no sooner hung up than Amy was walking into the office with the list. She must have been waiting for him to get off his call. It had taken a little longer than he expected. She sat down in her chair across from him and waited for him to get out a notepad and pen. Jason always liked to take his own notes when they had important meetings about things. Amy started to go through the list. Jason could see that she had about eleven things listed, and she had paragraphs underneath each of them containing information about the organization and what type of pro bono work they had available, and a rating from one to five.

They were working their way down the list, and nothing was sticking out to Jason or interesting him. But when Amy got to number nine, it caught his attention, as she read "the Exoneration Project." Jason had learned about the Exoneration Project in law school. They were an organization that worked to free the innocent, prevent wrongful convictions, and create fair, compassionate, and equitable systems of justice for everyone. They had studied a few cases in their criminal law class about people who were released from prison thanks to the Exoneration Project. Their mission statement was one of the questions on the test, and Jason still remembered it to this day.

Amy went on to read that the Exoneration Project only had a few true staff at the Minnesota branch, and that much of the work was done by volunteers. She finished reading the information about it and started to go on to number ten. Jason stopped her. "Wait! What else did you learn about that one?"

She paused and started to think back to what she had read earlier. "Umm, it had a number for the person to contact. It had testimonials from exonerated people and how long they were wrongfully kept in prison. I am not sure. I can go look for more, if you want?"

"No. It's okay. I will look at it and contact them about volunteering. I would imagine those cases have a lot of hours' worth of work. Plus, the whole reason I went to law school in the first place was because of my love for criminal law. Did you know that?" Jason asked.

Amy thought about it for a second. "I don't think so, no. I just figured you always knew you were going to be this big-shot attorney in a high-rise looking over Minneapolis," she joked.

"Well, I guess I never knew for sure what I wanted to do or what law I wanted to practice. But criminal law got me interested in the law and made me want to go to law school." He paused. "I guess once I was in the trenches of law school, I figured I should find whatever job could make me the most money." He paused again and looked down. "Wow, that made me sound shallow."

"No, it didn't," Amy assured him. "There is nothing wrong with wanting to have a high-paying job. You worked hard, and you have a gift. It would be a waste if you weren't using it."

"Yeah, I guess you're right," Jason conceded. "I am helping my mom and sisters out some with my salary. I don't think I would have been able to do that if I was working as a prosecutor. Maybe if I worked at a private defense firm, but who knows?" It sounded like he was trying to convince himself now more than Amy. Jason spent his time making rich people more money, not doing anything to help people in situations that he and his family had been in while he was growing up.

The Exoneration Project worked with people who were sitting in prison for crimes that they didn't commit. They helped people try to get their lives back. Maybe these pro bono hours wouldn't be so bad. Jason thought about it as the two of them sat there in silence. Those attorneys were really making a difference in the world, and he could be a part of that, even if it were on a temporary basis and he would be using it just to get his pro bono hours done. He was kind of excited. He couldn't remember the last time that something at work had made him genuinely excited. He was stuck in his normal routine every day and was looking forward to a small change of pace. He moved the mouse to awaken his desktop, searched for the Exoneration Project, and found the number for Dylan Franks, the supervising attorney. He picked up his phone to call Mr. Franks.

CHAPTER FIVE

In his conversation with Mr. Franks, Jason learned that the Exoneration Project was currently working on nine cases. One of them was nearing its end because they believed their motion for a new trial was going to be denied. The second case was waiting for the order to be signed granting them a new trial. There were a few preparing for a retrial. The last one was a case that they recently got approval to take, and was the one that they needed the most help with. Jason wanted to know everything he could about it, but Mr. Franks said that he couldn't go into details until Jason came in and signed some papers. He had to be officially on the case so that the confidentiality rules would apply to him.

Mr. Franks said, "Well, we got all the documents from the trial about a month ago, so everything is starting to ramp up. When can you get here?"

Jason looked at his calendar for the next day and saw he only had three appointments in the afternoon. "Mr. Franks, can you hold on one second?" He hit the hold button on his phone. "Hey Amy, can you clear my afternoon for tomorrow? I am going to go and meet with Mr. Franks."

"You got it, boss," came the response.

Jason took the phone off hold. "Mr. Franks, how does tomorrow at 1 p.m. work? I am having my assistant clear my schedule for the afternoon."

With a little more pep in his voice, Mr. Franks said, "Yes, that sounds great, Mr. Michelson. I will see you tomorrow."

They hung up, and Jason was already feeling like he had accomplished something meaningful for the day by agreeing to work on this case—a case for someone who was wrongfully convicted and sitting in prison because of it. He found it hard to find the motivation to finish the rest of the work that was already in front of him. Amy came in and said goodbye around 6:45 p.m.

Jason answered a few more emails after that and made it through half of a merger proposal. He decided that he was done for the night, so he got his stuff ready and was out to his car by 7:45 p.m. This was the earliest he had left the office in a while. When he got home, Jason did something else he hadn't done in a while. He took out his cellphone and called his mom.

The phone rang twice and then he heard his mom on the other end of the line, with a little panic in her voice. "Hello, Jason. Is everything all right?"

"Yeah, mom. I am great. I just figured we hadn't talked in a couple of weeks, so I wanted to call and check in."

He could hear the relief in her voice. "Oh, good. I was worried something was wrong. I rarely hear from you on weeknights. Things are going good on this end. Your sister is in town visiting with the twins."

Jason surprised himself when he heard the words coming out of his mouth. "Oh, cool. Maybe I could come visit. How long are they staying?" Who was this man saying that? It couldn't be me, Jason thought to himself. He couldn't remember the last time he had seen his sister and the twins.

His mom, clearly shocked as well, said, "W-what? That would be amazing. They are here until Sunday."

They made plans for Jason to go visit on Saturday, and after a few more minutes of talking they hung up. Jason went to his fridge to see what he could make for dinner. He was disappointed when he realized it only contained a twelve-pack of beer and an old bag of grapes. He grabbed a beer and went back to the couch. He opened his DoorDash app and ordered some Chinese from the place up the street.

His food arrived a half hour later, and Jason enjoyed a few beers while he watched the Twins play. He had heard that they had a pretty good team this year and might actually have a chance in the playoffs. Unless you are from Minnesota, you don't understand the heartbreak that their sports teams inflict on their residents. The teams will look so promising all through the season, playing like they have never played before. Then they get to the playoffs, and they shit the bed. It's like a whole new team has showed up to the playoffs, and that team has never played a professional game in their lives. Despite how good they were looking, Jason still knew not to get his hopes up.

Jason enjoyed watching the Twins play because it was something he used to do with his dad. He tried to go to at least one game a year because it made him feel close to his dad. He watched the rest of the game and then went to bed around 9:45 p.m. Jason didn't check his phone for emails. He just showered, brushed his teeth, and got into bed. *Friends* was on TV as he fell asleep, and it was the best night of sleep he had gotten in a long time.

At 12:30 p.m. the next day, Jason left to head over to the Exoneration Project office to meet with Dylan Franks. He pulled in and was surprised at how small the building was. It was in an older part of town and looked like it maybe had enough space for five offices at most. Jason wondered how could they do everything with so little space? He walked in the door and nobody seemed to notice

he was there. He was fifteen minutes early—Mr. Franks wouldn't be expecting him yet. Jason went to grab a chair in what looked to be the waiting area. The chair he was going to sit on had a big brown-looking stain on it, so Jason decided that he would just stand while he waited. He answered emails on his phone.

At 1:10 p.m. a man in khakis and a button-up came out to the lobby, looking around. He looked at Jason. "Are you Jason?" Jason nodded. "Sorry about that wait. I was waiting for you in my office. Most people just walk right in and find me. I didn't realize you were here. Follow me."

Mr. Franks showed him around the small space. It had three offices, a conference room, and a few tables that looked like they were used as desks strewn around the rest of the open area. After the tour was done, Jason said, "Mr. Franks—," but he was interrupted immediately.

"Mr. Franks is my dad. Call me Dylan."

Jason continued, "Dylan, I am very excited to get working on this case with you."

Dylan interrupted again. He seemed to be frazzled. "Oh, you won't be working with me. You will be working with attorney Rachel Nix. She is the head attorney on the case. She is still at a lunch meeting, but she should be getting back soon." Dylan led them back to the conference room. The table was cluttered with six big boxes with papers in them. There was a notepad out and loose papers all around it.

Dylan's phone started to ring. He looked at it. "Oh, I need to take this—it's the court. Just make yourself comfortable and I will come introduce you to Rachel when she gets back." With that, he left without waiting for a response. He answered his phone as he walked away. Jason chose a chair—none of them matched—and moved some of the papers in front of the seat. Jason preferred to keep things organized and in neat piles. The current state of the conference table was beginning to make him anxious. He looked at some of the papers and started to put them into piles.

"What do you think you're doing?" came a female voice from the doorway. Jason jumped a little and dropped what he was holding. He looked in the direction of the voice. He saw a brown-haired woman with glasses staring at him with a disgusted look on her face. She was wearing a navy-blue power suit with a white blouse underneath. She came closer, and Jason could see she had beautiful green eyes and cheekbones that looked like they belonged to a supermodel. He couldn't help but notice that she was beautiful, even as she was scolding him. Her angry face looked cute, and Jason felt himself smiling at her.

"Didn't you hear me? What are you doing?" she asked, as she grabbed the papers that Jason was just trying to organize. "Who are you?"

Jason registered what she was asking. "Uh, I am here meeting with Mr. Franks, uh, I mean Dylan. There is a case that I am volunteering on for my pro bono hours." Why had he said it like that, he asked himself? Why couldn't he have just said he was here to volunteer? Now she knew that if he didn't have to be here, he wouldn't be. She had him flustered. They were not off to a good start. He recovered with, "I am Jason Michelson."

"Well, Jason Michelson," she said, still aggravated with him, "do you make a habit of touching other people's work? I had everything where I needed it and you have messed it up. Dylan didn't say anything about you coming. You haven't even signed the documents yet to be able to look at all of this, have you?"

Jason didn't know what to say. He felt like he was in the principal's office being scolded. Just as he started to answer, Dylan returned. In a rushed voice, he said, "Perfect. You two have met. Rachel, this is Jason. Jason, this is Rachel. Rachel, Jason is here to help you with the Williams case." Rachel looked Jason up and down like she was deciding whether or not he was worthy of working on this case with her. He felt a little offended.

She finally relented, and held out her hand. "Hi. I am Rachel. I don't do well with people touching my stuff. I can tell by your suit that you are some attorney who works in corporate law, and like you said, are here for your pro bono hours." Her voice was ramping up to a higher volume. "The work that we do here is important and will need your full attention when you work on it. If you miss one piece of evidence, one sentence, it could be the deciding factor in a case. If you can't put the effort and time in, then you should probably fulfill your charity hours somewhere else." Rachel finished talking and looked at Jason like it was okay for him to talk.

Jason looked at Dylan and then back to Rachel. He couldn't remember the last time that someone had talked to him like that. He considered changing his mind and going to volunteer somewhere else. He wanted to respond to her in the same tone that she'd used with him, but decided that wouldn't get them anywhere. He realized that Dylan wasn't going to say anything to help him, so he finally said, "I am sorry, but you don't know me. How can you assume those things about me?"

Rachel rolled her eyes. "We get people like you in here all of the time. Expensive suits, no criminal law experience, and just hoping to get by with the minimum amount of work so that they can claim the hours. Well, that's not how it works with me. I am not going to let you mess up my case. I am going to expect you to work hard." She looked him up and down again. "Is that going to be a problem?"

Jason thought to himself that maybe this was too intense for him. Was he really ready and able to commit his time and full attention to this project? Most attorneys just had a few pro bono clients that they did court appearances for. Their assistants did the rest of the work, and the attorney got credit for the hours. Did Jason really have a hundred hours of his own time to devote to this? Rachel and

Dylan were both staring at him. She looked at him impatiently. "Well?" she asked.

Jason took in a deep breath and responded. "I am here to assist you in any way possible. I want to be here and want to do the work. Just let me know what to do." He paused, and then felt the need to explain. "I will let you know that you were right about one thing. Other than my criminal law courses, I have zero relevant training apart from what I learned on *Law & Order*." He chuckled, trying to lighten the mood in the room.

Rachel looked back at him with a blank stare, clearly unamused. Dylan cut in. "All right. Now that we've got that settled, I will get you the paperwork to sign."

Rachel went around and sat in the chair by the pad of paper on the table. The two sat in silence as they waited for Dylan to come back. Dylan returned with a single sheet of paper. Jason was expecting there to be more to it, like the fifteen-page retainers that they used at Goldstein Brandt Miller and Fredrickson. He read over the paper, which contained boilerplate confidentiality language. Jason signed it and handed it back to Dylan, who grabbed the paper and headed for the door. "I will let you two get down to it. Let me know if you need anything." He left.

Rachel was back to reading the documents from where she had left off before her lunch, ignoring Jason. Jason admired her as she worked. Her face was no longer tight with the disgust he had caused earlier. She was very focused and intently read what was in front of her. She must have felt him staring at her, because she looked up suddenly. "What?"

"Nothing," Jason said, as he looked around the table at the boxes and papers. "I, uh, just don't know what you need me to do."

She seemed annoyed again as she said, "Just let me finish this page and then we can go through some stuff." She looked back down to start reading again. She mumbled under her breath, but it was clear that she meant Jason to hear. "It looks like I will have to add babysitting to my resume after this case."

She had taken another shot at him. Jason was starting to get upset. Who was she to be rude to him? He was here to help her. She clearly needed it, based on the number of boxes and papers on the table. Why was she treating him like that? He thought about giving her a piece of his mind and voicing these thoughts, but decided against it. No use in making things worse. That wouldn't help anyone and could make their working together even more awkward. He sat, waiting until she looked up at him again.

"Okay," Rachel said. "So, have you really done nothing in criminal law?" Jason looked a little ashamed as he shook his head no. She breathed out harshly. "We have our work cut out for us, then." She thought for a moment, searching for a way to help him understand and to get to a point where he could assist her more than her having to teach him. She grabbed a piece of paper. "Let's start with a summary of the case." Rachel readjusted in the seat, pulling her legs up and crossing them. She took off her suit jacket, revealing her blouse was sleeveless. Jason could see the colors of a tattoo on her forearm, but couldn't see the image properly the way her arm was facing.

"You're going to want to get comfortable." Rachel paused, waiting for Jason to make some type of movement. When he didn't, she said, "You aren't going to take your jacket off?" When Jason shook his head no, in a nonchalant way, Rachel shrugged her shoulders like she couldn't care less. She started, "His name is Maxwell James Williams. He was convicted in 1982 of three offenses."

Jason interrupted her. "Do you have an extra notepad and pen I could borrow?" Rachel looked around the table and found a notepad with a few pages left in it. She grabbed that and an extra pen and slid them over to Jason. She looked at him, waiting for the cue that he was ready for her to keep going. He quickly wrote "Maxwell James Williams – 1982" at the top of his page and looked up at her to signify he was ready. Rachel continued. "Like I was saying, he was convicted of three offenses. Burglary in the first degree, first-degree murder, and sexual assault." Jason continued to take vigorous notes.

"The victim in the case was Amelia Marie Jackson, a twenty-three-year-old nursing student. She attended the University of Minnesota. Amelia was killed on March 23, 1982, in her home. The State's theory of the case is that Maxwell knocked on the door, and Amelia let him into the apartment. He went on to rape and kill her and then left her in her apartment on the bed. Her roommate, Casey, came home a few hours later and found her body."

Rachel paused for Jason to catch up with his notes. "Wow," he said. "Why did they suspect our client?" She looked down at the summary sheet again, but Jason could tell that was just for show. He had a feeling Rachel had the sheet memorized already. There was something about her that gave off a vibe that she had studied this case inside and out. She had a focused look on her face, but Jason could also see a hint of sadness as well.

"Maxwell and Amelia had been in an on-again, off-again relationship for three years at the time of her death. Witnesses saw them fighting the night before she was killed. Maxwell told the police he was at home alone during the time the medical examiner determined Amelia was killed. There was something about him having food delivered a little while before that time, but the prosecutor showed he would have had enough time to get to Amelia's and kill her after the food was delivered."

Rachel put down the sheet and looked at Jason, waiting for his questions. He couldn't think of anything good to ask, so he just said, "Where do we start?" Rachel got a slight smile on her face like she approved of the question. As she smiled, a dimple appeared on each cheek, and her eyes lit up a little bit. They looked less serious, almost playful.

"That's what I like to hear," she said, still smiling. Rachel looked around the table and grabbed a criminal appellate procedure book. She handed it to Jason. "How much do you know about appellate procedure?" she asked.

Jason opened the book. "Just what we learned in school, and that was 1L year, almost seven years ago now."

Rachel seemed to be warming up to Jason a little bit. He thought that was a good sign that they were making progress.

Rachel said, "Okay, well, it's probably best if you understand what we are asking for and how it works procedurally, before you get into the facts of the case. It will help you know what things are important. Start with the Petition for New Trial, based on DNA evidence. There was semen found at the scene, but this case began prior to DNA evidence being admissible in Minnesota criminal cases. Minnesota started accepting DNA evidence in cases in 1989. Before that, it was not considered valid science."

Jason, feeling the anticipation rising as he prepared to start digging into the Williams case, asked, "Was the semen tested?" After he asked, it started to seem like a stupid question. He had read on the Exoneration Project website that there were stringent criteria that a case had to meet for the organization to take it. They received thousands of letters and calls a year from inmates or family members asking the Exoneration Project to take their cases. Cases had to survive an extensive screening process to qualify. They wouldn't have taken the Williams case if there wasn't something to give him a good shot at exoneration.

"Yes!" Rachel exclaimed, seemingly annoyed again. Jason thought to himself how easy it was to set her off. He was going to have to be more careful with what he said. "They tested it, and we got the results back six months ago. It was not a match for Mr. Williams. There is no match in the database, however, so that complicates things."

"How so?" Jason asked. "If the semen isn't Mr. Williams's, isn't that enough to show he didn't do it?"

"No. Haven't you ever watched any crime show on TV? A jury could still find him guilty based on the rest of the evidence. There are many theories that could explain why there was DNA present that wasn't his." Rachel went on. "Don't get me wrong. The DNA not matching is strong evidence and should be enough to get a new trial, but we need more."

Rachel looked down at her notes; this time it looked like she was actually searching for something. "We need to find something that his attorney missed. Mr. Williams was only twenty-four years old at the time and was a student himself. He didn't have money for an attorney, so he had a public defender. It is customary with appeals like this that we argue inefficient assistance of counsel, especially when a public defender is involved."

"Do the previous attorneys get angry if you claim that? Has anyone ever come back and argued that they did the best they could?" Jason asked.

"No, that hasn't happened since I have been here. Attorneys realize that if their clients get convicted then an inefficient assistance of counsel argument is going to follow. It is easy to make arguments that an attorney did something wrong or missed something in a case. We are essentially looking at the case with twenty-twenty hindsight, as the saying goes. We can see everything, all the testimony, all the evidence, things that the defense attorney was not necessarily fully aware of when prepping for trial." She continued, "It is especially easy to argue inefficient assistance of counsel when the client had a public defender. Public defenders typically have too heavy caseloads and too few resources to provide an adequate defense in cases like this. This is well known by the courts as well, and I feel like courts give the client the benefit of the doubt because of it."

Jason continued to take notes here and there for things to look up in the procedure book. "That should be enough to get you started for today," Rachel said. "I am sure you have a busy schedule to get back to at the office. You can take the book with you if you want."

Jason stood up, and she thought he was getting ready to leave. She was surprised, however, when he started to take off his suit jacket and hang it on the back of the chair next to where he was sitting. He sat back down. "I had my assistant clear the rest of the day. I would prefer to stay here and work on this, if that's okay with you." Jason looked at her hopefully. Rachel shrugged like she was fine with it, and she went back to her reading. Jason opened the book and found the statutes for new trial petitions.

CHAPTER SIX

Jason and Rachel had been working silently for almost two hours when she got up to stretch. "How's it going?" Her voice was sweeter than in their earlier conversations. "Are you figuring out the procedures?" She leaned down, stretching to touch her toes, and held that position for about ten seconds before she came back up again to look toward him.

"Good. I think I am almost finished up with it." He smiled. "I forgot how much I like researching right from the books. I can't remember the last time I didn't use Westlaw for my searches. I may have to keep doing it the old-fashioned way."

"I love having the physical copy of something in front of me. It seems more, oh, what's a good way to describe it? More real, I guess? You see all the papers in front of you. You can see all the statutes and rules, and you can get a better understanding of how they intertwine with each other when you read it in the book itself. When I was in law school, I realized that when I read cases or things online, I wouldn't comprehend them as well. It was almost like I was just skimming," Rachel said. Jason could hear the passion in Rachel's voice as she spoke. He was amused, and thought she was cute when she got passionate.

Rachel paused and looked down. "Sorry. I get really into this stuff." She seemed embarrassed.

"No, I like it. I get that way too!" Jason reassured her.

Rachel was still looking down, and Jason thought he could see her blushing a little bit. Before he could think about it too much, she looked back up and was right back to business. "So, what did you learn about the process?" she asked.

Jason started, "Well, we would be using Minnesota Statute Section 590 for post-conviction relief. That statute allows for a petition for a person convicted of a crime if there is scientific evidence that wasn't available at trial that establishes the person's innocence. Since DNA testing was not around at the initial trial, that qualifies as new scientific evidence that was previously not available. There is an explanation on how to get the DNA testing done, but since you told me that a test was already done, and the DNA doesn't match Mr. Williams's, I am guessing that someone else already brought that motion?" He paused to get some type of assurance that he was on the right track.

Rachel looked amused and nodded yes. "That was done prior to our involvement. We must have the testing done already for the cases to qualify for our services." She paused, indicating that Jason should keep going.

"The time limits for post-conviction relief seemed very stringent at first, and I was worried that this case would not qualify since it is so old. However, we could argue that the DNA results are newly discovered evidence under subd. 4(a)(2), or under subd. 4(a)(5)'s catch-all provision that states that the petition is not frivolous and is in the interest of justice. Justice will not be served if an innocent man continues to sit in prison for a crime that he did not commit." Jason continued, gaining enthusiasm: "I have flagged the pages with the requirements of the petition, and the procedures that we have to follow after we file the petition."

"Is that all you learned in the last two hours?" Rachel asked, with a hint of sarcasm in her voice.

"No, I also read some of the case law referenced in the notes and history section, and have outlined the cases that I think would be beneficial for us to cite in any memorandum we attach to our petition," Jason countered.

"Now that is what I would expect from a big-firm lawyer," she teased.

She smiled at him, her eyes twinkling and her dimples deepening on her face. "Well, now that you understand the procedures we will need to utilize, time to start reviewing the file." Rachel stood up to look in a box. She picked it up and handed it over to Jason. He looked inside and saw three big stacks of paper. The first page of the top stack was labeled "*State of Minnesota v. Maxwell James Williams*" and "October 23, 1982."

"I have already read through the transcript, and I knew someone else was going to be assigned to help me, so I printed off a clean copy of it. It's all in there. Why don't you start there?" she offered.

Jason picked up the first stack of papers and started reading the first page. Rachel looked at him, a little shocked. "Don't you need to get back to your office?" She realized that came out harsher than she meant. "Sorry, that's not what I meant. I just mean you don't have to do all of it right now, today. I know you probably have a lot to catch up on." She gave a weak smile to make up for her harsh comment.

"You're fine. I get what you meant. You are probably right. I should probably get back to it." Jason looked at his watch and saw it was almost 3:45 p.m. Even though Amy had cleared his whole day, Jason didn't want to overstay his welcome. He started to pack everything up and put the notepad he was using for notes in the box with the transcripts. "Is it just us working on this case?"

"No. I have a law student, Mia Drake, who is volunteering as well. Her law school sent her over a week or two before we got approved to take this case."

"When was that?" Jason asked. He remembered Dylan saying that it was approved recently.

Rachel thought for a second. "Um, about five months ago, I think." Jason was surprised, and it must have showed on his face. "What?" Rachel asked.

"Nothing. Dylan had said this case was just approved, so I thought it was maybe a few weeks ago." Jason thought back to the old saying that the wheels of justice grind slowly. Boy, was that right. Jason thought better of sharing the quote with Rachel. She might have been offended by it.

"So, is this Mia Drake any help?" Jason asked.

Rachel thought about a way to answer the question. "I guess so. She is very green and sometimes oversteps."

"What do you mean 'oversteps?'"

"Well, I get the impression that she thinks this case would not be able to proceed without her. Like I am just here to supervise her while she works on the case."

Jason just nodded, not sure what to say to that. Based on his interactions with Rachel so far, he couldn't see her letting that kind of behavior from someone fly. "How often does she volunteer?" he asked.

"She is here twice a week usually. Sometimes three days a week, depending on her workload at school." Rachel pointed to the transcripts Jason had. "She has already read through all of those and done a lot of research into the DNA evidence and petition. I had her start with the background research, just like you. She didn't get it done as quickly as you did." Rachel smiled at him.

Jason smiled back at her. "I'm a seasoned pro. What are the next steps? I review these, and then we get back together for me to go over more of the file?"

"Yeah. That would probably work best." Rachel grabbed a card off the table behind her. "Here's my card. It has my cellphone number on it. Don't try the office phone. I never check the voicemail, and I'm rarely in my office. There isn't enough space in there to spread out. I am usually in here, or I bring everything home and spread things out on my tables. I have a war room set up at my place."

"That is so awesome!" Jason exclaimed. "I have always wanted to have a war room set up. I do transactional commercial law, so I rarely go to court. No need for a war room in my line of work. I would love to see it some time." He paused, looking like he had put his foot in his mouth. "Sorry, I didn't mean to invite myself over to your house." He stopped again before he made it worse.

Rachel let out a little giggle, enjoying Jason's struggling. "Yeah, that was a little presumptuous. At least take me out to dinner first," she joked. "And I think you would play well in court. You have that whole pretty boy look about you."

Jason felt his cheeks blushing, and he wasn't sure why. He was used to getting compliments from women. He wasn't sure what it was about Rachel, but she intrigued him. She wasn't the typical type he went for. To be honest, he was into blondes who looked like they would walk the runway. Rachel had dark hair and glasses, and had more of an edgy look to her. She had a curvy, athletic body, and her blouse fit her well. She was beautiful in her own way, but it wasn't her looks that intrigued him. It was something about her attitude and the passion he could see on her face. He wanted to learn more about her, more than just what he would learn as they worked together on the case.

He registered what Rachel had said, and he decided to take a shot. He asked, "Would you like to get dinner some time?" There were a few seconds of silence with no answer, so he quickly added, "Maybe a working dinner. We could order some food and work on the case."

She thought about it for a few more seconds. "Sure. We could do that. How about once you're done with the transcripts, you text me and we will plan a night to order in some food here and go over everything we have learned so far?"

"That sounds great." Jason's watch started buzzing to signify he was getting a call. He looked at his Apple watch and saw it was Amy calling from the office phone. "Sorry, I have to grab this." Rachel nodded and looked back down at the document she was reviewing. "Hey, Amy, what's up?" he said as he answered his phone.

"Hey, Jason. Mr. Brandt is looking for you to go over a new case he wants you to take the lead on. He's wondering when you are going to be back. What can I tell him?" Amy asked.

"I am just packing up here and will be heading back. I should be there by 4:10 p.m. I can stop by his as soon as I get there. See you soon!" Jason hung up, got up from his chair and put his suit jacket back on. "Rachel, I appreciate everything, and it was great meeting you. I look forward to working with you." He reached out to shake her hand. She took his and shook it back.

"Just text me when you're done with those, and we will get something set up," she said. Jason grabbed the box and headed out the door.

"Talk soon," he said with a nod.

Jason walked into his office and put the box on his desk. He grabbed a notepad and pen and headed over to Zachary's office. He stopped to talk with Juliette, the assistant. "Hey Jules, is he available to meet on that new file?" Jason asked. Juliette was a petite blonde thirty-year-old who had been working for Zachary for about two years. She had a beauty mark on her cheek that was dark brown in color. She always wore high-end designer clothing and was very put together. Jason wouldn't describe her as beautiful, but she was cute in her own way.

Jason and Juliette had hung out a few times outside of work. It started when they were at the yearly party the firm had when they were trying to impress potential incoming associates. There were law students who were interviewing to be summer associates, as well as potential new hires who were newly licensed attorneys. All employees were required to attend and be welcoming to these potential newcomers.

This was the first year that Juliette was with the firm, and she'd had a few too many drinks. She walked over to Jason, who was talking with some other associates, and put her arm around his waist. "How's it going, boys?" she said a little too loudly, slurring her words a little. The other associates looked at each other, not sure what to do. Jason had dealt with this situation before. His sister Kylie had gotten really drunk at a family gathering when she was seventeen, and Jason had had to get her out of there before anyone noticed.

Jason looked around to see where Zachary Brandt was. He put his arm around Juliette's waist and leaned over to whisper in her ear. "You are drunk and being loud. We need to get you out of here before any of the partners notice."

"I'm not drunk," she said, even louder this time. A few people who were close by started to look over. Jason looked around and noticed that she was beginning to make a scene.

He turned back to the other associates. "I am going to get her out of here. If anyone asks, just say she was sick, and I offered to take her home." The associates nodded. "You guys have a great rest of your night." He started to lead Juliette from the party to the parking ramp to his car.

"Where are we going? I was just starting to have fun," Juliette said, her words still slurred.

As they were walking out, they passed a table, and Jason grabbed two waters for her to drink. He'd only had two drinks in the three hours they had been there. "We need to make sure you still have a job next Monday, so I am going to get you home," Jason told her as they walked out to the elevator.

"What do you mean? Why wouldn't I have a job?" Juliette hiccupped as she stumbled forward. Jason had to catch her. Grasping harder to steady her, he pushed the button on the elevator to go down to the lobby so they could get on the regular elevator and get to his car.

"Here, drink this," he said, as he handed her one of the water bottles. She started chugging it but had to stop a few times to hiccup. Then she burped. "Oops, sorry." She giggled, and kept drinking the water.

They got down to Jason's car and he helped her buckle her seatbelt. He handed her the second water. "What's your address?" he asked, putting his own seatbelt on, getting ready to take her home.

He looked over and Juliette's eyes were already closing as she passed out. Jason shook her arm a little bit. "Hey! Don't go to sleep yet. What's your address? I need to get you home." When he realized she wasn't going to answer, he sighed. What was he going to do now? His only option was to bring her back to his place to sleep it off. He backed out of his parking spot and headed for his apartment. She was soon snoring quietly next to him.

They got back to Jason's place, and he carried her up to his apartment. He thought about how bad it would look if one of his neighbors came back and saw him carrying a random, passed-out girl to his door. He put that thought aside and got her inside. Jason laid her down on the bed, took her stilettos off and placed them on the floor next to her. He grabbed another bottle of water from the fridge and put it on the bedside table next to her. Finally, he grabbed the mop bucket from under the kitchen sink and put it next to the bed, just in case.

After he got her all settled, he grabbed an extra blanket out of the closet and the extra pillow from the bed and brought them over to the couch. He grabbed his laptop and logged in remotely to his desktop at the office. He had been working for about three hours when he heard a noise from his bed.

"Oh, I don't feel so good." Juliette sat up too quickly and looked like she was going to throw up. She stood up to run to the bathroom. Jason followed her and held her hair while she puked into his toilet. That went on for a few minutes, then he helped her back to bed. Jason made her drink the last bottle of water before she lay back down. Juliette didn't seem too concerned about where she was, and she went back to sleep.

Jason went back over to the couch and realized it was almost two in the morning. He had been planning on going back to the office in a few hours. It was a Saturday, and Jason always got the most done on Saturdays when there were fewer distractions. He would have to bring Juliette back to her car anyway, so nothing should really get in the way of him going to the office in the morning. It might just be a little later than planned. He decided to lie down and try to get a few hours of sleep.

Jason's alarm on his phone went off at 8 a.m. and he rolled over to turn it off. He wiped the sleep out of his eyes and looked over toward his bed, where Juliette was still sleeping. He went to the bathroom and got ready. Then he heard her start to move around. He walked out of the bathroom, and she looked at him, confused. Then she looked down and saw the bucket next to her and the blanket on the couch where Jason had slept. As she pieced together what must have happened, a mortified look came across her face. "Oh my gosh, Jason. I am so sorry. I don't even remember what happened last night."

He walked back over to the bed. "You got pretty drunk and were getting kind of loud, so I figured I should get you out of there before Mr. Brandt saw."

"Thank you so much. I really appreciate it. Did we . . . ?" Her words trailed off, and she looked at him curiously.

"No. I slept on the couch," Jason answered quickly, not wanting her to get the wrong impression about him.

"Oh. Okay. Thanks for taking care of me," she said. Jason thought Juliette almost sounded disappointed that they didn't hook up.

"We should probably get you back to your car at the office. I planned on going in today to get some stuff done. We could stop for a quick breakfast on the way if you want," Jason said, hinting at them getting ready to leave.

Juliette took the hint, stood up out of the bed and ran her hands down the creases on her dress. She started putting her shoes back on. She looked around for anything else of hers that was around the apartment.

"I wasn't sure where your purse was. You didn't have it with you at the party, and you were too drunk to answer any questions when we were leaving."

She put her face in her hands. "I am such an idiot. I am so sorry, Jason. I don't know how things got so out of control. I don't usually drink much." She hesitated, seeming to contemplate whether she should say more. "We found out yesterday that my dad has been diagnosed with Stage IV cancer. I guess I was still dealing with that news and went a little overboard." She turned, so he wouldn't see the tears coming to her eyes.

"It's okay," Jason said, coming closer to put a hand on her shoulder. "I am sorry you are going through this. Don't worry about what happened last night. It could happen to anyone. Really!" he reassured her.

"You're just being nice," Juliette said, as she wiped away a tear from her cheek. "I owe you big time."

"No problem. Let's stop and grab some breakfast on the way." He gathered the rest of his stuff for the office, and they headed to the car.

They stopped and bought some smoothies on the way. When they got to the office, Jason said, "Maybe you should go up first and get your stuff. It might look bad if we both show up at the same time and you are still in your outfit from last night."

"Good idea," Juliette said, as she got out of the car. She leaned back through the door and kissed him on the cheek. "Thanks again, Jason. I don't know what I would have done if I had made a fool of myself and ended up being fired."

"No problem," he said, as she shut the door and went to the elevator. Jason waited and went up to the office ten minutes later.

Two weeks later, Juliette emailed Jason to see if he wanted to go get drinks as thanks for him saving her that night. They went out that evening for happy hour. Jason asked her about her dad, and it sounded like things weren't going well. He listened to her as she talked about her childhood and what it was like around the house with her dad. She described him as if he were already gone and these were the only good memories she would have of him.

They went back to the office that night after drinks. He walked Juliette to her car, and she surprised Jason when she leaned in and kissed him. He wasn't ready for it and was taken aback. He didn't kiss her back.

She pulled away. "I'm sorry. I just, I thought, maybe you were interested in me?"

"I, uh," Jason stammered. "You are a great girl, Juliette. I just don't see you that way. I don't have time to date, and I don't think dating someone from work would be a good idea. I'm sorry if I gave you the wrong idea."

"No. It's my fault," Juliette responded. "I shouldn't have assumed. It's just not often you meet such a nice guy, and I misread the signals."

After that night, Jason attended Juliette's dad's funeral, and they hung out once more after that, but it was strictly platonic. Juliette started dating another guy a few months after her dad died, and that made Jason more comfortable hanging out with her again.

CHAPTER SEVEN

Juliette smiled at Jason. "He is just finishing up on a call, Jason. Then he will be ready for you. Where have you been this afternoon? He went to your office a few times and had me page Amy."

"I started my pro bono hours this afternoon. I am volunteering for the Exoneration Project. It's a case where a man was wrongfully convicted of sexually assaulting and killing his girlfriend," Jason explained.

"Wow, that sounds interesting! Just a tip. Don't bring up the new pro bono requirement and how you don't like it or think it's unfair. He has already heard that from half the office, and he is not happy about it," she cautioned.

"Thanks for the heads-up," Jason said, as Zachary Brandt's voice sounded from his office. "Okay, Jason, I am ready for you. Come on in." Jason walked into the office and sat down in the chair across from Mr. Brandt's desk. "Where were you off to this afternoon? I tried to find you a few times."

Jason answered, making sure not to make it seem like he had a problem with the pro bono hours. "I started my hours at the Exoneration Project today, so I was over there for a few hours meeting the staff and starting the casework."

Mr. Brandt seemed relieved. "Thank you for not complaining about the requirement changing, and just getting right to it. The named partners believe it is important for our firm to show stronger community involvement. A study came out that correlated law firms that are involved in the community with overall higher satisfaction from clients. Apparently high-paying businesses like to know that their attorneys have a soul or some shit."

Jason nodded. "That makes sense, I guess."

Mr. Brandt moved on to other business. "All right, we have a new client, and they requested you take the lead. It's a health and wellness company that is working to go public. The CEO is a woman who grew up in your hometown, I believe. She said she knew you, and that's why she chose us as a firm."

"Oh, really. Who is she?" Jason asked curiously. He looked at his notes. "Emily Cruze."

Jason thought about the name but couldn't place it. "I'm not sure I remember her. I will have to look her up and see if she rings any bells."

"You do that. She is coming in first thing tomorrow to meet with you." Mr. Brandt handed Jason a folder. "Here is the preliminary report that her accountant sent over. Review it in preparation for the meeting." He looked back at his computer as though the conversation was over. Zachary Brandt had a way of doing that. Once he got out what he had to say, he was right on to the next thing. Never any time for small talk or questions. He gave his orders, and then expected them to be followed.

There was one time that Jason and Mr. Brandt had gone out to eat after a late night at the office. They had just closed a $9.4 million deal, and they were celebrating. Jason soon found out that once Zachary Brandt had a few beers in him, he was a talker. He told Jason how the only reason he went to law school was because his dad was an attorney. His real passion was animals, and he wanted to open a nonprofit to take in animals with disabilities and those that families didn't want to adopt. If it were up to him, Zachary Brandt would be a veterinarian right now, not running a law firm.

Jason enjoyed getting a small look at who his boss was outside of the office. He would never have guessed that he was such an animal lover, or interested in operating a nonprofit. Jason remembered thinking that Mr. Brandt would never have the time to do that—he was too busy running the firm. That was the only time that Jason and Zachary Brandt had spent together discussing things other than work. It seemed almost like he wanted to keep up a boundary to have things remain professional between them. Jason didn't mind it too much.

Jason took the cue, grabbed the folder, and got up to leave. "Thanks, Mr. Brandt." He walked back to his office. Amy followed him in. They both sat down at the desk. Jason told her about the new case, and filled her in about the wellness CEO and how she had requested him because they had gone to school together. They looked her up on Facebook, so Jason could see if it triggered anything.

"She looks kind of familiar," Jason said, as he scrolled through her photos. He went back and found some from high school. "Oh, here we go. Yeah, she was in my science class, I think, but I think she was Emily Baer back then. She must have gotten married since then." Jason handed Amy the folder. "Can you do a summary sheet on this for me before you go tonight? I guess she is coming in first thing tomorrow for a meeting."

"Of course, boss." The two of them went over everything else that needed to get done in the day, plus the calls he had missed, and then she asked, "How did it go at the Exoneration Project?"

"It went all right. The lead attorney's name is Rachel. She didn't like me very much at first. She gave me a really hard time, but I think by the end she realized that I was actually going to try on this case." Jason went on to relay the summary of the case that Rachel had told him. He pointed over to the box on the other side of his desk. "The trial transcripts are in there. I am going to work through them, and then Rachel and I are getting together to go over everything."

Amy listened intently, and Jason could tell she was intrigued and waiting to ask something. "So," she started, "tell me more about this Rachel."

Jason rolled his eyes. "We are working together. I wasn't focused on anything other than that. Plus, I don't have time to gossip right now. I have a lot to get done, since I was there this afternoon instead of here working."

"Just answer one question. Is she cute?" Amy smiled.

Jason sighed and gave in. "Yes. She is cute, okay? Can I get back to working now?"

Amy got up and left the office with a wink. Jason couldn't help but think back to his time with Rachel. She *was* cute, beautiful even. Had she agreed to have dinner with him just as a working dinner? Why did he even ask her to dinner in the first place? That was so unlike him. Jason didn't have time to think about that, though. He had work to catch up on and transcripts to read.

Amy came in to say goodbye before she left, and Jason went down to get some food. He ordered a burger and went down to get some coffee. When he got back to his desk, he grabbed the summary Amy had put together for Emily's case.

Emily had started the business in 2017, a few years after high school. She started by making YouTube fitness videos. From there, it expanded to activewear, smoothies, and now full meal kits. Jason was impressed. Emily had made a successful business for herself. He was happy that she had chosen him to represent her as she took her company public. This move would make her a lot more money, and in turn make him and the firm a lot of money. Jason thought about the additional work that taking a company public would be for him in addition to his work with the Exoneration Project, but then he realized that two of his big mergers were going to be wrapping up soon, so he should have the time.

His food was delivered, and he ate quickly as he read through a few other reports for other clients. He looked at the clock. It was almost 11 p.m. He rubbed his eyes and blinked a few times to let them adjust after looking at the computer screen for so many hours straight. He stretched out his arms and leaned back in his chair. He saw the box of transcripts out of the corner of his eye. Jason had planned on starting on those tonight. He thought about it and assessed how tired he was. He had been through plenty of all-nighters beginning in law school, then while studying for the bar, and now since being hired at Goldstein Brandt Miller and Fredrickson. He asked himself, did he have enough energy to pull another one tonight?

Jason made up his mind that he was going to at least try to get through the opening statements in the transcripts. He decided that it would be better for him to head home first, shower, and change into something more comfortable to make his reading more enjoyable. He gathered his things and headed for the door. He was the only one left in the office at that hour. He rode down to the lobby, and the security guard on duty walked him out to his car. Their offices were in a nice part of Minneapolis, but it was still Minneapolis. It was necessary to have a security guard walk everyone out to their cars after hours, especially this late at night.

After driving home, once Jason got out of the shower, he slipped on some gray sweatpants and grabbed the first book of transcripts. He sat down on the couch with a highlighter and pen on the end table next to him. The transcript started out with the date, time, and the judge putting everyone's name on the record. This was followed by some material about jury selection. Jason decided that he didn't need to read those parts right now. He skimmed to see where the opening statements started.

He got to page 102. Perfect, he thought. I am already a hundred pages in. Jason laughed to himself about the thought. The transcript read, "Mr. Jackson"—the county attorney on the case at the time—"are you ready to proceed with opening statements?"

Phillip Jackson: "I am, Your Honor. Ladies and gentlemen of the jury. We are all here today because of the events that occurred on March 23, 1982, in a North Minneapolis apartment. Twenty-three-year-old Amelia Marie Jackson was sitting in her home studying for a school exam. Amelia was a nursing student in her last year at the University of Minnesota. The exam was the following day, and she was ready to ace it. Amelia was a straight-A student, and she was on track to graduate with honors at the end of the semester. She was working for Fairview part time and was hoping to get a full-time RN position with them once she graduated and passed the nursing exam.

"Unfortunately, Amelia would never get to live out that dream. She would never get an A on that test, she would never graduate nursing school, and she would never go on to pass the nursing exam and start her dream job. Not only that, but Amelia would never grow up and get married or have kids. Her life was cut short in a tragic series of events.

"The State will show you evidence throughout this trial to prove beyond a reasonable doubt that Maxwell James Williams pushed his way into Amelia's home, sexually assaulted her, and stabbed her, leaving her to bleed out on her bed until her roommate came home to find her later that day.

"The defendant and Amelia were in an on-again, off-again relationship for three years at the time. Nobody can say for certain if they were together or not the day that she was murdered. However, you will hear testimony that the defendant and Amelia were out together the night before at a bar. There were witnesses who saw them arguing and yelling at each other. Things got heated and the couple went outside. They continued to argue, and Amelia ended up slapping the defendant in the face. After that, Amelia stormed off and called her roommate to come pick her up. She told her roommate, Casey True, all about the fight that happened between her and the defendant.

"Ms. True will testify that it was not unusual for the defendant and Amelia to fight. She will tell you about the many fights that she witnessed between the couple, and that it often got loud and dramatic. She will testify about coming home that day and finding Amelia, her skin starting to turn colors, her body covered in blood. It is something that no twenty-two-year-old should ever have to see, and it will stick with her forever. This is the second life that the defendant changed forever.

"Amelia's family and friends are also forever changed. She had two loving parents, who are in the courtroom today. She had a younger brother, who is a freshman at the University of Minnesota, and an older sister who just had her first child. Amelia was an aunt and a godmother to her niece. This family will never get their daughter, sister, and aunt back.

"Amelia had countless friends from high school and college who will forever be changed and who miss her dearly. The acts of the defendant that cold March day have forever changed the lives of all these people, and he needs to pay for his crimes.

"The evidence will show that Amelia died between 1 and 1:45 p.m., with the cause of death being sixteen stab wounds to her body. Yes, you heard me right, sixteen. The evidence will show that after their fight the night before, the defendant tried to call Amelia three times that morning, and she ignored all his calls. He was angry with her for not answering, so he went over to her apartment. He knocked on the door, and when she opened it, the defendant pushed his way into the apartment. He struck Amelia to knock her off guard. You will see autopsy photographs showing the impression on her head.

"The defendant then brought Amelia over to her bed, ripped off all of her clothes, and raped her. He didn't use a condom. The defendant held Amelia down by the wrists as he forced himself inside of her. We have no way to know how long the sexual assault lasted, but we do know that it was long enough for the defendant to leave a semen sample in her. Can you just imagine the fear and confusion that Amelia was feeling during those moments? The man she thought loved her had broken into her apartment, assaulted her, and was now raping her.

"If that wasn't enough, the defendant took his rage further and found a knife in the kitchen. In the meantime, while he was in the kitchen, Amelia tried to cover herself up with a blanket. The defendant came back and began stabbing her—stabbing her over and over again with her own kitchen knife. Amelia's body will show that she struggled during a few of the stabs, based on the wounds left in her body. He didn't stop until he had stabbed her enough times that she was no longer moving. She was no longer able to fight back. The defendant left her body on her bed covered in blood, half of her covered by the blanket she had tried to put over herself. He left her there for Ms. True to come home and find.

"The defendant forced his way into Amelia Jackson's apartment, hit her, raped her, and murdered her. The State is confident that at the end of this trial, it will be clear what the defendant did. I will stand up here and ask you to find the defendant Maxwell James Williams guilty of burglary in the first degree, first-degree murder, and sexual assault. Thank you."

Jason put down the transcript and took a deep breath. That was a very powerful opening statement. If the evidence did support what Mr. Jackson said, Jason wasn't surprised that the jury convicted Mr. Williams of the charges. Jason looked at the time; it was past midnight now. He had enough time to read through the defense opening and still grab a few hours of sleep before going back into the office. He picked up the transcript again.

Judge: "Mr. Duncan, are you ready for your opening?"

Cole Duncan: "Yes, Your Honor. Ladies and gentlemen of the jury, Mr. Jackson paints a pretty horrific picture of what he thinks happened that day in Amelia Jackson's apartment. The truth is, he doesn't know what happened that day. He is just guessing based on what other people have told him about my client and Amelia. Nobody was there to witness when Amelia was attacked and died. There were no witnesses who saw my client at her apartment, or near the building. The State has no witnesses who place my client with Amelia at any point after she left the bar the night before. There is nothing to suggest that Mr. Williams even talked with Amelia after that point.

"Yes, he did call her three times, and she never answered him. That was typical for them when they would fight. Mr. Jackson is right. There are witnesses who will be able to testify that the relationship between Mr. Williams and Amelia was not always healthy. They did fight a lot. However, there is no witness who can get up here and say that Mr. Williams ever got physical with her. The State tries to paint this as an abusive relationship, but the fact of the matter is Maxwell Williams was not abusive. Couples fight. These two were young, in their early twenties. They fought. Sometimes things escalated too much, and things got loud. The two of them would break up, go home to cool off, and eventually talk things out and get back together.

"None of that proves that Mr. Williams was the one in Amelia's apartment on March 23, 1982. Amelia had been cleaning with bleach earlier that day, which left only a few sets of prints once she was done. There were no fingerprints in the apartment that matched my client's. There is no way to prove who the DNA belonged to. The only reason the State thinks Mr. Williams committed this crime is because they were in a relationship and had fought the night before. If that were all it took to convict someone of murder, there would be a lot more of us in prison. I know I would be. My wife and I get into heated arguments. What couple doesn't?

"There is something that Mr. Jackson conveniently left out. Mr. Williams was in his own apartment at the time Amelia was killed. He had ordered food from a local restaurant down the street. It was delivered at 12:30 p.m. that day. The delivery driver will testify to that fact. He will testify that he didn't remember Mr. Williams acting strange or like anything was out of the ordinary. Mr. Williams took the food inside his apartment and ate it. Then he started studying for the history exam he had coming up later in the week.

"Mr. Williams didn't leave his apartment during that time. He was home for the entirety of the time during which the medical examiner will testify that Amelia died. My client even tried to call Amelia again at 3:02 p.m. that day. He wasn't aware of what was going on until the police came to his apartment at 9 p.m. that night to question him.

"If my client had committed these crimes, why wouldn't the delivery driver have noticed him acting weird? If he was about to go assault and kill his girlfriend, wouldn't you think he would be acting funny or anxious? Why would he order food before he went and did all of those things? If Mr. Williams went over to Amelia's apartment, don't you think someone would have noticed him? It was in the middle of the day, and Mr. Williams had been to Amelia's apartment before. People would have recognized him if he were there. Why would he have called her three times earlier in the day, and again after she had been killed and left bleeding in her bed? He's no criminal mastermind trying to set up any sort of defense. He honestly had no idea what had happened, and he was calling Amelia during a study break to try to reconcile.

"The simple answer is that Mr. Williams wouldn't have done any of those things. The story the county attorney gave you just doesn't make sense. Mr. Williams had no reason to kill Amelia. They had a fight the night before, so what? That was common for them. They would likely get back together the next day like they always had. That is why Mr. Williams had called her that day. He was calling to apologize. He wouldn't do that if he planned on going to her apartment and killing her.

"The State made a lot of promises about the evidence and what it was going to show you. Ignore what Mr. Jackson has told you and the narrative that he is trying to push. You listen to the evidence and make the decision for yourselves what that evidence means. If you look at it all from a neutral perspective, you will see the evidence doesn't add up to what Mr. Jackson says it does. Mr. Williams did not commit these crimes. He did not go into Amelia's apartment that day. Mr. Williams did not rape her. Mr. Williams did not kill Amelia. Mr. Williams is not guilty of the charges brought against him today.

"We will be asking at the end of this trial that you review all the evidence: all the physical evidence, or lack thereof, all the witness testimony, and the timelines. After you review all that, we will ask you to find that the State has not met its burden of proving Maxwell Williams guilty beyond a reasonable doubt. Because of that, we will be asking that you find Maxwell James Williams not guilty.

"Thank you."

Jason put down the transcript again, but this time on the end table next to the couch. He was entranced with this case already. Now that he had read the defense's opening statement, he wasn't so sure about what he thought. Of course, he would read about the evidence and testimony that came in during the trial and make his final determination at that point. He thought the public defender's opening statement was very good, and he remembered back to something he'd read about arguing inefficient assistance of counsel and how that was always an argument to make on appeal. Rachel had also mentioned this and indicated that they would be making that argument in the petition.

After reading that opening, Jason didn't see how they could argue inefficient assistance of counsel. Mr. Duncan's opening was strong. He seemed like he knew the case well and was representing his client efficiently. Again, there were a lot of transcripts left, but these were Jason's initial thoughts. One thing was clear: Jason was looking forward to reading the rest of the transcripts and working on this case. The love of criminal law that had started when he was younger watching *Law & Order: SUV* was back, and he was anxious to get to experience this world for himself.

Jason got up from the couch and went over to the bed. He took off his shirt and sweatpants, leaving him in just his boxers. He set his alarm to 6:30 a.m. He would give himself an extra hour of sleep, since he had worked so late. He got under the covers and went to sleep with the remnants of what he'd just read still swirling in his mind.

CHAPTER EIGHT

Jason walked into the office at 7:05 a.m., probably the latest he had arrived since he started working there. Amy was already at her desk when he walked in. "Nice of you to join us," she joked as she followed him into his office. "Did you have a late night?"

"Yeah, I stayed up reading some of the transcripts on the Williams case. Then I got a few hours of sleep before my meeting with Emily. I read your summary of her company—it is pretty impressive."

Amy smiled. "Very! How well did you know her in high school?"

"I didn't know her well at all. I think we just had that one class together. I was surprised we were friends on Facebook. I am not sure how she even knows that I work here or practice commercial law."

"Don't you post about work at all, or have it listed on your profile that you work here?" Amy offered as an explanation.

Jason thought about it for a minute. "I don't think I have posted anything. I guess someone may have tagged me in photos from one of the firm parties and she could have seen those. I'm not sure. I will ask her. Will she be here right at 8 o'clock?"

"That's what Juliette told me to put on your calendar. I have conference room B reserved for you. I think it's just her coming to meet with you, so you won't need conference room A," Amy said.

"Thank you. I appreciate it." Jason turned on the monitor on his desktop. "I think I am going to grab some coffee. Do you want something?"

"I am the one that is supposed to get you coffee, boss," Amy teased. "I'll come with you." They both got up and went to the firm's Starbucks.

Jason came back to his office and made his to-do list for the day. He was reading through a vendor contract when Amy paged his office phone. "Emily Cruze is here waiting for you in the conference room." Jason looked at the time. It was 7:45, fifteen minutes early. Maybe Emily had the same rule drilled into her about being early to places. He put a tab where he'd left off reading and closed the contract he was looking at. Jason picked up his notepad and headed to conference room B.

As he walked in, Jason saw that Emily was immersed in a document. She was wearing a navy-blue sleeveless dress. Her brown hair was covering some of her face as she looked down. She reached up and put a strand of hair behind her ear, unaware that Jason had walked into the room, she was so focused on what she was reading. He could see her leg shaking up and down as she read, likely a nervous tic. Jason couldn't blame her—taking a company public was a big deal and a very scary jump to make.

Jason cleared his throat. "Hello, Ms. Cruze." Emily looked up at him and smiled, genuinely happy to see him. The smile showed off her perfectly straight, white teeth. She got up and walked over to him. Jason got ready to shake her hand, but was shocked when she went in for a hug. He paused for a minute before putting his arms around her to hug back.

"Jason, it is so good to see you again." She stepped back from the hug and went back to sit at the table. "This place is pretty impressive," she said, looking around the room. Jason took a seat across the table from her.

"You're one to talk. This business you have built is amazing, Emily." He took the fact that she had called him by his first name as permission to go ahead and call her by hers. She blushed a little bit and looked down at her papers again.

"It is doing pretty well. I never imagined it would get this big. I just started as a small business out of my parents' house. That started doing so well that I began adding more things to the business. I started adding employees, and things just took off. I can't believe I am sitting here to talk with you about taking my company public. I don't even know where to start on that, what it entails, anything like that. I will need a lot of guidance on this," Emily admitted.

Jason smiled. "Well, you have come to the right place. I am the expert in this area. Do you have any idea on when you want to go public?"

Emily and Jason talked for another hour, discussing what the process would look like, how Jason would assist, and what she should expect. Then they got to the least fun part of the conversation: retainers and billable hour amounts. Jason went over his standard fee arrangement for taking a company public, which included a fee schedule as an example of what an average case would cost. He explained that this was just an example and not a guarantee of what the cost in her case would be. That depended on the actual time spent on the file.

Jason always watched how people reacted to the fee schedules and agreements. He had gotten good at reading whether the potential client was overwhelmed by the dollar amounts or if they were unbothered by them. Usually, the ones who seemed overwhelmed were the ones who couldn't continue paying their bills in the long run. Emily didn't seem to flinch. Jason hadn't looked at her books yet, so he had no idea what her profits and losses were. But based on what he had seen, and the fact that she was considering taking the company public at all, he reckoned she likely had a significant excess of profits in her company.

"Do you have any questions about the fee agreement?" Jason

asked. Emily kept looking down at the papers as if she was considering things. "I don't want you to feel pressured to move forward since I am here with you, or because of our history. This is a big decision, and if you need time to think about it or talk with other firms, I won't be upset."

He tried to go on to say more, but Emily interrupted him. "Jason, you don't have to sell me on it. There was never a doubt I would go with you. Your fee agreements could have been double what they are, and I still would have gone with you and your firm. This business is my first baby. I am not going to trust something this big with just anyone. I need you. I trust you."

Jason was taken aback. Yes, they had known each other in high school, but the way Emily was describing things, she made it seem as if they had had some strong relationship back then. She trusted him with her life's work based on having had a class together and maybe talking on a few occasions. He tried to think back to something else that might have happened with them that he wasn't remembering. He didn't think they'd hung out with the same friend group. Nothing was coming to mind. Nonetheless, he was flattered.

The two of them finalized and signed the retainer and fee agreements, and the attorney-client relationship was formed. They made plans for Emily to bring over all the books from since the start of the business for Jason to review, plus all the contracts, loans, leases, and anything else that showed the details of how her business was run. After they came up with the plan of action, Emily closed her folder and asked, "So, now that business is done, what have you been up to since graduation? Obviously killing it to be working here."

"I guess so." Jason was being modest. "I finished undergrad and went right to law school at Mitchell Hamline in St. Paul. Had a few offers from big firms here and a few in different states, but in the end, I chose to come here. I have loved it ever since. How about you? You are no longer Emily Baer."

Emily laughed. "You are very observant, Jason Michelson. I ended up getting pregnant a year after graduating from University of Minnesota with my master's in business administration. I got married to my boyfriend before the baby was born. We had another baby a little over a year ago."

"Wow, congratulations. That is a lot of exciting changes. All of that in addition to running a growing and thriving business. You are very impressive!" Jason complimented her.

"Thanks," Emily said, but then she seemed to hesitate a little. It was like she was deciding whether or not she was going to say what else was on her mind. She started again, "Once my business started to really take off, my husband decided to stay at home with the kids. He ended up getting bored with that arrangement and was not a fan of my long work hours. Long story short, he found another woman and we are currently going through a divorce." Emily couldn't make eye contact as she spoke.

Jason felt a pull in his stomach. He felt bad for Emily and felt an awkwardness in not knowing what to say. He could see the hurt on her face and hear it in her voice. How could someone do that to their wife and the mother of their children? Jason never understood cheaters. "I am sorry, Emily. You don't deserve any of that."

She seemed to suck in all of her feelings, and said, "I appreciate that, but it's his loss. I have a great divorce attorney, and we are fighting to keep the company and just buy out his marital interest. That, or my attorney has thrown out the idea of giving him some shares of the company once it goes public, as his settlement from the business. She wanted me to go over all of that with you."

Jason listened and then said, "Well, I have zero experience in family law, but I could talk with your divorce attorney, and we could go over everything and what the different options would mean for the company."

"That would be great. She is the reason that I found out you worked here."

"How so?" Jason asked, as he tried to think of any female family law attorneys he knew. That was a short list.

"She gave me a list of business law attorneys in the area their firm has worked with. Your firm was on that list, and I came across your name when I was looking at the firm's website. I did some more digging and realized you were the same Jason Michelson I went to high school with, and from there the decision was easy. I called to set up a meeting right away."

"Well, I appreciate the business, Emily. I look forward to working with you and representing your company!" Jason exclaimed. He stood up to signify that the meeting was coming to a close.

Emily stopped him. "Jason, one more thing."

Jason sat back down. "What's that?"

"This company is everything to me aside from my kids. I know you don't practice family law, but my attorney is telling me that my husband has a good chance of getting more custody of the kids, since he was the stay-at-home dad and my work schedule is the way that it is. He is trying to take half of the business and take my kids. I can't let him do that. He is the one who ruined this marriage. I am the one who put my blood, sweat, and tears into this business. I don't want him to get half of what I created."

Jason nodded, not quite sure what to say. He finally said, "I am not sure how I can help on that side of things. Isn't that something that would happen in the divorce?"

"I don't know. This is all too much for me. I just needed you to know where I am at on all fronts. Maybe it will help you understand me better while we work through all of this."

"Of course. I am glad you shared that. Thank you. I will touch base with your family law attorney and see what things may fall into my purview, and how we can work together to get you the best outcome possible on all fronts. How does that sound?"

Emily gave a weak smile and nodded. She began gathering her things and stood. She grabbed the folder off the table and walked out the door. Jason put his hand on the small of her back, leading her out.

"I'll have someone run over copies of all the files you need before the end of the week," she said as she hit the button on the elevator.

"That sounds great. If you need anything in the meantime, my contact information is in the folder with the signed agreements. It was great seeing you again, Emily," Jason said, as she stepped on the elevator to leave.

"You too, Jason."

Two days later, Emily Cruze came walking back into the office. The front desk called Amy to let her know that Emily was there to meet with Jason. Amy checked Jason's calendar, even though she knew it backward and forward. She knew Emily did not have a meeting scheduled with Jason today. Amy let the receptionist know that she would be right there.

Amy walked up to the front desk and met Emily. "Hello, Emily. I am Jason's assistant. I'm not sure if you remember me?"

Emily looked like she had been crying and was in a panic. All she could do was nod yes.

Amy quickly grabbed her and ushered her into one of the smaller conference rooms. She shut the door behind them, and before she could ask what was wrong, Emily was crying loudly. "Oh, dear. Here, here, sit down." Amy led Emily to a chair. She grabbed the Kleenex box and handed it to her. "Is everything okay?"

"No. Everything is falling apart. My husband is trying to take my kids away from me. If that weren't enough, he is trying to take my company from me, too. He wants to take everything. He is the one who cheated on me, and now he thinks he can just take everything else from me. It just isn't fair."

Amy moved a chair next to Emily and put a comforting hand on her shoulder. She decided it was best to listen and let Emily get it all out before she said anything. This was not something that had ever happened before and was far outside Amy's scope of work, but she didn't mind. She saw a woman hurting and wanted to be there for her.

"I just met with my family law attorney, and she said that he will likely win if we go to trial. He is asking for so much. I just don't get it. I thought Minnesota favored mothers; how can he take my kids from me? They are talking about giving me the minimum, every other weekend and one night a week. I know I work a lot, but how can they think that is enough time? I carried these kids inside of me for over nine months, and I love them with everything inside of me.

"Yes, I work a lot and sometimes late into the night, but I am still always there for dinner. Most of the time, I am the one cooking. How can he say that I am not there for them? It—just—doesn't—make—sense," Emily said, with a sob between each word. She was now crying uncontrollably. Amy just sat there and rubbed her arm and let her cry.

After a few minutes, Emily stopped crying and seemed to be pulling herself back together. "I am so sorry. I don't know what came over me. That was so unprofessional."

"It's okay! I get it. There is a lot of pressure on us as professional women in the workplace who also have kids and a family at home to take care of. I have kids, too. It is really hard. There is nothing wrong with you wanting a successful career, too!"

Emily sighed in relief. "Thank you. You are so kind to me, and you don't even know me."

"You don't need to thank me. Part of being a good human is being there for others in their time of need. I am just doing that for you. You seemed to need it."

"You're a godsend!" Emily exclaimed. She thought for a minute. "Thank goodness Jason wasn't the one who came out. That would have been really embarrassing, to break down in front of him."

"It would have been fine. Jason is a great guy. He would have understood. You are under a lot of stress, and there is a lot going on in your life right now. There is no need to be embarrassed about anything."

Emily smiled. Amy asked, "Why were you looking for Jason today?"

"Oh, well, I don't know. I guess I just wanted to update him on things and relay the information that my family law attorney gave me." She paused. "You know what? I really think I was just looking for a friend who could be on my side. All of my friends are friends with both my husband and me, and it's hard to talk about things with them. I tried talking to my friend Kyra once, thinking it would be safe. Came to find out she went and told my husband everything I said, and he plans on using it against me in the divorce. Do you know how hard it is to not trust anyone who you considered your friend for the past ten years?" she asked, more rhetorically than anything.

"I don't know how that feels, and couldn't imagine. I'm sorry that you are going through all this." Amy thought for a moment. "Why did you come here, though?"

"Well, Jason and I were friends in high school, and he never met or knew my husband. I guess I just saw him as someone who was going to be solely on my side, and that's what I needed. After today, I even have doubts about my family law attorney being on my side. I just felt so alone. I needed someone familiar."

"I'm sorry. I may be confused. I thought you and Jason didn't know each other that well in high school?" Amy asked finally.

Emily laughed a little. "Is that what Jason said?" Amy nodded, not wanting to say anything that might hurt the attorney-client relationship. "I guess that sounds about right from his perspective. We were at a lot of the same parties in high school, but he was usually with a different group of friends. We talked at some of the parties, but I think he was pretty drunk most of the time. Well, at least at the parties that happened when the hockey season was over.

"In fact, we were talking once at a party, and he had mentioned that we should get food some time together. We made plans for the next weekend to go to The Cabin to eat—that was a local bar restaurant in Stillwater back then. I was so excited and got all dressed up and waited at the restaurant for an hour and a half before I finally left." Emily's shoulders sank like she was reliving the day over again.

"He never showed up. I guess he just didn't remember the conversation ever happening. I went to a party that next night, and he was there. He didn't even seem to know that we had talked before, let alone made plans. I know he had a lot going on back then with his family. Everyone in town knew about his dad and the troubles he had at home. It makes sense now, looking back on things, why he was drinking so heavily during those parties.

"It all makes sense now, and I don't hold any resentment about it. I know Jason is a good guy, he always was in high school. We can't judge people for how they act at their worst, you know?"

Amy was shocked. This did not sound like the Jason she knew at all. He had shared about his struggles with family stuff in high school and said he was the "player," but she couldn't see him standing someone up.

When a few seconds had passed, Emily looked up at Amy. "Oh, gosh. Please don't tell him that. I don't want things to be weird between us. I got over that a long time ago. The two of us actually worked on a class project together after that, and it went great. Please, I don't want this to affect anything now."

Amy thought for a moment about her ability to keep something like this from Jason. Not only was he her boss, but she considered him her friend as well. If Jason knew about this, he would be so hard on himself, and it would probably affect his work. Amy decided that it wouldn't do any good to tell him. "Don't worry. I won't tell him," she finally said.

"Oh, thank you, Amy. Thank you for listening to me and really being here for me. I needed it. In fact, if you could maybe not even tell Jason that I came by, I would really appreciate it," she said.

Amy, again, had to think about it. She didn't like keeping things from Jason, but decided that this would be harmless. "Okay. I guess I can do that."

Emily finished drying her eyes and stood up. She pulled herself back together the rest of the way, and walked out of the conference room with her head held high. Maybe this talk was exactly what she needed. She turned and gave a little wave and smile to Amy, then got on the elevator and left.

CHAPTER NINE

A few days after their meeting, Emily's assistant had brought over all the documents Jason had requested, and he was about halfway through them. After he left the office each day, he went home and worked his way through more of the Williams trial transcripts. Jason had already accounted for more than seventeen hours of his hundred-hour pro bono requirement. He was making quick progress on the transcripts. It was like a good book that he couldn't put down. Each night, he planned on reading for about an hour, and then it ended up being three or four hours each time. He just couldn't get enough of it.

A week and a half after first meeting Rachel at the Exoneration Project and getting the case assignment, he was nearing the end of the transcripts. It was a Wednesday night at midnight, and he looked through to see how much he had left. There were about a hundred pages for him to finish. He was averaging about that many pages a night, so he figured it would be a good time to text Rachel to set up a time to get back together. He picked up his phone and scrolled to find her name.

He tapped out a text: "Hey, Rachel. It's Jason Michelson. I am working with you on the Williams appeal. I have about a hundred pages of transcript left, so I should be done tomorrow night. Did you want to set up a time to get together to get dinner and go over it all?"

Before he realized how late it was, he hit send. Then seeing it was past midnight, he cursed himself for texting her so late. Why didn't he just wait until the morning? Not everyone stayed up late like he did. As he was internally scolding himself, his phone vibrated.

He looked at it. "I know who you are, Jason. Lol. You didn't have to explain. Wow! How did you get through it so fast? I could do Friday night around 6 p.m. at our office, assuming you don't have any plans?"

Jason laughed to himself for feeling stupid about his text. He had been so worried about sending the text late and not about the fact that the message itself made him look dumb. He responded, "No plans. That sounds great. I will see you then. Sorry for texting so late. Have a great night!"

"You too. See you Friday," came Rachel's response.

It was Friday at 5 p.m. and Jason was finishing up at the office. Amy came in at 5:15 with a binder of documents. She had changed her outfit from what she was wearing earlier. She had a short, tight-fitting black dress on and some matching high heels. "Wow," was all that Jason could say. He had to admit he wasn't blind; Amy was an attractive woman for her age. Obviously, he knew that, but he hadn't ever given it much thought. She was older, married, had a family, and most importantly he worked with her. Plus, Jason never really noticed those things much. He was usually too focused on work and was never great at the whole flirting thing, at least not since starting law school. There, he'd switched his focus to school and working.

In high school, on the other hand, he had been the typical hockey player. Jason stood at 6 foot 3, with sandy brown hair, dark brown eyes, and a muscular build. It was fair to say he had his share of girls who were interested in him. Honestly, he did take advantage of the opportunities, for lack of a better expression. Jason "dated" a lot in high school, using that term loosely. What he really did was go out on a few dates with a girl, if that; they would hook up, and then things would fizzle out. Jason didn't usually have feelings for them; it was just a way to pass the time and stay away from home longer.

Jason's home life wasn't bad in an abusive or neglectful way. Things just got rough after his dad came back from combat. He was never officially diagnosed, but the family knew that he had post-traumatic stress disorder (PTSD) from what he saw over there. Before that, his dad used to come home from work and play with Jason and his siblings. They used to go to Twins games in the summer, work on building things out in the garage, and go down to the ice arena to skate around. After his service, though, Jason's dad was withdrawn and always on edge, and something small could set him off. The days of doing things together were gone. Nobody, including Jason's mom, liked to be in the house when his dad was home. It got too hard to walk on eggshells all the time. Jason found it was just easier to be gone as much as possible.

Things got even worse when Jason's dad had an outburst at work and lost his job. It became even harder for their family to get by on just his mom's teacher salary. She ended up getting a second job, and in the summers she worked at a supermarket. His older siblings got jobs once they turned sixteen, and started helping with some of the bills too. All the while, his dad stayed home sitting on the couch, falling deeper and deeper into his depression. Jason tried to stay away from home at all costs after that. His best friend Elijah's parents were never home, so Jason spent the night there most of the time. He even had his own room at Elijah's. That also made it easier to hook up with myriad of girls.

Jason's dad died on April 14, 2010, when Jason was seventeen years old. Jason came home from working out at the gym and found his dad in the office. He had used his 9mm handgun to take his own life. Jason found him slumped over in the office chair, with blood splattered on the back wall. He couldn't even react when he walked into the office that day. Jason was numb as he dialed 911 and told the operator what he had found. Jason later found out in the therapy sessions his mom made him go to that he was disassociating at the time, because his brain could not deal with the trauma in front of him. He also realized in therapy that he wasn't completely shocked when he found his dad that day. A little part of Jason had always assumed that something like that would happen.

Jason's life was changed forever that day. He couldn't open up to people anymore. He put all his energy and focus into hockey and working out during the hockey season, and into partying in the off season. It boded well for him in the end, with him getting a scholarship to play hockey in college. Due to his dad taking his own life, the life insurance policies wouldn't pay out, and the family's financial burdens worsened. His mom had to move from the house that Jason grew up in, and she had to use the kids' college funds to get by. Things were a struggle, but instead of sticking around to help his family out, Jason went away to college and came back to visit once or twice a year. He got a job in the summers to stay in Mankato. It was just too painful to go home.

Jason continued in therapy through his first year of law school and worked through some of his issues. He realized that he felt bad for not contributing to the family, and that was why he now sent his mom a check each month from his salary. Not a huge amount, but enough for her to not have to work a second job anymore. He also sent the money to make up for the fact that he was not there in person. Jason sometimes felt bad about it, but it was just easier to throw all his attention into work. It was better for him to ignore those feelings from his childhood.

His therapist told him that was also why his relationships never lasted long. It was due to his family life being the way it was and the trauma that it caused him. Apparently, he had issues trusting and opening up to women. Between that and his work schedule, making it past a few dates was not likely. He had also pushed away most of his friends through the years. Outside of work relationships, he didn't have many people in his life. That was the way Jason preferred it, however.

CHAPTER TEN

Amy put the binder on Jason's desk. "These are the other documents from Emily Cruze. A runner from her office just dropped them off. He was very happy that there were people still here this late on a Friday."

Jason ignored what she had said about the binder and the delivery boy. "You look amazing, Amy. Big plans for tonight?"

"As a matter of fact, yes. My parents are in town to watch the kids, so we are having a date night," she explained. "David has been back to work for almost eight months now. Between us both working and the kids' schedules, we never have time for each other anymore. He got us tickets to a concert."

"Very exciting. Who's playing?" Jason asked.

"Carrie Underwood!" He could hear the excitement in her voice. Jason knew that Carrie Underwood was Amy's favorite singer. She had Carrie playing in the background at least half of the time when she was working on projects for Jason. Jason had admitted in the past that he was a fan too, and he could probably sing the words to a good number of her songs.

"I am jealous. That sounds amazing! I hope you guys have a great night. You deserve it."

"Do you need anything before I go?" Amy asked.

"No. You are good to go. I can handle everything here. I am heading out to meet with Rachel to work on the Williams case, anyway,"

Jason responded. Amy was waving as she walked out the door. He yelled after her, "Hey, Amy!"

"Yeah?" she responded, walking back in through the office door.

"Do me a favor and take tomorrow off too, okay?" He smiled.

She smiled back. "Will do, boss! Have a great weekend." Amy walked out and left for the weekend. Twenty minutes later, Jason was walking out the door as well. He left his suit jacket behind this time, hanging on the back of his office door. He turned off the lights and headed to his car.

Jason pulled up to the Exoneration Project office twenty minutes early, but grabbed the box of transcripts and walked in anyway. There was no point in staying out in the car. The motion sensor lights in the lobby turned on when he walked in. He could see the conference room light on and Rachel in there working. He walked over to the door and knocked lightly. "Hey. Sorry, I am a little early," Jason said.

Rachel smiled at him, her eyes catching the light perfectly. "Hey! That's fine. Come on in." She got up and moved some stuff out of the way from the spot next to hers at the table. She gestured at the spot, indicating that she had cleared it for him to sit there. Jason walked in and set down the box of transcripts. "How did you read through all of those so fast? Did you have the week off of work or something?" She laughed.

Jason laughed with her. "No. I just read most of it when I got home each night."

"Don't you big-firm boys work, like, crazy long hours as it is?" She was joking, but Jason could tell there was some seriousness to her question.

"Yeah. That is true. I usually get home late, but the transcripts were interesting, and I know they are important." He paused. "It is really amazing that you do this work all the time!"

He could see her starting to blush as she looked away to hide it.

She tried to sound as modest as she could. "Someone needs to help these people. I am just lucky I get the chance to be that person."

"Well, you're amazing," Jason said, and he reached out and put his hand on hers. She pulled her hand away instinctively, and Jason's cheeks started turning red.

Rachel looked at him apologetically and tried to move past the moment. "Thanks! I think it's pretty great that you are putting actual effort into helping on the case." She went on, "Most attorneys who come in here don't care about the case. They just want to get the hours as quickly as possible."

"Well, that's not going to be me," Jason assured her.

"I can see that." Rachel grinned. "You are in it for the right reasons. I can tell. Even if you originally did come because of your pro bono requirement." Jason didn't know what to say back. There was a long pause.

"So, should we order food before we get started?" she asked. "It usually takes a while during the dinner rush."

"Sure. That sounds good to me." The two decided on a restaurant and looked at the menus on their phones.

"I'm buying," he said, after they finished putting their orders in.

"You don't have to do that!" Rachel protested.

"It's okay. I've got it," Jason responded. "It says it will be here in about fifty-eight minutes. Plenty of time to get some work done. Where do we start?"

"What were your initial thoughts after reading the transcripts?" Rachel asked.

Jason thought a minute before answering, "I think that making the inefficient assistance of counsel argument is unwise. Both attorneys in this case did really well with the facts they had."

Rachel nodded. "I agree. Duncan did a really great job on this and picked up many points throughout the trial. Mia agrees with you that we shouldn't make that argument, but we still have to use the inefficient assistance of counsel in the motion. It is really just a standard thing, and I am sure we can find a few things that he could have done better. Duncan expects it to happen in appeals. I reached out to him when the Exoneration Project approved the case. He agreed to sit down with me—well us, now—to go over things, answer questions, and bounce ideas off each other."

"That will be beneficial, I think. Does that normally happen in these cases?" Jason asked.

"No. It is very rare. This is the first time I have even received a response back when I reached out to the original attorney. He said it was because he had a feeling in his gut that Williams didn't do it. He wants to help in any way he can," Rachel explained. "What else?"

"I know I am not the criminal law expert, but doesn't the State usually have to show the intent or what the motive would have been to commit the crimes?"

"The answer to those questions should be 'yes,' according to all the textbooks and statutes, but it's not that simple. Yes, the crimes have an intent element, the *mens rea*, in which the court is required to prove that Maxwell had the intention or knowledge of wrongdoing that constituted part of the crimes. A lot of times, people use intent and motive interchangeably because the motive can show why or how the intent was there. Unfortunately, with juries, sometimes even if the State can't prove intent with anything more than circumstantial evidence, they still find the defendant guilty."

She took a breath before starting on her next thought. "In this case, the county attorney didn't even touch on a real motive or intent, other than just saying that because of their on-again, off-again relationship, Maxwell attacked the victim. It was argued that Maxwell had been stewing overnight about whatever they had fought about the night before, and the next day he couldn't take it. His anger rose further when Amelia wouldn't answer his calls, until he couldn't contain the rage any longer. There was never any testimony about what was specifically said during their fight that I can recall.

"I just can't make the jump from that story, which had little to no corroborating evidence, to him going to her house, breaking in, raping and killing her. It just doesn't add up."

Jason jumped in. "I agree. It had me confused too, but then I started doing some research." He turned a few pages in his notebook to find more notes. "I found statistics and articles about defendants who don't testify. Even though the jury is given instructions about not taking that into account, and informed the defendant has the right not to testify, it plays a big role."

He read down his page until he found what he was looking for. "Jurors believe that defendants who don't testify have something to hide, and even if they are not guilty of this crime, they must be guilty of something." He paused and then said, "I can't believe that people admitted that to these researchers."

"I know. It's really sad, and not what was originally envisaged with jury trials. The jurors don't understand the complexity of what having a defendant testify in their trial really does." Rachel's passion was rising. "It's not fair that jurors can give a defendant's choice not to testify that much weight. I still wouldn't recommend to any defendant to testify, though."

"Why not? If the studies show that it hurts their case not to, why wouldn't you have them testify? He is innocent," Jason protested.

Rachel was about to say something when Jason's phone started to ring. He looked at it and answered. Jason talked with the person on the line for a minute and then got up.

"The food is here. He says the door is locked," Jason told her.

"It automatically locks to the outside at 6 p.m. You should be able to open it from the inside," Rachel informed him without looking at him. She seemed to be upset with him again.

Jason went to get the food and came back. Rachel was writing something on her notepad, flipping over to a new page. "Food is here," he said, setting the bags down on an open table that was up against the wall.

Rachel finished up what she was writing and looked up. "Sorry. I just had to get all of my thoughts down before I lost them." Jason knew how she felt. There were times when he would get an idea, or something would come to him, and he just had to write it down. If he didn't, he would sit and worry or think about it until he got it all written out. Jason realized just then that he and Rachel seemingly had a lot in common, at least when it came to their work ethic and how they thought, not so much with their organization skills.

Rachel started to move some of the boxes and things farther along the table, making more room for them to eat. "Did we get plates or anything with it?" she asked.

Jason looked in the bag. "It doesn't look like it, no. Well, there is silverware."

"Good enough. We can just eat out of the containers. I don't have cooties," she joked. Jason brought the food over and they sat down to eat. He started with the shrimp fried rice, and she took the chicken lo mein.

Rachel had a noodle sticking out of her mouth. She quickly shoved it in, and with the food still in there, she said, "Tell me about you, Jason. What do I need to know, since we will be working together so closely on this case?"

He finished the bite he was chewing. "There isn't much to know."

"That can't be true. Where did you grow up? What about your family?" she asked.

Jason hesitated. "I grew up in Stillwater with my parents and siblings." He didn't want to tell Rachel more about his family, so he quickly changed subject. "I played hockey and got a scholarship to Minnesota State University, Mankato. I got hurt and lost my scholarship, and I had to work full time to supplement my loans. After graduating from MSU, I went to Mitchell Hamline. Here we are."

"Well, that was definitely the Cliffs Notes version," Rachel joked as she put another forkful of food in her mouth. Then she handed the lo mein container over to Jason. "Want to switch?"

Jason grabbed the lo mein and handed her the fried rice. He also took an egg roll out of the bag and put it on a napkin, the grease from the roll soaking through the napkin quickly. "What about you?" he asked, directing the attention away from himself.

"I grew up in Duluth," Rachel started as she put down the fork. "My parents got divorced when I was a junior in high school, and I am an only child. I danced competitively through high school, and then was on the dance team at the University of Minnesota Duluth until my junior year. The summer before my junior year, I decided that I wanted to go to law school. I quit dancing at UMD and started working with a local law firm in Duluth, clerking twenty-five hours a week. I ended up moving to go to University of Chicago Law for my first year, and then transferred to U of M Law School my last two years." She took a bite of food as she finished.

"Why did you move back?" Jason asked.

Rachel got a sad look on her face and contemplated answering that question honestly. "Um, I was dating a guy I met my 1L year. He lived here, so when things started to get more serious, I transferred back here." She paused before continuing, "We broke up and called off the wedding the week before I took the bar exam." She looked down and went back to eating her food.

Jason caught the word "wedding" and realized how serious the relationship had gotten. He felt bad for asking. "Rachel, I am sorry. I didn't mean to pry. You don't have to talk about this if you don't want to." Jason felt terrible. He'd wanted the attention off his own family and tragic past, but he didn't want her to be hurting talking about her own past. He reached out and touched her hand to comfort her. This time she didn't pull away.

"It's okay. That was a few years ago. I have accepted it." She quickly changed the subject. "How about you? I don't see a ring. Are you in a relationship?"

"No relationships here. I don't get much time to date." Jason realized that sounded harsh. "I guess I have been focusing more on work than romantic relationships."

"That makes sense. I have been doing the same thing." Rachel finished up her last bites of food and wiped off her hands. "I'm going to get started again." Jason took one last bite, put the containers back in the bags, and moved them off to the other table.

They went through the other things that Jason had made notes about when he'd read through the transcripts. They got to the part about the lead officer on the case, Rockwell Swenson. When Rachel brought up his name, Jason's demeanor changed noticeably.

She looked at him, concerned. "Hey, are you okay?"

Jason was quiet, seemingly deep in thought. His face had gone completely flat. "I know Detective Swenson," Jason said, in almost a whisper.

Rachel's curiosity was piqued at how Jason knew him, and why it made him react the way he had. She didn't want to be nosy, but on the other hand she did want to know. She questioned what she should say next. Should she ask him how he knew Rockwell Swenson? Should she just wait and see if he was going to explain, without her asking? Rachel ultimately decided to wait, and see if he wanted to talk about it more.

Jason's hand was still on hers, and he continued looking down. It looked almost like he was about to cry. Rachel turned her hand in his and gave his hand a soft squeeze. He flinched, and pulled his hand away. Then he glanced up at her with an apologetic look. She could see the tears welling up in his eyes. "Sorry. I didn't mean to pull away." He shook his head as if he was trying to shake away the tears, and put his hand back out to take hers. Rachel placed her hand in his, and he gave her a weak smile.

"I never talk about this with anyone. Not even my family." He paused. "I mean, they obviously know that it happened, but since that day, we haven't talked about it." Rachel's curiosity grew. She could tell he was having a hard time finding the words. She squeezed his hand again to let him know she was there for him. "It was April 14, 2010. I was seventeen years old. I came home one day and found my dad in his office. He was an Army veteran and he had been deployed a few years earlier. When he came home, he wasn't the same anymore. We think he had PTSD, but he would never go in to get diagnosed. It got really bad, to the point where nobody wanted to be home."

Rachel felt her eyes widen unintentionally, as she tried to figure out where this story was going. Jason continued, "He shot himself in the head. I was the one who found him. Detective Swenson was the first officer to show up to our house. He picked me up off of the floor and got me out of the room. I guess I was in shock and couldn't hear when the officers were talking with me. That day is such a blur, but I still have nightmares about what I saw when I walked in there that day."

Jason looked up at Rachel. She had tears streaming down her face. "I don't even know what to say." She squeezed his hand again. "I can't imagine how that has affected you."

She got up and moved toward Jason. She gave him a hug, wrapping her arms around his neck. He hugged her back, feeling his body relax and lean into her. The embrace felt nice. The only other time he had talked about this was with his former therapist, and obviously she couldn't give him any type of physical contact to help him feel better. This hug was great, and Jason felt a sense of peace.

He had always thought that if he shared this story with someone, they would leave him. Rachel did the opposite—she comforted him.

Rachel pulled back from the hug and sat back down. She wiped the last of her tears away.

"Thank you," Jason said.

"For what?" she asked.

"I have never told anyone about that because I figured they wouldn't know how to respond. The way you responded, though, was more than I could have ever asked for." He smiled at her. "I really appreciate it."

Rachel smiled at him. "Do you want to move on to a different topic?" she finally asked, not sure if they should skip past talking about Officer Swenson and his investigation and testimony.

"No, it's okay. I think I was so shocked about seeing his name that I didn't pay much attention to his testimony. I will have to pay better attention when I review the police reports," Jason admitted.

"Okay. That's fine," Rachel said, as she grabbed another notebook from her pile. "I don't think there was really anything surprising in his reports or testimony. It just reiterates what circumstantial evidence was found, and then he testifies about the chain of custody for the DNA evidence."

"When you are working on the Petition and Motion, do you talk with the officers on the case?"

Rachel thought about it. "We have a few times, yes. It is helpful sometimes if there is any question about the police report or the officer's testimony. However, in this case, it was so long ago that he probably doesn't remember much outside of his report. If we do need to, I can go alone, though. I understand it might be tough for you."

"No. I could do it. I am all in on this case. I want to be a part of each step," Jason told her.

CHAPTER ELEVEN

Rachel and Jason got back to work and spent the rest of the night working through the case files. Around 9 p.m., Jason got out his laptop to check his emails. He scrolled through them. As he was scrolling, he saw an email from Emily and opened it. "Hey, Jason. Just wanted to make sure you got the files. Can you text me to confirm?"

Many people would think it was weird for an attorney to text their clients, but in Jason's office it was common. It was actually expected most of the time. The firm provided the phones, and the cellphone numbers were listed on the attorneys' business cards. This gave clients the feeling that they could always reach their attorney if any emergencies arose, which happened at times. Or at least what the clients thought were emergencies. Jason had had clients calling and texting him at 3 a.m. before. His clients often worked late into the night, and therefore so did Jason when necessary.

He got out his phone and texted Emily. "Hello Emily, it's Jason. I just got your email. Yes, we got your files. I started reviewing them but haven't finished them up yet. Planning to work through them tomorrow." He reread the text; he always proofread his emails and messages to clients to make sure there weren't any typos or mistakes. It looked good to go, so Jason sent the text. He started to get back to looking at emails to see if there was anything pressing that needed attention before tomorrow morning. It all could wait.

Jason's phone rang, and he looked at the caller ID. It was Emily calling. He looked at Rachel. "Sorry, I have to take this. It's a new client." She nodded her understanding without looking up from the report she was reading. "Hey, Emily."

"Hey, Jason. Thanks for the text. I am glad you got the files. We had a meeting run long, and I wasn't sure anybody would still be at the office when my guy brought them over." She was slurring her words a little.

"No problem. I am usually in the office late most days. If someone comes after 5 p.m., they can just let me know and I will give security a heads-up. They can escort them up to my floor."

"Wow." Emily let out a little giggle. "You are a pretty important person, aren't you, Jason Michelson? Security has to bring people up to you after hours." Rachel must have heard the giggle, or picked up on the tone in the call. She looked up to watch Jason talk. She felt something weird about the call, but couldn't name what the feeling was.

Jason laughed and said sarcastically, "Oh, yeah. I am a pretty important person, don't you know?"

Rachel felt that feeling rising. Almost like a jealous feeling, but she wasn't sure why that was happening. Jason was someone she was working with, a colleague. She didn't look at him that way, or at least she didn't think she did. Maybe him opening up about his father's death had changed things. Had that and the hug changed things for her? Had it changed things for him? She looked back down at her work, but continued to listen.

Emily laughed again, and Jason could hear some people in the background having a conversation. The sound got louder and then softer again. "Are you still at work?" he asked her.

"No. I am out at a bar blowing off some steam and celebrating," Emily said.

"Celebrating what?" Jason asked.

"My husband had his deposition today, and it went really well for me. At least that's what my attorney tells me. So I am deciding to celebrate the little wins because this whole process is depressing. I don't want it to consume me." She paused to talk to someone else, then she said, "Hey. What are you doing? You should come out. I am at Brothers, downtown. Stephanie Michaels from high school is here too. We could all catch up."

Jason thought for a minute, trying to put a face with the name Stephanie Michaels. He wasn't sure he could remember her. "I'm actually working right now."

Rachel could hear Emily on the other end of the line, begging Jason to come out. She felt happy when he told her he couldn't and that he was going to stay back here with her. Emily begged, "Please. I'm sure you are always working. Whatever it is can wait."

"It's not just me working. Plus, it is sort of time-sensitive. We are trying to get an innocent man out of prison," Jason explained.

"You what?" Emily said. "I thought you just did business. Who is we?"

"I do, primarily. This is a pro bono case that I am working on. The head attorney on the case, Rachel, and I are working through the file right now."

"Bring her with!" Emily said after a brief pause.

Rachel looked up when she heard that. Jason looked at her and could see she was hearing the whole conversation. "I guess I could ask her. Let me talk with her and then I will text you. Are you staying at Brothers for a while?" He said this more as a way to get off the call than anything.

"I think so," Emily said. "If we move, I will text you. Just let me know." She hung up without saying goodbye.

Jason looked back to Rachel. "That was Emily, my new client. We actually went to high school together. She is going through a nasty divorce and had a good deposition today. She's out celebrating with another girl from high school. They want us to come meet them."

After he'd explained everything, Jason sat back down and went back to working. He wasn't sure why he felt the need to explain all that to Rachel.

"Well," Rachel said, and Jason looked back up at her. "Do you want to go?"

"Umm. I guess I wasn't really considering it. We have a lot of work to do here. I don't really go out to the bars anyway. Not my scene."

Rachel thought about it. "It could be fun. We have made a lot of progress today. Maybe we should go!" She looked at her outfit and then over at his. "We would probably have to change first, though. We might not fit in very well in our suits." She laughed. Jason looked at her and locked in on her smile. He decided he liked it when Rachel smiled. He smiled back at her.

Jason looked down at his watch. It was only 9:20 p.m. He considered it and decided, why not? "Sure. Let's do it. It could be fun." He honestly was fine with any excuse to hang out with Rachel outside of working on the case.

Rachel started packing up her things, excited about going out. It had been at least a month since she had gone out, or even had a drink other than the occasional glass of wine. The last time she'd gone out was for a bachelorette party, and that had gotten a little crazy. That led to a little hiatus from the bar scene. Tonight wouldn't be crazy like that. "I'm in."

"Well, it doesn't make sense to take two cars. How about I go home and change? You text me your address, and I will come pick you up and drive us downtown. That way, we only have one car and don't have to pay for parking twice." Parking in downtown Minneapolis typically cost $20 or $25. That was considered cheap compared to the daytime rates.

Rachel thought about it for a minute. Would it be weird if Jason was picking her up and dropping her off? She guessed not. "Sure," she said. "Let's pack up and get going."

Jason texted Emily that he and Rachel were going to come meet up with them. He let her know that they had to go change first and then would be on their way. She texted back a smiley face and a thumbs-up. Jason and Rachel left to head home.

A half hour later, Jason was at Rachel's apartment to pick her up. He had changed into dark jeans and a blue button-up. He texted Rachel to let her know he was outside. Jason looked at his emails on his phone while he waited. He could see something out of the corner of his eye, so he looked up. Rachel was walking toward his car. She was wearing a red dress that clung to her curves and fell well above her knees. She wore black heels and a black jacket over the dress. She looked amazing. Jason had noticed Rachel was attractive when they were working together, but this was a whole new level.

Jason jumped out to walk around to the other side of the car and open the door for her. "You look amazing," Jason told her.

Rachel blushed. "Thanks. That's so sweet. I can't remember the last time a guy opened my door for me." She stepped down from the curb and got into the car. Jason waited until she was all the way in, then shut the car door. He went back to the driver's side, buckled his seatbelt, and started driving to the bar.

"So you went to high school with the girl we are meeting. Were you guys good friends?" she asked. But Rachel was really trying to find out if the two had dated. She had realized while she was getting ready that she did have a little crush on Jason. This was the first crush since her nasty breakup with her ex-fiancé. It scared her.

"Can I tell you a secret?" Jason asked. Rachel nodded. "I didn't really remember her. When my boss told me that Emily had asked for me because she knew me, I had no idea who she was. My assistant and I had to look her up on Facebook. I recognized her at that point, and I think we had one class together in high school. Not really friends, just acquaintances," he explained.

"Oh, cool," Rachel said. She smiled, feeling happy that there wasn't some complicated past between the two. "And don't worry, your secret is safe with me that you didn't know who she was." She laughed.

Jason looked at her and smiled. "Thanks. I appreciate it." He went on. "We don't have to stay very long if you aren't feeling it. Whenever you want to go, just let me know, and we can go."

"That's fine. It should be fun. I haven't been out in a while. The last time I was, I went a little too hard. I will behave tonight." She winked at him, but wasn't sure he noticed.

"Oh, really?" Jason was interested. "What happened last time?"

"It was a bachelorette party. Let's just say I got a little too drunk. You know those TikToks where all the girls go on the camera and guess who is going to be the drunkest that night?"

Jason looked at her, confused, and felt embarrassed to admit, "I don't have TikTok."

"Well, all of the girls come on camera and guess who is going to be the drunkest. Typically, all of the answers are the same and everyone says the same girl is going to be the drunkest. We did one, and everyone said me because I had just gotten done with one of my other cases, and I let everyone know I was letting loose. Once I heard that everyone thought I would be the drunkest, I just went for it." She paused, considering whether she should tell the rest of the story. "I, uh . . . ended up leaving with a random guy. My friend came with, because, you know, safety in numbers or whatever. Well, we were in the Uber and the night started catching up with me. I puked on the guy in the Uber, and he kicked us out. We had to grab another Uber to take us back to the Airbnb we had rented. The next day, I had the worst hangover ever."

Jason laughed. "That is a great story. Please don't puke on me tonight," he joked.

"Oh, I won't." Rachel laughed too, happy that the story was funny to Jason. "That isn't even the worst part. He texted me two days later to tell me how expensive the outfit was that he'd worn that night, and that I ruined it when I puked on him. He asked me to pay for it."

"No way!" Jason was shocked. "What a douche."

"That was also when I decided to write off guys." Rachel paused and then laughed. "Well, probably the fourth time in my life I've decided that." Jason laughed too, and nodded that he understood.

They pulled up to the bar and chose a parking lot to park in. They got out and walked into the bar. It was packed with people taking shots, waiting at the bar to get drinks, and dancing. Jason looked around to see if he could find Emily. He couldn't see her, so he took out his phone and sent her a quick text to see where she was. Then he looked at Rachel. "What do you want to drink? I'm buying."

"You already bought dinner. Let me get the first round," Rachel protested.

"No. Believe me. I never do this or spend money. I got this." Rachel could tell Jason wasn't going to give in. Plus, she knew he had to earn way more than she did. If he wanted to pay for drinks, she should let him. She gave him her order, and they went up to the bar to wait in line. They got their first round and then went to find Emily and her friends.

Emily saw Jason walking over. She ran up to him and threw her arms around him, giving him a hug, leaning into him as she did—more like falling into him. Jason could smell the alcohol on her. It was very strong. Emily was wearing black leggings and a low-cut white short-sleeved blouse. Her hug lingered a little long, then she finally pulled back. "Sorry. I'm a little drunk" she slurred, laughing.

Jason took a step back to put a little more space between him and Emily. Even though they had gone to high school together, and that was the pretense he was there under, she was still a client. He didn't want to cross any lines. It was against an attorney's ethical rules to date a client. Jason prided himself on being an ethical attorney, and he didn't want to overstep any lines or cross any boundaries.

"Emily, this is Rachel. Rachel, this is Emily."

Emily smiled at Rachel and gave her a hug too. It was an awkward hug, but it made Jason feel better about the one Emily had just given him.

"Come on," Emily said, grabbing Rachel's hand. Rachel followed, and Jason was right behind them. They went to a booth where four other people were sitting. Jason vaguely recognized Stephanie. Introductions were made for everyone at the table. Stephanie didn't seem to know Jason much either, or she just didn't care because she was too focused on the guy she was talking to. Rachel ordered everyone a round of Fireball shots.

"I'm driving," Jason stated. "I probably should take it easy tonight. Plus, I have to get into the office tomorrow morning to start reviewing those files," he added, directing the comment to Emily.

The other people at the table booed him. "My files can wait, Jason. We have to wait now until 'the D word' is done anyway," Emily said.

"The D word?" Rachel asked, confused.

"Yeah. Divorce. I don't like how negative a word it is, and I don't want it to bring me down, so I refer to it as 'the D word,'" Emily explained.

"Oh. That makes sense," Rachel said. "Well. I will take a shot." She looked at Jason. "Just do it. We can take an Uber home if we need to."

That comment piqued Emily's interest. "You guys could take an Uber home? I thought you were just working on a case together?"

"Oh, no," Jason said.

Rachel simultaneously said, "No. That's not what I meant."

They looked at each other. Jason went on, "We just drove here together to save on gas and parking."

"Oh, okay. I guess that makes sense," Emily said. Rachel noticed that Emily looked a little relieved. That was weird to her.

Their shots arrived and were passed out to everyone at the table. One was put in front of Jason. He thought for a moment, then said, "What the hell. Let's do this." He grabbed the shot. They all tapped the shots on the table, put them up to cheers, tapped them on the table again, and downed them. They burned as they went down. Some of them made disgusted faces as they swallowed the shots. "That will warm you up," Jason said.

The night went on, and everyone was drinking and taking more shots. Jason got to the point where he knew that he wasn't going to be able to drive anymore, so he just gave in and figured he would enjoy himself. He almost never had opportunities to just let loose and forget about work. He was with a fun group of people, so why not? He was still young and deserved to act like it sometimes.

At one point, Emily and Rachel were talking. Rachel asked, "So were you and Jason close in high school?"

"No, not really. We used to party together some, and he asked me on a date once." She paused. "He stood me up, though." The alcohol made her forget that this was supposed to be a secret.

Rachel's eyebrows raised. That didn't seem like something that Jason would do. Then she thought about it. She really didn't know Jason all that well, not well enough to have an opinion on how he was in his dating life. "Oh, really? That's too bad. Did he ever apologize?"

"No. I don't think he even realized he did it. He was pretty drunk when he originally asked me out. He was going through a lot after losing his dad," Emily explained.

Rachel just nodded. It made sense that Emily would know that, since she went to high school with him. It also made more sense for Jason not to have intentionally stood Emily up. Rachel's idea of Jason as a good guy was restored.

Without more prompting, Emily said, "You know, when I saw him on the firm's website, all those feelings I had for him back in high school came back. He is so handsome. Between you and me, I even considered not using him as an attorney so I could try and ask him on a date after my divorce was finalized." She laughed. Emily was clearly drunk and oversharing. "But then I realized that was a farfetched idea, and I would probably be better off with him being my attorney than hoping he would say yes to a date. I mean, I didn't even know if he was single."

Rachel just nodded, listening to Emily talk.

"Who knows, though? He agreed to come tonight. Maybe that's a sign that I should go for it," Emily said.

Rachel shook her head no, and started to say, "I don't think that's such a great idea."

Emily didn't hear her, though—she was already walking back to the bar to get another drink. Rachel shrugged and walked back over to the rest of the group.

It was around 12:30 a.m. when the music got turned up in the bar, and Emily wanted to go dance. She convinced a few of the others, including Jason and Rachel, to join. The DJ put on "Pour Some Sugar on Me" by Def Leppard, the signature stripper song. The drinks continued to flow, and everyone was clearly drunk at this point. Jason found himself dancing between Rachel and Emily. Both were way better at dancing than he was. He sort of just bounced his knees and swayed back and forth and let everyone else dancing around him make him look better.

All of a sudden, Emily was moving back into Jason, trying to grind on him. Rachel noticed and looked at Jason, her eyebrows raised. He took a step back away from Emily, but she kept backing up toward him. When she realized that he was moving back, she turned around and moved forward toward him. She put her arms around his neck and leaned in to kiss him. Her lips touched his, and it was like time stood still for a second. Jason pulled away and put his hands on her arms, taking them off his neck. He felt heat rising into his face, and his ears felt red. He was in shock about what had just transpired.

This crossed so many lines, and things had moved so quickly. Why did she think this was okay? He was her attorney, and she was married. "What are you doing?" Jason said, a little too harshly. He looked back at Rachel to see if she'd seen what just happened. Rachel was looking back at him with her mouth open. He looked back at Emily, who was stunned, and he could see the hurt in her eyes.

"I'm sorry. I thought we were drinking and having a good time. I just went for it. I shouldn't have. Let's just forget it happened," Emily begged.

"This is really not okay," Jason said. "This can't happen. You're my client."

"I know. I'm sorry. Let's just forget about it," Emily repeated.

Jason looked at Rachel. "I think it's probably best if we head out," he said, more to Rachel than to Emily. Rachel nodded in agreement.

"No. I am sorry. Don't let it ruin the night. It was just a stupid kiss," Emily pleaded.

"I think it's best if we leave. It's getting late, anyway," Jason said. "We can touch base next week, Emily." Jason's head was spinning, half from the alcohol, half from replaying the night and how they had ended up here. This was partly his fault. He should never have agreed to meet with a client for drinks, whether they were once classmates or not.

Rachel walked back to the table to get her coat, and the two of them walked out of the bar. Rachel pulled out her phone to order an Uber. She could tell by the look on Jason's face that he was replaying what had just happened and imagining the potential repercussions. "It's going to be okay," she said. "You were both drunk. She just said to forget it happened. Maybe it's best you just do that." She put her hand on his shoulder.

"I don't think I can just forget it happened. The ethics rules are very clear. She is my client. Nothing like that can happen. I was already worried about the hug when we got there. I should've known it was a bad idea from that point on. In fact, I should never have agreed to us coming."

The Uber pulled up, and they both got in. It took them back to Rachel's apartment. They rode in silence on the way back. As they were getting close, Rachel said, "Well, I was having a lot of fun tonight. Since neither one of us does this often, why don't you come in and have another drink or two so we can end the night on a good note? I don't want my drinking experiences to keep ending poorly," she joked, referencing the conversation earlier in the night.

"I don't know," Jason said. "I have a lot of work to get done in the morning. I also have to figure out what to do about this situation. I don't know if I can represent her anymore. It's all a mess."

Rachel put her hand on Jason's. "It's going to be okay. The work will still be there tomorrow at whatever time you decide to go in. You work really hard, Jason—you deserve a break. Just come up and have another drink and relax."

He thought about it as the Uber pulled up to the apartment. They sat there for a minute before Rachel started to get out. She looked at him, waiting for his decision. Jason opened his door and got out of the Uber. "Fine. You're right."

Jason leaned in and tipped the driver, and they walked into the apartment building and rode up to her floor. Rachel led Jason down the hall to her apartment and put her key in the lock to open the door. The door opened, and they walked into the apartment.

CHAPTER TWELVE

One or two drinks ended up being three or four. Jason and Rachel were getting along great, talking about their childhoods and what it was like in law school. Two drinks in, they started playing kings in the corner. Jason was ahead four games to three. "I dated Elizabeth throughout 1L year, and then things just didn't end up continuing after that," Jason explained. They were talking about their last relationships. "It wasn't a good match anyway. She just wanted to get her law degree because her dad and brother both had theirs. She likely wasn't even going to use it. I think her plan was to find a husband in law school who was going to make a lot of money. That was the lifestyle she was used to." Jason realized that sounded harsh. He really didn't care at this point. He had completely opened up to Rachel, and he liked it. He thought the alcohol probably played a big part in that.

Rachel nodded as though she understood. "My last relationship ended a few years ago. I was engaged to a guy I met during law school."

"I'm sorry things didn't work out. Was he in your year?" Jason asked.

"Well, I didn't meet him in law school, just when I was in law school. He was older. He actually worked at Cooper Schwartz and Filstone. I met him when I went to interview with them for the internship after 1L year. I was planning on coming back home for the summer." Cooper Schwartz and Filstone was another big firm in Minneapolis that took on summer associates after their first year of law school. The information surprised Jason. You needed to be in the top of your class to qualify for the summer associate positions.

He thought through his questions out loud. "If you had a summer associate position, how did you end up at the Exoneration Project instead of a big firm like Cooper Schwartz and Filstone?"

Rachel thought about how to answer that. "I worked there through my 3L year. Like I said before, I moved back to Minnesota for my last two years of law school. I had my offer, contingent on passing the bar exam, obviously. One day when I was studying for the bar exam at a coffee shop, I overheard a conversation between the people at the table next to me. It turned out to be an interview between a guy from the *Pioneer Press* and another man who was talking about his time in prison. I was intrigued, so I eavesdropped. The guy was sent to prison for fifteen years for the rape of a thirteen-year-old girl. He didn't do it, though, and he was exonerated by DNA evidence."

"Let me guess," Jason interjected, "by the Exoneration Project?"

"Yup." Rachel went on. "After the interview was over, and they both left, I took a study break and looked up the Exoneration Project and that man's case. I was researching both for hours. Over the next few weeks, I did more research during study breaks and realized that I wanted to take my first year after the bar exam to work with the Exoneration Project."

"And you just ended up staying there for good?" Jason asked.

"Sort of," she said. "As I'm sure you know, big firms give a year off to their associates if they are going to clerk for a judge. I thought maybe they would give me a year off to work with the Exoneration Project. Cooper Schwartz and Filstone are big on pro bono hours, and I thought they could maybe make an exception because it would make them look good down the line, having an associate who worked for a year freeing innocent people. Unfortunately, they wouldn't make an exception. They said that if I wanted to take a year to do the Exoneration Project my position wouldn't be saved for me, and I would be required to apply for one again if it became available."

"That's shitty."

"Yeah. My fiancé was not happy. We had life planned out. We were both going to work at the same firm. The relationship had already been disclosed and vetted by human resources. He was going to make partner. We would get married two years after I passed the bar. It all sounded so great. Until he didn't agree with my idea about the Exoneration Project. He always was into the status and salary that came with working at a big firm. He's the type of attorney who hands off his pro bono work and then takes the credit for the hours. I should have known that we were fundamentally different, and it wouldn't work out."

"How did it end?" Jason asked, figuring they were this far into the conversation, and he had been sharing personal details and stories all night. It should be fine to ask.

"I passed the bar and went to work at the Exoneration Project. I fell in love with it. He kept urging me to apply every time a position opened up at the firm, but I was happy where I was. It caused a lot of fights between us. He started sleeping at the office. The wedding date got pushed back a few times. We finally had a huge fight one night, and he said that I wasn't living up to my potential. I should be working at a big firm making big money, and I was wasting my time trying to get dirtbags out of prison." Jason could tell from Rachel's expression that she was reliving the fight. "After that, I was done. I moved my things out. Left the ring on the bedside table. We have only talked once since."

"Wow," Jason said in shock. "I am so sorry."

"Oh, it gets better," Rachel said as she finished the rest of her drink. There was half left before she chugged it, and they were making some very strong drinks at that point in the night. "He is now engaged and has a baby on the way. I later found out that when he started sleeping at the office, or I thought he was sleeping at the office, he was actually sleeping with his assistant."

Rachel laughed and got up to make another drink, but as she stood up, she was unsteady on her feet. She almost fell as she tried to walk. Jason put out his arm to catch her. There was a moment where Rachel looked into Jason's eyes, and he was looking back into hers. They just stayed there for a moment, looking into each other's eyes. The energy between them was electric. Neither one leaned in any farther.

After a few more moments, Rachel steadied herself and got back up. "Sorry. It all just hit me when I stood. Maybe I don't need another one." She walked back and sat down again. She pushed a strand of hair back behind her ear.

Rachel had changed when they got back to her apartment. She was in sweatpants and a sweatshirt from Yale. Jason had wondered why she had these when she first came out after changing, but he never ended up asking. He figured it could have just been a gift from someone. It didn't matter anyway.

Jason finished the drink in front of him and pushed his glass to the side. "You are right. We both have probably had enough."

Rachel got up, more steady this time, and grabbed two water bottles out of the fridge. They started playing another game of cards, and Rachel ended up winning. Jason looked at his phone to see the time. It was almost four in the morning. "I should probably get going soon."

Rachel looked at the time. "We have to play a tie-breaker. Plus, it's so late. There won't be any Ubers out anymore. Why don't you just stay here, and then I can take you to get your car in the morning? That way, you don't have to Uber home then Uber to get your car."

Jason thought about it. That plan did make sense. On the other hand, he had already made one mistake tonight by sticking around at the bar after Emily hugged him. That mistake hadn't ended well. He didn't want anything to happen with Rachel that would cause any awkwardness in their professional relationship. Ultimately, though, he decided to just stay. "Okay. I guess you're probably right. Thanks for the offer!"

"Perfect. Let's play one more game and then we can head to bed. I think I have some of the Liquid IV water stuff to help prevent a hangover. I will definitely need one, want one too?" Rachel offered.

"Yeah, I will take one. Thanks!" Jason said.

She got up and grabbed them both another bottle of water and a Liquid IV packet each. Jason had never used one of them before, so he watched as Rachel poured the full packet into the bottle of water and shook it up. Then she chugged it. Jason mimicked her actions and finished up his bottle of water as well. "Does this stuff actually work?" he asked.

"Yeah, I think so. My best friend swears by it, and she goes out drinking a lot. I should have used it that day of the bachelorette party but didn't. I figured it works for my friend, so I picked up some to keep on hand for occasions like this." She laughed.

Rachel and Jason were finishing up their tie-breaker game of cards. They each had two cards left. Jason picked up his card at the start of his turn. He played that card, and moved one pile over. He checked the piles to see if there was any way he could win during this turn. When he realized there wasn't, he put down one of the cards into the empty spot. It was Rachel's turn. She picked up her card and got a big smile on her face. Jason knew what that meant. She was going to beat him.

Rachel played her cards and won the game. Jason took it graciously on the outside, even though he was a sore loser on the inside. She finished up the second water and got up to go to the bathroom.

Jason could hear her brushing her teeth. Her apartment was about three times the size of his. It had two bedrooms, one with her bed in it. The other was her home office, or "war room" as she called it. It had a big desk in it and papers all over. Rachel had given him a tour earlier when they got back to her apartment. Her war room was the same as the conference room at the office: messy. Jason didn't get how she could function with her desk like that.

The apartment had a full kitchen with an island and a separate dining room, where they had been playing cards. Jason was checking his phone and noticed a text from Emily. It had come in at 2:14 a.m. She must have sent it when she left at closing time. He was nervous, but opened the message. It read: "Jason Sry bout 2nite. Shoud not have kiss you. Will come 2 office tmorow to tlk bout case."

Jason rolled his eyes. He didn't want to think about Emily and what had happened earlier that night. The rest of the night had been going really well, and he didn't want his anxiety about Emily to ruin things. He decided to ignore the text message and deal with it in the morning. He was just putting his phone back down when Rachel walked back out of the bathroom. She had changed into pajama shorts and a tank top. The shorts were shorter than fingertip length and had pink and purple stripes running downward. Her tank top was pink, with the words "Maid of Honor" in white cursive writing on the front. Jason figured the shirt was from the bachelorette party Rachel had told him about earlier.

Jason leaned back and started to get comfortable on the couch. She looked at him, waiting. "Aren't you coming?" she asked, beckoning toward her bedroom.

Jason didn't know what to say or think. Did Rachel think this was more than it was? They were just hanging out tonight as friends, weren't they? Yes, there had been a few moments where Jason thought maybe there was something more, and he was very attracted to her, but hooking up would be a very bad idea. "Oh. I just thought I would be sleeping on the couch."

She smiled. "Jason, we are adults. I have a king bed, we can share it. There is no reason for you to sleep on the couch. We won't even touch each other while we sleep. Come on. It's way more comfortable in here." Jason was still hesitant. "I promise I don't bite. Nothing is going to happen. We will just get a good night's sleep and go get your car in the morning."

The alcohol kicked in again, and Jason gave in and decided what would it hurt? It seemed like they were on the same page about not hooking up. Was that something she wanted, anyway? He grabbed his phone and followed her into the bedroom. Her king bed had a white bedspread and duvet that she took off. Underneath, there were light gray sheets on the bed. Rachel grabbed an extra blanket from the closet and handed it over to him. "I'm not great at sharing blankets. I tend to hog them."

He took the blanket and smiled at her. "Thanks. I am going to run to the bathroom quick." He left the room and went to the bathroom. He saw her mouthwash and used a little bit of that to clean out some of the alcohol he'd drunk that night. Even though they weren't going to be doing anything, he didn't want to scare Rachel off with bad morning breath. He splashed some water on his face and used the bar of soap to wash up. He ended with going to the bathroom and walked back into Rachel's room.

Jason gestured to the light switch, asking if he should turn it off. She nodded yes. He turned off the light and walked over to the bed. He started climbing into bed and she looked at him. "Are you seriously going to keep your jeans on? How is that comfortable?" Rachel asked.

"I just . . . I just didn't want things to be uncomfortable or to overstep any boundaries," he said as he stood back up.

"Jason, I want you to be comfortable. Like I said, we are both adults. Just get comfortable so you can get some good sleep. You look like you could use it." She laughed, smiling at him.

Jason took off his jeans and pulled his shirt over his head. Despite not getting to work out as much as he used to, Jason still had a chiseled chest, and he was very fit. He noticed Rachel staring at him for a minute before she turned to plug her phone in. "Do you want me to set an alarm?" she asked.

"Umm." He thought about it as he crawled into the bed, feeling the soft warm sheets against his body. He hadn't realized how tired he was until that moment. Based on Rachel's comment, it must have shown on his face. Jason decided that he could sleep in tomorrow, especially since he'd had a long night tonight. "No. Let's just see when we wake up." He turned toward her and put his arm under the pillow, getting comfortable.

Rachel set her phone down on the end table and turned toward Jason, putting her arm under her pillow as well. She looked at him, their eyes locking again. "I had fun tonight."

"I did too. It's so easy to talk to you. I really appreciate you letting me stay," Jason said, his eyes feeling heavy. "This is a really comfy bed."

She smiled. "Thanks. I bought it when I was still working at the firm, so I had some extra money lying around. I went big and got the comfiest bed I could find. I thought that if I was going to be working long hours at the office, I needed a comfortable bed to come home to."

Jason thought back to the bed at his studio apartment that he'd had since he was in high school. He'd just brought it with him from his mom's house when he moved to college and then to law school. "That makes sense," he said, making a mental note that it was time for him to buy a new bed.

Rachel scooted over a little closer to Jason, getting more comfortable. She closed her eyes and sighed, signifying that she was relaxed.

Jason watched her and felt his smile widen. There was something about this girl that was pulling him in. He felt so comfortable around her, and like there was a sense of something he hadn't felt in so many years. Jason felt at home and as if Rachel could be trusted with anything that he said. She was smart and funny, compassionate, and had a competitive side to her, just like him. He had a lot of fun with her. He realized that he wanted to do this more often.

Rachel opened her eyes, and Jason was looking at her, smiling. "What?" she asked.

"Nothing," he said, and looked away. "Sorry."

"No, tell me!"

Jason thought about it. Between the alcohol and the tiredness, he blurted out, "You look really cute right now."

She smiled big at him, her dimples really popping out, and he could see her eyes sparkling even though the lights were off. "Thank you," she whispered. She leaned over toward him. Jason's heart began to pound. The closer she got, the more he was ready to just give in and let whatever happened happen. He closed his eyes. Then he felt her kiss him on the cheek.

Jason let out the breath he had been holding. As he felt her soft lips, the anxiety from his anticipation left his body. He wasn't disappointed, and the feel of her lips on his cheek gave him a rush. Rachel moved back to where she was on the bed before. She closed her eyes. "Goodnight, Jason," she whispered.

He smiled. "Goodnight, Rachel."

With that, they both closed their eyes and went to sleep.

CHAPTER THIRTEEN

Jason woke up and was confused for a minute when he didn't recognize his surroundings. He looked over, and he had his arm around Rachel, who was sleeping peacefully next to him. She had her back facing him; she must have backed up into him in her sleep. His arm then found its way around her and she placed her hand on his. He waited for the aching headache and upset stomach that normally come with a hangover, then he remembered that they'd drunk the Liquid IV water before turning in. When the headache didn't come, Jason was impressed with the supplement's effectiveness and made a note to get some for the apartment for use on the few occasions when he did drink.

Jason left his arm around Rachel for a few minutes. It felt good to have human touch. Jason hadn't felt that in a long time. He hated to admit it, but he did miss it. He finally took his arm off her, and Rachel started to stir. She rolled over to face Jason, and a tired smile crossed her face. "Good morning." She yawned. "How did you sleep?"

Jason smiled back at her. "Better than I have in a long time, honestly. How about you?"

Rachel stretched her arms out, her shirt pulling up to show her belly button. She let out a little moan. "Like a baby!" She pulled the blanket back up over her shoulder again. "I could use another few hours, though."

Jason sighed and settled back into the bed. "That does sound pretty good. You weren't kidding, this bed is really comfortable. I think it's time I get a new one."

"I can help you pick one out," Rachel joked. "Clearly I am good at choosing beds!"

Just as she finished saying that, Jason's phone began to ring. He groaned and turned to look at it. "Oh, good. It's my assistant." He answered his phone. "Hey, Amy. What's up?"

"Jason. I just got to the office. Where are you?" Amy asked.

He paused and looked at Rachel, wondering what he should say about the situation. He decided to go with, "I am still in bed. I decided to sleep in for once. I thought I told you to take the day off?"

"I was going to, but we got an email from Emily Cruze with the topic saying "urgent." She said she is coming in to meet with you at 11? What's happened since I left last night?" Amy asked.

"Oh, shit," Jason said.

Rachel looked at him and mouthed "What?" He held up a finger, telling Rachel to hold on. Getting back to Amy, he said, "Rachel and I met Emily and a few friends out at a bar last night, and some stuff happened. I told her I would have to get back to her next week about my representation. It's a long story. I will explain it when I get there."

He looked at the time: 9:49 a.m. "We have to go get my car, it's still at the bar," he said, thinking out loud. "I will be there soon."

"We?" he heard Amy ask as he went to hang up, her curiosity piqued.

Jason ignored her question. "I will see you soon." And he hung up. He looked at Rachel. "Emily emailed my assistant and me last night, saying she is coming in at 11 o'clock to discuss everything. I am not ready for that conversation."

He started to get up and put his shirt back on. He caught Rachel checking him out as he did so, but acted like he didn't notice. Jason knew he looked good, and he was flattered that she noticed. Maybe she was feeling some of what he was feeling about her. He finished putting on his shirt and pants.

Rachel started getting out of bed. "I guess we better get you back to your car, then." She went over to her closet and grabbed a t-shirt and shorts. Before he knew it, she was taking off her tank top, facing away from him, her smooth, bare back showing. Jason couldn't help but watch. She put on a sports bra and slipped her t-shirt over her head. Then she slipped her shorts down, revealing her bright pink, lacy thong. It was like she didn't remember that Jason was in the room watching all of this take place. Or maybe she was doing this on purpose.

She put the shorts on and turned around. Rachel noticed Jason staring at her. He quickly looked away. "Sorry. I didn't mean to watch."

She smirked. "Sure you didn't." Rachel started walking out of the bedroom. "Come on. Let's get some food on the way to your car." Jason followed her and they put their shoes on to go out.

On the way to get food, they talked about the things that had happened the night before with Emily. "What do you think you're going to do?" Rachel asked.

"I don't know. I feel like her kissing me was past the line and violated the ethics rules. But if I tell her it can't happen again, maybe it's okay. Then it wouldn't be an ongoing relationship or anything close to that, and I can still represent her." Jason started thinking out loud. "What if she doesn't take me seriously, though, and it happens again? I don't want to be put in a situation like that. The money will be good, though, from her attorney fees. My boss is the one who assigned me the case, and if I drop her, I will have to explain everything. He will probably be mad that I agreed to go meet her out. I don't know. What do you think?"

Rachel thought about it as she pulled into the Burger King

drive-through. They finished ordering, got their food, and started eating before she responded. "I think you are probably fine as long as you don't go out socially with her again while she is your client. If I were you, I wouldn't put myself in that situation again, since she crossed the line once already."

"Yeah, I think you're right!" Jason said as he took a big bite of his breakfast sandwich.

They both ate their food and listened to the radio while they finished the drive back to Jason's car. Jason started to get out of the car. He leaned back in. "Thanks for the ride. Are you planning on working at all today?"

She laughed at him. "It's Saturday, Jason. Some people have lives outside of work." She paused and then followed up with, "But, yes, I am planning on going into the office this afternoon. I am going to sweat off some of the alcohol first at the gym."

"Want to meet up to work on the case more?" he asked.

A smile crossed her face. "Oh, you have time for little old me in your busy day?" She laughed.

"I think I can make some time." He smiled. "I'll text you after my meeting and touch base. Sound good?" Jason asked.

"Works for me." She took a drink of her coffee as Jason waved and shut the door. Rachel watched him unlock and get into his car, making sure that he could get in before she drove away. She smiled to herself, thinking about the night before. Rachel had to admit that her small crush was growing.

Jason pulled into his parking spot and went up to his office. Amy was in the middle of a phone call, so he walked by her quickly, hoping to brush past her last question from the phone call. He sat down at his desk, turned on his desktop monitor and scrolled to the email from Emily. It had come through at 3:36 a.m. She was clearly still drunk when she sent it.

Amy walked in as he finished reading it. He rubbed his hands up his face to his forehead and sighed audibly. Amy sat down across from Jason. "Well?"

"Well, what?" he asked.

"What happened last night? Who is 'we'? Why is a client emailing in the middle of the night saying she is coming in on a Saturday to discuss her case?" Amy paused, then said, "Let's start there."

"Emily called when I was at the Exoneration Project working with Rachel to make sure we got the files. She was going out with a girl we went to high school with and a few other friends, so she invited us out. Rachel and I went, and everyone got drunk. Emily kissed me. I pulled away and told her that wasn't okay, and I didn't know if I could represent her anymore. She stayed at the bar and probably continued drinking, got home, and sent that email," Jason explained.

Amy took in all that information and considered what to say next. "Okay," is all that she could manage to say. "Are we going to continue representing her?"

"I think so. I don't know. We probably should run the decision past someone else at the firm to get their determination on it. She needs to understand that this cannot happen again. If she doesn't, we can either refer her to a different attorney in the firm, or a different firm altogether. Hopefully, it won't come to that," he said.

"On to the next question then. Who is this 'we' you referred to this morning on the phone? What happened the rest of the night after you left the bar?"

"I was talking about Rachel and me. We took an Uber back to her place after the bar, because I drove us there and was too drunk to drive home. We had a few more drinks and played cards. By the time we were done, it was too late to get a ride home, so I stayed over. Then she drove me back to my car this morning." He said it quickly and nonchalantly, as if it was just another normal Friday night. Then he got up and grabbed the files Emily had had dropped off the night before, signaling that he didn't want to talk about the topic anymore. "I better get to reviewing this before she gets here."

Amy started to get up. "That conversation isn't over, mister. Do you need me to do anything before she gets here?"

"No. Just whatever else you were working on is fine. How long are you planning to stay today?" Jason asked.

"I am free until 2 p.m. Then we have family plans."

"Can you sit in on this meeting with Emily, please? I think it would be best to have a witness to the conversation."

"Sounds good, boss. I will be there!" She left the office and went back to her desk. Jason started reviewing the files and getting ready for the meeting.

About an hour later Jason's phone started ringing. He looked down at the caller ID. It was Emily. He picked it up. "Hello, this is Jason."

"Hey, Jason. It's Emily," she said somewhat quietly. Jason could hear the embarrassment in her voice. "I am downstairs. The security guy needs verification that I can come up."

"Tell Fred I will send him an email verification now." Jason hung up the phone, really dreading this meeting. He sent a quick email to Fred, the security guard, confirming that Emily was there for a meeting with him and that she could be escorted up. He got up from his desk and walked out of his office. "She's on her way up. You ready?" he asked Amy.

Amy finished reading the page she was working on and grabbed her notepad. "Yup. I will meet her at the elevator. You head into the conference room. We will meet you in there."

Jason walked into the conference room and sat down at the table. He was wearing jeans and a short-sleeve polo shirt. He could dress casually on weekends at the office. He was waiting a few minutes before Amy and Emily walked in, talking about their respective kids. Emily was dressed in jeans and a sweater. Gone was the fancy outfit from the night before. Hopefully that meant that the flirtations were also gone.

Jason admitted to himself, while he waited in the conference room for them, that he did really want to continue working on her case. He liked what he saw from his review of the file, and her company looked like it was at the perfect stage to go public. There were admittedly a few wrinkles, though. One being the pending divorce and what effect that would have on the company. Then there were the happenings from the night before. He was pretty sure they could move past the kiss, if someone else at the firm signed off on the decision. The divorce, on the other hand, was something that he didn't know much about. Of course, he'd taken family law in law school and had to study that subject for the bar exam. He knew that both parties in a divorce are entitled to an equitable division of the marital assets. However, outside of that, he did not know much at all about family law. Good thing Emily's divorce attorney was willing to help him out on that end. Jason made a mental note to get that attorney on the phone sometime next week.

Amy and Emily finished up their conversation as they sat down at the table. Emily's demeanor changed to some kind of mixture of let's-get-to-business and embarrassment. She opened her mouth to say something and then paused, seeming to rethink what she was going to say. She finally said, "Jason, I am really sorry about last night. I know what happened wasn't okay. As you know, I am going through this divorce, and things are not going well. I'm hurt and scared and was out drinking a little too much. None of that is an excuse, but an explanation for why it happened. I just want you to know that nothing like that will ever happen again. I know our relationship is strictly business, and I won't cross that line again. I'm sorry." It sounded like one long run-on sentence as she said it, with no breaths or pauses. She breathed a sigh of relief for getting it all out.

Jason was speechless for a minute. It was like she had just summed up the whole conversation that he had envisioned in his head. He finally said, "I accept your apology. I would like to keep working on your case, but I think I need someone else at the firm to review the situation and give the go-ahead for me to keep working with you."

Emily nodded her head, understanding what Jason was saying. She was upset with herself for jeopardizing the professional relationship between them, and letting her emotional state and the alcohol cloud her thinking.

"We will have to wait for that official determination," he said. "But in the meantime, I guess we could discuss your case some more. I finished reviewing your files this morning. My initial review leads me to the conclusion that your company is prime for going public. You have hit all the benchmark numbers that I usually look for. Your growth is phenomenal, and overall, as a company, you have many profit-making avenues. In other words, if one of your streams of revenue in the business were to take a dip, or struggle, you have enough else going on to make up for that fluctuation." He finished looking at his notes to see if there was anything he had missed. "The only issue is, how is the divorce going to affect all of this?"

Emily sighed loudly. "I know. Like I said yesterday, my attorney thinks the deposition went well, but I don't think we are close to getting the divorce finalized." She thought for a moment. "Obviously, we can't take it public before the divorce is finalized—or that would not be advisable, because he would then get a much bigger payout. Worst-case scenario, if I have to pay him out half the company's worth, would we still be able to go public at that point?"

Jason thought about it, trying to run the numbers in his head. "I don't know," he finally said. "I haven't gone through that as a possibility yet. We have time—should we go through the numbers now?"

"Sure, I have time," Emily said.

The three of them spent the next two hours going over all the numbers and analyzing what it would look like if Emily's husband took half the equity of the company. They finished up, and Jason said, "I guess the conclusion is, if you lose half the equity in the business in the divorce, you will need to bring your company back up at least 32 percent before we would advise to go public."

Amy looked at Emily. "Are you really okay with your husband getting $1.4 million of your business?"

Emily looked defeated. "No. But I don't know if I have a choice. My attorney is making the overall outcome look bleak on my end." She looked to Jason, and said, "That 32 percent is a huge number. I don't know if I could make that work. Not in a short period of time, at any rate."

Jason tried to ease some of her concern. "That's just the worst-case scenario. It doesn't mean that is what will happen. Let's just stop there for today. Give Amy the contact information for your divorce attorney, and I will talk it over with them next week, assuming I get the okay from whoever reviews the issue from last night. Maybe there is a way that we can work something else out in your divorce that would make better sense business-wise. Just don't panic now."

Emily seemed to cheer up a little bit, and nodded her head in understanding. She got a business card out of her purse and handed it to Amy. After that, she packed up her things and started to stand up. "Thanks for everything, Jason. Again, I am really sorry about last night. I hope we can get past it, because I need you on this business deal with me." She began walking out of the conference room, with Jason and Amy following her out.

Jason assured her, "I hope to be working with you on this deal as well. It will all work itself out. You just focus on your kids and running the business. Your divorce attorney and I will work out the rest."

The elevator door opened, and Emily stepped inside to leave. Jason and Amy walked back to his office, and she stopped at her desk to sit down. Jason went into his office and sat down. He grabbed his phone and saw a text from Rachel. It was a selfie of her post-workout, a sweaty mess, with her tongue sticking out like she was exhausted. He smiled and opened the text. It read, "Sweating all of that alcohol out. Never drinking again," with a tongue-out emoji.

He chuckled, and texted back. "Looks like you got it all out of your system. Just finished up with my meeting. Have about two hours' worth of work to get done. Still want to meet up to work on Williams?" He set his phone down and started to go to his computer, when his text tone went off. He picked up his phone again. Rachel's text read, "Sounds good. My place at 4?" He replied with a thumbs-up emoji and put his phone down. It was then he noticed that Amy was standing in his doorway smiling at him.

"And who are you texting with that big goofy smile on your face?" she teased.

Jason blushed. "It's just Rachel. We are getting together at 4 to work on the Williams case."

Amy came in and sat down again, with a look on her face like she was waiting for Jason to go on and explain more.

"What? We are colleagues." He paused. "Well, I guess friends too, at this point, since we shared a bed last night."

Amy almost shot out of her chair. "You what?!"

"It's not a big deal, we are both adults," Jason said, stealing Rachel's explanation from last night. "Nothing happened. We just hung out, drank, played cards, and went to bed."

Amy had a mischievous smile on her face. "Okay, Jason, whatever you have to tell yourself." She looked down at her watch. "I am going to head out. Do you need anything before I go?"

"Nope. I think I am good. I'm just going to work through these emails and then do my brief on the Callikson matter. Thanks for everything, Amy. Have a great rest of your weekend. See you Monday!"

Amy smiled at him. "You have a great weekend, too. Enjoy your time with Rachel," she teased, as she walked out the door. Jason shook his head at her, but he had to admit, he was excited to see Rachel again.

CHAPTER FOURTEEN

Jason pulled into Rachel's apartment complex at quarter to 4 and texted to let her know he was there. She texted back that she would buzz him in. He got up to her door, and it was propped open for him. Jason stopped for a second, feeling weird for just letting himself into her apartment. Then he rationalized that she had left it open for him, so it was okay. He knocked lightly as he walked in. "Hello?" he called out.

Rachel's voice came from another room. "I am in the war room. Come on in. Grab something from the fridge to drink, if you want." Jason did as he was told and grabbed two water bottles from the fridge. He walked into the office to find Rachel surrounded by stacks of papers, her hair up in a messy bun, a sweatshirt and shorts on. She was sitting cross-legged on her chair.

Jason handed her the water. "You look in the thick of it."

"Yeah, I got a head start when I got home at 2 p.m." She took the cap off the water and took a sip. "Thanks! I've been working on another case at the office and had all those files spread out in the conference room there. I figured it would be easier to spread everything out here. Thanks for meeting here instead of at the office."

"Of course," Jason said, as he pulled up a chair to the table. He had gone home and changed into a sweatshirt and athletic shorts before making his way to Rachel's house. He wanted to be comfortable in case it was another long night, which he was secretly hoping it would be. He also considered throwing an extra set of clothes and a toothbrush into his car in case this turned into another overnight stay, but then he reconsidered and decided that would be presumptuous and a bad idea. He reminded himself that they were just friends, nothing more.

"What are you working on?" he asked her. "And what do you want me to work on?"

She finished the page she was reading, grabbed a pile of papers, and handed them over to Jason. "These are the police reports. If you are still fine with coming along to talk to the officer, review those."

Jason nodded and took the police reports. There were about 200 pages in the stack. They sat in silence reviewing documents and making notes for about an hour, before Rachel threw her pen down and rubbed her eyes. "How could a jury convict him of this? There is literally no evidence other than their relationship and the fight the night before. It just makes no sense."

"That's good, right?" Jason asked. "That should make our arguments easier to make."

"Yeah, it will. It just really frustrates me that juries can convict people with little to no evidence," Rachel said, passion rising in her voice. Jason smiled at her. She noticed his smile and looked upset about it. "What?"

"Nothing. I just like it when you get passionate about it. It's cute." He said that last part without putting much thought into it. It just kind of slipped out.

She didn't seem to hear his compliment, or she was choosing not to acknowledge it. Her face did soften, though, and she gave him a little smile. "How much more do you have to go through? After this pile," she waved her hand at a pile of papers with about a hundred pages left in it, "I'll be done with my second review of the file."

"I have this much left," Jason said, pointing to the small stack. It had about forty pages left in it.

"Okay, perfect. The next steps are the follow-up interviews with Mr. Duncan and Detective Swenson, for sure." Rachel started writing a list.

"Do we track down and talk to the witnesses who testified at trial?" Jason asked.

"No, not yet. That comes only if our motion for a new trial is successful. Do you want to be part of the meeting with Duncan, as well?" she asked.

"Yeah. If I can. Like I said, I want to be as involved as possible in this case."

"Okay. So, game plan is finish going through these tonight, and we can work on scheduling those meetings on Monday," Rachel said. She looked at her clock: almost 6 p.m. "Wow, time is flying by. Want to order dinner?"

They decided on pizza, put in their order, and got back to work. They took a break when the pizza came and ate it out on the couch, with the TV on as background noise. "How was the meeting with Emily?" Rachel finally asked.

Jason finished chewing the bite he'd just taken. "It went fine. She came in and apologized right away, said she knew it could never happen again, and that was pretty much the whole conversation." Rachel nodded. "Then we went over her business for the next two hours. I am going to have someone at my firm review the situation and make sure I am good ethically to keep working on her case. I am sure they will have her sign a CYA letter or something." He took another bite of his pizza.

"A what?" Rachel asked.

"A cover-your-ass letter. You know, when we put it all in writing to make sure that if anything ever goes wrong, we have written proof," Jason explained.

"I would think you wouldn't want written proof, in this case," Rachel said.

Jason thought about it for a minute. "Yeah, you are probably right. I don't know. I will ask whoever is doing the review what we should do if they decide I can still represent her. She promised, though, that it won't happen again, so I just hope that is the case."

"That's good, I guess." Changing gears, Rachel said, "Now tell me more about your personal life."

"You already know more than anyone else in my life. What do you want to know?" he asked, hesitant to talk about himself again. He was still new at opening up to people when it came to his intimate life.

"When's the last time you saw your family?" she asked.

"My sister was in town a couple of weekends ago, and I went to my mom's to see them. Before that, it had been probably six months," he said, ashamed. "How about you? I don't think we talked much about your family," he continued, realizing their previous conversation had been mostly about his family.

"I told you about my ex," Rachel said defensively.

"Yeah, but what about your family?" Jason asked.

Rachel took another bite of food and seemed to chew more slowly than she had been, probably contemplating how to respond to that. "We talked about my family some. My parents divorced when I was younger. My dad got remarried and ended up having a few more kids. So I guess I was wrong before. I technically do have a few half-siblings, or had."

"Had?" Jason asked, treading lightly.

Rachel adjusted her position on the couch. "Four years ago, my dad was driving us home from a Twins game that went extra innings. We didn't leave until around 11 at night and it was raining. A guy ran a stoplight and t-boned us. He was drunk." Rachel wiped away a few tears that had begun streaming down her face. Jason instinctively reached out his hand to comfort her. "My half-sister and -brother didn't make it to the hospital." She choked back tears, trying to keep from completely losing it.

Jason pulled her in for a hug as she began sobbing. That went on for a few minutes, as he hugged her and rubbed her back. He didn't say anything, but just sat there letting her cry. When she finally pulled away, she wiped her nose on her sweatshirt sleeve, her eyes red. "I'm sorry. I didn't mean to cry."

"Don't be sorry. I can't imagine what that was like," Jason reassured her. "Were you okay, physically I mean?"

"I spent three days in the hospital. I was in the seat farthest from the impact, so I got out with some injuries, but nothing too bad." She sniffed, clearing up the rest of the evidence from her crying.

"I'm glad you were okay," Jason said, rubbing her arm. He looked into her eyes for a few seconds, then looked away and took his hand off her arm. He grabbed his water and took a drink, hoping to move past this moment. He wasn't the best at this emotional stuff. That is why he normally chose not to deal with his own feelings. Rachel looked back at the TV, and they sat there quietly for a few minutes, finishing up their pizza.

There was a sadness through the rest of the night, as they finished reviewing their respective piles of paper. It took about another hour for Jason to finish his up. He looked at Rachel. "How much more do you have left?"

She held up the stack of papers in front of her, about fifteen more pages. It was clear that there was nothing more happening tonight after they were done working. "Do you want me to do anything else before I head out?" Jason asked.

Rachel looked up at him, considered the question for a minute, and shook her head no. "I think that should be good. I will email Mr. Duncan and Detective Swenson and cc you, so we can get those scheduled."

Jason was sort of wishing that Rachel had asked him to stay, or come up with an excuse for him not to go. But the mood was somber, so he decided it would make sense that he head home. He packed his stuff and said goodbye as he walked out. She didn't offer to walk him to the door.

Jason decided to go to bed at a decent hour, because he had a lot to catch up on at the office on Sunday. The Exoneration Project work had been cutting into his normal work hours, and he had a lot to do to make up for it. He figured his Sunday at the office was going to be a long one. Before he went to bed, he decided to send Rachel a quick text to check in on her.

"Hey. Just wanted to see if you were doing all right?" the text read. He waited for about twenty minutes, but when he didn't get a response, he decided to just head to bed.

CHAPTER FIFTEEN

Rachel and Jason had scheduled their meetings with Duncan and Detective Swenson back to back for that following Friday. The first meeting was with Detective Swenson at 11 a.m. They were meeting at Jason's firm because he had another meeting right before. Rachel showed up at 10:30 and was escorted up to Jason's floor. The secretary showed her to Jason's office and introduced her to Amy.

Amy smiled. "So you are the famous Rachel? It's nice to meet you."

Rachel began to blush, put her hand to her face and looked away slightly. "I don't know about famous." She let out a little laugh. "I have heard a lot about you, Amy. It's great to finally meet you."

The two went on talking for ten minutes, then Amy's phone started to ring. She answered it and said, "Can you hold on one minute?" to the person on the phone. She clicked the hold button on her phone and turned to Rachel. "This call will last a bit. You can head into Jason's office and wait at his desk if you want." Rachel nodded. Amy smiled and then went back to her phone call.

Rachel walked into Jason's office, looking around at the decorations on the walls. It was very clear that a designer was used, because no man she had ever met would have picked out such beautiful things. Jason didn't seem like the type to care about art or color schemes. She looked around to see if she could find any family photos, but didn't see any. Based on what Jason had shared about his family, it shouldn't have been a surprise that he didn't have any on display.

After snooping around some more, not looking at files or anything confidential, she sat down in the chair across from Jason's. She got out her phone and started looking at emails. She had one from the detective, letting her and Jason know that he was going to be about ten minutes late. She emailed him back a quick "Thanks for letting us know. We will see you soon."

Rachel was scrolling through her other emails when she heard Jason's voice coming from out in the hallway. She turned to see him as he walked in. Jason seemed startled to see her in his office. Amy was still on the phone, so she couldn't have warned him that she was there. "Oh. Hey, Rachel," he said, startled.

"Hey. Sorry, I got here early, and Amy had a call, so she said to just wait in here," Rachel explained.

"No. That's fine. I was just shocked to see anyone in here," he said, as he walked around the desk to sit down. He moved his mouse to wake up his desktop. The two of them hadn't seen each other since the night at Rachel's house when she broke down in front of him. They had texted back and forth a few times, but only about things related to the case. This interaction was awkward, and Jason didn't like it. He tried to move past it. "How are you today?"

"I'm doing all right. We got an email from the detective. He is going to be a little late."

Jason scrolled through his emails, a focused look on his face as he scanned through them. "Okay. That's fine. There shouldn't be too much for him to add to his reports anyway, right? Especially since it was so long ago," he said.

Rachel nodded her head. "Yeah, they usually don't remember much more, or they say 'if there was anything else that happened, it would be in the report.' Cops are kind of assholes sometimes." She looked away, as though she was ashamed of saying that.

Jason looked at her and picked up on her mood shift. "I hear you there," he said, trying to lift her back up. "I bet it doesn't help that your job deals with a lot of mistakes that cops make that lead to these innocent people being sent to prison." He paused. Rachel looked up at him and smiled a little, catching on to what he was doing. "From my interactions with him, Detective Swenson seems like a good guy. Obviously, we didn't meet under the best of circumstances, and he could treat criminals and investigations completely differently. But I am going to be optimistic."

"I like your attitude," Rachel said, her smile widening on her face, her cute dimples coming out. "I need some of that positivity to rub off on me sometimes, especially in my job."

As time had gone on, Jason had started to find Rachel's smile more and more contagious. He found himself smiling back at her. He was looking at her for a few seconds before he caught himself. "Well, since we have a little time, I am going to try and get through a few of these emails. Is that okay?"

"Yeah. That's fine. I have a few to get through too," she said as she went back to her phone. The two of them worked on their respective emails for the next fifteen minutes, until Amy came in to let them know that Detective Swenson was in the conference room. They made their way there.

"Jason Michelson. I thought I recognized the name. How are you, buddy?" was the greeting Detective Swenson gave. There was a sad smile on his face, likely due to him remembering the last time he'd seen Jason.

All the feelings and emotions came rushing back to Jason from the last time he'd spoken with Detective Swenson. He felt a knot coming up his throat, and there were tears at the backs of his eyes, fighting to make their way out. Jason hadn't expected this reaction in himself at all. It had been a long time since his dad's death and when he'd seen Swenson. When Detective Swenson called him "buddy" it was like he was back there that day, after finding his dad.

Jason shook his head and cleared his throat, pushing all those feelings back down. "Hello, detective. I am doing well. How have things been with you? This is Rachel Nix." He motioned to Rachel as an introduction.

Detective Swenson nodded his hello to Rachel. "I've been doing all right. I have been retired now for about ten years, so I am living the good life," he joked.

"Wow. Congratulations. It's nice to meet you, detective," Rachel said, as she and Jason sat down at the table. Rachel was carrying the police reports with her. She set them down on the table and pushed them forward a little, making room for her notepad. The small talk continued for a few more minutes, in true Minnesotan fashion, then Rachel said, "Well, should we get down to business?"

Detective Swenson's demeanor changed; the kindhearted joker was replaced by the professional detective. "Of course we can. That's what I am here for, right? What do you want to know?"

Rachel took the lead. "We have read over your reports. I know officers are very thorough with their reports, but we were wondering if you could remember anything else that maybe wasn't included there, or in your testimony at trial?"

The detective looked like he was pondering her question and looking back through memories deep in his brain, dusting off the cobwebs. "It was a long time ago. I was new to the homicide division, and this was one of my first homicide calls." He grabbed a file folder that he had sitting on the chair next to him. Neither Jason nor Rachel had noticed it before that point. Detective Swenson opened the file and started looking through things. He stopped on a page, and Rachel looked at it more closely.

"Hey. Can I see that?" Rachel asked, the confusion clear on her face.

The detective looked confused, but slid the paper across the table to her. "Sure. What is it?"

Rachel studied the paper to confirm her suspicion. She turned it to see if there was a back page. "I've never seen this before. This wasn't in the original file the defense attorney had." She looked over at his file folder. "In fact, that looks like it has a lot more in it than what the prosecutor turned over back then."

Detective Swenson looked down at his folder, confused. "How could that be? Are you sure?" He handed the rest of the folder over to her. "This is the complete file that the police station had. I grabbed it from storage to review it all when you reached out."

Rachel began flipping through all the pages, clearly flustered with this new revelation. She pulled a few pages upward so the top of each page was higher than the rest, as she was going through them. Jason and the detective sat there quietly while Rachel finished her inspection of the file. By the end of it, she had about thirty pages exposed above the rest of the file. "I will have to double check, but I am pretty sure I have never seen these pages before. They weren't in the documents the prosecution gave Mr. Duncan."

Detective Swenson seemed to be thinking back again. "You know what?" he said. "That makes sense. There were a lot of things that Mr. Duncan did not ask about while I was on the stand. I remember thinking it was odd that he wouldn't bring certain things up."

Jason spoke up for the first time since they had started talking about the case. "What types of things?" He began making notes.

"Well," Detective Swenson started. "We had a few other suspects right away, when the investigation began. Usually, defense attorneys will follow up on those leads and figure out why we didn't pursue them further, and how it was we ruled those people out. Mr. Duncan didn't do that in this case."

"I never read about any other leads. That must have been some of the missing pages," Rachel said, looking back through the pages that she had marked as new. "Can we make a copy of this?" Rachel looked up at the detective and asked.

"Uh. Sure, I guess," he stammered. "You legally should have had all that already. It shouldn't be a problem if you copy it now."

"Jason. Can you have Amy copy this for us? Two copies," Rachel asked. Jason got up, grabbed the file, and walked out to give the folder to Amy for her to make the copies.

"I don't understand," Detective Swenson said. "How could the prosecutor not give the full file to the defense in the case?"

Rachel thought about it. "I'm not sure. It is against all the discovery rules. Why would he have to withhold them?" She asked this more rhetorically than to the detective specifically.

Jason walked back in with the copies, then handed the originals back to the detective and a copy to Rachel. He sat down with his copy and started flipping through the pages himself.

"Who were the other suspects?" Rachel asked, as she got to one of the new pages in the reports. "Mathias Fillmore, Jacob Caldwell, Casey True, and Jesus Cabrera." She thought for a minute. "Wasn't Casey True Amelia's roommate?"

Detective Swenson nodded his head and looked for a page of his notes. "Yes. Casey True was the roommate who found Amelia. Jesus Cabrera was her boyfriend at the time. Mathias Fillmore was the maintenance man in her apartment building." He turned the page. "And Jacob Caldwell was the neighbor across the hall."

Rachel looked at the same pages that the detective was reviewing. "It doesn't look like any of those leads were pursued far. There aren't many notes about them. What happened?"

"Amelia's father, Cordwell Jackson, was working his way up the political ladder. I think he pulled some strings and had the chief relay the message that our attention should only be on Maxwell Williams," Detective Swenson explained.

"Why did he want you to focus on Maxwell?" Jason asked.

"I always got the impression that Cordwell wasn't a big fan of Max, the way that he talked about him. He always made it seem like Max wasn't good enough for Amelia, and as though he knew something like this would happen if they stayed together. It also sounded as if some of the fights between Amelia and Max got pretty bad. Once Cordwell had talked to the chief, we were told to only focus our attention on Mr. Williams. We couldn't go against the chief, and it seemed like Maxwell might have been the one who did it anyway." Detective Swenson stopped, almost looking remorseful.

"It wasn't my call," he said, almost as if he was trying to convince himself. "The chief gave orders, and we had to follow them."

"Nobody is blaming you," Jason assured him.

Rachel tipped her head. "Maxwell Williams might."

Jason shot her a look as though he couldn't believe she'd just said that. Her response was a shrug.

Detective Swenson sighed. "No. She's right. I still should have investigated the other suspects further. I should have figured out something was wrong when the defense attorney didn't ask about those things." You could hear the emotion in his voice rising. "If I could go back and change it, I would. I would have stood up to the chief and told him that I wasn't going to get tunnel vision and only focus on one suspect. Especially so early in the case."

Rachel could tell that the detective felt bad about it, and felt guilty for her comment, and her tone with him. "I am sorry. We get that the chief gave an order. It's not your fault that the prosecutor left out parts of the file. This isn't your fault."

Amy walked into the conference room. "Mr. Duncan is here." She hesitated, as she read the mood in the room. "What?" she asked.

Jason said, "The victim's dad pushed for Williams to be the only suspect during the investigation, and the prosecutor didn't turn over the whole police file in the case."

Amy looked confused; she was clearly unfamiliar with criminal law outside of what she saw on TV. "So, that's bad, right? Does that mean you will win your motion or whatever?" she asked.

"It definitely helps," Rachel said. "You can tell Mr. Duncan to come in. He is going to want to see this."

Attorney Cole Duncan was led into the room, then brought up to speed on what the group had discovered. "I always thought that there were pages missing from the reports. Something just didn't add up." Amy made him a copy of his own to review. "Maxwell Williams didn't do this, did he?" he asked, coming to that realization.

Rachel looked at him. "Is this the first time you are realizing that?"

"I mean, he always said he was innocent, but a lot of defendants say that. I just take it with a grain of salt. I gave the case my all, but once a jury verdict comes back guilty, I can't worry about my client anymore. I had too many cases back then to dwell on the losses." Cole tried to make excuses for himself. "I did the best I could with what I had."

Detective Swenson's phone began to ring. He stepped out to take the call. When he came back, he said, "I'm sorry, I have to go. Just let me know if you need anything else from me."

"Thank you for everything," Rachel said. "You have helped tremendously."

"It's no problem. I wish I would have done more back then," Detective Swenson said as he walked out of the conference room, waving goodbye to the rest of the group. After he left, Jason, Rachel, and Cole spent some time looking over the new pages.

Cole finally said, "Well, this should all be enough for you to get your motion granted, in addition to the normal arguments. I am not sure what else you may need from me, but I have another meeting to get to. Can you guys just touch base later if you need anything after processing all of this?" He didn't seem like he wanted to be there any longer, even though they were just getting started and he hadn't added anything new to the investigations. He had to use the table to help him get back up, showing his age a little.

Jason looked at Rachel. This was all way beyond what he'd

expected when he'd started to work on the case. Obviously, he had seen plenty of *Law & Order* shows where crazy things like this happened. He never thought they happened in real life, though. He was stunned and reeling, as he considered all that had transpired today, and he wasn't 100 percent sure what it all meant. He knew it helped the case, but he didn't know the full extent of it yet.

"Yes. That's a good idea. There is a lot to digest here and figure into our strategy. Thanks for coming," Rachel said. Cole gave a nod and headed out the door. After he left, Rachel sat back in her chair with an amazed look on her face.

"Wow," was all that she could muster up. "I have never had anything like this happen before."

That admission made Jason feel better; he wasn't the only one shocked about everything that had come to light over the last few hours. Jason could see the wheels turning in Rachel's head as she considered what steps to take next and what all this meant.

Amy walked into the room. "Sorry to interrupt. Jason, your next appointment is on the line. Do you want me to reschedule?"

Jason looked at his clock. It was 1:30 p.m. already. He looked at Rachel as though he was trying to figure out what was best to say. Rachel cut in. "No, it's okay. You take your call. I am going to take this stuff and grab some lunch. I need to look at these reports further and figure out how this changes things. What is your night looking like?" she asked Jason.

Amy looked at Jason with amusement, something that Rachel surely noticed. "I was planning on working here until about 7:30 and then heading to the gym. I can skip the gym, though, and come work on this stuff," he said.

"That sounds good. I will text you around 7 to let you know where I am at. Does that work?" she asked.

"Yeah. That's fine. Let me know if you want me to pick up food on the way," Jason said, as Rachel packed up her things to leave.

Jason walked back to his office, with Amy close behind. He was glad that he and Rachel were getting together again, and hopeful that they were over the awkwardness. Amy looked at Jason and smiled. "Don't even start," he said to her.

"I like her," Amy said, and she left it at that. She sat down at her desk. Jason walked into his office and sat down to take his waiting call. He couldn't focus, though, as his mind was racing, thinking about everything they had just uncovered and how it all fit together. Jason had to admit he also couldn't get Rachel out of his mind. He was excited to be spending time with her again that night.

CHAPTER SIXTEEN

The rest of the day flew by. Jason was finishing up an internal memorandum to Mr. Brandt when he heard his text tone ding. He looked at his phone and it was from Rachel. "Meet at my house and bring food please :)."

Jason smiled at his phone and texted back, "What do you want to eat?"

The response came almost immediately. "Surprise me!"

Jason quickly finished up the rest of his memorandum, then gave it another once over before sending it to Mr. Brandt. He packed up the rest of his things and headed down to his car. He waved goodnight to Fred, the security guard, and went on his way. He decided on Thai food. In the past, Jason would have been worried about ordering or picking out food for girls. They were always so picky, and he didn't want to get the wrong thing. He thought about that and realized he didn't have any of that apprehension with Rachel. He had spent enough time with her and shared enough meals to have a good idea of what food to order for her.

He picked up the order and pulled up outside Rachel's apartment. She let him in, and he walked in and sat at the table. Jason started to pull all the food out of the bags. Rachel was in her work attire when she first opened the door. Now she was coming out of her bedroom in short shorts and a tank top. The tank top was low cut and Jason could see Rachel's cleavage peeking out of the top. She looked beautiful, as always, even in just this simple outfit. Jason admitted to himself that Rachel looked good in everything she wore.

The more time he spent with her, the more he found things that he liked about her. It was funny to say, but he liked that she was stubborn and hardheaded. She could argue with the best of them, and sometimes that scared him. He never wanted to get into a fight with her. She was well put together, and even if her organization of files was not always the best, she seemed to know where everything was. Rachel had this fierceness about her that showed through when she was getting passionate about a case. But the thing that Jason liked most about her was her compassion. She had to be one of the most compassionate people he knew, and it made sense why she worked doing what she did. Jason admired her and had admitted to himself that he really liked her.

Rachel sat down at the table, her legs criss-crossed on the chair underneath her. "Oooh, Thai food, one of my favorites."

She started to open all the containers to see what Jason had gotten. "This all looks so good. Thank you!" she said as she started eating. Jason could tell that Rachel was excited about everything that they had found out that day. She was more upbeat than normal. He was amused as he watched her eat quickly, figuring that she wanted to finish eating so she could get back to the work.

That was the first time that Jason came to the realization that Rachel was a workaholic, much like him. She was always working late hours, she had a war room at her apartment, she focused all her attention on work above personal relationships, and she lived off takeout food, from what he had learned about her. He smiled at her.

"You seem extra excited about everything," he said.

She swallowed her bite. "You have no idea! We have so much to go over. Get eating!"

They ate in near silence and as quickly as possible, so they could get back to work. Jason finally sat back in his seat and exhaled. "I ate too much."

Rachel laughed at him. She got up and put the leftover into the fridge for later. Jason was sticking his stomach out to make himself look pregnant with a food baby. Rachel walked by and poked her finger into it. She grabbed his hand. "Come on." She led him to the war room, where the new files were already spread out and highlighted. Jason felt her warm hand in his and it felt natural. He liked it every time she touched him. She dropped his hand, and sat down at her seat across from him. He sat down, too.

"So," Rachel started. "We talked about those other suspects that Detective Swenson mentioned. We can get back to those later. I have a theory on who did it, and why, based on the new police reports. The fact that Amelia's father had undue influence in the investigation is another argument for us to add to the petition to show that the investigation was never fair to begin with. It strengthens the confirmation bias argument." She started talking faster and faster, as her excitement rose.

She took a deep breath before going off on her next tangent. "The fact that the prosecutor in the case did not disclose the full file is not only an ethical violation, but in itself would likely be grounds for a new trial. We have this in the bag!" she exclaimed. "I have never been so confident about a petition before. I talked to Mr. Williams today and gave him an update on the case. He was so happy that he cried." A pause. "Well, I cried too, if we are being honest. We have got this one, Jason!"

Rachel stood up, walked over to Jason and pulled him up from his chair. She put her arms around his neck, and he thought she was pulling him in for a hug. To his surprise, Rachel closed her eyes and went in for a kiss. Her soft lips pressing against Jason's. He felt the warmth from her face being close to his, pushed his lips back into hers, and kissed her back. He brought his hands to her hips. The kiss only lasted a few seconds, but they were a great few seconds. When it was over, Jason's face was hot.

Rachel pulled back, with her arms still around his neck. She looked at him as if she were questioning whether it was okay that she kissed him or if he was on a completely different page than her. Jason answered by bringing his hand to her cheek and pulling her in for another kiss, this time more passionate. He was completely giving in to the moment, Rachel going up on her tiptoes to get a better angle. The second kiss lasted almost a minute, before they parted again and smiled at each other.

"That was nice," Jason said.

"Yes, it was," Rachel said, as she pulled her arms back down and went back to sit down at her spot. Jason laughed. "What?" she asked.

"All of that, and then you're right back to business. I love it."

"Oh, throwing out the L word already?" she joked. "I must be one hell of a kisser."

Even though he knew she was kidding, Jason's face flushed with the mention of the word "love." Jason hadn't used that word in this context since high school. He smiled and sat back down at the table. "What's next?"

"Next, we draft the petition and submit everything to the court," Rachel said.

"Okay. What do you need me to do?" Jason asked.

"Well, I will draft the petition and then you can review it. I have a bank of all the legal arguments that we need to make, so I just have to put it all together. Then I will send it over to you to read over, edit, add to, all that good stuff."

"That sounds like a good plan," he said.

"At some point soon you will probably have to come in and meet Mia. She is going to be even more involved from this point on if the motion is granted, which it will be."

"Okay. That sounds good to me. Has she read through everything now? Even the updated stuff?" Jason asked.

"No. She has been out studying for finals. I will fill her in when she comes back into the office."

Rachel started to organize the papers on the table into a semblance of strategic piles. Jason's phone started to ring. He looked at it; it was Mr. Brandt. He picked up his phone. "Hello, Mr. Brandt. How are you?"

"Good, Jason. Hey, I just read through your internal memo. That looks good. I had a last-minute thing come up, and I need you to come to the office to help me with something."

"Right now?" Jason asked.

"Yes, right now. It is urgent."

"Okay. I am on my way," Jason said, and Mr. Brandt hung up on his end.

"You have to go?" Rachel asked.

Jason sighed. "Yes. My boss needs me for some emergency."

"Does that happen a lot?"

"Sometimes," Jason admitted. "Ugh. I wanted to stay and hang out."

"Me too," she admitted. "It's okay, though. Duty calls. Rain check!"

"Rain check," Jason agreed. He wasn't sure if he should hug her goodbye or give her another kiss. This was all new territory that he wasn't used to. While he was deciding what to do, Rachel stood up and came over to him. She leaned up and gave him a quick goodbye kiss.

"Text me later?" she said.

Jason leaned down and kissed her quickly once more. "I will." He grabbed his stuff and walked out of her apartment. He ran home to change and made his way to the office to help Mr. Brandt with his emergency.

CHAPTER SEVENTEEN

Jason was busy the next few days helping Mr. Brandt with his emergency. He had been texting with Rachel here and there, and they had made plans to get together for dinner after work on Friday. They were going to a fancy steak restaurant in the city, and Rachel was very excited. She said it had been years since she had been to a fancy dinner. They pulled into the restaurant fifteen minutes early. Jason leaned over to give Rachel a kiss in the passenger seat.

Jason walked around to the passenger door and opened it for her. Rachel was wearing a skintight black dress that had a little sparkle to it when the moonlight hit it right. She looked beautiful. As Jason looked at her, he couldn't remember the last time he had felt this excited about a woman. He was wearing a navy-blue suit jacket and dress pants. He was actually dressed down from his normal work attire, but Rachel didn't mind. She thought he looked handsome.

They walked into the restaurant, and Jason opened the door for Rachel again. She thought to herself how she could get used to this chivalry. After they checked in, she went to the bathroom to freshen up before they sat down. She came back out just in time for the hostess to call Jason's name. They started walking to their seats, then and all of a sudden Jason noticed Rachel's face go pale. She stopped walking for a minute. "What's wrong?" Jason said.

At the same time as he asked, a man in a full black suit called out, "Rachel Nix. How are you doing?" He stood up and looked like he was going to give her a hug. Jason vaguely recognized him, but couldn't place where he knew the face from. Rachel started walking toward him again and reluctantly gave him a half-hearted hug. He pulled away from her. "Rachel, this is Melinda." He gestured to the woman sitting with him. She was a pregnant blonde-haired girl with big fake boobs. She was wearing a black dress that looked like it was intentionally two sizes too small.

Rachel nodded her hello, but looked mortified and like she couldn't find the words to say anything. The man cleared his throat. "Melinda is my fiancée," he said, looking to Rachel for a reaction. When he didn't seem to get the one that he was expecting, he turned to Jason. "And who are you?"

Jason waited a second for Rachel to introduce him, and when she still seemed too stunned to say anything, he put out his hand to shake the man's. "I am Jason Michelson. Nice to meet you." He paused, waiting for the man to introduce himself back.

"Matthew Cox," he said, answering the question that Jason had not asked. That name rang a bell, and now Jason realized how he recognized him. They had gone up against each other in a case his first year at the firm. Jason had won the case, and he felt a sense of accomplishment that he had beaten the man who had broken Rachel's heart. Matthew didn't seem to recognize Jason back, or if he did, he was playing it off like he didn't.

During the whole interaction, the hostess was waiting patiently. Rachel still had not said anything, so Jason finally said, "Well, it was great seeing you both. We should get to our table." He put his arm around Rachel's waist, and they walked to their table and sat down.

"Are you okay?" Jason asked Rachel.

She had finally found her voice again. It was a little shaky as she said, "I'm sorry."

"No. Don't be sorry. We all live in the same town. It isn't a huge surprise that we would run into him eventually," he assured her.

"Not that. How I reacted. I just haven't seen him since I moved out. And I . . ." She paused. "I wasn't ready to see her."

"You are way better," Jason told her, trying to make her feel better. Rachel gave him a small smile, as thanks. "I mean it. She has nothing on you. And she probably can't even spell 'litigation,'" he joked. That got a bigger smile and a little laugh. Jason wanted to do anything he could to cheer her up. The waitress came over and they ordered some drinks, hers a white wine, his a Jack Daniel's and Coke.

By the time the drinks came, Rachel had shaken the encounter off and seemed to be back to normal. "I am not going to let this ruin our night," she finally said. She gave Jason a big smile and held up her glass to toast him. He raised his glass and clinked it together with hers. They spent the rest of the dinner talking about the places where Rachel had traveled. They were getting to the end of their meal, and Rachel asked, "So, when am I going to get to see your place? You have been to mine a few times now."

Jason was surprised by this. His apartment was nothing compared to hers, and he felt a twinge of embarrassment. Things were so new with them; he didn't want to bring her back there. "Um, I don't know about that."

"Why not?" Rachel asked. "Do you have a wife and kids you are hiding from me?" She was trying to joke, but there seemed to be a little curiosity in her voice.

"Let's just say I still live in the studio apartment that I lived in during law school. It is about the size of your living room and is a little embarrassing," he admitted.

Rachel heaved a little sigh of relief. "I don't care about the size of it," she said, trying to convince him not to be ashamed. Jason didn't say anything more, but seemed to be considering her suggestion. Rachel reached over and grabbed his hand. She gave him her best puppy dog eyes. "Pleeaase?"

He rolled his eyes. "Fine," Jason relented. "I guess we can go there."

"Good," Rachel said, feeling like she had won.

Jason paid the bill and they drove back to his apartment. They walked up to his door, and he paused for a minute. "Okay. Remember, it's nothing special. I am rarely here, so I figured that there was no point in getting some fancy apartment, when I would never be there."

Rachel pushed him playfully. "Don't be so worried. I am not going to judge you because of your apartment. I have plenty of other things to judge you about." She winked at him.

They went in and Rachel looked around. "Oh my gosh. This is so bad," she said.

Jason turned around to look at her, with a sinking feeling in the pit of his stomach. Once he saw her face, he knew she was joking. His heart stopped racing. She walked over and plopped down on the couch. "I like it! Simple and clean." She patted the spot on the couch next to her, signaling to him to come sit down. Jason smiled at her and walked over.

"You're just saying that," he said. "I know it's nothing special." He sat down on the couch next to her and put his arm around her shoulders. She snuggled into him.

They sat there in silence for a few minutes, and then Rachel turned to look at Jason. "I have a question." He looked at her curiously and nodded, signaling for her to go ahead and ask. Rachel paused and looked as though she was considering how to put things. "I know we just started hanging out as more than colleagues, and I am not saying there is anything wrong with it if you are. I was just curious—are you seeing or talking with anyone else?" Rachel looked away, breaking eye contact.

Jason laughed a little. "I definitely am not seeing or talking to anyone else." Rachel sighed a little sigh of relief and smiled. "Nor do I want to. I mean, I don't want to put any added pressure on this, whatever it may be, but I am only interested in talking and spending time with you."

Rachel's smile widened, her dimples becoming very pronounced. "Okay, good. Me too!" She leaned in and kissed him quickly on the lips. She looked a little more serious, and said, "I know it is new, and I don't want to put any pressure on it, on us." She paused. "But I am at the point in my life where I've already been engaged once, and I don't have the time or the desire to just mess around with anyone." Rachel looked at Jason to gauge his reaction.

Jason took in what she was saying. He hadn't been in a serious relationship for more than six years, and had never considered marrying someone he was dating. Jason wasn't against getting married, and he did have feelings for Rachel. He wanted to be honest and transparent with her, though. "I do have feelings for you, and I like spending time with you. I am not against marriage by any means, but I have never really considered getting married. At least not to anyone that I have dated in the past."

Jason was worried that this was going to end whatever was going on between them before it really got started. Rachel considered what he was saying. She finally smiled at him and said, "Well, I am not saying we have to get married or make that decision right now." She laughed. "I just wanted to make sure you knew where I was at and that I am not in a place where I want to just date casually anymore."

"I am not in a place for that, either. I don't have the time or energy to date casually," Jason joked. Rachel pushed at his chest playfully. Then she moved over and straddled Jason's lap, her legs on either side of his. She leaned into him and kissed him deeply, her hands on his cheeks. Jason wrapped his arms around her waist and leaned into the kiss. They sat on the couch like that, making out for a few minutes. Suddenly Jason picked Rachel up, her legs going around his waist, and walked them over to his bed, their kiss not breaking through the walk. Rachel felt his strong arms around her waist.

Jason laid Rachel down on the bed, and she kept her legs wrapped around him. He put his arms on either side of her and lowered himself down to kiss her again. He kissed her all around her face, then moved down and gently kissed and sucked on the side of her neck. He felt Rachel's body instinctively pulling up toward his, a soft moan escaping her lips. She ran her hands down his chest and started to tug on the bottom of his shirt to untuck it. She brought her hands back up and started unbuttoning his dress shirt. Jason sat up on the bed, shrugged the shirt off his shoulders and threw it to the floor.

He had a white tank top on underneath. Rachel leaned up and pulled it off over Jason's head. She threw it on the floor next to the dress shirt. She unhooked her legs from around his waist, then stood up and turned around, signaling to him to unzip her dress. He stood up behind her, kissing the back of her neck and down her shoulder blade, making every moment calculated and meaningful. He slowly unzipped her dress, the top of her black lacy thong just peeking out from the slit in the dress. She took out one arm and then the other, and let the dress fall to the floor.

Rachel turned around to face Jason, looking deep into his eyes. She was standing in front of him in a matching bra and thong. He wondered if she had planned to wear a matching set in hopes that this would happen. He looked her up and down, taking it all in. He smiled at her, a hungry smile, his hands finding their way back to her body. He ran them slowly down to her hips. Rachel reached for Jason's dress pants and unbuttoned them. She pulled them down past his waist and let them fall to the floor. Jason stepped out of them, and the two made their way back onto the bed.

Rachel rolled over so she was on top of Jason, straddling him. She leaned down and kissed his neck. She then started making her way down his chest, softly kissing a line downwards. She kissed across his waistline, teasing him, then kissed her way back up his chest.

She could feel him growing underneath her hips. She leaned up with her hands on his chest. She looked down at him, smiling, then bit her lip. Rachel reached around and unhooked her bra, letting it fall to the bed. She could feel Jason's heart rate quicken underneath her hand.

Rachel leaned back down, and they began kissing again. It wasn't rushed, the way Jason was used to doing things. His past experiences were quicker, where he and the woman hastily took their clothes off and got it done fast. This was not like that at all. They were taking their time and enjoying each second of it. Rachel's hand made its way down to the top of Jason's boxers. She looked at him, silently asking with her eyes if he was okay with her taking them off. Jason gave her a little nod. Rachel pulled them down and threw them on the floor. She was in control.

Jason put his hand on the small of her back, picked her up and turned her so she was lying back on the bed. "Are you sure you want to do this?" he asked her. She put her hand behind his neck and pulled him down for a kiss instead of answering his question out loud. He reached down and pulled her underwear down. Rachel kicked the thong off to the floor, and they went back to kissing passionately, their hands exploring each other's bodies.

A half hour later they were sprawled on the bed. Jason had his arm extended, with Rachel lying on it, the blankets pulled up around their shoulders. She turned to face him, and he turned to look at her, a big smile on his face. She leaned in closer to kiss him once more.

The two of them stayed up talking until a little after midnight. Rachel finally yawned and asked, "Should we get some sleep?"

Jason nodded. "Yeah. I guess so." He turned over to the nightstand and grabbed his phone. He plugged it in, and asked, "What time do you want to get up?"

Rachel thought about it for a minute. "I guess 5:30." Jason set the alarm and set his phone back on the nightstand. He rolled onto his back and put his arm back out for Rachel to cuddle into. She lay down, put her hand on his chest and asked, "Is there any chance you can read through and edit the Williams petition tomorrow? I want to get everything finalized by Monday."

Jason smiled at her. He found it adorable how she was just as committed to work as he was. "Yeah. I can make time for that."

"Thanks!" Rachel said as she closed her eyes, her breathing getting heavier. Jason watched her fall asleep, taking in her beauty as she slept. He thought back to meeting Rachel a month and a half ago. Never in a million years did he think he would end up where he was tonight. Jason was genuinely happy, for the first time in as long as he could remember. He fell asleep with a smile on his face, Rachel in his arms.

CHAPTER EIGHTEEN

Over the next three weeks, Jason and Rachel spent a few more nights together, but they were both busy. Jason reviewed and edited the petition for Maxwell Williams, and they submitted everything to the courts. They anxiously waited to hear back about the appeal. There were a few different things that could happen. The court could approve the petition outright, they could have oral arguments, or they could deny it outright. Jason and Rachel were fairly certain that the court was not going to deny it, so they were just waiting to see if they would have to prepare for an oral argument hearing or not.

It had seemed like work was taking over, and they hadn't been spending as much quality time together as either of them would have liked. They did send each other "good morning" and "goodnight" texts, but Rachel wanted more than that. As she had told him, she wasn't looking for casual dating. She wanted something more serious, and she wanted it with him.

With Thanksgiving a week and a half away, Jason and Rachel were having dinner at Rachel's place. Since the Williams case was at a standstill, waiting on the court, they didn't have to focus on work as much when they were together now, which they hoped would help. It would give them more time to get to know each other and spend quality time with one another.

"What are you doing for Thanksgiving?" Rachel asked as they were eating their spaghetti dinner.

Jason finished chewing his bite of garlic bread. "I don't usually do anything, at least not since starting law school. What are you planning on doing?"

"I was thinking maybe we could go to your mom's," Rachel said as she swirled up another forkful of spaghetti and put it in her mouth.

Jason dropped his fork unintentionally, and looked at her. "Oh, really?"

"Yeah. You told me that Thanksgiving was always a big holiday in your house and that your mom still does it every year. I think it would be nice if we went." Rachel touched Jason's hand.

The two of them had talked about working things out with their families and trying to see them more. Jason had been talking with his mom more the past few weeks, and he had to admit that it had been nice. Jason finally decided. "I guess we could do that." Rachel got a big smile on her face as she leaned over to kiss him. This was all new to Jason, and he felt a little nervous about it. He had never brought a girl home before.

After dinner, they decided to call Jason's mom and tell her the news and ask what they could bring to Thanksgiving. "Hey, mom," Jason said.

"Hey, Jason. How's it going, son?" his mom asked.

"Good. I just wanted to let you know that my girlfriend, Rachel, and I are planning on coming to Thanksgiving this year."

That was the first time Jason had referred to Rachel as his girlfriend. Her heart jumped in her chest just hearing him say it. Rachel blushed, and felt like a teenager with her first crush again. The phone was on speaker. "Oh, Jason. That is just great news. Everyone will be so excited to see you and meet Rachel."

"She's very excited to meet all of you too. She's here now," Jason said.

"Hello, Ms. Michelson," Rachel said.

"Oh, hello, Rachel. I have heard a lot of good things about you from my son. I look forward to meeting you at Thanksgiving," Jason's mom said.

"I have heard a lot of great things about you too," Rachel said. "What can we bring with us for Thanksgiving?"

"Oh, just yourself, dear. We have got everything covered. You getting my Jason here for the holiday is more than enough."

Rachel smiled at Jason with an I-told-you-so look on her face, rubbing in that this was a good idea. "Are you sure? We can still bring something," Rachel stated.

"I promise. Just bring the two of you here, and we will take care of the rest."

Jason cut in, "All right, mom, that sounds good. Well, we are excited to see you guys."

"Everyone here will be so excited too. Talk to you soon." And with that, his mom hung up the phone. The conversations between Jason and his mom, though more frequent now, were still short. They were working on building that relationship back up, slowly but surely.

Jason pulled into the driveway, and took a deep breath. He looked over at Rachel. "Are you ready to do this?"

She smiled back at him. "Of course. I am really happy we are doing this!" Rachel wasn't nervous at all. She wanted to meet Jason's family and learn more about him.

Jason walked around and opened Rachel's door for her, and they went into the house. The second they walked in, it was a commotion. Jason's sister Kylie came running to the door to greet them. She gave Jason a big hug and then went straight to Rachel and gave her one too. Rachel didn't mind, and embraced it. She had told Jason that she was looking forward to meeting his siblings the most because she missed her half-siblings so much. Jason was glad that Kylie had hugged Rachel right away. He hoped it made her feel like she was at home.

Next came the twins, running toward their uncle. They both jumped on him and began trying to tackle him. Jason pretended like he was being overtaken. He fell to the floor, and everyone laughed.

Jason's mom came into the entryway. "Kids, get off your uncle and go wash up for dinner." They obediently followed their grandma's direction. She walked over and gave Jason her hand to help him off the ground. He took it, and stood up and gave her a big hug. Next, she hugged Rachel and whispered in her ear, "Thank you so much for getting my son back to me. It has been a long time."

All Rachel could do was smile and nod. She was happy to have made a positive impact in Jason's life. She realized how truly important it was for her to get closer with her family too. Originally, when she and Jason first started talking about reconnecting with their families, she had mostly agreed to the project so that Jason would talk more with his. She didn't actually put much thought into seeing and talking with her own family more. After Thanksgiving with Jason's family, she changed her mind about that. She needed to get closer with her family again. More importantly, she *wanted* to get closer with them.

CHAPTER NINETEEN

Thanksgiving with Jason's family went well. It brought Jason and Rachel even closer together. They were spending more and more nights together. Some nights they were going out to dinner, other nights they were just in the same room as they worked on their respective workloads. They were comfortable together, and everything felt so natural. Jason was starting to see a future with Rachel, and surprisingly that didn't scare him. Despite having that conversation with Rachel about their intentions with the relationship, Jason had never committed to the idea that it could get serious, but he had been open to it. Neither one of them had thought it would go this well and move this fast. One night, they even talked about Jason's lease being up in a few months and the possibility of him moving in with Rachel.

One night, they were eating dinner at his place and Jason felt like she was looking at him. He looked up, and she was. She had a smile on her face and looked deep in thought. He grabbed her hand and kissed it. Rachel thought about what a gentleman Jason was, and that she was lucky to have him. She could feel herself starting to fall for him. While it scared her, she was ready to let it happen. Jason wasn't her ex, and she couldn't hold someone else's wrongs against him. She was excited to see where this was going. In that moment, Rachel could honestly say that she had real feelings for Jason Michelson.

They ended the night cuddling on Jason's couch, watching some movie on the Hallmark Channel. Christmas was approaching, and the Hallmark Channel was continuously playing those Christmas movies that all tended to have the same plots that ended in a happy love fest. Jason had never seen any of them before, and he seemed to be enjoying the movie, even though it was cheesy. Rachel had always secretly loved these movies and tried to watch as many as she could every year. They helped get her in the Christmas spirit.

It was getting close to midnight, and the next movie was about to start. Rachel looked up, and Jason was sleeping. She lay there and just enjoyed the moment. He was so peaceful looking when he slept. The worry and stress that he usually carried on his face were gone and he had an almost childlike calmness to him. It was nice. Rachel leaned up and kissed him on the cheek. Jason's eyes shot open.

"Sorry, babe. I didn't mean to wake you. You were sleeping so peacefully." She stroked her hand across his cheek.

"It's okay," he said in a groggy voice. "Want to head to bed?"

"Sure," Rachel said. They both went and lay down together, and a few minutes later they were both asleep, snoring softly.

The next day, Jason sat at his desk. It was December 17, 2021, and he was working on a brief for a merger that one of his clients was considering. His phone started ringing; it was Rachel Facetiming him. He hit the save button on the Word document, and answered the call. "Hey, babe. What's up?" Rachel normally didn't call during work hours.

"Did you see it?" she asked, sort of out of breath.

"See what?"

"The email from the court. They granted our petition on

Williams. He is getting a new trial!" She was yelling now, her excitement palpable.

"What? Really?" Jason said, his voice getting louder as well. Amy heard the excitement and walked around the corner to look in and see what was going on. "We are getting a new trial," Jason said to Amy.

"Congratulations!" Amy said.

"Is that Amy?" Rachel said, the excitement still in her voice.

"Yes. I am so proud of you two!" Amy said into the phone. "We need to go out and celebrate!"

The three of them made plans to go out to dinner and drinks at Manny's. They spent the night celebrating and drinking. It was a Friday night, so they decided to let loose and have some fun. Amy's husband was home alone with the kids, so she ended up leaving around 9:30 p.m., while Jason and Rachel continued to drink at the restaurant. When Manny's closed, they took an Uber back to Rachel's apartment, where they continued the celebrations.

They were lying in bed that night after having sex. "What's next?" Jason asked.

"Now comes the hard part. We prepare for a new trial."

CHAPTER TWENTY

Mia Drake was scheduled to return to volunteering after the holiday break. Jason still hadn't met her yet, but he was interested to see how the interaction would go, based on what Rachel had shared about her. Jason had to get in his certified statement for his hundred pro bono hours by December 30. Rachel and Jason were sitting down in the Exoneration Project conference room on December 22 accounting for all of his hours. Once they had calculated it all out, he let out a sigh of relief. "It's 116 hours," he said.

"That is pretty impressive in such a short period of time," Rachel said.

"No wonder I fell in love with you, with all of that time we spent together on the case." Jason caught himself as he heard those words coming out of his own mouth. He had never said that to Rachel before. He had never said it to any girlfriend before, and really meant it.

Rachel's head snapped up from her review of the statement. "What did you just say?"

He looked at her again and grabbed her hands from across the conference room table. "This is not how I pictured saying it for the first time. But I love you, Rachel."

Rachel stood up, jumped into Jason's lap and kissed him. "I love you too!" They continued to kiss for a few more minutes, before stopping to finish up what they were working on and head back to Rachel's apartment.

The next day, Jason went into the office early because he had a meeting at 8 a.m. sharp with Emily Cruze. After a review of everything that had occurrd, the ethics liaison who worked at the firm had decided that there was no ethical violation stemming from what had happened between them at the bar that night. She did initially reprimand Jason for deciding to go out drinking with a client, but then reasoned that since they were former classmates, it was okay. Attorneys can represent family members and friends, and aren't thereby required not to drink or spend time with those people, so this should not be any different.

Emily did have to sign an acknowledgment stating that if anything else occurred that would hinder the professional relationship between her and the firm, she would have to go elsewhere for representation. The whole situation was embarrassing, and neither Jason nor Emily wanted to talk about it ever again.

They hadn't talked much since their last meeting anyway, because they were waiting for things in her divorce to proceed. Jason had talked to her divorce attorney and gone over the various options involved. The goal was for Emily to keep as much of her company's equity as possible.

Emily arrived at 7:50 a.m. and walked into the conference room where Jason was waiting. She sat down across from him at the table. "Hey, Jason. How are you?" She laid her papers down on the table in front of her.

"I am doing well, thanks. How about you, Emily?"

"Honestly, not great. This is the first Christmas with us being separated, and the kids aren't doing very well. They are with my husband and his family this year, so I won't see them until they get back." Emily started to get choked up. She pushed it back down, reminding herself that she needed to keep things professional. "It's going to be okay, though. They will have fun, and we will celebrate when they get back." She was still trying to convince herself of that fact.

Jason gave her a sad smile. "You are strong. Kids are resilient. They will be okay."

Emily nodded. Then she picked up the papers, looking to change the subject. "Okay. The reason we are meeting. My attorney thinks we have a solution to the problem of dividing the business."

"That sounds promising. What is it?" Jason asked.

"He will end up getting way more than I am comfortable with, but this seems to be the only way that it will work, where I can still keep the company's equity and take it public right away," Emily explained.

Jason was growing a little impatient with the suspense game. "What is that solution?" he asked.

"He is going to get some of the shares once we go public," she finally said, still sounding a little unsure about the decision. "Is that a possibility?"

"Of course it is. Like you said, though, that could be giving him a lot more money over time. Are you sure that's the best outcome in the grand scheme of things?" Jason asked. "I know I don't practice family law, but that doesn't seem like a very equitable division, if he gets a continuous part of your future profits."

Emily shook her head almost regretfully. "It's the only way. We have gone through all the scenarios, and this is the only one that allows me to take the company public within the next year and still have joint custody of the kids. My kids are what is most important. I have made my decision. I have to live with it."

"Is it finalized already?" Jason asked, feeling a bit of concern and regret for Emily.

"Almost. We are hoping to finalize the last details and sign in January."

"How many shares is he getting?" Jason asked.

"A fifth of however many shares we agree on making."

"A fifth!" Jason exclaimed. "Why didn't your family law attorney reach out to me about this before you guys agreed? That is going to amount to big money, way more than he would otherwise be entitled to." Jason did a quick calculation in his head. "Based on the numbers I have been running, that could be almost $5 million in shares if he cashed them in the day after going public. If he took half the equity now, it would only amount to $1.4 million. You would be better off in the long run just paying him out of the company's equity and postponing taking it public."

"He isn't willing to take that as an option. Once he saw the numbers that my attorney legally had to send over to him, it was a done deal in his eyes. His offer was joint custody of the kids, and he gets a fifth of the company shares once we go public. My attorney told me that this is a good deal and I should take it." She was near tears now.

"I don't think your attorney realizes how much your husband will be getting," Jason protested.

Emily just shook her head no, signifying to Jason that the decision had already been made and she couldn't debate it any further. She didn't have it in her. "The only question is, can we still take the company public as planned, with him having a fifth of the company?"

Jason sighed. "Yes. There will just be fewer shares to offer to employees and ultimately sell off."

"Then this is what we are doing, Jason," Emily said in a matter-of-fact tone. Jason conceded on that point, and they spent the next two hours working through the initial details of taking the company public.

Amy walked in to let Jason know that his next appointment was waiting in the lobby. Emily packed up her things and began walking out of the conference room. Jason called after her. "Have a great Christmas, Emily. It's all going to be okay."

Emily turned back and gave him a weak smile. "Thank you, Jason. You have a great Christmas too."

Jason worked until 10 p.m. that night to try to get ahead on things. He was only working a half day the next day, since it was Christmas Eve. Jason was going to spend Christmas Eve with Rachel's family, meeting them for the first time. To say he was nervous was an understatement. The last time he'd met a girlfriend's parents, it didn't go very well. The girl's dad bluntly told Jason that he was not good enough for his daughter unless he made a certain amount of money per year and could sustain the lifestyle she was used to. Jason should have known that the relationship wasn't going to work out after that, but he had stuck it out a few more months.

This time, it ended up going much better. Rachel's family loved Jason and told him he was welcome any time. They had gotten to Duluth right after 3 p.m. Rachel's dad was outside fixing the Christmas lights on the house. Jason immediately ran out to help him, which started things off on the right foot. Rachel's stepmom saw that they were there, and she opened the front door to call out to them.

"Rachel, come on in here, honey. I haven't seen you in so long, I need a hug." Rachel walked over and gave her a big hug.

About an hour later, Rachel's mom pulled in. Rachel had convinced her and her father that they should all get together as one big family for Christmas this year. They had reluctantly agreed, mostly because this was the first time Rachel had been back home for a holiday since her breakup with her ex-fiancé. That, and they knew there was no sense in arguing with Rachel.

The group ate ham and mashed potatoes and had some delicious pie for dessert. After dessert, they made their way to the living room and sat by the fire talking. Jason watched as Rachel opened up some presents from her family. He noticed that she seemed very happy to be home. He was glad to be a part of all this. Jason felt proud that he had played a small part in making this happen.

It was starting to get late, and Rachel said that they had to get going. Her family protested and renewed their offer for the two of them to stay. Rachel had already told them no thank you, and that they had to get back to the Twin Cities. Jason had told her that he didn't mind staying if she wanted to, but Rachel wasn't ready for that yet. She said she wanted to take it one step at a time. Jason got a sense that Rachel had not told him about some things that were keeping her from being close with her family. It seemed like there was more to it than her being busy and the grief the family felt from losing her half-siblings.

Everyone was hugging and saying their goodbyes. Jason promised he would be back soon. Rachel and Jason drove back to her apartment that night. Christmas Day was spent watching movies in bed and eating takeout, their new tradition. They were both making progress with reconnecting with their families, and that was in big part thanks to each other. They truly did make each other better versions of themselves.

The day after Christmas, they were sitting talking and Jason asked, "What happened with you and your family?"

"What do you mean?" Rachel asked, confused.

"I mean, it seems like there is something there. A reason why you haven't been close with them the last few years. I'm just curious what it is."

"It's none of your business," Rachel shot back.

Jason was taken aback. He hadn't seen this side of her since that first day at the Exoneration Project. He didn't know what to say, but settled on, "I'm sorry. I didn't mean to upset you. I just thought it was probably something I should know."

"Why do you think you should know? It's none of your business. It doesn't concern you," she shot back again.

Jason was so confused. Where was this coming from? Why was Rachel reacting this way? "I mean, it doesn't concern me necessarily, but it is something that happened in your life, so I thought it was probably important for me to know." He paused. "Why are you acting like this?"

"Acting like what?" she barked.

Jason walked over and tried to put a hand on her shoulder, but she pulled away. He was hurt by this reaction, and it must have showed on his face. Rachel noticed, but it didn't seem to matter at first. The two sat there silently for a few minutes, neither one sure what to do next.

Rachel took a deep breath and seemed to calm down. "I'm sorry for getting snappy with you. There are just some things I am not ready to talk about yet. This is one of those things."

All Jason could do was nod. He understood that she wasn't ready to share, but he was not sure who this person was. He hadn't seen her like this since they had got together, not even a glimpse of this kind of reaction. He figured that the secret had to be something really bad. Still Jason felt hurt, and like Rachel was blowing this whole thing out of proportion. He didn't think he deserved to be treated the way Rachel was treating him right now. They were supposed to love each other, and they'd just shared these great days and holidays with each other's families. He was really confused.

Jason stood up, and said, "I think I am going to head out and get some stuff done at my apartment."

Rachel looked at him, her face now showing less anger and a little bit of sadness. Jason was expecting her to ask him not to go, to just stay and work this out. When she didn't do that, he was even more upset about the situation.

All Rachel said was, "Okay. Sounds good." She didn't offer to walk him to the door, or even get up to kiss him goodbye.

Jason decided that if she wasn't going to make an effort to get up, then he wasn't going to make an effort either. He didn't lean down to give her a kiss or a hug goodbye. He just packed up his things and walked over to the door. Jason looked back at Rachel one more time as he grabbed the door handle. "Bye. I love you," he said, in a last attempt.

Rachel did not get up off the couch or reply. Jason's head dropped and he said it again in a louder tone: "I love you!"

Rachel huffed and finally said, "I love you too."

Jason had never been more confused. Why was he having to force her to say "I love you" back? What was so bad about things with her and her family that just his asking about things had led to all of this? He decided that he was too upset with Rachel right now to worry about it anymore. He opened the door and left the apartment. Jason got down to his car, feeling hurt. He was still not comprehending what had just happened, and he was honestly surprised that she hadn't run down after him. He gave it a few minutes longer, and when Rachel didn't come down, he drove away and went home.

Two days had gone by, and other than the occasional text, Rachel and Jason hadn't communicated at all. They had not discussed the fight between them and where it left things. Jason knew Rachel was stubborn, but so was he. He wasn't going to be the first one to apologize. He didn't think he had done anything wrong. All he did was ask a question, and a reasonable one in his mind. Why shouldn't he be able to ask questions about her relationship with her family? Rachel was the one who'd said she wanted a serious relationship, and ultimately a marriage. How could she expect that, and not be willing to answer a simple question?

Jason was still upset about everything, and he was focusing more on work to try and keep his mind off of it. It was New Year's Eve, and he was sitting in his office. The firm was surprisingly quiet that day. He was getting some contracts reviewed when Amy walked in. She had noticed that Jason had been a bit irritable lately, but when she had tried to ask why, Jason had said he didn't want to talk about it. It killed Amy to see him like this, but she respected his wishes and didn't ask about it again.

"Hey. The receptionist just called. Rachel is here. Do you want security to bring her up?" Amy asked.

Jason looked up, surprised. He didn't know she was coming. He thought about it for a minute too long, and Amy chimed in, "You should really talk to her. Let her come up, Jason."

All Jason could do was nod. Amy was right. They needed to get this fight behind them and try to move on. They had a lot of work coming up on the Williams case, and they didn't need their relationship issues getting in the way of what they were doing. It was too important, and this was such a stupid fight.

A few minutes later, Rachel walked into the office. Amy said hello and then went back to her desk. Jason stood up to greet Rachel but didn't want to make the first move. Rachel walked over to him and gave him a big hug. "I'm really sorry about everything. I don't know why I reacted that way. You had every right to be upset with me. All you did was ask a question."

Jason hugged her back.

Rachel pulled back from the hug and looked down. She sat on the edge of Jason's desk and sighed. "I'm still really upset with them for what they did. I thought I could get over it, but it was really hard to be around them."

"Really? I thought you seemed happy," Jason told her.

"I was," she reassured him. "I know that I need to move on and work on the relationship with them, but it's still so hard."

"Rachel, what happened that was so bad?"

Rachel seemed like she was ready to just give in. She started to speak in a defeated tone. "They sided with him."

"What do you mean?" he asked.

"They sided with Matthew. They said that if I was going to lose my job and lose him, that I should just go and find a big firm to work at." A lone tear fell down her face. "It killed me that they took his side."

Jason leaned down and hugged her. "Rachel. I am so sorry. That is terrible." He couldn't picture the people he had just spent Christmas Eve with treating their own daughter that way. It didn't make sense.

Rachel continued, "They apologized a few weeks after, and said they were just worried about me, that I worked so hard. They felt like I was throwing it all away. They just don't get what I do and how important it is to me."

Jason was trying to figure out what to say. "Do you think they mean it that they are sorry?"

"Yes. I know they are. I am just having a hard time getting over it all."

"I don't blame you for that." Jason rubbed her arm to comfort her. "Hey, thank you for sharing this with me. I really appreciate it. I love you."

"I love you too. I'm really sorry about the fight. It was completely my fault. I hated fighting with you. I just want us to be okay again. Can we?" she asked, her eyes hopeful.

Jason laughed. "Of course we can."

Rachel's phone rang, and she took it out of her pocket. "Oh, it's Dylan. I have to take this." She answered her phone. "Hey, Dylan, can you hold on one second?"

Jason couldn't hear the reply, but then Rachel took the phone away from her ear. "I have to go, but can we do something tonight?" she asked hopefully.

"Of course. Text me later," Jason responded.

Rachel waved, and got back to her phone call as she walked out of Jason's office. He sat back down at his desk and let out a long sigh. He was relieved that things seemed to be better between them. Amy walked in to check on things. "We are good," Jason said, and she smiled at him and walked back out to let Jason work. He appreciated that.

He started getting back to his work , then decided that he needed to do one last thing. "Hey, Amy?" he called.

Amy popped back in. "Yes?"

"Can you please order some flowers and see if they can still be delivered to the Exoneration Project today? If not, have them ready for me to pick up around 5:30?"

Amy smiled at him. "Sure thing, boss. I'll get right on it."

CHAPTER TWENTY-ONE

It was the start of the new year, and Jason was going to the Exoneration Project at 3:00 p.m. to meet Mia Drake. He walked into Rachel's office at 2:45, and saw she was on the phone. He gave her a little wave as he moved some messy folders from the chair by her desk and sat down. Rachel hung up the phone and walked over to give Jason a kiss. "Hey, babe. You're early," she joked.

"Oh, you know me. Less than fifteen minutes early and I am late." He put his arm around her waist and pulled her back in for another kiss. She pushed him away in a teasing fashion.

"Okay, let's go introduce you to Mia. She's in the conference room reviewing the new files," Rachel said, grabbing Jason's hand, leading the way. They walked into the conference room, and there was a woman sitting at the table. She looked to be in her mid-forties, dressed in a pink suit jacket and matching pants. Jason was taken aback, not only by her outfit, but also by the fact that she was older than the traditional law student. She was not exactly what he had pictured when Rachel had told him about her.

"Jason Michelson, this is Mia Drake. Mia, this is Jason." Rachel said.

Mia seemed to look Jason up and down, and then, making a decision of some sort, she stood up to shake his hand. Instead of the "Nice to meet you" Jason was expecting, Mia's first comment was,

"Well, that is a fancy suit you have there, Jason. You definitely don't work here."

Jason was surprised and not quite sure how to answer that. Was it a compliment? Was it a diss directed at Rachel? He looked to Rachel to see her reaction. Rachel shrugged. "Well, she's not wrong. Nobody working here could afford that suit." She laughed, trying to ease the awkwardness.

Jason put his hand out and shook Mia's hand. "I guess that's true. Nice to meet you, Mia. I am just a volunteer here."

Rachel jumped in. "He is just gracing us with his presence to get his pro bono hours." She said it in a joking way, but Mia retracted her hand from the handshake quickly, as if that was all she needed to know about Jason. They were not getting off to a great start, to say the least. Rachel caught the reaction and said, "I'm just kidding. Well, he is here to get his pro bono hours, but he's not like that. He is fully invested in this case and is doing his share of the work."

Mia looked uninterested by this and went back to what she was working on. Jason looked at Rachel again, his expression conveying that the exchange hadn't gone as planned. Rachel shrugged and pulled out a chair to sit down at the conference table. Jason followed her lead and did the same.

Rachel started to say, "So, the game plan," but before she could finish her sentence, Mia put up a finger to indicate that she should stop talking until she was finished with what she was reading. Rachel looked at Jason, who rolled his eyes, clearly annoyed.

A minute or two went by and Mia finally looked up. "Okay, go," was all she said. Jason's annoyance with Mia was rising. She was the legal intern, but was acting like she was in charge. To say that she rubbed Jason the wrong way would be an understatement. He pushed those feelings aside momentarily. This wasn't his show to run—it was Rachel's. He didn't want to step on any toes.

"All right," Rachel said, not seeming to let the way Mia was acting get to her. "We got notice from the court that the prosecutor for the new trial is Jeff Malone. I have never heard of him before, but he reached out to set up a meeting for next week."

Mia took out her phone and opened her calendar app. "What day and time?"

Rachel looked at her phone and opened an email. "It looks like Tuesday at 2 p.m. at his office."

Jason pulled out his phone. "I am in mediation all day that day, so I won't be able to make it. Should we try to reschedule? I don't know if I need to be there for it. Do I?"

"No. It should just be a quick meeting to touch base and talk about the flow of the case. I can go alone, it's no big deal."

"I can make it work," Mia chimed in.

"Oh, okay, perfect. Mia will come with, then," Rachel said. "Let's talk about the theory of the case. I found some things in the pages that were left out of the original case file. I think I have an idea of who actually killed Amelia Jackson."

They spent the next two hours going over her theory of the case, the strategy, and what each of them would be working on as the new trial approached. Rachel stood up once they were done. "Do you have any questions for us, Mia?"

Without looking up, Mia responded, "No. I understand what we are each doing." She went back to what she was working on before. Jason got up to follow Rachel out of the conference room. They headed back into Rachel's office, closing the door behind them.

"Well, she's lovely," Jason said, as soon as the door was shut. "What is wrong with her attitude?"

"She's just different," Rachel said, searching for a word to describe Mia. "I think she has a difficult time taking direction from me, since I am younger than she is."

"It's not just that. She is straight-out rude. It was hard for me to hold my tongue. I don't know if I will be able to handle working with her often," Jason admitted. "I know I won't be able to deal with her being disrespectful toward you."

"It's okay. I can handle her. If I need to, I can talk to her about it. If things keep going this way, I can always have my supervisor reach out to the law school and let them know it just isn't a good fit. I don't want her attitude to hinder our work on the case in any way," Rachel explained.

Suddenly, Mia walked into the office and said, "I am heading out for my night class. Can I take the case file with me?"

Rachel said, "Interns can't take anything from the office with them. It's company policy. Sorry."

Mia looked disgusted and said, "Well, how do you expect me to catch up on the case and be part of the litigation team, then?"

Rachel let out a big sigh. "Mia, let's head into the conference room and talk alone, quick." Mia looked back at Jason and then walked out to the conference room.

Ten minutes later, Rachel walked back in and shut the door behind her. Her face was flushed, and she sat down at her desk. "Well, that didn't go the best, but she has one more chance before I kick her off the case."

"What was said?" Jason asked curiously, with a small smile across his face.

"I told her that I oversee this case and that we appreciate her help, but she is not going to be as big a part of the case as she was expecting. She got angry and tried to argue that she has all this experience as a paralegal, and she can do more than just push our papers around," Rachel went on. "I calmly explained what her place was and that she only had so many hours and things that she would be assigned to do. At one point, she got up and was pacing and almost left. Then she calmed down and sat back down."

"How did it end?" Jason asked.

"Well, I told her what we expected of her and that she needed to respect both of us."

"You put her in her place. That's kind of hot," Jason said, a mischievous smile coming to his face.

"Shut up, you dork!"

Jason looked down at his phone. "All right. Well, I have to head back. What time do you want to eat tonight?"

"I am making chicken parmesan, and it should be done," she paused and looked at the time, ". . . probably about 7:45 or 8 p.m."

"Oooh, chicken parmesan. My favorite. Can't wait. That time should work great." He stood up and gave Rachel a quick kiss goodbye.

Jason got back to his law firm a little before 6:30 p.m. and walked back to his office. Amy stood up and followed him in. "Mr. Brandt was looking for you earlier. He said he is leaving at 7 p.m. but wanted to talk with you quick before he leaves." Jason stood right back up as fast as he had sat down in his chair.

"Did he say what about?" he asked, as he grabbed his notepad to head to Brandt's office.

"No. He didn't say."

Jason walked over to Mr. Brandt's office and said hello to Juliette. She gave him a big smile. "Hey Jason. Go ahead in, he's been waiting for you."

"Thanks."

Jason knocked on the door as he walked into the office. Mr. Brandt looked up. "Oh, Jason. Good. Come take a seat."

Jason sat down, feeling a little wary about the conversation. He instinctively started to silently cycle through all the things that this could be about. He went through a mental checklist: his billable hours were still above everyone else's in his year; he got his pro bono hours done for last year; he was consistently bringing in new clients; and his to-do list on cases for Mr. Brandt was all caught up on. He couldn't think of anything that would lead to this meeting.

Mr. Brandt finished up the document he was reading and then looked up. "Sorry about that. Have to get this out before I leave. So, I know this is going to feel rushed and not like a proper way to do this, but you know how I am. I am not big on the whole rigmarole of things." Jason's confusion was growing. Mr. Brandt went on, "The partners had their monthly meeting this morning. We discussed your future at the firm, and it was ratified that you are the newest junior partner at Goldstein Brandt Miller and Fredrickson." He let his words sink in for a minute and waited for a reaction.

Jason was stunned. He didn't think he was hearing Mr. Brandt right. "But I haven't been here for the required number of years yet," was all Jason could get out. The traditional trajectory at Goldstein Brandt Miller and Fredrickson was junior partner at five years, senior partner around year eight or nine. Jason had only been there about four years.

"Jason, you bring this firm more money than most of the existing junior partners do. You are my go-to person when I need assistance on cases. You deserve this. The partners all agreed. You are the newest junior partner, effective tomorrow afternoon."

All Jason could do was nod, still not fully comprehending what he was hearing. Mr. Brandt looked at his computer screen, seeing a notification that had popped up. "Look, Jason, this is not the big official meeting that normally happens or that you deserve. We are doing a lunch with the partners tomorrow, and they will tell you officially then, but I wanted to be able to tell you, so you weren't blindsided tomorrow. I know I hate being blindsided, and I would appreciate the heads-up in your shoes. Congratulations, son." Mr. Brandt said it in a way that seemed to hint that the conversation was ending. "I will have Juliette send the details for lunch to your assistant."

Jason got up to leave the room. Mr. Brandt sent him on his way with "Jason, I am very proud of you. You deserve this! Do me a favor and act surprised tomorrow."

Jason walked out of the office, a blank stare on his face. Juliette got up and gave him a big hug.

"Congratulations, Jason!" she squealed a little too loudly. She looked behind her to make sure Mr. Brandt hadn't heard. She pulled back from the hug, and looked at Jason. She smiled. "Still in shock?"

"That is an understatement. I thought I was getting in trouble for something." Things were starting to sink in just a little.

"Juliette?" Mr. Brandt called from his office.

"Ope, that's my cue to go. Congrats again! I'll talk with Amy about the lunch details for tomorrow." She waved to Jason as she walked into Mr. Brandt's office.

Jason walked back to his desk, trying to process everything. He walked by Amy, who looked up, concerned about the look on his face. She followed him into his office and closed the door behind her. "What is it, Jason?" she asked, with concern in her voice.

Jason sat down in his chair. "They're making me junior partner," he said, just above a whisper.

"What?" Amy said excitedly.

"I am the newest junior partner," Jason said a little more loudly, gaining confidence in saying it. He thought maybe if he said it more confidently, it would help him believe it himself.

Amy's jaw dropped. "Are you kidding me?" she said, her voice rising with excitement. Jason shook his head. She ran around to hug him. "Jason, that's amazing. Congratulations!" Her voice had risen, almost to a yell.

He hugged her back. "I think I am in shock. I . . . I don't even know what to think or say. I wasn't expecting this for at least another year."

"You have always been a trailblazer around here. You work way harder than anybody else. You deserve this!" Amy assured him.

"It's not official until tomorrow. He just wanted to give me a heads-up. They are telling me at a big lunch with the partners. Juliette is going to email you to get it on my schedule."

"What does that change mean, other than the title?" she asked.

"I don't even know. I am assuming they will go over all of that with me." His mind started racing with all the questions. "I think there is probably a buy-in too. I wonder how much that will be?" Jason started talking faster, his anxiety rising. When an attorney is asked to be a partner at a firm, they are required to pay a sum of money as a "buy-in" to the firm. It is a way for the new partner to have a financial stake in the firm, in addition to the "sweat equity" they have already put in. Jason knew that he could afford the buy-in, whatever it was. He had been living in his small apartment and not spending most of his salary and bonuses since starting at the firm.

After working through that question in his mind, Jason then jumped to what changes this would make to his day-to-day work. Would he have his own associate attorney whom he could push some of his work onto? Would he still have to do all the grunt work on his own? What other things would they require from him? There were so many thoughts and questions running through his mind that he barely heard what Amy said next.

Reading his mind, she said, "Hey. Slow down. This is a great thing. Don't worry about all those things right now. It will all be fine. Just go and tell Rachel the good news!"

Jason shook his head a little bit, getting out of his head and back to being present in the room. "I can't believe this is happening."

"It's happening," Amy said, putting a hand on his shoulder. "Now come on. Get out of here. This stuff can wait." Jason grabbed his jacket and left his office, shutting off the light. Amy sat down at her desk.

"Hey. You should head home too!" Jason said to her.

"I am just going to finalize the details for lunch tomorrow, and then I will head out. You get out of here. Go tell Rachel!" Amy urged.

Jason got to his car and drove to Rachel's. She had left the door open for him, so he walked in and took off his boots and winter coat. Rachel called hello from the kitchen. "I wasn't expecting you so early. I have about ten more minutes on this." Jason walked around the corner, and Rachel turned to look at his face. Her face fell. "What's wrong?" Rachel turned her attention to him and walked over to him, placing a hand on his shoulder.

"They are making me junior partner."

Rachel smiled and asked, "Are you serious?" She threw her arms around him. Jason whisked her into the air, as he hugged her back.

"Mr. Brandt called me into his office at the end of the day and just nonchalantly came out and said it. It isn't official until tomorrow. The partners are taking me to lunch to tell me. Mr. Brandt wanted to give me the heads-up and be the first to congratulate me." He put Rachel back down, but she kept her arms around his shoulders.

"Have they ever made someone junior partner this fast?" Rachel asked, her voice still high and excited.

Jason shook his head. "I don't think so, no."

"Babe!" She hugged him again, tighter this time. "I am so excited for you. Congratulations. You deserve this!" She pulled away from the hug and gave him a kiss, putting her hands on his cheeks. When she pulled away, he could see a small moment of sadness on her face before her smile grew wide again.

"What is it?" Jason asked with concern in his voice.

"Nothing." Rachel smiled. "I am so, so proud of you."

"Tell me!" he persisted.

"I don't want to take away from this moment. You deserve to be excited and happy. I am all those things for you too."

"Rachel. What is it? You're worrying me."

"It was just a momentary sense of regret. I would most likely have been a junior partner now if I had stayed at Cooper Schwartz and Filstone. It was always my goal, up until I left there for the Exoneration Project." She paused for a moment, letting the sadness pass. "I made my choice, though, and it was the right choice for me! Now, back to celebrating you!"

Jason looked at her cautiously. "Are you sure you're okay? We can talk about it if you want. I am technically not going to be junior partner until tomorrow, so we can wait to celebrate until then. I don't want you to be upset."

"Don't be silly," Rachel said, smiling again, seeming to have moved on from the moment of sadness. "We are celebrating tonight!"

With that, the conversation about Rachel's moment of regret was over, and she led him over to the stove where the food was cooking. She grabbed the wooden spoon, stirred the red sauce, and then scooped up a little on the spoon. She blew on it for a few seconds to cool it down, then pushed it toward Jason's mouth. "Here, try this." Jason tasted it and smiled, feeling the warm sauce hit his taste buds. Rachel is a really great cook, Jason thought to himself.

"That is so good. I can't wait to eat!" Jason said, kissing Rachel again. She smiled at him, and his stomach suddenly growled loudly. They both laughed.

A half hour later, they were finishing up dinner and Jason looked at Rachel seriously. "Hey, babe. Do you ever regret not staying in a big firm? Be honest."

Rachel thought about it for a minute and sighed. "I would be lying if I said no. I do regret it sometimes. That's all I pictured while I was in law school, working at a big firm. Spending all day, night, and most weekends working my butt off. Working my way up the ladder. I think if they would have let me take a year off and do the Exoneration Project, and then go back to the firm, as though it was a clerkship, maybe things would be different. I know how hard it would have been to just apply to a position and get in after the fact. I wasn't going to give in and not pursue the Exoneration Project." She paused, a melancholy look on her face. "Everything happens for a reason, though, right? I am doing amazing things for people, where I am now. I'm making a difference in their lives. Plus, if I wasn't at the Exoneration Project, I would have never met you." She smiled at him.

Jason felt a moment of sadness; the way she said that made it seem like he was some consolation prize. He felt some type of self-consciousness that he had not felt before. He asked himself if Rachel was just settling for him. He shook those thoughts away, and realized it was just his anxiety getting to him. She didn't mean it in that way. He was overthinking it. He smiled back at her. "That's true. I wouldn't have liked that!"

Rachel held up her glass of wine. "Cheers to the newest junior partner at Goldstein Brandt Miller and Fredrickson." Jason clinked his glass with hers. The two of them spent the rest of the night drinking wine and enjoying each other's company. As they lay in bed that night, Jason couldn't fall asleep. The anticipation of the lunch with the partners tomorrow was keeping him awake, his mind wandering. It was almost 4:30 a.m. when he finally turned on some music on his phone to help him fall asleep. His last thought as he drifted away was how damn proud of himself he was.

CHAPTER TWENTY-TWO

The next morning dragged on as Jason tried to keep himself busy until lunch. Lunchtime finally arrived, and Jason met the partners out at Manny's. They were all enjoying a drink on the firm, and after they'd ordered their steaks, Mr. Brandt cleared his throat. The table all turned their attention to him. He explained again how the partners had talked and voted that Jason be the firm's newest junior partner. Everyone looked to Jason, who gave his best fake surprised look. He knew he wasn't fooling anyone. Everyone clapped for him, and he could feel his cheeks getting red in embarrassment from all the attention on him.

It was time for Jason to say something. He cleared his throat and tried to think about what to say. He hadn't practiced this part of the lunch. "I will keep this short and sweet. I just wanted to thank each one of you for making this decision. I am very appreciative, and I look forward to continuing my work for the firm, beside all of you." Jason raised his glass to cheers to the firm's name. Everyone clinked their glasses together and then their meals came.

Once the food arrived, everyone was back to being focused on other conversations, and Jason sat there eating and trying to make small talk with the senior partner sitting next to him. At around 1:30 p.m., people started to get up to head back to the office. Jason stood up to leave, and Mr. Brandt called over to him, "Jason, stop by my office later today and we will go over the logistics."

"I will. Thank you, Mr. Brandt," Jason responded, and then he left the restaurant.

He got back to the office, and Amy wasn't at her desk, which was weird. He walked into his office, and was caught off guard by some shouting. "Surprise!" came a unanimous yell. Rachel, Amy, Juliette, Mia, and a few other staff from the firm were in his office waiting for him. They had a big banner that read "Congratulations," and a few of them had noisemakers like those used for New Year's Eve. There was a cake on his desk that read "Congratulations, Junior Partner."

Jason had a big smile across his face. "Thank you, everyone! This is great." He walked over and put his arm around Rachel. He leaned down to kiss her on the cheek and whispered in her ear, "I hate surprises."

Rachel smiled at him and whispered back, "I know. It was Amy's idea. I couldn't say no."

"Well, let's eat some cake!" Jason exclaimed. Amy got out plates and utensils and handed out pieces of cake. As each person grabbed some cake, they said their congratulations and then headed back to their offices. By the end, it was just Amy, Rachel, Jason, and Mia. Mia had been much better since her talk with Rachel. Jason was surprised to see her there, but then he thought about it; it was her day to volunteer at the Exoneration Project.

"Congrats on the promotion, boss," Mia said. She had started calling him "boss" as a sign of respect.

"Thank you, Mia, and thanks for being here." Jason looked back and forth between Amy and Rachel. "And thank you two for all this, and the support you have both given me." He hugged them both.

Mia and Rachel got up to leave. Rachel gave Jason a quick kiss goodbye, said "We will celebrate more later!" and winked.

Jason smiled back at her and nodded.

Amy looked at Jason as she sat down across from him. "You did it!" she said.

"*We* did it," he corrected her.

CHAPTER TWENTY-THREE

Two weeks later, Rachel was taking Jason to meet Maxwell Williams for the first time. The COVID regulations on visitors had finally relaxed to the point that both of them could go at once. Rachel had been going at least once a month to visit with Maxwell, and wanted to be there the first time he and Jason met. They got checked in at the prison, their belongings were searched, and they were led into a ten-by-ten concrete room. It had a cold feeling to it. Jason instantly felt uncomfortable as they sat down in the cheap plastic chairs on one side of the table.

A few minutes later, two guards brought in Maxwell Williams. He was handcuffed by his hands and feet, and he shuffled along as he walked. He wore his standard prison scrubs and black flip-flops. Maxwell was a tall man with a big build. He wasn't overweight, but had a solid frame and looked like he worked out daily in his cell.

Rachel smiled. "Hello, Maxwell. How are you today? This is Jason Michelson."

Maxwell was led over to the table and sat down in the chair across from them. One of the guards took off one of his handcuffs and locked it to the table. Maxwell nodded to Jason and seemed to be sizing him up.

Rachel looked at the guards and waited for them to leave. Once they did, she said to Jason, "Maxwell doesn't talk when the guards are in here. I told him not to."

Jason nodded and Maxwell said, "It's nice to meet you, man. I really appreciate all the hard work you have been doing on my case." He looked down at his handcuffed hands. "I would shake your hand if I could."

"It's nice to meet you too. Don't worry about it. Thank you for letting me work on your case. It is an honor to work for you and work to get you out of here."

"Rachel tells me we have a pretty solid case."

"It seems like it to me. I think the evidence on the case is sparse. I don't understand how they convicted you in the first trial," Jason said.

"I've never understood it either. I guess the jury couldn't see how a black man from a poor family could end up with a white girl from a prominent family. It was a different time back then, man."

"I get that, but still, it wasn't fair. You shouldn't have been here all this time. You had so much going for you, with school and your life. It's a real tragedy that you spent your time in here. I just don't even know what to say," Jason said, genuinely at a loss.

"Hey, man. It's not your fault that I'm here. Don't take that burden on."

"I know. I just hate that I am in a profession that could be so blind and unjust." He paused, not sure if he should ask what was on his mind. "Maxwell, if you could go back, knowing what you know now, would you still have dated Amelia?"

Without hesitation, Maxwell responded, "Absolutely. I will love that girl with my whole heart until the day I die. If I could go back, I wouldn't change a thing about our relationship." He thought about that for a minute, and corrected himself: "Well, I guess I would change that last night we were together, so that we weren't fighting. Maybe none of this would have happened. She would have been at my house studying that day if we wouldn't have fought the night before." He looked down.

"It's not your fault," Rachel assured him. "You don't deserve any of this."

At one of their last meetings, Maxwell had been having a bad day and shared with Rachel that he thought he deserved to be here and that it was all his fault. He blamed himself for the fight the night before Amelia died. He was convinced that if it hadn't happened she would still be alive, and they would be living happily ever after, married with kids. Rachel had shared this with Jason, but told him not to say anything. She didn't want Maxwell to feel like his conversations with her were shared with everyone.

"So, Rachel told me last time that the team had to talk about things for the trial, and then the two of you would come here and go over it with me. What is the consensus?" Maxwell said.

Rachel looked at Jason, who shrugged. She started explaining. "After reviewing all of the evidence, I have a theory of what actually happened." Rachel and Jason had discussed this at length, and were on the same page about what they thought potentially happened the day that Amelia Jackson died. The thing they didn't agree about, however, was whether they should tell Maxwell, because if it was what really happened it could change so much. Jason was adamant that they should not tell Maxwell. Rachel thought that he deserved to know their theory of the case, and that if he didn't know it would hinder their defense.

Jason and Rachel had gone back and forth arguing about this for days. This was by far the worst argument that they had had yet. Jason was very concerned that if Maxwell knew what they thought happened he would see Amelia differently. Jason liked to think of the worst-case scenario in situations, so that if that was the outcome at least he was ready for it. He was worried that Maxwell would be so depressed and upset about their theory that he would not want to fight anymore. It would change the idea that he had had about Amelia all of these years. There was no telling how he would react.

Rachel held fast to her position, and her stubbornness prevailed. She essentially told Jason that she was the lead on the case and the one who does this every day. She was also the one who had been meeting with Maxwell, and she thought he could handle it. Jason ended up relenting, and here they were.

"Now, we don't know for sure if this is what happened, but we do think it is very plausible. I want to caution you that what I say is going to be upsetting, but I don't want it to change anything," Rachel continued.

"What do you mean 'change anything?'" Maxwell asked, starting to get concerned.

"We don't want you to think about Amelia any differently or stop fighting to get out," Jason explained.

"I don't think anything could do that, man. I have never been more hopeful to get out of here, and Amelia could do no wrong in my mind. She was my soulmate, no matter what."

Rachel smiled. "Okay, good." Then to Jason, "See, I told you. You were arguing with me for nothing."

Jason rolled his eyes, and Maxwell said, "Ah, man. You guys were arguing about me. Don't do that. Rachel tells me that you are her Prince Charming. Please don't let my case ruin that. Love conquers all. Just remember that."

Jason smiled. "You are very wise, Maxwell. We are fine, don't worry. It's going to happen sometimes when you have two attorneys in a relationship. If it wasn't obvious, attorneys like to argue." He laughed.

Maxwell laughed too. "Let's get into it, then. Break it down for me."

Rachel decided to start out with the ending. "We think that Casey True killed Amelia." She waited for a reaction.

"Really?" Maxwell said, but he didn't seem too surprised.

Jason looked at him, reading his reaction. "You've contemplated that before, haven't you?"

"I mean, when you have been locked away as long as I have, you run through every possible scenario. I think I have considered every single person we knew who could have killed her at one point or another. How do you think it happened?"

"Here is the part that may be upsetting to you," Rachel cautioned. Maxwell nodded at her to continue. He was ready. "We think that she was having sex with Jesus Cabrera." She paused to let that sink in. Maxwell didn't have any initial reaction. He seemed to just be pondering that thought. Rachel decided to keep going when he didn't say anything. "We think that she was upset with you and was vulnerable when Jesus came over that day. Casey wasn't home for some reason, and so Jesus and Amelia started talking. He was comforting her, and one thing led to another.

"They ended up sleeping together. Either during it, or after they had just finished, Casey came home and caught them. Amelia didn't have time to get her clothes on, so she wrapped her bedsheet around her. Casey confronted the two of them, and she struck Amelia with something. Amelia fell backwards, either knocked out or temporarily dazed. Casey went to the kitchen and grabbed a knife. She came back and stabbed Amelia.

"Jesus either tried to stop her or sat watching, horrified and in shock. There is really no evidence to show what he could have been doing at the time. The stab wounds do show that Amelia tried to fight back at some point, though. Three of the wounds show a pattern that she wasn't just lying there as she was being stabbed."

At that point, Maxwell started to tear up, and he said, "Amelia always was a fighter. It doesn't surprise me that she fought in the end."

Rachel nodded. "That's what the evidence showed, too. We think that after reality set in, and Amelia was dead, the couple covered for each other and came up with a bogus story that would give each of them an alibi."

After a few seconds of silence, Jason asked, "What do you think? You knew these people. Does that seem plausible?"

"Oh, definitely. Casey was always jealous of Amelia. Amelia was smarter, had more money, had a better internship, better grades, she was prettier. Casey used to yell at Jesus all the time for noticing Amelia. It got to the point that we didn't spend time at Amelia's apartment because it was so awkward. It was either Jesus trying to flirt with Amelia in front of me and Casey, or Casey yelling at him because of it. I think if Casey came in and found out that they had hooked up, she would have snapped and lost it. It's very plausible."

"Do you think that Amelia would have slept with Jesus?" Rachel asked. Jason shot her a look, signifying that that was going too far. Rachel shrugged it off.

"Yeah, probably. Amelia liked to get back at me when she was mad. She had slept with people in the past when we were broken up for a few days after a fight," Maxwell explained.

"Did that make you mad?" Rachel asked.

"I mean, of course it made me mad, but we were on a break, technically, so what could I do? Plus, like I said, that girl could do no wrong. I loved her no matter what."

They talked more specifically about the evidence and their trial strategy for the next two hours. It was about time for Rachel and Jason to leave so that Maxwell could go to dinner. Jason said, "Maxwell, I can't shake it, I have to know something."

"Yeah, what's that?" Maxwell asked.

"What were you and Amelia fighting about the night before she died?"

Maxwell sighed. "The same thing we always fought about: her dad. He had called her and wanted to take her out to dinner to talk about something important. This was the day after I'd gone to him and asked him if I could have his blessing. I was worried that he was going to tell her and ruin the surprise. I told her that I didn't want her to go. We had been drinking, and she was stubborn. She told me not to tell her what to do, and it escalated from there."

Jason said, "I know how it is dealing with a stubborn woman. I'm sorry that's the last time the two of you talked."

Maxwell laughed, and looked at Rachel. "She is a stubborn one, isn't she? I like it. It's a good characteristic to have."

Rachel rolled her eyes. "Okay, you two, quit ganging up on me. We have to get going, Maxwell, so you aren't late to dinner. You already don't get enough time to eat. We will be back once more to go over trial prep and what to expect. Do you need anything else before we go?"

"No. Thank you both."

CHAPTER TWENTY-FOUR

The New Trial

It was Thursday, May 12, 2022, the first day of Maxwell Williams's new trial. Maxwell was led to the courtroom at 8:15 a.m. after changing into the suit that Jason and Rachel had brought for him. When he walked in, they were already there waiting. The table in front of them was covered with binders and notepads, and they both had their laptops open. Maxwell took a deep breath as he walked over to see them. They both stood up. Jason shook his hand and did a once over of the suit Maxwell was wearing. He nodded his approval. Rachel gave him a quick hug.

"Are you ready?" she asked him.

"I think so," Maxwell responded as he sat down at the table between the two of them. Rachel started to go over a rundown of how the proceedings would go. They had already done this a number of times, so she was mostly doing it as a way to calm her nerves. "We will start with the jury selection. That will take most of the morning. That should get us to the afternoon break. Next, opening statements, and then the State will start calling their witnesses. Any questions?" she asked.

"Nope. I got it. I'm just ready for this show to get on the road," Maxwell said.

Rachel addressed Jason next: "Remember, I will look to see if you have anything else when I am questioning witnesses. And then you will do the same when you're questioning."

"That's the plan," Jason said. It was clear from the quaver in his voice that he was very nervous. Jason was not a trial lawyer, nor a criminal lawyer. This was all new to him. One thing he was good at was preparing for cases and knowing them backwards and forwards. Jason knew this case, the theory and strategy of it by heart. He had prepared as much as he possibly could, short of participating in an actual criminal trial. He could do this. At least that's what he kept telling himself. If all else failed, he would have to fake it until he made it. It was not like there was a man's freedom at stake or anything, he kept thinking to himself.

Jeff Malone, the prosecutor on the case, walked in followed by a woman. Jason, Rachel, and Maxwell turned around to watch them once they heard the doors open. Rachel's and Jason's mouths dropped open when they recognized the woman who was walking in with Jeff. Maxwell sensed the confusion and looked from Rachel to Jason and back again. "What is it?"

"She can't work on this case with him!" Jason exclaimed, with panic in his voice. "That's against the ethics rules. She knows things about our theory of the case." Rachel's face was pale, she looked like she was in shock, and she couldn't find any words. Jason looked at her and asked, "Rachel, are you okay?"

"Who is she?" Maxwell asked again, his voice louder and more concerned. Jeff came through the swinging doors and sat down at the prosecutor's table, which was placed farthest away from the jury box. The woman sat down in the first row of the gallery behind Jeff. She wasn't yet sworn in as an attorney, so she could not be up at the counsel table with him. She put down her bag, pulled out some documents and a laptop, and got settled in. She must have sensed that they were all looking at her, because she looked over at them and smiled—a vicious smirk—seemingly knowing what was going through Rachel and Jason's minds. She held their stares for a minute, and then went back to what she was doing.

Jason finally stood up and walked over to where Jeff was seated. "She can't be working for you. It's a conflict of interest."

Jeff Malone looked up and feigned confusion. "What do you mean? Our office can hire any interns we want."

"You know what I am talking about. She was working with us on this case before she came to work for you. She worked directly on the case. That is a conflict of interest," Jason shot back.

Jeff smiled slightly. "I'm not in charge of the conflict-of-interest checks for the interns. HR is responsible for that. She must have lied on the form." He turned to look at the woman, who still had the smirk on her face, and shrugged.

Jason could feel his blood boiling and his face getting hot. He had to remind himself that he was in a courtroom and had to keep his temper in check. He didn't do a great job at that, as he said, "That's bullshit, and you know it. Are you really that afraid to lose that you can't play a fair game? You have to fight dirty? What is it with you prosecutors, you can't win a case, so you rig it to favor you?" His voice was rising with every word.

Jeff stood up, looking like he was ready for a fight. The bailiff, who had been standing in the corner of the room, was already up and rushing over. Jason felt a hand on his shoulder. He turned to look—it was Rachel. She had some of her color back now, and she was urging him to walk away. The bailiff made it over to them and pushed both men back. "What is going on over here?" he bellowed, his voice echoing throughout the courtroom. He was an old man, probably around seventy, and if Jason and Jeff Malone were actually going to fight, the bailiff would have no chance of breaking it up.

A month earlier Rachel had reached the last straw with Mia. She had walked into the conference room one day just as Mia was trying to leave. Mia had copies of the trial transcripts and their outline of the case strategy in her hands. "What do you think you are doing? I made it very clear, Mia, interns cannot take things with them."

Mia shot back, "I am more capable and involved than the other interns, Rachel, and you know it. I am good enough to break the rules for."

"No. Just no. For one, I don't break the rules the organization has set. They come from the New York division, and they apply to every division of the Exoneration Project, not just us. Second, I would not say you are worth breaking the rules for. You have undermined me every step of the way, overstepped your boundaries, and are honestly a rude person. You are insufferable to work with." Rachel had held it all in too long, and now it was all coming out.

"Seriously, do you even know how stupid you look right now, Rachel? I am ten years older than you and have been a paralegal since the time you were in middle school. I am more than capable. Much more capable than you are."

Rachel sneered, "Wow. You are unbelievable. Do you really think that way? Just get out. You're done here."

"What? You can't do that," Mia protested. "I am a part of this case, and Dylan is the one in charge. You don't have the authority to fire me."

"I'm not firing you, because you never worked here. You are a volunteer. A volunteer under my supervision, on my case. If I say you are done, then you are done. Leave, now!" Rachel said, getting louder. A few other people at the office started to overhear and looked over to see what was going on.

"Screw you, Rachel. You are going to regret this."

"Don't count on it," Rachel called after her as she walked out of the conference room. They hadn't talked since. Dylan had backed Rachel up and told the law school that Mia was no longer welcome as an intern. Rachel assumed that there was some kind of fallout with the law school, since Dylan had informed them a little about what happened. She never could have imagined this would be the outcome.

Rachel finally found her voice. "We need to go out to a conference room with our client to discuss something. And then we will need to discuss something with the judge before we call in any prospective jurors."

The bailiff turned to look at the clock on the wall and nodded. "Okay." Then he looked back and forth between the two men. "You two need to keep it under control. This is still a courtroom, even if the judge isn't in here yet," he scolded. Both nodded their understanding.

Rachel walked out through the swinging doors and motioned for Jason and Maxwell to follow her. They went out of the courtroom and found a conference room open, and the three of them filed in and sat down. They talked about what was happening and what it meant for the case. They had to explain it to Maxwell a few times, because the rules didn't make much sense to him. Then once he understood them, he didn't understand how the prosecutor could just disregard the rules and play dumb.

Maxwell started to tear up. "How can the State screw me over again?" He had to pause a minute and collect himself. "It's just not right. I am an innocent man and have spent almost half my life in prison for a crime that I didn't commit. They pulled some shady shit on me the first time around, and here we are again. What are we going to do?"

"We are going to talk to the judge," Rachel said, trying to sound reassuring. She had never dealt with this before. She didn't want to admit to Maxwell or Jason that she was scared and not sure what to do. Would this completely screw up their whole case? Were they going to lose this? Was this all her fault? Mia had told her that she would regret it. In this moment, she definitely did.

When she had walked into court that morning, Rachel had been confident that she had a good chance at winning this, more confident than with any other new trial she had had over the past few years. The evidence was nonexistent in this case. She had it in the bag. Now, there was someone with inside knowledge of their case strategy on the other side. This wasn't fair, or right, but was there anything that could be done to fix it at this point? Rachel wasn't so sure.

The bailiff came and knocked on the door to the conference room. Jason stood and opened the door. "The judge wants you back in chambers to talk with him about whatever is going on." The three of them got up and walked back into the courtroom and through the swinging doors. Jeff and Mia were not there. The bailiff led them into the judge's chambers. Jeff and Mia were already in there, sitting with the judge, who looked annoyed. The three of them walked in, and Rachel sat down at the remaining seat. Jason and Maxwell stood.

"The bailiff informs me that you have something to discuss with me before we proceed. Is that correct, Ms. Nix?" the judge asked.

"Yes, Your Honor." Her voice cracked a little, and she cleared her throat. "Mr. Malone's intern used to work at my office. She worked on this case with us."

The judge's demeanor changed from annoyed to out-and-out angry. He turned his attention to Jeff. "Is that true, Mr. Malone?"

Jeff sighed. "Judge, like I told them, I don't do the conflict-of-interest checks at the office. How was I supposed to know that she worked with them on the case before she came to work at our office?"

Jason noted that Jeff didn't say he hadn't known that she worked on the case, just "how was he supposed to" have. He'd known, of course he had. She'd probably told him all about their whole theory of the case, what their strategy was, and what jurors they wanted on the panel.

The judge put his hands together and looked back to Rachel. "How much work did she do on the case at your office?"

"Almost all of the preparation, Your Honor. She worked with me on the case from the start, and was with us until a month and a half ago." Rachel's voice started to sound pleading, but she wasn't sure what she was pleading for.

The judge looked at Mia. "Is that true, Ms. . . . ?" He paused, letting her fill in the blank with her name.

"Drake," she said. "Mia Drake. Yes, it is true. I worked with Ms. Nix and Mr. Michelson up until I was wrongfully terminated a little over a month ago." She threw in that little dig because she knew the court reporter was transcribing the meeting.

"Fired," Rachel almost snorted. "You weren't fired. You didn't even work for us or get paid. It was an internship."

The judge looked back to Rachel. "Ms. Nix, what led to the term . . ." He stopped himself, and looked at the court reporter. "Strike that. What led to Ms. Drake no longer volunteering for the Exoneration Project, Ms. Nix?"

"When Ms. Drake started volunteering, it was clear that she thought she should be a bigger part of the case than she was authorized to be. Nor did she have the time to be that involved. She got upset when I told her she couldn't take the files home and she was overstepping her bounds. We had to have a talk about her role and what she was able to do. It was better for a few months. Then about six weeks ago, we had a blow-up at our office and she went off on me after she tried to sneak the transcripts and our trial strategy documents out of the firm. Ms. Drake had already been warned about not taking files home, and the outburst was unacceptable. It was decided that she was no longer welcome as a volunteer."

The judge thought about it for a moment and then said, "How much was she aware of in the case? Anything outside of what the files said?"

"Yes. She was there for meetings where we went over our theory of the case and what jurors we wanted to try and get on the panel. She was very involved, Your Honor," Rachel replied.

"Is that true?" the judge asked, his attention back on Jeff and Mia. Jeff shrugged and looked back at Mia, signaling for her to answer.

She nodded her head slowly. "Yes, it is." She looked down at her feet. The confident smirk from earlier in the courtroom was long gone, and she was now realizing the magnitude of what she had done. Or at least that was what she was trying to portray.

The judge took his glasses off and put his hands over his eyes, rubbing them up to his forehead. He kept his hands there for a moment, and then said, "Well. I guess we only have two options. We can postpone the case." He paused to let that option sink in and get any responses.

"Your Honor, with all due respect, we can't postpone this. My client has been sitting in prison for forty years, wrongfully convicted. He has fought for this new trial, and he deserves for it to happen now. Plus, postponing the trial won't change anything. Our theory of the case and strategy will be the same," Rachel explained.

"Postponement would be fine with us, Your Honor." Jeff took the opportunity to talk after Rachel paused. "I am fine proceeding, as well. Either way." He seemed indifferent and bored with the conversation. Jeff knew that the defense team wouldn't agree to a postponement of the trial. As Rachel said, it wouldn't change anything. Jeff had known this would be the outcome when he first met with Mia, and she told him that she knew the defense's strategy on the Maxwell Williams case. He'd been very hesitant about bringing the new trial with the evidence he had. But his boss made the call that they had to retry Maxwell. When Mia Drake came to him and said she had just finished working with the Exoneration Project on the case and knew everything about their strategy, it was like he was being delivered a gift. He still had time to adjust his case to get ahead of their arguments.

"Cut the act, Mr. Malone. I don't believe for a second that you have been working with Ms. Drake for the better part of six weeks without being aware that she worked with the defense on this case. I will be referring this issue to the ethics board." The judge paused for dramatic effect. "I understand your position, Ms. Nix. Is that how Mr. Williams wants to proceed?" he asked, looking at Maxwell, who had felt invisible up until this point.

Maxwell looked at Rachel, who indicated that he could talk. "Well, sir. I just don't understand all of this. The State withheld evidence in my first case, and now this? How is it fair?"

"Your Honor," Jeff almost yelled. "That needs to be stricken from the record. I was not the prosecutor on the first case. That can't be on the record. We already argued about this in pretrial motions. Nothing about the missing evidence in the first trial gets to come in."

Maxwell looked down, ashamed. "I'm sorry, sir. I didn't mean to say something I shouldn't. I just don't understand what is going on and how this can happen."

The judge held up his hand to silence everyone. "It's okay, Mr. Williams. You are right. This isn't fair and should not have happened. Mr. Malone and his office will have to deal with the ethics board about it. The issue we must decide now, though, is if you want to proceed with the trial today?"

"I do, sir. I have been waiting for this day for over forty years. I have never been more ready. I know I am innocent," Maxwell said with confidence.

"Your Honor." Jeff stood up this time. "That needs to be stricken as well! Mr. Williams is not testifying subject to cross-examination right now. He cannot be claiming his innocence on the record."

"Sit down, Mr. Malone. You are already on very thin ice this morning. Do you want to push for sanctions?" the judge barked. Jeff sat back down sheepishly. "Mr. Malone has made his objections. I am overruling both of them. The statements will stay on the record. We are not in front of a jury yet, Mr. Malone, so please stop the theatrics. Besides, it is your office's fault that this issue arose at all."

The judge looked down at his gold watch, and the time read 8:47 a.m. "Okay. Mr. Williams has stated that he wishes to move forward; Ms. Nix has also agreed to proceed. Let's take a ten-minute break to gather our composure, and then we will start with jury selection. Anything else to put on the record before we go to break?" the judge asked, looking to both sides of the room. When nobody spoke, he dismissed them from his office.

The bailiff led the group back into the courtroom. Jeff and Mia started walking out and Rachel yelled after them, "I am going to notify the board about your conduct in this as well, Mia. You won't pass the character and fitness portion, even if you pass the bar." Mia looked back, and Rachel could see the realization on her face. Mia had not thought about that as a possibility when she went to work with Mr. Malone. That one decision was now going to ruin her career and any prospect of her practicing law in the State of Minnesota.

Jeff didn't seem to hear Rachel's comment, and he was already out of the courtroom door before Mia turned back around to walk out. Jason and Maxwell sat down at the defense table, and Maxwell looked to Rachel. "What do we do now?"

Rachel took a deep breath and gathered all the confidence she could, and said, "Now, we fight for your freedom."

CHAPTER TWENTY-FIVE

The jury was picked and sat at 12:17 p.m. on the first day of trial. It was clear that Jeff knew the defense's strategy for jury selection. He ended up striking all of the people Rachel and Jason really wanted on the panel. Rachel was not feeling so optimistic anymore. The jury consisted of eight women and six men: seven white, three Black, three Asian, and one Hispanic. Two of them were alternates—one of the Black men and the Asian woman—but they didn't know it yet. The alternates are not told they are the alternates until the end. It prevents them from not paying as much attention to the trial as they should.

The defense's perfect juror would have been a black male between the ages of eighteen and thirty-two. Only one of the jurors fit that description, a twenty-nine-year-old, and a schoolteacher. They wanted to have black men on the jury who might be able to understand what Maxwell was going through, and what it might have been like for him dating a white woman in Minneapolis in the 1980s. While that age group would not have been alive back then, they likely had family members that told them stories. They almost definitely had a better chance of understanding all this than older white gentlemen, of which there were three on the jury, ages forty-seven, fifty-nine, and sixty-three. Rachel was worried about them, especially the sixty-three-year-old. Some of his answers to questions during voir dire seemed to have racist undertones to them. They lost their for-cause objection to remove him, and there were even worse options that they were forced to use their challenges on.

There was nothing they could do now. They had their jury. Rachel and Jason had used their peremptory strikes on members who had answered questions with a very clear and open bias. Those people simply couldn't be on the jury. The older man who was left over was the lesser of the evils. At least, they hoped that was the case.

The judge informed everyone that it was time for a lunch break, and they were expected to be back in exactly one hour to start opening statements. The bailiff permitted Maxwell to go with his attorneys to talk about the case during all breaks, including lunch. Jason and Rachel had brought bagged lunches from home for themselves, but they asked Maxwell what he wanted to eat. He hadn't had food from outside of the prison for more than forty years. It was very overwhelming that first day to choose what to get. There were also so many more restaurants available now that he had never heard of.

He decided on Subway and McDonald's both, and asked if that was okay. Jason laughed. "Of course it's okay. Let me just order it quick from DoorDash."

"What's that?" Maxwell asked.

"It's a food delivery service. They will go pick up food orders for people from most restaurants, and then deliver them on the stores' behalf. It's pretty slick." Jason looked at Rachel. "We use it a lot when we are working late."

Rachel laughed. "More than just when we are working late. I probably use it for ten meals a week," she admitted. Maxwell still looked confused but let it pass. Jason ordered the food; it was going to be delivered in twenty-two minutes. "Do you want us to wait and eat with you?" Rachel asked.

"No. You guys eat. I am sure you have work to go through. Or things to discuss about the jury."

Jason and Rachel ate their ham sandwiches and looked at their juror maps laying out which juror sat where. Rachel nodded as she went through each person and remembered what they had learned about them during their research. The court sends out the list of prospective jurors up to a week before the trial. Once the attorneys get those juror lists, they drop everything and go to work trying to find out about each person. Some attorneys and their clients hire jury consultants who do a deep dive into each prospective juror to learn everything possible about them. The consultants then sit in during the trial and give updates on what they have observed from the jury.

The Exoneration Project didn't have a budget for any jury consultants. The duo's research on the prospective jurors for this case had included social media searches, Minnesota Court Information System (MNCIS) record searches, and good old Google searches. Even though it was not as effective as having a jury consultant, Jason and Rachel were able to find out enough about each of the seventy-five prospective jurors to have a good baseline understanding of who they were and what their views might be. For example, prospective juror number seventy-two, Mason Cromwell, was active in racial hate groups, and they would not want him on the jury under any circumstances. Rachel and Jason lucked out because they had their jury seated through the first twenty-nine people, so they didn't have to use any of their peremptory strikes on Mr. Cromwell.

Rachel finished eating and said, "Well, it is clear that Mia shared our strategy for jury selection." She paused. "I think it still turned out okay, though." She was trying to convince herself more than anyone else in the room. She could tell Maxwell was less than confident with her tone. "The facts are still in our favor. The State only has circumstantial evidence, and they know it. Why else would they risk the ethical complaints by having Mia on the case? They're scared, and they should be."

Maxwell's food was delivered, and he opened everything and

placed it out on the table. He got a footlong B.M.T., chips, a cookie, and a bottle of Sprite from Subway. From McDonald's he got a Big Mac, large fries, and a milkshake. Jason and Rachel watched as Maxwell took in the sight of his food. They weren't expecting it, but Maxwell's eyes got misty as he looked it over. He tried to keep back the tears, but one escaped and rolled down his cheek.

It was in that moment that Jason realized the reason that Rachel did this job, the reason she had declined a big-firm job offer promising more money a year than any one person could need. She'd lost a fiancé because of that. None of it mattered, because what Rachel was doing was more important than any of that. She was helping people fight to get their lives back. People like Maxwell Williams were sitting in prison for decades for crimes that they didn't commit, most of them only allowed outside of those prison walls a maximum of three hours per day. Something as simple as fast food had brought this man to tears. Food was supposed to be a basic necessity, and Jason could not even fathom the quality of the food that Maxwell had become used to.

Jason felt a tear rolling down his cheek, and he quickly wiped it away. Rachel was looking at him, and noticed it before he could pull himself back together. She gave him a knowing look. Jason knew that she had been in this position before. The mood was a little more somber after that, but Maxwell didn't notice. He was too busy devouring his mountain of food. Twenty minutes later he was slurping up the last bit of his chocolate shake. He sat back in his chair and stuck his stomach out, and let out a big, satisfied sigh.

Jason and Rachel looked at him and smiled. "You are going to have to put some thought into what you want to eat over the next few days. There are so many great options around here, and I'm buying. Whatever you want to eat, say the word, and I will get it for you. I can even bring you food for breakfast before court starts each day, if you want," Jason offered.

"Ah, man, you don't have to do that. This was amazing, I don't expect it every day."

"I won't hear it," Jason stopped him. "You have put up with prison food for too long. You deserve some good food."

Maxwell nodded. If Jason wanted to buy him good food to eat every day, he wasn't about to argue, especially after eating his lunch and remembering how amazing food on the outside was. He couldn't help tearing up when he tasted it. Maxwell had never thought about the food he was eating before he was sentenced to prison. It was one of the many things he realized that he had taken for granted.

One of the other things he had always taken for granted, probably the biggest one of all, was the ability to hug his family whenever he wanted. He hadn't had physical contact with his mom since the day of his sentencing. He was allowed to give her a quick hug as she sobbed in the courtroom right before they took him away to prison. His mom would come and visit him, but they were always on opposite sides of the glass and talking through two phone receptors.

As the years went on, the number of visits started to decrease. His mom was not able to get off work for the first day of trial, but she was going to be there tomorrow. Maxwell didn't know about it yet—Jason and Rachel had wanted to keep it as a surprise. They also didn't want to get him overwhelmed with too many things at one time. He still needed to be focused on the trial and getting through the process.

The bailiff came and knocked on the door to the conference room. Jason gave him a nod, saying it was okay to come in. "I just wanted to let you know I am opening the courtroom door. You have about ten minutes before the judge goes back on the record."

"Thank you. We will pack up in here and head back in," Rachel said, as she started cleaning up the wrappers and garbage from the table and throwing it all into the small trash can in the room. As she stood up, Maxwell stood quickly too and wrapped his arms around her, holding her in a big, tight embrace. Rachel was not expecting it and flinched at first, caught off guard. Once she realized what was happening, she felt the warmth and emotion in the hug, and let Maxwell hug her for a few more seconds before he pulled away.

When he pulled back, he had tears streaming down his face again. "Thank you," was all that he could choke out without it turning into a full-fledged sob. Rachel had tears streaming down her own face. They took another minute to compose themselves, then they all walked back into the courtroom, heads held high, confidence exuding from them. They sat back down at the defense table. Rachel took a deep breath and grabbed her notes from her opening statement.

Jeff and Mia walked in and took their seats again. Jeff was looking through all his papers and notebooks and seemed like he couldn't find what he was looking for. He turned back to Mia and whispered something to her. Mia got up, walked through the swinging gates and searched the table. She apparently found what she was looking for, because she had a few pages of papers that were stapled together in her hand. She handed these to Jeff, who thanked her, and went back to her seat in the gallery.

The judge walked in, and the bailiff called, "All rise." Everyone stood until the judge was seated.

"Please be seated," he called from up on his perch behind the bench. "Is there anything we need on the record before we call the jury in?" he asked, first looking to prosecutor Jeff Malone.

"Not from the State, Your Honor," Jeff said.

He then looked to Rachel. "Nothing from us, Your Honor," she said.

"Are you ready for opening statements?" the judge asked. Both attorneys nodded, and the judge turned to the bailiff. "All right, let's bring in the jury."

The bailiff went and opened the door to the jury room, and the jurors filed in. One by one, they took their seats in the jury box, some of them making eye contact with Maxwell, Jason, and Rachel, a few making eye contact with Jeff, the last few not making eye contact with anyone. As they sat down, they each grabbed their notepads and pens, and looked up to the judge, not quite sure what was going to happen next.

"Members of the jury. It is now time for opening statements. The State will go first. Mr. Malone, the floor is yours."

CHAPTER TWENTY-SIX

Jeff stood up with purpose, grabbed his papers, and walked to the lectern.

"Members of the jury. This case is simple and straightforward. The facts are clear and should leave you with no doubt that Maxwell Williams is guilty of the crimes that he is charged with today. On March 23, 1982, Amelia Jackson was brutally murdered in her home. She was sitting at home, studying for upcoming exams, when she heard a knock at the door. She went to answer and saw it was her boyfriend, Maxwell Williams. They had been fighting the night before at the bar, but that wasn't uncommon for them.

"Amelia let the defendant into her apartment, and they resumed their fight from the night before. Things escalated, and the defendant struck her and pushed her down onto her bed. Amelia was resisting and did not want him near her. The defendant," he paused and gestured towards Maxwell, "was 6 foot 2 and 200 pounds back then, similar to his build now. Poor Amelia Jackson was 5 foot 7 and about 110 pounds. It was not hard for the defendant to overpower her and take what he wanted.

"The defendant held Amelia down on her bed and raped her forcefully. He didn't stop until she was injured and bleeding. If that wasn't enough, the defendant got up, left Amelia in her bed crying, and went to the kitchen. He grabbed a butcher knife and came back to the bed. The defendant stabbed Amelia sixteen times. You will hear the medical examiner testify that Amelia could not have been alive when that last stab came. It was overkill, quite literally, sometime after the sixth or seventh time he stabbed her.

"You will hear testimony that it is customary in a crime of passion for the offender to stab their victim multiple times, more than is required to kill them."

After that statement, Rachel's head shot up. Had she really heard him right? Did Jeff just refer to the crime as a crime of passion? He was a seasoned prosecutor; there was no way that he could have made that mistake. In Minnesota, if a Defendant claims that a death occurred in the heat of passion, that is a valid defense to a first-degree murder charge. Typical examples being a spouse or significant other walking in on their partner cheating, or a heated argument that goes too far. Jeff referring to this as a crime of passion could affect the first-degree murder charge. She felt a grin cross her face, but she quickly stifled it, looked back down at her notes and continued writing.

She sneaked a quick peek at the jury to make sure nobody had witnessed her reaction. They were all watching Jeff, entranced with his narrative. Rachel turned to Jason, who was taking his own notes and had not seemed to catch the mistake Jeff Malone had just made. She considered how this should be addressed, and whether she should bring it up in her opening or not. The plan was to be convincing, but not give the jury all the facts or their theory of the case during the opening. The idea was to pull bits and pieces of the truth out from each witness as they testified, and then tie it all up with a nice bow during closing arguments.

Jeff continued. "That is exactly what happened in this case. The defendant and Amelia had been in one of their intense fights the previous night at the bar. You will hear testimony from people who witnessed it. He went over to her house the next day, and the fight continued. You will hear that they were fighting about Amelia's father not wanting them to continue with their relationship—a fight that they had had many times before.

"This was the last time the defendant wanted to have that fight. Three years' worth of rage and hatred for Amelia's father came out that day. He raped her and murdered her in cold blood that night. The defendant went over to her house with the intent to kill Amelia. At the end of this case, it will be clear that is what happened. The physical evidence and testimony will show that."

"The defense," he again gestured toward the defense table, "will try to distract you and make up stories that may confuse you. Don't let them do it. Don't let them take away from the hard facts and actual proof. The defense will try to make it seem like there is no possible way that the defendant could have committed this crime. However, they are wrong. It will be clear when you review the evidence that Maxwell Williams is guilty of these crimes. That is why, at the end of the trial, I will be asking you, the jury, to find Maxwell Williams guilty beyond a reasonable doubt of the charges against him."

Jeff looked down at his notes for the first time since he'd gotten up to begin his opening statement. He skimmed his notes and then looked satisfied with his performance. He looked back up to the jury, nodded his head, and said, "Thank you." Jeff gathered his notes and walked back to the table. As he passed the defense table, making sure his back was to the jurors, he smirked a little at Rachel and Jason.

"Thank you, Mr. Malone," the judge said. "Ms. Nix, are you ready for your opening, or are you planning on waiting until the start of the defense's case?"

Rachel and Jason had spent some time making this decision. They had the opportunity to either give their opening statement right after the prosecutor, or wait until the State was done with their case. In the second case, they would give their opening before they presented the defense's case-in-chief.

Ultimately, they had decided that they wanted to get their information to the jury as soon as possible. They didn't want to leave them with the narrative that Jeff had just given them. There was too big a risk that the jurors would only pay attention to the evidence and testimony that fit that narrative, a type of confirmation bias. They weren't going to let that happen. Rachel needed to put in some doubts to keep them questioning everything throughout the State's case.

"I am ready now, Your Honor," Rachel said as she stood. She didn't need her notes. She had decided not to bring them up with her, as a show of confidence in herself and the defense's case.

"Go ahead, Ms. Nix," the judge instructed, and Rachel walked up to the lectern. She took a deep breath, smiled at the jurors, and started. She made sure to make eye contact with each individual juror throughout her opening, to make that initial connection and build their trust in her and her client. She was a seasoned pro at this point, and it was clear that she knew what she was doing.

"Ladies and gentlemen," she started, her voice confident and clear. At that moment, Rachel decided to make a minor change to her opening statement, and she said, "Mr. Malone asked that you pay attention to the physical evidence and the testimony that you hear during this trial. We want that same thing. We want you to be observant, take notes, and pay careful attention to the things you see and hear. If you do that, and really think about what has been presented to you, the evidence will show you that Maxwell Williams did not commit these crimes." She pointed over to Maxwell as she made that statement. Almost on cue, Maxwell looked over at the jurors and had a look on his face that portrayed innocence.

Rachel continued, "It is true that Maxwell and Amelia had been dating on and off for three years. Yes, they did have an argument at the bar the night before. What couples don't fight?" She let that question hang in the air for a moment before she continued. "Just because you have a fight with your significant other doesn't mean that you go to their house and kill them, does it? I am sure most of you have fought with your spouses. You didn't kill them because of it—of course not. That is not what people do.

"That is not what Mr. Williams did, either. He did not go to Amelia's house that day and kill her. The evidence will show that he didn't go to her house at all. He hadn't seen her since they went their separate ways after their fight at the bar. The evidence will show that he tried to call her a few times the day she died, to try and make up, as they had so many times before. None of his calls were answered, so he assumed that she was still mad at him.

"He then ordered takeout, and the delivery person was at Maxwell's apartment about a half hour before the time that the medical examiner later determined that Amelia had died. The prosecutor wants you to believe that his food was delivered and he then left his apartment to go to Amelia's. He made it there, they fought, and he assaulted and killed her, all within a half hour to an hour. That just doesn't make sense.

"Another thing that doesn't make sense: why would he kill his girlfriend? They had been dating for over three years, and he loved Amelia. He would never hurt her. You will hear testimony from his friend that he was planning on asking Amelia to marry him after graduation. His best friend had gone ring shopping with him, and Maxwell had something picked out. He was taking on more shifts at work, and he went and purchased that ring. Does that sound like a man who is going to kill the woman he loves? No!

"The State has nothing more than a theory, and they are trying to make the circumstantial evidence fit their narrative. You will hear testimony about another possible scenario regarding what happened the day Amelia Jackson died. You will see that the evidence supports this narrative more than the one that the prosecutor is trying to tell you. The prosecution has a high burden in this case. They must prove that Maxwell Williams is guilty of the crimes he is accused of beyond a reasonable doubt. They have nothing more than circumstantial evidence that doesn't add up to what they are trying to sell you. That is why, at the end of this trial, we will be asking you to find Maxwell Williams not guilty on all charges.

"This isn't his first trial in this case. Maxwell Williams had his first trial almost forty years ago in this same courthouse. Science wasn't as advanced back then as it is now. There was no way to test the evidence in the case. That's right, there was DNA evidence found on Amelia that day, DNA that does not match Maxwell William's. It's interesting to me that Mr. Malone didn't include that information in his opening statement." Rachel paused, knowing what was going to happen next.

Jeff shot to his feet. "Objection, Your Honor." He continued before the judge could say anything. "She is getting close to matters that cannot be discussed."

"Sit down, Mr. Malone. Your objection is overruled. Ms. Nix is allowed to discuss the evidence in the case and point out things that your opening did not address," the judge explained. Jeff sat back down in his seat, looking defeated. Rachel had set him up for the trap, and Jeff had played right into it. Not only did Jeff get shut down by the judge for interrupting her opening, but he let the jury know that there were some things about the first trial that the judge had decided the jury couldn't hear. It also put more emphasis on the DNA evidence, another huge mistake on Jeff's part.

Rachel was now gaining confidence and momentum. Even if Jeff Malone did know their theory of the case, he was still making missteps left and right.

She continued with her opening. "As I was saying before Mr. Malone interrupted, the DNA does not match Maxwell Williams's. The one thing that could put him there that day in the apartment does not put him there. So, what else does the State have against my client? That's a good question—one that we have continued to ask ourselves since I took on this case. The same question that Maxwell Williams has been asking himself ever since he was arrested after Amelia's murder. The same question he asked himself every. Single. Day. For the last forty years as he sat in a prison cell.

"He has been in that prison cell for forty years for a crime that he didn't commit. Maxwell Williams was a college student, close to graduation, and ready to start his life and career. He was going to propose to his longtime girlfriend, who was also going to graduate in a few short months. They were talking about moving in together. Their lives were all planned out for them. Amelia Jackson tragically lost her life on March 23, 1982, but she was not the only one. Maxwell Williams also lost his life that day when the police came to his apartment, handcuffed him, and brought him to jail.

"He didn't have money for bail, so he sat in that jail cell until his first trial started. The jury was told in that trial to just assume that it was Maxwell Williams's DNA on Amelia, because who else's could it be? Now we know they were wrong. Yes, the jury did find him guilty at the first trial, but that isn't really a big surprise, is it?

"We can all agree that 1982 was a different time in this world. Maxwell Williams was a black man accused of raping and killing his white girlfriend. His white girlfriend whose father was a prominent member of the community, who had forbidden his daughter to date Maxwell. Interracial relationships were not accepted in 1982, and it is easy to understand how a jury back then could find Maxwell guilty of the charges against him. Something bad happened to Amelia; the first suspect is always the significant other. In this case, her significant other happened to be a black man who was fighting with her the night before. It just made sense to convict him, even though the proof wasn't there. They were wrong.

"I like to believe that our society has come a long way since 1982, and that racial biases, whether conscious or subconscious, will not cloud your judgment when you are deliberating at the end of this case. Don't let the fact that Maxwell is a black man and Amelia was a white woman distract you from the evidence in this case. Moreover, don't let it distract you from the *lack of* evidence in this case. Maxwell Williams is not guilty of the charges against him, and he has been sitting in prison for the last forty years paying for someone else's debts. It is up to you to set him free. You have the power to do that. Each and every one of you has the power to set him free at the end of this. All you have to do is find him not guilty. It is the right thing to do, and it is the right verdict in this case. Thank you!"

Rachel smiled at the jurors and made eye contact with each of them once more. She thought a few of them were nodding along as she gave her opening statement. A few looked somberly at Maxwell as though they felt sorry for him. This was a good sign. Rachel walked back to the defense table, and Maxwell had tears in his eyes, the thankfulness evident on his face. She felt tears welling up behind her eyes, but she pushed them back. Rachel had to stay professional and in charge—she couldn't be caught getting emotional.

Jason gave her an encouraging nod as she sat back down in her seat and set her notes to the side. Rachel believed that she had just given the best opening statement of her career. Things were starting to go her way now, but she had enough experience to know not to get ahead of herself. In trials, anything could change at the drop of a hat. She had lost trials in the past. Just because a defendant is granted a new trial doesn't always mean that it will result in a "not guilty" verdict. Getting the new trial granted is the easy part of a case. The trial is the hard part. They were now in the hard part, and it was going to be a nasty one.

CHAPTER TWENTY-SEVEN

Jeff's first witness was Detective Swenson, who explained to the jury about his experience and background as an officer back in 1982 when he investigated the case. He described to them the steps he took and things he learned through interviews with witnesses and friends of Amelia Jackson. Detective Swenson explained how he got the call to go to Amelia's apartment, and when he got there, found her lying on her bed, half covered by her white bedsheet. She was naked and bloody, her eyes open and her head facing the door. She was staring at him as he walked in. He said he still remembered the chill that went up his body. He stated that it was his first homicide case, and those always stick with you.

Jeff didn't ask the detective about any of the other potential suspects that they had. In fact, his questioning mirrored that of the prosecutor in the first case. It seemed like he was possibly just reusing the questions from the transcripts. None of the missing information that was withheld in the first trial came out in Detective Swenson's direct examination. This was going to be even more fun, Rachel thought to herself. It is going to seem like the prosecution is trying to hide things. Jeff should have got out ahead of that information, and tried to spin it before it could come out during Rachel's questioning.

It was time for Rachel's cross-examination; she stood up and began. "Hello, detective. Mr. Malone didn't ask you about certain parts of your investigation, did he?"

In cross-examination, the goal is to ask questions that only lead to yes or no answers from witnesses. And the number one rule of litigation is never to ask a question that you don't already know the answer to. Rachel was confident that she could go a little off yes or no questions with Detective Swenson, because she considered him one of the good ones. If it weren't for him, the defense would still be missing out on a lot of key evidence. Rachel had no doubt that Jeff would have left out the additional police reports, and they would never have seen them if it weren't for Detective Swenson.

Rachel felt bad that she was going to have to be hard on Detective Swenson, because he had been so helpful and was a nice guy. But it was her job, and she was sure the detective knew it. She presented a few more preliminary questions about the information that Jeff didn't touch on, and then said, "You said this was your first homicide case. Is it possible that you missed some things or made mistakes?"

Detective Swenson had been around long enough to know that this was coming. He gave the standard answer: "I followed the protocols of the department and direction from my supervisors."

"That's not what I asked, detective. Is it possible that you missed something or made mistakes?" Rachel repeated.

"I don't think I missed anything or made any mistakes, no," Detective Swenson answered confidently. He was playing right into her questioning—the detective was going to look combative.

"Again, detective, that is not the question. It is a yes or a no. Is it *possible* that you missed something or made a mistake, since it was your first homicide case?" The detective finally answered, "Yes. Anything is possible, Ms. Nix."

Rachel decided to move on from the point. "Isn't it true that you had other suspects when you initially started investigating the case?"

"That is true," the detective agreed.

"In fact, Amelia's roommate, Casey True, was a suspect at first, correct?"

"She was."

"Her boyfriend, Jesus Cabrera, was another suspect?" Rachel asked.

"Yes, he was."

"There were a few other suspects as well. Mathias Fillmore, the maintenance man, and Jacob Caldwell, the neighbor from across the hall. Is that right?"

"Yes, that is correct," Detective Swenson said.

Here is where Rachel felt confident enough to move away from the yes and no questions. She asked, "What did your investigations into those suspects tell you?"

"Well, we didn't pursue those leads much past the first few hours, so there was not much investigation into them at all," the detective admitted.

Rachel feigned surprise. "What do you mean, you didn't investigate them much at all?"

"Well, my supervisor came to me and told me—"

"Objection, Your Honor. Hearsay." Jeff stood. "He is going to testify about what his supervisor told him."

"Your Honor," Rachel started. "It is not being offered for the truth of the matter asserted, it is being offered to show why the investigation continued the way that it did."

The judge didn't take much time to think about it and said, "Overruled. You may answer." Jeff sat down loudly to let the jurors know he was upset with the ruling.

The detective continued. "My supervisor told me that he spoke with the victim's father, and we were only supposed to focus on the boyfriend, Maxwell Williams."

"Was it odd to you that you were being directed by the victim's father about whom to solely focus the investigation on?" Rachel asked.

"Yes and no. Part of our job during an investigation is to ask witnesses, friends, and family if they know who could have done this. Most of the time, that leads to us focusing on some suspects more than others. However, it doesn't usually lead to us ignoring all the other suspects altogether," Detective Swenson explained.

"Did it seem weird to you at the time that your supervisor was telling you to stop looking into the other suspects?" Rachel asked.

"Yes. I asked him why we were dropping the other suspects, especially because I thought the evidence wasn't completely pointing to Mr. Williams at that time."

"How did your supervisor respond?"

"Objection, Your Honor. Hearsay," Jeff tried again.

The judge said, "Overruled. You may answer."

Detective Swenson continued, "He told me it was because Amelia's dad, Cordwell Jackson, was a political figure in the community, and he wanted us to focus on the boyfriend."

Rachel let that fact sit in the jurors' minds for a minute, as she paused and faked looking at her notes. "So, let me get this straight. Amelia's father was an important person in the community, and he told your supervisor to focus only on Maxwell Williams. That led to all other suspects falling to the side, and Mr. Williams becoming the one and only suspect. Is that right?" Her voice rising, Rachel expressed her disbelief clearly.

"That is correct, Ms. Nix," the detective said clearly into the microphone.

"You didn't see anything wrong with that?"

"I did, but it wasn't my call at that point. The supervisor, my boss, had given me an order, and I had to follow it," he rationalized. "I could have lost my job if I had not listened."

"Hmm. Well, that's interesting." She paused theatrically. "Let's move back a little bit. You said that you didn't think the evidence was pointing to Maxwell Williams, is that correct?"

"That is correct, yes."

"Can you explain why that is?" Rachel asked, taking a big risk in leaving that much of an opportunity open for the State's witness to create a narrative.

"Well, there was no forced entry, which didn't necessarily have too much significance, since Amelia would likely have let Mr. Williams into the apartment. There were a few missed calls on Amelia's phone from Mr. Williams, just like he had told us, including one from after Amelia had died. There was also nothing that would signify that Mr. Williams was in the apartment that day."

"Who did you think were more plausible suspects at first?" Again, Rachel was out on a limb here because she didn't know the answer, but she was hopeful that Detective Swenson was a good enough investigator back then that he had thought the same thing as she was thinking now.

"Honestly, after interviewing the roommate, Casey True, and her boyfriend, Jesus Cabrera, I decided their stories didn't really make sense or fit with the evidence, so they were my top two suspects at the time," he admitted.

"Objection, Your Honor. Speculation." Jeff rose, almost yelling.

"Overruled. The witness may answer," came the judge's immediate response.

"What did you mean by stating that their stories didn't make sense?" Rachel asked. She was happy that his interpretation of the evidence back then was the same as her theory now.

"Objection, Your Honor. Hearsay." Jeff tried again, desperately trying to keep the testimony out.

"Overruled."

Detective Swenson answered the question. "If I remember correctly, they had different timelines for when they went places and even where they went that day. Amelia's roommate, Casey, made some comments that didn't sit well with me about her relationship with Amelia. I couldn't quite put my finger on it, but something just felt off that led me to want to investigate it further," he explained.

"Kind of like that gut feeling that detectives often get?" Rachel asked.

"Exactly."

"Did you suspect them more than Mr. Williams at the time?" Rachel asked.

"Yes, at the time, they were higher up on my suspect list than Mr. Williams was."

"Do you know what confirmation bias is, detective?" Rachel asked. She believed that she had scored enough points with his testimony, so she was going to wrap it up.

"Yes, I do." Rachel nodded to him, conveying that she wanted him to explain what it was. "Confirmation bias is where you have a suspect, and you look at the facts in such a way as to confirm the suspect you have is the one who committed the crimes."

"Do you believe that occurred in this case, detective?"

"Unfortunately, since we weren't looking at any other suspects after a certain point, I do think it is possible, yes," the detective admitted, his voice softer now.

"Thank you, Detective Swenson. I have nothing further for this witness, Your Honor." Rachel nodded a silent thanks to the detective, who understood and nodded back to her. In a way, this was the only way that the detective could make up for the many wrongs that happened all those years ago. He just hoped that he had done enough.

"Mr. Malone, any redirect of this witness?" the judge asked.

Jeff looked over at his notes and looked as though he was contemplating his decision. He decided that any more questions could just hurt his case more, so he said, "No, Your Honor. We release Detective Swenson from the subpoena."

"Thank you, detective, you are free to go," the judge said. The detective got up from the stand and walked down past the counsel tables and out the swinging doors, then sat in the gallery to continue watching the trial. The judge looked at his watch, seeing that it was 4:47 p.m. He continued, "All right. I think that is a good spot to stop for today. Members of the jury, you are free to go home tonight, but make sure that you do not do any research on this case or on the first trial. You are ordered not to talk about this case with anyone, even your family. If anyone asks you, you can confirm you are on a jury for a criminal trial, but nothing more than that. Is that understood?"

When the jurors nodded their understanding, he said, "If anyone from either the prosecution or defense team tries to contact you, or anyone else you think is related to this case does so, I want you to report it to the bailiff immediately. The members involved in this case are not allowed to have any contact with jurors during the trial, not even a 'good morning' or 'hello.' So if you see them out getting coffee tomorrow, don't be offended if they don't say 'hello.' I want you all back here at 8:30 tomorrow morning. Any questions?" When nobody said anything, the judge finished with, "You are excused."

The jurors all filed out of the courtroom as the lawyers and Maxwell stood watching them go. None of them turned around to look back as they left. Once they were gone, the judge asked, "Is there anything we need to put on the record? Mr. Malone?"

"No, Your Honor. Thank you," Jeff said.

"Ms. Nix?"

"Yes, Your Honor. I just want to make a record regarding Mr. Malone's opening statement," Rachel said. Everyone, including Jason, looked at her inquisitively.

"Go ahead," the judge said.

"Your Honor, Mr. Malone referred to what occurred to the victim as a crime of passion. He characterized what allegedly took place as being done in the heat of passion. The State has now introduced the crime-of-passion defense to a first-degree murder trial.

I would request that we instruct the jury on the crime-of-passion defense, and how interpreting events like this will make the crime a second-degree offense if they do find Mr. Williams guilty."

"Your Honor," Jeff said, "Crime of passion is a defense, she is correct. However, just because I mentioned that phrase in my opening doesn't warrant an additional jury instruction being read. Unless Ms. Nix is going to change her client's plea to guilty and claim that as the defense?"

Rachel shot back, "I don't have to do that. The fact that you brought it up as a defense for the crime warrants the jury instruction being added. The jury has a right to know that crime of passion is a defense if they do believe that he committed the crimes."

Jeff started to argue back again, but the judge stopped him with his hand up. "I am inclined to agree, Mr. Malone. You are the one who brought up the defense, and if that is your interpretation of the facts, then the jurors have a right to know about the potential defense. I am going to grant the request." He turned to his law clerk. "Please draft the proposed jury instructions and send them out to both attorneys by the end of the day tomorrow." His clerk nodded.

"Anything else from either of you?" When both attorneys shook their heads, he said, "Let the record reflect that neither attorney has anything further. I want you both back here at 8:15 a.m., and we will see if there is anything more to put on the record before we bring the jury in. Thank you, you are dismissed."

The judge and his staff walked out of the courtroom. Rachel and Jason started to pack up their things, and Jeff walked over. "You're pulling a lot of cheap shots, aren't you?" he sneered.

Rachel and Jason ignored him, and he finally walked out, with Mia right behind him. They decided to leave their exhibit binders in the courtroom, but packed up their laptops and notepads. They went back to the conference room to explain to Maxwell what had happened in court today and about what to expect tomorrow. They said their goodbyes, and he was taken by the deputy back to the jail for the night.

Rachel and Jason walked out to his car in the court parking ramp. When they got settled in the car and started to pull out of the ramp Jason said, "That was amazing. You killed it today!"

Rachel smiled and put her hand on his. "Thank you, babe. I was just doing my best. Jeff made a lot of missteps that helped us, too."

"Yeah, that's true. He didn't do himself any favors, but you were masterful in there. You caught all his mistakes. I didn't catch a lot of them. I don't think the judge did, either. This really is your calling, you know that? You were meant to do this work."

Her smile grew bigger. "Thank you. I really appreciate that. You finally understand why I do it now, don't you?"

"Yeah, I do. Watching Maxwell with his food today, it really hit me. His whole life was taken away from him for forty years. If it weren't for you, that would be the end of the story."

"If it weren't for us," Rachel corrected him, squeezing his hand.

Jason smiled back at her. "What time do you want me to pick you up tomorrow?" They had already decided that they would sleep at their own apartments during the trial. Rachel liked to focus and prepare for the next day in court, and Jason had a lot of work to do for the firm when he got home.

"I want to meet with Maxwell before we go in. The courthouse opens at 7:30 a.m., so maybe get here at 6:45 and we can grab some coffee and go over a few things in the car before we go in?"

"That works for me." They pulled up to her apartment building. "Do you want me to walk you up?" Jason asked.

"No, that's okay. I know you probably have a lot of work to get to." She smiled at him. She got out of the car and walked into her building. Jason drove home, excited to see what the next day had in store.

CHAPTER TWENTY-EIGHT

Day two of the trial started with the medical examiner. Jeff took him through the steps and the results of Amelia's autopsy. He spent a great deal of time on each individual stab wound and on which ones would have killed her.

"In your professional opinion, can you say with a reasonable degree of medical certainty that Amelia Jackson would have died without the last few stab wounds?" Jeff said.

"That is correct," the examiner opined. "I can say with a reasonable degree of medical certainty that any of the six stab wounds that we discussed would have killed Amelia by themselves within a matter of minutes."

"Did Ms. Jackson struggle at all during the attack?"

"Yes. Some of the stab wounds are consistent with the victim trying to defend herself."

"How so?" Jeff asked.

"When a knife goes straight in and out, it is a clean cut." The medical examiner, who had prepared a slideshow, used his laser pointer to point to a wound that indicated that type of stab. He moved it to a different wound. "Now you see here, this wound is wider and signifies that the knife was put in straight, but came out at an angle. This happens when someone fights back or is trying to get away."

"Thank you, nothing further," Jeff said, and sat down.

"Dr. Wright," Rachel said as she got to the lectern, "isn't it true you don't know what order the stab wounds occurred in?"

"That is correct. There is no way to ascertain what stab wound occurred when."

"There was also a head wound on Ms. Jackson, wasn't there?"

"Yes, there was a wound to the right side of her head. If you go back to the second-to-last page of my report, please." The medical examiner got his laser pointer out. He made a circle around a spot on Amelia's head that was sunken in. "There was a skull fracture right here on her head."

"Do you have an opinion on when that injury was sustained?"

"I believe that it was sustained by a blow to the head prior to the stab wounds," he answered, going on to explain how he came to that conclusion based on the slight bruising, which would not have occurred if the blow came after the stabs. He explained in great detail about the blood flow, and how bruising would not have occurred on the head if the intense blood loss had happened prior to this injury.

"Thank you, Dr. Wright. Based on your experience, do you have an opinion on how this blow occurred?" Rachel asked.

"I believe it came right before she fell to the bed. Someone hit her with a blunt object, which likely caused her to fall."

"You testified that Ms. Jackson had defended herself during the stabbing, correct?"

"That is correct," the medical examiner responded.

"There has been testimony saying my client was 6 foot 2 at the time and 200 pounds," Rachel explained.

"Okay."

"Amelia was 5 foot 7 and about 110 pounds."

"Okay."

"If someone of Maxwell Williams's size was on top of someone Amelia Jackson's size, in the same way that you have described this crime as occurring, do you believe that Amelia would have been able to fight back?" Rachel asked, knowing that this would be objected to.

"Objection, Your Honor. Calls for speculation." Jeff stood.

"Sustained," the judge called out.

It didn't matter. Rachel had got the idea out there for the jurors to think about. "Mr. Wright, do you have an opinion on whether the perpetrator was right- or left-handed?" Rachel asked.

"Objection, Your Honor. Calls for speculation," Jeff interjected.

The judge looked to Rachel for an answer to the objection. "Your Honor. He is a medical examiner, and he testified that he has twenty-seven years of experience and does approximately 700 examinations every year. He is a professional who can give his opinion based on the examination of Amelia Jackson's body."

"Overruled. You may answer, Dr. Wright," the judge ruled.

Dr. Wright replied, "Based on the wound and the trajectory that it would have taken to make this impression, I believe the person who hit Ms. Jackson was right-handed."

"One last question, Dr. Wright. Would this blow to the head have knocked Ms. Jackson unconscious?" Rachel asked.

"I cannot say for sure whether it would or not," he answered truthfully. That was okay. Rachel was ready to spin it either way.

Rachel finished her questions, and Jeff again decided not to ask any questions on redirect. Dr. Wright exited the stand and left the courtroom. The next witness for the State was the maintenance man, who testified about being in the apartment earlier that day to fix the fridge. He testified that Amelia had been cleaning and scrubbing the apartment while he was there. Rachel only asked what Amelia had been cleaning with, to which he replied bleach.

Jeff's next witness was a technician from the crime scene investigator's office. The original investigator on the case had passed away unexpectedly five years earlier from a heart attack. The investigator's office had had a new tech review the case, enough to be able to testify. They sent Malorie Kuch to testify that day. It was made clear to the jury that Ms. Kuch was not the one who initially investigated this case, but that the person who did had passed away. Ms. Kuch explained in depth what steps she took and what all she reviewed to get up to speed on the case to testify. Ms. Kuch testified about the blood spatter patterns and what they said about what had happened to Amelia. Specifically, she explained that the blood spatter on the wall above Amelia's bed showed that the person who stabbed her pulled the knife back out and over their head with some force each time.

She testified that they had found a lamp in Amelia's room that was used to hit Amelia. She explained that she knew this was the object because it had Amelia's blood on it , and had been compared against the indent in Amelia's skull during the autopsy. Rachel realized that she and Jeff had both forgotten to address the object with the medical examiner. Overall, Ms. Kuch's testimony was short and easy to follow. It didn't really hurt Maxwell's defense in any way.

In cross-examination, Rachel made sure to emphasize that Ms. Kuch was not the one who originally investigated this case. She wanted to show the jury that the State's case lacked credibility because of it. It meant Ms. Kuch's testimony only took about two hours, where normally a crime scene investigator would be on the stand for the better part of a day. This was also pointed out to the jury, despite Jeff's objection.

"Ms. Kuch," Rachel said, "did the CSI team find any fingerprints at the scene?"

Malorie Kuch double-checked her notes. This was normal even when the original crime scene investigator was the one testifying, but Rachel was hopeful that some jurors took it to mean that she was ill-prepared. "Yes. There were three sets of prints found at the scene," she finally answered.

"Do you know who those prints belong to?"

"Some belonged to the victim, Amelia Jackson." Ms. Kuch paused.

"And the other two?" Rachel led her.

"One set belonged to a Jesus Cabrera, and the other to Casey True."

Rachel looked at the jurors to see if there were any reactions to that information. She did not see anything on their faces. It would ordinarily make sense that Jesus's and Casey's prints would be there, but Amelia had just cleaned the whole house with bleach. Rachel would have to remind the jury of that fact. "How do you know the prints belonged to Jesus and Casey?" Rachel asked.

"Well, the original techs had them fingerprinted, since they were in the apartment that afternoon and were the ones who found her," Ms. Kuch explained.

"Where were the prints found? Strike that, sorry—that was a bad question. Where were Jesus Cabrera's prints found?" Rachel asked.

"Well," the investigator said, looking down at her notes again, "they were found on the handle of the fridge, on the counter, on the doorknob to the victim's bedroom, and on the victim's nightstand." She read from her notes.

Rachel looked up again, and saw a few looks of concern or recognition from the jurors. Rachel was hoping they were asking themselves why Jesus Cabrera's prints were on Amelia's doorknob and nightstand. "Where were Casey's fingerprints?" Rachel asked, hoping this would tie her theory together in the jurors' minds.

"Casey's fingerprints were on the victim's door and the bedpost of the victim's bed."

"Were there any fingerprints on the lamp that has been declared to be the object that struck Amelia Jackson?"

Ms. Kuch looked at her notes again. "No, there were no prints on the lamp. It looked to have been wiped down."

"Ms. Kuch, does it say anywhere in your notes if the defendant Maxwell Williams was fingerprinted?"

"Yes," came the brief response.

"Yes, what?" Rachel asked.

"Yes, he was fingerprinted as part of the investigation."

"Ms. Kuch, were Maxwell Williams's fingerprints found anywhere in the apartment?"

"No, they were not," Ms. Kuch admitted with a sense of regret in her voice, as if this fact was going to blow the State's case.

Rachel let that answer sit for a minute, hoping the jurors were taking notes or thinking about this testimony a little further. Then she asked, "Ms. Kuch, was there anything strange about the number of fingerprints in the apartment?"

Ms. Kuch looked confused. "I am not sure what you mean, Ms. Nix."

"Well, wouldn't there usually be fingerprints all over an apartment that two people were living in?"

"Oh, yes. Normally, there would be hundreds of prints all over the apartment if it was being lived in," Ms. Kuch admitted.

"Do you know why there weren't hundreds of prints in this apartment?" Rachel asked.

"Yes. There was a significant amount of sodium hypochlorite, or bleach, as it is commonly known. It was found out later by questioning witnesses that the victim had been cleaning her home earlier in the day with sodium hypochlorite. That would have cleaned away any prints."

Rachel had to connect the last few dots, in case the jurors hadn't. "So, Ms. Kuch, if the apartment was cleaned with bleach a few hours prior to Amelia dying, it would make sense that her fingerprints were in the home, correct?"

"Yes. My understanding is that she stayed home after cleaning to study, so she would have touched many surfaces in the house after cleaning."

"What about Jesus Cabrera? Could his fingerprints have been

there prior to Amelia cleaning, and she just missed those spots?" Rachel asked, already knowing the answer.

"No, that is very unlikely. The evidence showed that the victim had cleaned the home very well. The likelihood of the prints being from earlier is slim. The evidence shows that they were made after the cleaning occurred."

"So, those prints would have appeared once Jesus came back to the apartment that day?" Rachel asked, taking a shot.

"Well, the fingerprints don't tell me that, but based on the physical evidence, in conjunction with the witness statements—yes, that is the most likely outcome."

"Does the same apply for Casey's fingerprints?"

"Yes," Ms. Kuch responded.

Rachel looked at her notes to see if she had covered everything. She thought she had, and looked back at Jason to see if he had any other questions. He shook his head. "Nothing further, Your Honor. Thank you."

Jeff had a few follow-up questions, and then Malorie Kuch was released from her subpoena and left the stand. Rachel was feeling very confident after that testimony.

CHAPTER TWENTY-NINE

"Your Honor, the State calls Cordwell Jackson," Jeff declared, and Mr. Jackson made his way to the stand. He was dressed in a navy-blue suit with silver cufflinks. He was a tall, powerful, dark-featured man of about 6 foot 5, boasting an athletic build even though he was at least seventy-five years old. Rachel had to admit to herself that he was a very attractive man for his age, as he walked confidently through the swinging doors and up to the witness stand. She could already tell that the jury was going to be captivated by him. He was a politician, good looking, and well put together. Add all that to the fact that his daughter had been tragically killed; the jury would give him sympathy for that.

"Mr. Jackson, I am so sorry for your loss. Can you please tell us about your daughter, Amelia?" Jeff started. It was a smart move, starting off by conveying sympathy. That would help the jury get into that mentality.

Rachel sat back for a minute. This was the worst part of the trial, when the family took the stand and raved about what a great person the victim was and what plans they had for their future. Technically, none of the information was relevant to the case, but judges always let it in. Rachel knew better than to object. The judge would overrule it, and it would make her look bad and as if she was trying to keep the jury from hearing the good things about Amelia.

Cordwell Jackson choked up, almost on cue, and said, "Amelia was my whole world. Her mother and I were so proud of her. She was going to graduate near the top of her class and go on to make a big impact in the world." He went on for another five minutes about her future and what a tragedy it was to society that she was not still here to impact the world. He ended his monologue with, "If Maxwell Williams hadn't taken my baby from us, the world would have been a better place."

"Objection, Your Honor. Mr. Jackson has no firsthand knowledge about the crime or who committed it."

"Sustained. The jury will disregard the last comment from the witness." The judge looked to Mr. Jackson. "Sir. You cannot testify about things that you don't know about firsthand. You are not allowed to make legal conclusions or speculate on things. Is that clear?"

"Yes. I understand," he responded.

Jeff looked discouraged and scanned through his questions. He clearly had planned on asking more speculative questions of Mr. Jackson, and his opinion on why Maxwell Williams committed the crime. He finally asked, "Mr. Jackson, why did you tell the officers to focus their attention on Mr. Williams?"

Rachel contemplated the question and whether to object. She decided to let Mr. Jackson answer, with hopes that his racial bias would come out in his response.

"I never liked him. He wasn't good enough for my daughter. My family has money and status, and that boy was just some no-good kid from the hood. My daughter wasn't going to end up with some black kid, no matter how much she thought she loved him." You could practically feel the hatred in the air.

Rachel looked to the jury box and could see the disgust on some of the jurors' faces. They were not fond of Mr. Jackson or his mentality, and that would bode well for the defense. Not objecting to the question had ended up working out great.

Jeff decided to stop there, before things got worse. "Uh. Nothing further from me, judge."

"Ms. Nix, your witness."

Rachel walked up and took a deep breath. She had to tread lightly. Mr. Jackson was already riled up, and the jury didn't like him. She didn't want to spend too much time with him and let him regain any credibility. "Mr. Jackson, isn't it true that you told your daughter many times she couldn't date Mr. Williams?"

"That's right. I told her at least once a week that she had no business being with that low-life."

"Did you ever threaten Mr. Williams?"

"Of course I did. He had no business being with my daughter, and he needed to know it," he answered, looking as though there was nothing wrong with what he was saying.

"You were a political figure in the community, correct?"

"Yes, I was working my way toward being the mayor," he responded.

"Did that afford you certain power over the police, and did you use that power in this case?"

"I suggested the officers look at Maxwell Williams," Mr. Jackson gave as his non-answer.

Rachel tried to come at it a different way. "Did you know that the police would follow your suggestion, since you were a political figure?"

"Yes."

"Did you know the supervisor on the case personally before the day your daughter died?"

"Yes, I did," he answered.

"Did you specifically tell the supervisor to only look at Maxwell Williams as a suspect?"

"Yes."

Rachel looked through her notes and figured she had made enough headway. "Nothing further, Your Honor."

Jeff asked a few questions on redirect, but didn't make up any ground. He was allowed, over Rachel's objection, to talk about Amelia and her character a little more, to paint a picture for the jury of this bright, talented young woman. Rachel was upset, as it was far from relevant at this point, but she let it go.

The judge released them for lunch and Jason, Rachel, and Maxwell went back to their conference room to order food. Maxwell decided on Red Lobster for lunch. He'd had Denny's for breakfast that morning. At this rate, he was going to gain ten pounds by the end of the trial, but he didn't care. He was eating like a king.

Jason ate quickly and started to review his notes. He was going to cross-examine Casey True. They went back and forth on it for a long time, because Jason didn't feel he was ready to question such a key witness in the case. Rachel won the argument and pointed out that Casey might take better to a handsome man questioning her than some young woman.

Maxwell agreed with Rachel, based on what he knew about Casey back in the day. She would find Jason attractive and be more trusting. She would be easier to trip up if Jason was the one questioning her. Jason finally relented, but was already regretting it. He couldn't remember a time when he had been this nervous.

They all finished eating their food in silence. The bailiff came back in to tell them the judge was ready to start the afternoon. They cleaned up their garbage and headed back in. Jason was a little unsteady on his legs as they walked back inside.

Jeff called the DNA expert next. He made the right choice by getting out ahead of the DNA evidence, since it was the most damning for the State's case. It also would look bad if he didn't deal with the DNA at all in his case-in-chief. They spent the first two hours going through the expert's training, what DNA tells us, and how the tests are performed. The jury, at first appearing excited about the testimony, eventually grew bored and lost interest. A few of them looked like they were falling asleep.

Jeff finished his direct examination with, "Just because Maxwell Williams's DNA was not found on the victim doesn't mean he didn't commit the crime, correct?"

Rachel thought to herself that that was a double negative, and he was going to confuse the jury. The DNA analyst answered, "That is correct."

It was Rachel's turn. She stood. "Maxwell Williams's DNA was not on Amelia Jackson, correct?"

"That is correct. He was not a match for any of the samples on the victim."

"Any of the samples?" Rachel questioned. "How many samples were there?"

"There were two samples. One that belonged to a male and one to a female."

"Were you given any other DNA samples to compare with the samples on Amelia Jackson?"

"No. I was only given Mr. Williams's DNA for comparison."

"And that was not a match for either sample?" she confirmed.

"Objection, asked and answered," Jeff shouted.

"Overruled."

"That is correct. There were no matches for Mr. Williams."

Rachel was done with her questions, and the analyst left the stand. She had got the main point across that Maxwell's DNA wasn't there, and that was all she needed from the witness. No use in dragging it on and the jury falling asleep from boredom.

They took their afternoon break, and then Jeff called Yvonne

Chule to the stand. She was one of the witnesses who had seen Amelia and Maxwell at the bar the night before. She testified on direct about witnessing the fight that got very heated. Most of the things she testified about were hearsay, but Rachel let it all in. She figured that the judge would overrule any objection anyway.

"What was your impression of the altercation?" Jeff asked.

"Objection, Your Honor. Speculation," Rachel interjected.

"She can testify to her present sense impressions," Jeff shot back.

"Overruled. The witness can answer."

Yvonne looked to Jeff, confused about what was going on. Jeff gave her a nod, telling her it was okay to answer. "I mean, it was a long time ago, but I remember thinking that the fight got really bad. It was one of the worst I had seen between Amelia and Maxwell. They fought a lot, but this one was scary."

"What were they fighting about?" Jeff asked.

"The same thing that they always fought about, Amelia's dad. He didn't want them to be together. Amelia was really torn up about it because she loved him, but she didn't want to be cut off."

After she said that, Jeff looked up, seemingly surprised, as though that was new information to him. He tried to redirect the conversation. "Ms. Chule, you described the fight as scary, correct?"

"Yes. I had never seen Maxwell so mad. He looked like he was going to hit Amelia at one point, and that's when my boyfriend, Kyle, stepped in to break it up. He told Maxwell—"

Rachel interrupted her. "Objection, Your Honor. This is going to be hearsay. Ms. Chule cannot testify about what she heard her boyfriend tell Mr. Williams."

"Sustained. Next question, Mr. Malone," the judge ruled.

"Ms. Chule, after your boyfriend talked with Mr. Williams, what happened next?" Jeff asked, trying to regain control of the witness.

"They both left the bar," she said.

"Did you ever see or talk to Amelia again after she left the bar?"

Yvonne looked like she was trying to bring some tears to her eyes, but it wasn't working. "No. That was the last time I ever saw her."

"Nothing further," Jeff said, and walked back to sit down.

"Your witness, Ms. Nix," the judge said.

"Your Honor, Mr. Michelson is going to cross-examine this witness," Rachel informed the court.

"Very well. Mr. Michelson, please proceed."

"Thank you, Your Honor," said Jason, his voice cracking a little. He cleared his throat and walked up to the lectern with his notes. "Ms. Chule, you never witnessed Mr. Williams physically hurt Amelia, did you?"

"No, I did not," she admitted.

"You testified that Amelia was afraid that she would be cut off. Did her dad threaten that?" Jason asked.

"Yes, he threatened that all the time. Amelia always complained about it, saying how her dad would say if she stayed with Maxwell, she would be cut off and have to pay for college herself."

"Objection. Hearsay, move to strike," Jeff yelled.

"Your Honor," Jason said, gaining some momentum now that he had started with the questions, "Ms. Chule was allowed to testify about hearsay on direct. It is only fair that it goes both ways."

"Overruled. The witness's answer will stay in the record."

Jason continued, "Despite that threat from her father, Amelia continued to date Mr. Williams, right?"

"Yes, she did."

"Did Amelia and Maxwell leave together from the bar that night?" he asked.

"I believe they did, yes."

"Did Amelia seem afraid at all to go with Mr. Williams?" Jason asked.

"No, she wasn't acting afraid," Yvonne begrudgingly admitted.

"You weren't in Amelia's apartment the day she died, were you?"

"No," Yvonne replied, a little confused.

"Before the police came to you to ask for your statement, would you have ever thought Mr. Williams could do something like this?" Jason asked.

"Honestly, no," she answered.

Jason felt confident with his cross, but looked back to check with Rachel if she had anything else. She shook her head no, and Jason said, "Nothing further, Your Honor."

Jeff had a few follow-up questions. "Just because you didn't think Mr. Williams would do that doesn't mean he didn't, right?"

"Right."

"In fact, you said Mr. Williams looked like he was going to hit Amelia, correct?" Jeff asked.

"Yes. That was the first time I had seen him get to that point of anger with Amelia. When I thought he was going to hit her, that is when my boyfriend went over to break it up."

"At some point, did you believe that Mr. Williams raped and killed Amelia?" Jeff was gaining momentum again.

"Objection, speculation," Rachel said.

"Sustained."

"Nothing further for this witness," said Jeff.

Yvonne was excused from the witness stand, and her ex-boyfriend, Kyle Smith, went next. His testimony only confirmed what Yvonne had said. He testified that he told Maxwell to knock it off and that it was time for them to go home. Jason cross-examined him and got Kyle to admit that he had never actually seen Maxwell hit Amelia and that they had left together, appearing fine.

After Kyle was done with his testimony, the judge called it for the day. He gave the same warnings as before to the jurors before letting them leave for the night, telling them to return at 8:30 a.m. After they left, the judge asked, "Do you anticipate the State resting tomorrow, Mr. Malone?"

Jeff looked down at his notes. "Yes, Your Honor. Potentially before the lunch break, depending on the cross-examinations."

"Very well," the judge said. "I will see you all back here tomorrow at 8:15 a.m. Oh, was there anything else we needed to put on the record?"

"No, Your Honor," Rachel and Jeff said almost in unison.

"We are adjourned. Have a great night, everyone."

Rachel and Jason packed up and went and talked with Maxwell before they went home for the night. They asked the bailiff if they could work with Maxwell for about an hour and a half, and the bailiff said that was fine, but they would have to do it at the jail, because the courthouse needed to be locked up. They all made their way down to the jail part of the building, ordered Maxwell some food from Pizza Lucé and got down to work.

As they were waiting for their food to be delivered, Maxwell asked, "That went well today, right?"

"I think so," Jason said.

"Yes, it did," Rachel said. "We scored a lot of points with the witnesses today. We also started to lay out some breadcrumbs leading the way toward who really committed the crime. Or at least who we think did it."

"If the jury finds me not guilty, will the investigation open again? Will they look into it and charge the real killers?"

Rachel sighed. "Unfortunately, that's not likely. The police in this town are already overworked, so they don't have time to reopen an investigation on a forty-year-old murder. And even if they did, they likely couldn't prosecute anyone."

"Why not?"

"The State has already told the world that you are the one who did it by bringing charges against you, twice. The fact that you were convicted the first time, even though the evidence wasn't there for the conviction, will give anyone else an easy out. It wouldn't be hard to convince a jury that there was reasonable doubt that anyone else could have committed the crime. The cops and first jury thought you did it. Therefore, most jurors will have reasonable doubt based on that fact alone. The prosecution would never get a conviction."

"That's really dumb!" Maxwell said, with anger in his voice. "So, I sit in prison for forty years for a crime that I didn't commit. If we win this and get me out of prison and prove my innocence, there is nothing more? The crime just goes into some file cabinet, and Amelia's real killer, or killers, go free?" He shook his head. "That just doesn't make sense, man."

"I know it doesn't. It is one of the many pitfalls in our criminal justice system. That is why people often refer to it as 'the unjust system.' There are so many flaws," Rachel said sadly.

The food arrived, and Maxwell ate his large meat lover's pizza as Rachel and Jason talked about the witnesses testifying the next day. When Maxwell was done eating, Rachel looked at him and said, "I think it is time we talk about the biggest decision in this case." She paused to make sure she had his attention. "Are you going to testify?"

CHAPTER THIRTY

Jeff Malone called Casey Cabrera to the stand. "Good morning, Ms. Cabrera. Can you please state your name for the record?"

"Casey Josephine Cabrera."

"Where do you live?"

She gave her address, and Jason felt his nerves creeping up on him. This was going to be his witness, and he needed to catch her in her lies on the stand. He noticed what she gave as her last name and looked at his notes. Her maiden name was True. He hadn't even realized that she was now Casey Cabrera, which meant she had married Jesus, her boyfriend from forty years ago. His intuition was telling him that this was an important fact, so he made a note to ask Casey a question about it, if Jeff didn't.

"How do you know the defendant, Mr. Williams?" Jeff continued.

"Mr. Williams was dating my college roommate, Amelia Jackson. He used to be at our apartment a lot, and he and Amelia hung out with me and my now husband. We would go out on double dates a lot." Jason went to cross off his note about following up on her marriage, but then he thought to himself that he should still draw more attention to it.

Jeff spent the next hour going through the history of the four of them hanging out together, and the fights that Maxwell and Amelia would have. Casey mentioned the fact that Amelia's father did not approve of Maxwell, and the stress that this caused the couple. The jury was loving her. She was a beautiful woman, even at sixty-three years old. She would still turn heads. She was about 5 foot 4, petite, with long dyed blonde hair that was curled to perfection, and was wearing a knee-length black dress.

Casey was confident up there on the stand, and she knew that she had everyone's attention. When Jeff started to ask her about the day that Amelia died, her mood changed, and she started to cry. It started out as a few sniffles and stray tears running down her face. By the time she was into the heart of the questions, she was full-on ugly crying.

"Please take us through what happened that day when you got back to the apartment," Jeff led her.

"It was the worst day of my life. I'll never forget it." She stopped to wipe her nose theatrically. She looked over at the jurors with a sad look on her face, like she was putting on a show for them. "Jesus, who was my boyfriend at the time, and I came home, and we walked up to the apartment door. We were surprised to see that the door wasn't closed all the way. I looked at Jesus, confused, and he decided to walk in first to investigate what was going on. I walked in right behind him and I just screamed. He tried to shield me from it, but I still saw her."

She was sobbing and making gasping noises like she couldn't catch her breath. Jeff let her cry for a few more minutes and then finally said, "What did you see when you walked into the apartment?"

"At first, all I saw was the blood. It was everywhere. It was pooled underneath Amelia's bed. There was so much blood. I think I was in shock at first and didn't even notice that she was there. Then, when I realized that Amelia was there on the bed, and the blood was hers, I screamed again and almost fainted. Jesus had to catch me as I fell back a little." Jason made a note to follow up on that point.

"I walked over to the bed and just stood there looking at her. I didn't know what to do. We called 911 and then the police came to the apartment. They talked to Jesus and me and asked us what we knew. Then I found out that they had arrested Maxwell, I mean the defendant, a few hours later."

"Do you believe the defendant committed this crime?" Jeff asked.

Rachel shot to her feet. "Objection, Your Honor. Calls for speculation." Unfortunately, Rachel was too late, and Casey's answer got out before the objection.

"I know he did," she said confidently.

The judge declared, "The objection is sustained. The jury will disregard the witness's answer." Rachel sat back down, and her head fell slightly. She knew how it worked. The jury would not disregard what they heard.

Jeff let that answer hang in the air while he pretended to review his notes. You could see the minds of the jurors racing as they took in that last comment by Casey. Some wrote down notes. As the silence continued, a few started to look uncomfortable and shifted in their seats. Jeff finally looked back up to the witness stand. "I have nothing further, Your Honor."

"Mr. Michelson, it's your witness," the judge said.

Jason took a deep breath and stood, trying to exude confidence as he walked forward. He placed his notes in front of him and cleared his throat. "Hello, Ms. Cabrera." He paused and flashed her a smile, utilizing his perfect white teeth and dimples to soften the witness.

She smiled back at him. "Hello." The tension that was previously in her body was now gone, and it was clear that she was more comfortable than when Jason was walking up to the lectern. This was a good sign. The plan was working, Jason thought to himself.

"You just testified that you know that Mr. Williams did it, correct?" Jason jumped into an additional question that was not in his notes, taking a chance in going off his script.

"Correct. I know he did it."

Rachel gritted her teeth. That was a mistake. The previous answer had been stricken from the record because it was speculation. But now that Jason had brought it back up during his cross-examination, not only did the answer stand, but it allowed Casey to reiterate her position on the matter. Rachel began to rethink the decision to let Jason cross-examine this important witness. She contemplated asking the judge for a recess, so she could take over questioning Casey.

"The only way you would know that is if you were in the room when she died, isn't that right?" Jason asked. Rachel contemplated this next question, and decided that maybe it wasn't so bad that Jason had reintroduced Casey's speculation.

"What do you mean?" Casey asked, confusion coming across her face. Jason thought he could also detect a little sense of panic in her expression.

"You say you are sure that Mr. Williams committed the crime, but you would only know that if you were in the room when it happened, right?" Jason reiterated. Rachel looked toward the jurors and they looked intrigued, like they were anxiously awaiting a response.

"I don't know," Casey said, a slight quiver in her voice. Her cheeks began to flush.

"Well, were you in the room when Amelia Jackson was killed?" he asked, being careful not to use the word "murdered."

"I . . . uh." She looked over at Jeff nervously, begging for assistance with her eyes. Jeff was looking down at his notepad and didn't even notice that she was looking at him.

When Casey realized that Jeff wasn't going to help her, she said, a little softer now, "No. I wasn't in the room when she died."

"Then you can't possibly know who killed Amelia, right?"

"I guess not," she said, and looked down at her hands in her lap.

"Was your now-husband Jesus Cabrera in the room when Amelia died?" Jason took a shot.

Jeff seemed to be listening now, as he shot up. "Objection, Your Honor. Calls for speculation. She just testified that she wasn't present."

Without allowing any further argument from Jason, the judge ruled, "Sustained."

That's okay, Jason thought to himself. The whole point of the question was to get the idea out there that Jesus and Casey were in the apartment when Amelia was killed. Jason paused to look down at his notes, letting the question bounce around the room. Rachel watched as a few jurors made notes on their pads. She subconsciously nodded her head slightly. The plan had worked, and a few seeds of their alternate theory had been planted.

Jason changed gears. "What time did you get home the day Ms. Jackson died?"

Casey looked like she wasn't expecting that question. "I don't know exactly," she finally answered, after about thirty seconds had passed.

"What time did Mr. Cabrera get there?" Jason continued quickly, not letting Casey have much time to think between questions.

"I don't know," she said, then she quickly added, "The same time as me."

"What way was Ms. Jackson facing on the bed when you found her?" Jason continued.

"I don't remember."

"Who walked into the room first, you or Mr. Cabrera?"

"I don't remember."

"You don't remember? Didn't you testify on direct examination that Mr. Cabrera walked in first?" Jason asked, his voice rising to emphasize the fact that Casey was now changing her story.

"Um. Yes. That's right. I got confused. Yes, he went in first because the door was open, and we weren't sure why."

"Did you touch the body?"

"I don't think so, no."

"Did Mr. Cabrera touch her body?"

"I don't recall."

"Mrs. Cabrera, you testified earlier that it was the worst day of your life, and you will never forget it, didn't you?" Jason looked her in the eyes as he asked the question.

"Yes. That is correct."

"If you can never forget the day, why do you now seem to be forgetting everything?" The disbelief was palpable in Jason's voice.

"Your questions are confusing me," she said, trying to look innocently toward the jurors as if she really was confused.

"I am sorry. I will try to go through things slower, so as not to confuse you. Just let me know if you don't understand the question." Jason came back with that same sweet-guy smile.

"Okay. Thank you," Casey said, smiling back at him.

"So, where were you before you came home the day Ms. Jackson died?" Jason started again, asking his question more slowly this time.

"We were out at a restaurant, eating," Casey answered.

"At a restaurant, okay. What time did you leave the restaurant?"

"Um. I don't know. Some time after noon, I think." Jason nodded. He was getting somewhere by locking her into a story.

"How long was the journey from the restaurant to your apartment?"

"About five minutes. We were just up the street," she said.

"Did you drive or walk?"

"We drove. It was still chilly outside."

"Who drove the car?" The back and forth was going smoothly now, and it was clear that Casey was comfortable, and her memory was miraculously coming back.

"I think Jesus did."

"What time did you get to the apartment?"

"I don't remember," she answered.

Jason sighed, exaggerating his frustration. "Well, you left the restaurant sometime after noon. Was it before 12:30 p.m.?"

"Yes. I think so."

"Was it after 12:15 p.m.?"

"I think so."

"Okay. So, you left sometime between 12:15 p.m. and 12:30 p.m., correct?"

"That sounds right." Casey nodded.

"It is a five-minute drive back to the apartment. Therefore, you got back to the apartment between 12:20 p.m. and 12:40 p.m., correct?"

Casey thought about it for a minute. "Yes, I guess that is right."

Jason thought about pointing out that Casey just admitted that she was in the apartment at the time of death, but he didn't want to give her a chance to explain that fact away. They could make that argument in their closing. "Between 12:20 p.m. and 12:40 p.m., when you walked into the apartment," he reiterated the timeline again, "you testified that you saw Ms. Jackson right away, correct?"

"Yes. That is correct," she said confidently.

Jason faked looking down at his notes. "And you screamed?"

"Yes. I did."

"How did you see her right when you walked into the apartment?"

Casey looked at him, puzzled again. "What do you mean?"

"Well, you walked into the apartment between 12:20 p.m. and 12:40 p.m. How did you see her when you walked in?" Jason reiterated the timeline one last time. He knew from his time in law school that if a fact or comment is stated three times, it sticks in people's minds. Rachel noticed a few people making notes after Jason asked that last question. Jason was doing a good job, she thought to herself.

"I saw her lying there covered in blood." Casey said with a slight rise in her voice, making her answer sound more like a question.

"You saw her right when you walked into the apartment?" Jason clarified.

"Yes," Casey said, gaining confidence.

Jason walked back to the defense table and put an exhibit up on the projector. It showed the layout of the apartment that Amelia and Casey lived in forty years ago, the apartment that Amelia died in. The building had been torn down about fifteen years ago. "I am showing you what has been marked in the record as State's Exhibit 58. Do you recognize this?"

"Yes. It's our apartment layout," she said, the confusion still in her voice. She clearly had not caught on to what Jason was getting at.

"This shows that you and Amelia both had your own separate rooms, correct?"

"Yes?" she said, her voice rising again to make the answer more of a question.

"You both had doors to your rooms?" Jason asked, portraying the question as simple, with no significant meaning.

"Yes, we did."

"Was her door open or closed when you walked into the apartment that day?" Jason asked. Rachel could see it on some of the jurors' faces: they'd realized where Jason was going with the questions.

"I don't remember," Casey answered. She was still clearly confused and not sure what Jason was trying to point out.

"You don't remember if Amelia's bedroom door was open that day?"

"No. I am not sure."

"Well, how could you have walked in and seen her right away if her door was closed?" Jason asked. At last, his plan was coming to fruition.

Casey responded, "Oh, that's right. It was open."

Jason nodded. "It was open. Okay. And that's how you saw her right when you walked into the apartment?"

"Yes. That's how I saw her," she confirmed, gaining her confidence again.

"How many steps did you take into the apartment before you saw Ms. Jackson?"

"What? I don't know!" The confusion was back.

"Isn't it true that it wouldn't matter how many steps you took, because the placement of Ms. Jackson's bed made it impossible to see it from anywhere in the living room?"

Casey got nervous and was shaking slightly. "I don't know if that's true or not," she finally said.

"You don't know if that is true or not? You just testified multiple times that you saw her right when you walked into the apartment. For that to happen, you would have to be able to see her from the living room, correct?" Jason was perfectly laying the groundwork for their theory of the case.

"I guess so, yes."

Jason pointed back to the layout of the apartment. "Amelia's bed was up against this wall, underneath a window, correct?"

"Yes."

"The placement of the bed made it impossible to see her bed from the living room, right?" Jason asked again.

"I don't remember."

"You don't remember?" Jason asked, with disbelief and slight annoyance. "Okay, then." He walked back to the defense table and pulled up a picture on the screen. "This is State's Exhibit 52, which the jury has already seen. This is a picture of Amelia's room, correct?" Jason made sure to choose a picture that didn't have Amelia's dead body in it. The blood was still on the bed and on the floor, but it was worth the risk of showing the jury the picture again to make his point. The picture showed Amelia's bed underneath a window on the far side of the room, away from the door. It was clear that there was no way to see her bed from the living room.

"Yes. That is her room."

"And that is her bed?"

"Yes," Casey admitted.

"Isn't it true that you couldn't see her bed from where you would have been standing in the living room?"

"I don't remember."

"It's interesting that you are back to not remembering things," Jason commented.

"Objection, Your Honor. Mr. Michelson is testifying and badgering the witness," Jeff stated, without standing.

"Sustained. Move on and ask a question, Mr. Michelson," the judge warned.

"Yes, Your Honor. Mrs. Cabrera, you testified before that you weren't in the apartment when Ms. Jackson died. Do you not remember that now either?" Jason spoke quickly to get the question out before Jeff could object.

"Your Honor!" Jeff yelled; he was on his feet this time. "Objection; he is badgering the witness."

"Sustained," the judge said, with his voice raised and in a reprimanding tone. "Mr. Michelson, I said it is time to move on."

"Sorry, Your Honor. You said to ask a question; I thought that was what I was doing." Jason looked up at the judge with a face of innocence, and when the judge just stared back at him angrily, Jason looked down at his notes. He knew he was going to upset the judge, but it was worth it if he could get his question out. He just hoped the jurors had caught on to his point.

Jason looked through his notes one last time and decided that was a good place to stop his questions. He had gotten his points across and had made Casey Cabrera look like an untruthful witness. Or at least he thought he had portrayed that well enough. He just had to make one last point.

"Mrs. Cabrera, you and your husband were dating at the time Ms. Jackson died, correct?"

"Yes. That's correct," she answered, again seemingly confused.

"Some time after that, the two of you got married?"

"Yes. A few years after Amelia died, Jesus and I got married."

Jason started to walk away, then turned back. "Oh, yeah. One more question, Mrs. Cabrera. Are you right-handed?"

Casey looked at him, confused again. "Yes. I am."

"I have nothing further, Your Honor," Jason said as he picked up his notes and walked back to the defense table to sit down. Rachel gave him a little nod of approval as he did so.

"Redirect, Mr. Malone?" the judge asked.

Jeff thought about it for a minute, as he looked down at his own notes. He decided that it was better to get Casey Cabrera off the stand. "No, Your Honor."

The judge turned to the witness stand. "Thank you, Mrs. Cabrera, you are excused."

Casey gathered her composure, stood tall, and walked down off the witness stand. She walked confidently through the middle of the courtroom and out the swinging doors. She had the same confidence in her step that she had had when she first walked up to the witness stand. If you hadn't just witnessed her testimony, you would have never known that she had struggled on the stand.

The judge looked at his watch. "It's 12:17, let's take our lunch break. Members of the jury, please be back in the jury room and ready to go at 1:25 p.m. We will have a slightly longer lunch today since we missed our morning break."

After the jurors left, the judge took off his glasses and rubbed his eyes. The morning had clearly taken a toll on him, and he had most likely allowed the extra time for lunch because he needed the break. Rachel knew the judge also probably had other cases to attend to during his lunch break. She did not envy him one bit.

"Let's have the attorneys and Mr. Williams back in here at 1:20 p.m. and see if there is anything to put on the record at that point, okay?" he suggested, and the attorneys nodded. "We are adjourned."

CHAPTER THIRTY-ONE

It was 1:23 p.m. when the judge finally came back into the courtroom. He walked in and sat down on the bench, adjusted in his seat, and looked at his court reporter. "Are we ready to go on the record?" When he received an affirmative nod from the court reporter, he began, "Okay. We are back on the record in *State v. Williams*. Does either party need to make a record before we proceed?"

"No," Jeff said.

"No, Your Honor," Rachel answered.

"Okay. Who are you calling as your next witness, Mr. Malone?" the judge inquired.

"Your Honor, the State intends to rest at this time."

"What?" Rachel and Jason both said at once, lookingover at Jeff. He still had Jesus Cabrera to call to the stand.

"Your Honor," Rachel said, "Mr. Malone said yesterday that he had two more witnesses to call. He has only called one. He has not called Jesus Cabrera yet."

The judge looked unamused. "Mr. Malone?"

"Yes, Your Honor. Mr. Cabrera is on our witness list. We intended to call him, but after some consideration over lunch, the State has decided that we do not need Mr. Cabrera's testimony, as it would be duplicative of Mrs. Cabrera's."

The judge looked back to Rachel. "Ms. Nix. The State has the right not to call people on their witness list."

"I understand that, Your Honor, but he was a firsthand witness who found the victim. It is our position that they need to call him as a witness," Rachel argued, the panic rising in her voice. They needed Jesus to testify to bring out further information about their theory of the case. They also needed to catch him in his lies and point them out to the jury.

Jeff started in before waiting for a cue from the judge. "Your Honor, it is duplicative of what Mrs. Cabrera testified to. They both found her at the same time. The State is confident that they have met their burden, without the need for Mr. Cabrera's testimony."

Rachel broke in right after Jeff was done talking.

"We need to cross-examine him, Your Honor," she insisted. "It is important to our defense." Her palms were starting to sweat. This had never happened to her in a trial before.

"I understand that, Ms. Nix. Is Mr. Cabrera on your witness list?" the judge asked.

She grabbed the witness list that she had prepared for trial. She scanned the sheet, not finding his name. She got to the end, where she had put in the boilerplate language, "Any and all witnesses listed by the State." She breathed a sigh of relief. "Yes, Your Honor. He would fall under the catch-all at the bottom: any and all witnesses listed by the State."

The judge nodded. "Mr. Malone?"

"That is fine, Your Honor. We have no objection if the defense wants to call him in their case-in-chief. Just for the record, we have released him from his subpoena, so he is no longer in the courthouse or required to appear," Jeff said, a smirk slowly coming across his face as he looked to see Rachel's reaction.

Rachel felt like she had been punched in the stomach, as the air left her lungs. If Jesus was no longer under a State subpoena, that meant they had to find him and try to serve him with their own subpoena. Without that, there was nothing directing Jesus to come to court and testify. Not only was that a problem, but none of their other witnesses had been subpoenaed for today. Rachel and Jason had expected Jesus's testimony to take the rest of the day, with them starting with their case the next morning.

Her panic was rising. She took a deep breath to calm her nerves, before speaking again. "Your Honor, we had no idea that the State was going to pull this stunt. There was no reason for us to subpoena Mr. Cabrera because we believed the State was going to call him. They stated yesterday that that was the case. The defense planned for Mr. Cabrera to be called to testify, and for that testimony to take the remainder of today. Our first witness is not scheduled to be here until tomorrow. Additionally, we have not prepared our arguments for directed verdict or any other matters. We do not believe it is acceptable for the State to not call a key witness, based on the circumstances."

"Ms. Nix, I cannot force the State to call any witnesses. The fact that they have released Mr. Cabrera from his subpoena is outside of my control. There is nothing legally obligating Mr. Cabrera to be at court at this time. The only way that he will be testifying is if you can get him here during your case."

Rachel let out a defeated sigh. "I understand, Your Honor. The Exoneration Project does not have the resources that the State has at its disposal to find and serve Mr. Cabrera. Can we have some time to try and execute that task?"

The judge thought about it, and looked at his computer. "I hate to keep the jurors waiting even longer than they already have been. They've been here for days now, and I am sure they want to get back to their normal routines and lives." He paused again. "You know what? This is what we will do. We will put that the State rests on the record, and the defense can make any necessary motions. Ms. Nix, you are a well-versed defense attorney, and I have faith that you can make the necessary motions and arguments without more preparation. After that, I will take matters under advisement until the morning.

"You will have the night to find Mr. Cabrera and serve him with a subpoena to appear tomorrow, Ms. Nix. If you cannot do that then you will have to forgo calling him as a witness. We will start with the defense's case tomorrow morning at 8:30 a.m."

Rachel nodded in defeat. It was a lot to ask for them to find and subpoena Mr. Cabrera in a night. She also still had to prepare the rest of her direct examination questions for her witness, determine whether Maxwell was going to testify, and work on their closing argument.

The judge continued, "Let's call the jury back in here to get back on the record for the State to rest their case." The bailiff went and brought the jurors back into the courtroom. It was now 1:48 p.m. Once they were all seated, the judge said, "Mr. Malone, please continue."

Jeff stood, straightened his suit jacket for dramatic effect, and said loudly, "The State rests, Your Honor." The jurors looked confused and not sure what that meant. They looked to the judge for guidance and explanation.

"Members of the jury," the judge said, "the State has rested its case. That means that they are done calling witnesses, and it is the defense's time to call their witnesses, if they have any. At this time, the lawyers and I have a few things to discuss without you here. You are all going to be dismissed early today, with the understanding that you are to be back here at 8:30 tomorrow morning to start back up. Remember, you are not to do any research on this case or talk to anyone about anything you have heard. You are not to talk about the case in any way, not even to family members. Is that clear?" The jurors were nodding their understanding. The judge dismissed them all, and they filed out.

Once they were gone, the judge continued, "Ms. Nix, please go ahead with your motions."

Rachel stood. "Yes, Your Honor, thank you. The defense motions for a judgment of acquittal. The State has failed to prove beyond a reasonable doubt that Maxwell Williams is the one who committed the crimes that he is charged with.

"The State has failed to call necessary witnesses, and they have not proved the elements of the crimes. The DNA found at the scene did not belong to Mr. Williams. There are no witnesses who can place him at the scene of the crime at any point during the day that Ms. Jackson was killed. There are no witnesses who saw Mr. Williams with Ms. Jackson at all that day. In fact, the last time anyone saw them together was over twelve hours earlier.

"The State's witness, Mrs. Cabrera, was less than a credible witness, and her story simply did not make sense. The Court should find her testimony to be uncredible, thus excluding anything that she testified to during her direct examination. Without Mrs. Cabrera's testimony, or any additional testimony from Mr. Cabrera, the other witness who allegedly found Ms. Jackson, the State has failed to prove additional elements of these crimes.

"Simply put, Your Honor, the State has failed at every turn to prove that Mr. Williams committed the crimes that he is charged with. We believe that the court should grant Maxwell Williams a judgment of acquittal, based on these arguments."

Rachel finished and sat down. Jeff stood up and started his response. "Your Honor, the jurors are the ultimate deciders of the facts and whether the State has proved Mr. Williams guilty beyond a reasonable doubt. Despite the defense's claims, the State has proved its burden.

"Witnesses had seen the couple fight the night before at the bar. This was not a rare occurrence. Mr. Williams was still upset with Ms. Jackson and tried to call her multiple times the day of her death. When he didn't get an answer, he went over to her apartment. He went in to confront her, and he ended up assaulting and killing her.

The evidence is there. The police officers, medical examiner, and the rest of the State's witnesses have testified to those facts.

"We ask that the court deny the defendant's motion for directed verdict and allow the jurors to decide what evidence is sufficient. They are the ones charged with the ability to determine witnesses' credibility and whether the State has proved its burden. There is nothing at this point to warrant the court granting a motion for acquittal. Thank you." Jeff sat down.

Jeff had made the standard arguments that every prosecutor makes in response to a motion for acquittal. To be fair, he was just going through the motions. Rachel was doing the same thing. They knew that the judge would not grant the motion. A judgment for acquittal is made when the State has failed to meet its burden of proof and there is no way that a jury could reasonably convict the defendant beyond a reasonable doubt. It consists of the judge stepping in and deciding that the jury will not be needed and the charges are dismissed. Jeff was right: it was up to the jury to decide the truth about everything Rachel had brought up in her argument.

Judges rarely grant a judgment for acquittal, especially in cases like this. They don't want to take the chance of having the judgment overturned on appeal. The jury had already heard this much of the case, and it was more beneficial for everyone involved if they continued to hear the case and made the ultimate decision on it. This would not only prevent a potential appeal, but put the heat on the jurors to decide, and not the judge.

Everyone knew that the arguments were useless, and the judge would deny the motion. This was just one of the steps that a defense attorney must take in a case. There honestly was no reason for the judge to consider the matter overnight. However, that was his decision, and Rachel accepted that. The parties were dismissed for the day a few minutes later, and the search was on for Mr. Cabrera.

Jason, Rachel, Dylan Franks, and Amy were out from the time

court adjourned until midnight looking to find Jesus Cabrera. Rachel had quickly emailed Dylan asking him to draft the subpoena and start looking, before proceeding with her motion that day. He had looked for additional people to join in on the search, but the backing was just not there. Detective Swenson, who had continued sitting in the courtroom watching, offered Rachel his help. He used his resources to try to locate Jesus in every way possible without violating his Fourth Amendment protections against unusual search and seizure. It was no use. He ended up going home at about 9:00 p.m. that night, when he had to go take care of his sick wife.

Jason and Rachel thanked him profusely for his help. It got to the point where everyone had to go home and get some rest. It seemed very unlikely that they were going to find Jesus Cabrera, and they still had a trial to conduct the next morning. Their efforts to continue looking were useless at that point. They had to get some rest. Dylan had a friend on the police force working nights who agreed to try to look for Jesus a little longer if he had a slow night. It was their last hope of finding him.

CHAPTER THIRTY-TWO

It was 8:32 a.m., and the jurors were all seated and ready for the next day of trial. They looked well rested and as though they had enjoyed the early dismissal the day before. The judge looked less exhausted as well. Jason and Rachel, on the other hand, had had a long night looking for Mr. Cabrera, and it showed on their faces and through their body language. They had both had three large cups of coffee that morning and gotten a total of two hours of sleep between the two of them.

They had to shake that all off as they started their case-in-chief. The judge had already put his denial of the motion for directed verdict on the record prior to the jury entering the courtroom. There was no surprise there. His reasoning followed the same boilerplate arguments that Jeff had made during his argument.

"Please call your first witness, Ms. Nix."

"The defense calls Wyatt Thielsen," Rachel said confidently. She had come to terms with what had happened the day before, and she had to portray confidence during their case. If she couldn't, she didn't even want to think what that might mean for Maxwell.

Wyatt Thielsen entered the courtroom, escorted by a court deputy. He was wearing jeans and a collared button-up. He was sixty-four years old, 5 foot 7, with a big beer gut. He had long, shaggy hair and a long beard that was about two weeks past needing a trim. He was not a physically appealing witness. Rachel knew that Jason had tried to convince Mr. Thielsen to clean up some for court. He obviously had refused.

Mr. Thielsen was sworn in; he spelt his name for the record. He gave his address, date of birth, current employment, and all the other details that witnesses initially go over. Rachel then directed him to the day of the crime. He confirmed that he had been working at a restaurant as a delivery driver. He had delivered food to Mr. Williams that day at 12:30 p.m. Yes, he rspecifically remembered Mr. Williams answering the door.

His direct testimony was short at less than fifteen minutes. Jeff stood up. "Just a few questions, Mr. Thielsen. Did you review your statement to the police from that night in preparation for your testimony today?"

"Yes, I did," he admitted.

"After you delivered the food to Mr. Williams, did you stay with him at his apartment?"

"No, why would I?"

"I am just asking to make sure I understand, that is all," Jeff explained nicely. "Are you aware if Mr. Williams left his apartment at any point after you left?"

"I am not."

"So he could have left his apartment right after you delivered the food, correct?" Jeff asked.

"Objection, calls for speculation," Rachel said, but instantly regretted it. She had fallen into Jeff's trap. He wanted her to object to call more attention to the point he was trying to make.

"Sustained," the judge said, but the mistake had already been made.

Jeff smiled. "I have nothing further for this witness. Thank you."

The witness was excused and left the courtroom. Rachel was upset with herself for making such a rookie mistake. She knew better. She was so tired from not sleeping the night before, and she had gone back to being frustrated about what had happened the previous day. She had to get over it and move on. The information that they needed from Wyatt Thielsen had been extracted, and that was what was important. The fact that Jeff had got his point in didn't matter. Rachel and Jason had gotten in many points of their own during their cross-examination of the State's witnesses. It was all part of the back-and-forth of trial.

"The defense calls Michael Ellers." Michael walked up to the stand, was sworn in, and went through the same customary questions as Mr. Thielsen had. He was better put together, wearing a gray suit and tie. He was clean-shaven, and his afro was neatly styled. He was a 6-foot-4 Black man who was now a banker at a Wells Fargo branch.

"Mr. Ellers, how do you know Maxwell Williams?" Rachel asked.

"Maxwell and I met at freshman orientation. We were friends right off the bat, and we did everything together. As often as possible, we would take the same classes, go to the same sporting events, work out together. People used to say, if you saw one of us, the other was not far behind." He smiled weakly, remembering the better times in life before they got here, the carefree times of two young men hanging out, without a care in the world aside from their schoolwork and what to do that night after work.

"When did you meet Amelia Jackson?"

Michael's smile faded, and a somber look came across his face. "I met Ms. Jackson pretty early on in the relationship between her and Mr. Williams. They went out I think twice before the three of us hung out together. I can't say exactly when it was, but it was early on in their relationship."

"How often would you see them together?"

"All of the time. Like I said before, Maxwell and I were always together. So, when Maxwell and Amelia were together, I was often there, too, at least when we were all out in public doing stuff together. They obviously spent alone time together at their apartments and on dates and stuff without me. But I would say I was with them a good amount of the time."

"We have heard testimony about some of the fights that the two of them had. Did you witness any of that?"

Michael sighed. "Yeah. Unfortunately, they did fight sometimes. Amelia's dad didn't approve of her dating Maxwell. That caused a lot of disagreements between them."

"Do you know why Mr. Jackson didn't approve of them dating?" Rachel asked.

"Objection, Your Honor. Calls for speculation."

"Overruled. He can answer, if he knows," the judge stated.

Rachel nodded to Michael to signify that he could answer. "Yes. He didn't like Maxwell because he was black and his daughter was white. He would say derogatory things and that—"

"Objection, Your Honor, hearsay," Jeff said, without standing.

"Sustained. The witness's testimony needs to be only on what he observed, not things he heard."

Michael nodded his understanding. Rachel and Jason had gone through all of this with him during their witness prep. He knew what to expect, and that the judge likely wouldn't let him talk about some things.

"How did that disapproval from Amelia's father affect their relationship, based on your observations?" Rachel asked the question in a way that Jeff could not object to.

"They would break up sometimes because of it, but they always got back together."

"Did you ever witness Amelia and Mr. Williams arguing about things other than her father's views on the relationship?"

"No. That was all they argued about," Michael said quickly. Jeff was standing up, but he was too late to object, and the jury had already heard the answer. He sat back down in his seat and let the testimony stand.

"Based on what you observed, was Mr. Williams going to let Mr. Jackson's opinion of him get in the way of his relationship?" Rachel asked, starting to get to the meat of the testimony.

"No. Absolutely not," Michael answered confidently.

"How do you know that?" Rachel asked.

"Objection, calls for speculation." Jeff knew what was coming and was trying to keep this witness's testimony away from the jury.

"Overruled," the judge said. "The witness may answer."

"Maxwell was planning on proposing the night after graduation," Michael said. He paused to let that sink in, just as he had practiced with the team, then started again. "He had bought a ring and everything. I went with him to pick it out. Maxwell loved Amelia more than anything, and he was going to marry her, despite her father's objections."

Rachel started to ask a follow-up question, when Michael remembered something else that he was supposed to say. "Maxwell had even gone to ask for Mr. Jackson's blessing. He knew he likely wouldn't get it, but it was the right thing to do. This was two weeks before Amelia's death."

"Objection; this is all hearsay, Your Honor," Jeff said, annoyed at what information was coming into the trial.

"Your Honor," Rachel said, "if you let me ask my next question, I can show that this is in fact firsthand knowledge."

"Overruled. You may continue."

"Mr. Ellers, how do you know about all of this?" Rachel led him.

"I was there for it all. I was there when Mr. Williams called Mr. Jackson up about meeting him, and was there at the meeting too. He didn't feel comfortable going alone, so I went with. I had met Mr. Jackson a few times before. Well, not met him, but been there when he was around. He was never interested in being introduced to me because I am Black."

"Objection, Your Honor. Speculation, move to strike," Jeff said.

"Sustained. The last comment about Mr. Jackson's attitude toward the witness will be struck and disregarded by the jury."

"What happened when the two of you went to meet with Mr. Jackson?" Rachel asked, not skipping a beat.

"Maxwell asked for his blessing. Mr. Jackson said there was no way in hell that his daughter was going to marry a hoodlum like Maxwell. He said he should keep dreaming," Michael said quickly before another objection could be made. Jeff remained silent, clearly wanting the moment to pass as soon as possible. Rachel wanted the opposite, so she let that sit for a minute.

She read through her notes. There was nothing else she could say that wouldn't be objected to. Rachel decided this was a good spot to stop. "Nothing further from me." She went back and sat down.

Jeff walked up to the lectern. "Mr. Ellers, you say you and the defendant were best friends, correct?"

"Yes," Michael answered, short and sweet.

"You went with him to talk to Mr. Jackson because he was scared to go alone, right?"

"Yes, that is right."

"Would you have been afraid to go talk to Mr. Jackson alone?"

"I guess so," Michael admitted.

"But you went with because Mr. Williams was your best friend and he needed you?"

"Yes."

"Isn't it true that you would do anything for Mr. Williams?" Jeff asked.

"I wouldn't say anything, no."

"Were you with the defendant the day Amelia Jackson was murdered?"

"I was not."

"Did you talk with him at all that day?"

"No. I did not."

"You have no idea whether he was in Ms. Jackson's apartment that day, do you?" Jeff asked.

"I cannot definitely say one way or the other, no," Michael reluctantly agreed.

"You cannot say for sure that he did not commit the crimes that he is accused of, right?"

"I know he didn't do it. He loved her. He could never do those things to her," Michael argued.

"Objection, Your Honor: nonresponsive and speculative. Move to strike," Jeff said.

"The objection is sustained. The jury will disregard the last statement by the witness."

"You were not there the day Ms. Jackson was murdered, were you, Mr. Ellers?"

"No. I was not."

"Nothing further, Your Honor," Jeff said and made his way back to his seat. He had scored some points during his cross-examination. Jason had a pit in his stomach. He knew that the information that just came in would hurt their case. Jeff was right; Michael wasn't there, so he didn't know what had happened that day. Hopefully the fact that Maxwell had bought a ring and was going to propose, despite Mr. Jackson's protests, was enough to sway the jurors' minds.

"Redirect?" the judge inquired.

"No, Your Honor," Rachel said.

"Let's take our morning break. Be back in here and ready to go at quarter to eleven." The jurors left the courtroom. Then the attorneys left to go to their separate conference rooms to discuss the next steps in the case.

Rachel checked her phone and had no missed calls or texts. She opened her email app to see if she had anything there. She had to see if the people from her office had found Mr. Cabrera to serve him his subpoena. They had not.

CHAPTER THIRTY-THREE

Court resumed at 10:52 a.m., and the judge asked Rachel to call her next witness. Rachel stood, took a deep breath, and looked around the courtroom one last time. "The defense calls the defendant Maxwell Williams to the stand." There was a small commotion in the room. Everyone was back at full attention at the notion that the defendant in the case was about to testify.

Maxwell had not testified in his first trial. After all, the burden of proof did not fall on him; it was up to the State to prove guilt beyond a reasonable doubt.

When Rachel, Jason, and Maxwell had discussed the pros and cons of whether Maxwell should testify this time, it was ultimately decided that he would. As people tend to assume that someone who has charges brought against them is guilty, and jurors tend to assume guilt when defendants don't testify—despite being explicitly told not to—Maxwell would be better off speaking up for himself.

On the other hand, when defendants testify, the State gets the opportunity to bring up everything they have done in the past. There is often more leeway to ask questions that they wouldn't normally get away with. It is almost like defendants so rarely testify at their own trials that when they do, judges let prosecutors ask them anything. This was one of the cons the three had discussed and argued about at length. However, Maxwell did not have any criminal history that Jeff could hold against him. It was already part of the record that Maxwell and Amelia would get into fights and break up. There was no proof that those fights had ever turned physical, because they never had.

The most important factor in the decision was that it was ultimately up to the defendant whether to testify. A criminal defense lawyer is supposed to inform their client about the pros and cons, but let the defendant have the final say on whether they are going to testify or not. Maxwell was surprised to hear it when Rachel told him it was up to him. He explained that his first attorney, Mr. Duncan, had not explained it that way. He just told Maxwell it would not be smart for him to testify and didn't call him as a witness.

Maxwell decided he wanted to testify. It was worth the risk to him. He was the one who had been sitting behind bars for forty years for a crime that he didn't commit. He was convicted of brutally assaulting and killing the woman he loved more than anything in the world—the woman he was planning to propose to a few short months later, the woman he was going to spend the rest of his life with. He wanted the chance to tell his truth. He said that if they found him guilty again, he would be upset, but he could make peace with that decision, knowing that he had told his story.

He got up on the stand and did just that. He told the jury everything. Maxwell spent two hours going through the relationship that he and Amelia had. The love that he had for her. How he would have never wished her any harm. His testimony was riveting and had the jurors on the edge of their seats the entire time. They seemed to connect with him. It seemed like the jurors liked him and were believing what he was telling them.

"Mr. Williams," Rachel said, "were you at Amelia Jackson's home on March 23, 1982?"

"I was not," he answered loudly and confidently.

"When was the last time you were in Amelia's home?"

"I had been in her apartment a few days prior to that. We were studying for exams together. We usually studied at my apartment or the library, though. Casey and Jesus spent a lot of time at Amelia's apartment, and they sometimes listened to music loudly. It wasn't easy to study there," Maxwell explained. "It also got uncomfortable sometimes because Jesus liked to look at Amelia too much. It caused fights between him and Casey."

Rachel nodded, surprised that Jeff didn't object to any of that. She continued, "So you hadn't been to her apartment since that time a few days prior to her death?"

"No."

"You were not there the day she died?"

"No. I was not."

"Did you sexually assault Amelia Jackson?"

"Never!" Maxwell answered, sounding appalled by the question.

"Did you stab Amelia Jackson?"

"Of course not. I would never hurt Amelia. I loved her more than life itself." He began to cry. It started as a sole tear running down his face. After that, it was like someone had opened the door to all of the emotions that he had been feeling the last forty years. He was grieving over the loss of Amelia, the trauma from the first trial, and the tragedy of being wrongfully convicted. He was feeling all the hurt and anger from spending the last forty years in prison at once up there on that witness stand. He had a chance to tell his story. To tell his truth.

He cried on the stand for what felt like an eternity, though it was only a few minutes. Rachel asked that the witness be given a break. She looked, and a few of the jurors had been crying as well. They had clearly been moved by Maxwell's testimony. His direct examination had taken about three hours at that point. They had taken a break for lunch about an hour in. The judge released everyone for the afternoon break, giving them an extra five minutes, making it a twenty-minute break.

Rachel was thankful for the extra time. Not only would the jury have more time to think about the testimony and the emotion that they had just witnessed, but it gave Maxwell time to prepare for the cross-examination. Jeff was also happy about the extra time because it gave him additional time to prepare.

It took about five minutes into the break before Maxwell could pull himself back together. "How did I do?" he asked. "And be brutally honest."

"You did great," Jason assured him. "The jury loved you and were very moved by your testimony."

"Okay, good. Any word on if they found Jesus?" he asked hopefully.

Rachel looked at her phone. "No. They can't find him. It's like he disappeared after he was released from the subpoena. I am sure Jeff told him to go away for a few days so we couldn't find him."

"Can he do that?" Maxwell asked.

"Technically and legally, no, he can't. But that wouldn't stop him. There really isn't any penalty enforced against prosecutors who do that sort of thing. Plus, it's hard to get proof. Just like people are rarely charged with perjury for lying on the stand, witness tampering is rarely a problem in practice," Rachel explained.

"This system is so messed up!" Maxwell exclaimed. "No wonder people call it the unjust system."

Jason nodded his head in agreement and Rachel said, "You're not wrong there. There is so much wrong with our justice system. That's why I do what I do. To try and make some of those wrongs right."

"You really are amazing, Rachel," Maxwell said. "I thank you and Jason from the bottom of my heart. You are the first ones to really give a damn about me."

They finished their break and went back into the courtroom. Maxwell walked back up and sat on the stand. The jury was led back in and took their seats. "Mr. Williams, let me remind you that you are still under oath," the judge said as he looked down at Maxwell on the witness stand.

"Yes, Your Honor," Maxwell said as he looked back up at him.

"I just have one more question for you, Mr. Williams," Rachel said.

"Okay," Maxwell responded.

"Are you right- or left-handed?"

"I am left-handed," he said. Some of the jurors looked at each other and made notes on their pads.

Rachel smiled. "Nothing further, Your Honor."

Jeff started to gather his notes and walk up to the lectern. Maxwell straightened in his seat, ready for a fight.

"Mr. Williams," Jeff started, "Isn't it true that you fought with the victim the night before her death?"

"Yes."

"That fight got physical, didn't it?"

"No."

"No? People saw you get into a fight, didn't they? You heard their testimony earlier today, didn't you?"

"Objection, compound question," Rachel said.

"Sustained. Ask one question at a time, Mr. Malone," the judge warned.

"Sorry, Your Honor. Mr. Williams, people saw you get into a fight the night before Amelia was murdered, correct?" he tried again.

"Yes." Maxwell was doing a great job, sticking to answering how they had practiced. Witness Prep 101 says to always tell clients to stick to the answers "yes," "no," "I don't know," and "can you repeat the question," on cross-examination. That way, the other attorney can't trip them up and try to impeach their credibility.

"You heard a witness testifying earlier that they thought it might get physical, correct?"

"Yes."

Jeff was getting frustrated. "Yes, you heard their testimony, or yes it got physical?"

"Yes, I heard their testimony," Maxwell answered calmly.

"It also got physical, didn't it?"

"No. I don't believe they stated it ever got physical either, Mr. Malone," Maxwell answered. Rachel was about to stand to object, but Maxwell answered perfectly, so she let it go and sat back down in her seat.

"You saw Ms. Jackson after you went home that night, didn't you?" Jeff moved on.

"No."

"You never saw her again after she was dropped off that night?" Jeff asked, his voice portraying his disbelief at the answer.

"No. I did not," Maxwell answered, still staying calm.

Jeff went through the day that Amelia died for the next hour and tried to get Maxwell to admit that he was at her apartment that day. Jeff's patience was obviously wearing thin, and he was clearly upset that he was not getting anywhere with Maxwell. Maxwell, on the other hand, was staying cool, calm, and collected, probably contributing to Jeff's rising anger. Jeff paused for a moment and then decided to go another way.

"Mr. Williams, you and your friend both testified that you went to ask Mr. Jackson for his permission to marry Amelia, correct?"

"Yes."

"When he said no, it angered you, didn't it?"

"I guess so, yes. But I wasn't expecting him to give his blessing."

"You were never going to get his approval, were you?"

"No, I don't think so," Maxwell admitted.

"Mr. Jackson told you that, didn't he?"

"Yes."

"He told you that nobody like *you* was ever going to end up with his daughter." Jeff put emphasis on the word "you." He was trying to get under Maxwell's skin. Rachel wanted to object, but there was nothing she could object to yet. This was all in line with what the other witnesses had testified to.

"He said that, yes," Maxwell said. His temper was beginning to rise a little. Rachel could see it on Maxwell's face as his cheeks reddened.

Jeff had obviously struck a nerve, and it appeared he noticed it. He kept going. "You were never going to be good enough for Amelia, were you?"

"I was good enough," Maxwell shot back.

"Mr. Jackson didn't think you were, though, did he?" Jeff asked.

"No, he did not," Maxwell said through gritted teeth.

"Mr. Jackson didn't think that you would ever amount to anything, right?"

"He said that."

"Amelia started to think that as well, didn't she?"

Maxwell looked up at him, a look of shock on his face. "No. She didn't think that."

"Are you sure about that? The two of you broke up the night before she died. Isn't it because she had finally come to her senses and was taking her father's advice?"

"No! That's not true at all. She didn't care what her dad had to say." Maxwell was almost yelling now. Rachel tried to get his attention to try and calm him down, but his eyes were locked on to Jeff.

"That's not true, though, is it? Amelia was very close with her father, wasn't she?"

"Yes," Maxwell admitted.

"The only thing that they fought about was you, wasn't it?"

"I believe so, yes," Maxwell admitted, his teeth clenched again.

"You two were broken up when she died; you weren't going to propose while you were broken up, were you?" Jeff asked.

"I mean, I was going to ask eventually. I had the ring."

"You had the ring, but the two of you were broken up. Her dad had not given his blessing." Jeff started to pace back and forth, talking more to the jury than to Maxwell. "You weren't going to propose anytime soon. Isn't it true that if you couldn't have Amelia, you didn't want anyone to have her?" he finally asked.

"What do you mean?" Maxwell asked.

"You didn't want Amelia to be with anyone else, right?"

"No. Why would I? I loved her."

Rachel saw where this was going. This cross-examination was going south quickly. She had to find something to object to.

"Exactly. You didn't want her with anyone else, so you made sure that she couldn't be."

Rachel shot up. "Objection, Your Honor. Speculation, argumentative, assumes facts not in evidence."

"Sustained," the judge said, his voice rising slightly. Jeff paused and looked over his notes. He decided that was the best he was going to get, and he had planted enough seeds for his closing. He looked up. "Nothing further for this witness." He made his way back to his seat and smiled at Mia as she gave him a thumbs up, presumably a sign that they had made progress on their cross of Mr. Williams.

"Ms. Nix?" the judge said as he looked at his watch. "How long do you predict your redirect will be?"

"Maybe a half hour, Your Honor," Rachel answered, as she walked up to the lectern to begin.

"Very well. Please continue."

"Mr. Williams," she began, "Mr. Malone is trying to imply that you wanted Amelia dead if she wasn't with you. Was that the case?"

"Of course not," Maxwell said with confidence, his voice calmer now. "I loved her more than anything."

"Did you go to her apartment that day?"

"No. I hadn't been there in a few days," he reiterated.

"Did you ever sexually assault Amelia Jackson?"

"No. Never."

"Was there ever any time that you physically assaulted Amelia Jackson?" Rachel asked, leading him through the charges against him.

"No. I would never lay a hand on a woman in that way."

"Was it common for you and Amelia to break up when you would fight?" Rachel asked.

"Unfortunately, yes. We would fight, mostly about her father, then we would break up. The next day, or a few days later, we would get back together, and it would be like nothing had ever happened," he explained.

"The day before she died, when you broke up, did you have any doubt that the two of you would reconcile like you always did?"

"No. Not at all. I knew it was just another fight."

"Was Mr. Jackson's decision not to give his blessing going to stop you from proposing to Amelia?"

"No," Maxwell said, looking at the jury. "Nothing was going to stop me from proposing to her."

Rachel looked back to Jason to see if he thought she should ask anything else, or just leave it at that. Jason shook his head, indicating he didn't have anything else.

"Nothing further, Your Honor," Rachel said, and she walked back to her seat. Jeff stated that he had no more questions for Maxwell, and he was released from the stand.

Maxwell walked back to take his seat between Rachel and Jason. The jury watched him take each step. Maxwell had seemingly done well on the stand. Yes, Jeff got under his skin, and he had gotten angry, but Rachel had made things okay again with the redirect. Or at least she thought she had.

"All right, everyone. It is about time to wrap up for the day," the judge said. He then gave the same speech he had given every day since the trial started. He continued, "Be back here at 8:15

tomorrow morning. I believe it should be the last day of trial. You are dismissed."

Everyone stood as the jurors filed out of the courtroom. The attorneys, court staff, and spectators all sat back down. "Ms. Nix, do you have any other witnesses?" the judge asked.

"No, Your Honor. The defense will rest in the morning." she said.

"Good. Any rebuttal witnesses, Mr. Malone?"

Jeff looked back at Mia, and said, "One moment, judge." He scooted back, and the two of them were whispering back and forth. Jeff scooted his chair back up to the table again. "Your Honor, we may have a rebuttal witness. We need to discuss it further."

"Okay. That's fine. Let's be prepared to get closing statements done with tomorrow if possible. I want to get the case to the jury." He looked at his watch again. "It's 4:15 p.m., so we have a little time. Let's go over jury instructions today." To the clerk he said, "Did you send a copy of the additional jury instructions to the attorneys?"

"Yes, Your Honor," she answered.

The spectators all cleared out as the judge and attorneys spent the next hour going over and fine-tuning the jury instructions. This was a very important, albeit boring, part of trials. These instructions were going back to the jury's deliberation room with them, and they would be reading them over and over again. It was their job to figure out if Mr. Williams had committed the crimes he was charged with. Every single word was important.

The judge dismissed the group for the night. Rachel and Jason ate with Maxwell at the jail, and then went over the people Jeff might call on tomorrow. They could not come up with anyone plausible, so they didn't spend too much time on that. They spent another hour going over their closing argument and what Maxwell should expect over the next few days. Jason and Rachel said their goodbyes to Maxwell and headed back to Rachel's apartment. They spent three more hours going over the closing. They practiced and tweaked it a few times before they came up with the final draft. Rachel was confident that they were going to get a "not guilty" verdict for Maxwell Williams.

CHAPTER THIRTY-FOUR

"The defense rests, Your Honor," Rachel said the next morning. The defense had again had no luck finding Jesus Cabrera.

"Any rebuttal, Mr. Malone?" the judge asked, and all eyes were on Jeff.

Jeff looked down at his notes and then back at Mia. The suspense was in the air, and Rachel figured he was doing it for effect. Jeff looked back at the judge. "No, Your Honor. We have no need for any rebuttal witnesses."

Rachel had to work to refrain from rolling her eyes. Jeff said it in an arrogant way that tried to show the jury he was confident in his case. He wanted to indicate to them that he had already proved his case, and there was no reason that he would need to call any rebuttal witnesses.

The judge then directed his attention to the jury. "Members of the jury. All the evidence has now been presented to you. The next step is for the attorneys to give their closing arguments. The State will go first, because they have the burden of proof. After that, the defense will give their closing. Mr. Malone will have the chance to give a responsive closing. After that, we will read through the charges and jury instructions. You will then go to the jury room to deliberate your verdicts." The judge looked down to make sure he hadn't missed anything. "Mr. Malone, are you ready to proceed with closing arguments?"

"Yes." Jeff grabbed his notes and went to the lectern. Mia got a slideshow up on the projector screen. Jeff spent the first hour of his closing going through each of the crimes Maxwell was charged with. He went through each element one by one, arguing that they combined to prove his guilt beyond a reasonable doubt.

Rachel had seen prosecutors do their closings like this many times. While she understood that they had to show that they had proved the elements of the case, she always thought that there was a better way to do it. The jurors were clearly bored and falling asleep. They knew the facts; they'd sat through days of trial. Jeff didn't need to spend as much time as he did reiterating each and every fact every time he went over a new charge.

He was getting toward his closing being two hours long, when he finally started to wrap it up. "The defendant knew that Amelia Jackson's father would never approve of him. He would never approve of them getting married. Mr. Jackson had told the defendant that he was not good enough, that he would never be good enough. Amelia and the defendant often fought about Mr. Jackson and the fact that he didn't approve of their relationship. You all heard the testimony. Amelia was close with her father and cared what he thought. It's plausible that she finally listened to him and had ended her relationship with the defendant for good. This is how he responded.

"Again, Amelia and her dad were close. Even if the defendant were going to propose - not a given, since they were broken up at the time of her death—do you really think that a young woman who was a daddy's girl, who looked up to her father and would do anything to get his approval, would marry a man her father didn't approve of?

"The answer is simple. No, she wouldn't do that. Amelia would never do anything that would permanently destroy the relationship between her and her father. Mr. Jackson testified that he and Amelia had talked about it, and she had promised him that they would never get married. Now, the defendant says that couldn't be true. But he wasn't there when the conversation happened. He didn't know the extent of the close relationship between Amelia and her father. He rarely saw them together, because frankly, he wasn't allowed to.

"The defendant knew that Amelia would never be able to marry him *and* keep a close relationship with her father. He knew that, even if he did propose, she was never going to say yes. He said it himself: If he couldn't have her, he didn't want anyone else to. Maxwell Williams knew that he was going to lose Amelia, that he wasn't going to have her anymore. They had a bad fight the night before her death. Witnesses described it as one of the worst fights they had witnessed between the two. They broke up and went their separate ways.

"The defendant called Amelia multiple times the next day and thought she was ignoring him. That angered him, so he went over to her apartment. He knocked on the door, and she let him in. They continued their fight from the night before. Amelia told him that she wasn't going to get back together with him and that they were done for good. He couldn't handle that. If he couldn't have her, nobody could.

"The defendant pushed her down onto the bed." Jeff paused, and Mia put the picture of Amelia's dead and bloodied body up on the projection screen. The jurors noticeably flinched at seeing the graphic image again. "He pushed her down on her bed and he raped her. The defendant knew that he was never going to get to have sex with her again, so he took what he wanted.

"After who knows how long, he grabbed a knife from the kitchen and stabbed her. Maxwell Williams stabbed Amelia Jackson once, twice, sixteen times." Jeff made a stabbing motion as he counted each and every stab wound. Mia put the autopsy photo up on the screen, which clearly showed each stab wound. "One of those stabs took Amelia's life that day. The medical examiner testified that she would have died at some point during the attack. The defendant stabbed her after she was already dead. He continued to stab her. If he couldn't have her, nobody else could.

"Amelia Jackson was likely scared beyond belief that day. She had no idea when she let the defendant into her apartment that he was going to brutally attack and murder her in cold blood. She had to look into the eyes of the man who was supposed to love her as he raped her and stabbed her so many times that she bled out in minutes. She had to have been so afraid. Did she call out for her father?

"Members of the jury, please don't let Maxwell Williams get away with his crime. Let Amelia's family know that their daughter's tragedy will continue to be avenged. Let them know that her life meant something. Show Mr. Williams that what he did was wrong and that he deserves to be in prison. The State asks that you find Maxwell Williams guilty beyond a reasonable doubt of the crimes that he is charged with." Jeff paused. "Thank you." He walked back to his seat.

Rachel had to admit that Jeff had given a very good closing argument. It was one of the better ones she had heard. She had a little knot in her stomach as she walked up for her closing. She took a deep breath and clasped her hands in front of her.

Rachel began, "I want to start off by thanking each one of you for being here for this trial. You have a very important job. You are the only ones who can do the right thing and find Maxwell Williams not guilty. You are the only ones who can end this hell that he has been living for the last forty years. You can fix the mistakes that the jurors in the first trial made. You have sat through the evidence, and you know the truth.

"The truth is Maxwell Williams was charged for crimes that he didn't commit. He was charged because he was the boyfriend of the woman who had died. He was charged because Amelia Jackson's father did not like him. He was charged because he was a Black man and Amelia was a white woman. They were not supposed to be together, so he was the easy suspect. It's as simple as that. Maxwell Williams wasn't charged because there was so much evidence against him that it was clear he committed the crimes. He was charged because Mr. Jackson, Amelia's father, was a powerful man in politics at the time of her death. He used that influence to steer the investigation of his daughter's death."

Rachel made sure to use Maxwell's full name as often as possible to make the jurors see him as a person. It was a tip that she had learned in a defense attorneys' seminar. The more you use the defendant's full name, the more the jurors see them as a human being, someone who exists apart from the charges against them. If jurors see the defendant in that light, they are more likely to have trouble finding them guilty.

"Mr. Jackson told the police to focus only on Mr. Williams. Because of his influence, the police stopped looking at all the other suspects they had. They stopped looking at people the investigating officer thought were more likely suspects. Detective Swenson testified that he did not feel good about having to solely focus on Maxwell Williams, because he didn't think it added up. You also heard him testify about confirmation bias and how the police could have made the facts fit a scenario where Maxwell was guilty.

"Two of the other suspects in this case were Jesus Cabrera and his now-wife Casey Cabrera. The two of them were just dating at the time. Casey was Amelia's roommate. You heard some testimony that suggests that the relationship between Amelia and Casey had gotten rocky. They weren't as close as they once were.

"Now, we didn't hear from Jesus Cabrera, who was allegedly one of the people who found Amelia Jackson that day, but we did hear from Casey. Casey testified originally that the day Amelia died was the worst day of her life and she will never forget it. However, when she was being questioned in cross-examination, she suddenly could not remember it anymore. She couldn't recollect simple facts about things that happened that day.

"Yes, it was more than forty years ago, but she had stated that she remembered that day clearly. When she was confronted with the hard facts, she faltered, and was unable to answer the questions posed to her. Are any of you asking why that is? I can tell you what I think happened. The evidence in this case show that the police should have followed up on Jesus and Casey as suspects, instead of focusing solely on Maxwell Williams.

"The evidence does not support a scenario where Maxwell Williams committed these crimes. What the facts do support is that Casey and Jesus Cabrera killed Amelia Jackson." Some of the jurors looked at each other with surprised expressions. There was movement in the gallery where the spectators were sitting. Rachel turned to see what the sound was. Casey Cabrera had stood up and was leaving the courtroom. Her fists were balled up, and she was crying loudly. Rachel had made sure she was there before she started her closing. She was hoping to get this kind of reaction from Casey.

Once Casey had left the courtroom and a few of the jurors had noticed her exit, Rachel looked at the jurors. They looked back at her. She kept going with her closing. "Casey Cabrera's recollection of the timeline for that day is a cause for concern. Her own testimony puts her and Jesus in the apartment at the time that Amelia was killed. Not only that, but her story doesn't make sense.

"Casey testified that the front door was open, so Jesus walked in before she did. She testified that right when they walked in, they saw Amelia's body, and she screamed. None of that is possible." Rachel looked back, and Jason put the exhibit with the layout of the apartment up on the screen. "Casey Cabrera wants you to believe that they walked into this apartment, and she was behind Jesus. Jesus was trying to shield her from whatever was inside. He was shielding her from seeing anything. Lie number one," she said as she put up one finger.

"Lie number two," she continued. "Casey said that they walked in and immediately saw the blood. There was no blood anywhere but in Amelia's room. Look at how the apartment is set up. There is no possible way for Casey and Jesus to have seen any blood from the entrance of the apartment. There is no way that they would see Amelia on the bed." Jason put up the picture of Amelia's bed, the one without her body. "Amelia's bed was up against the wall. There was no way to see it unless you were in the room. Casey is trying to make you believe that she not only saw Amelia and the blood while standing behind Jesus, but also from the entryway of the apartment. That just is not possible.

"The fingerprints," Rachel continued. "If you look at the fingerprint evidence, that negates the story that Casey told as well. The crime scene investigator testified that Amelia had just cleaned the whole house with bleach and done a pretty good job. The only plausible way that Casey's and Jesus's fingerprints could have been in that apartment was if they had been put there after they got back to the apartment that afternoon. If Casey and Jesus had just walked in and found Amelia, why would their fingerprints be where they were?

"Why were Jesus's fingerprints on the fridge handle, the counter, and in Amelia's room? Why were Casey's fingerprints in Amelia's room? It doesn't make sense. That is because Casey's story is not what happened. If they walked in and saw Amelia right away, which we know is not physically possible, why would their fingerprints be on the doorknob? The door would have been open. Casey testified, once her memory had apparently returned, that the door was open. There was no reason to touch the doorknob or to push the door open. More importantly, why were Mr. William's prints nowhere to be found in the apartment. If he was the one that killed Amelia, he would have left at least a few fingerprints. But there were none, keep that in mind while you deliberate.

"Casey Cabrera's whole story does not make sense. She is lying to you about everything, and that has shown throughout her testimony. First, she can't forget that day, then when confronted, she can no longer remember anything. Second, she has been caught in many lies. Third, her story cannot be true. She cannot see through walls; she cannot see through her now-husband. It's also likely not a coincidence that Casey and Jesus are now married. They had to stay together to make sure that neither of them would ever tell the truth.

"Oh, and don't forget that the medical examiner testified that whoever hit Amelia was right-handed. Who is right-handed in this case? Casey Cabrera. Maxwell Williams, on the other hand, is left-handed. Based on the evidence, Maxwell Williams is not the one who struck Amelia. By the State's logic, then, someone else hit Amelia, but Maxwell then came in and raped and killed her. But wait, that doesn't make sense either. The DNA found on Amelia did not belong to Maxwell either. There was no evidence linking Maxwell to the apartment that day because he hadn't been there in a few days, and Amelia had just finished cleaning the apartment with bleach. You heard that from the maintenance man.

"The truth is that Casey and Jesus Cabrera killed Amelia Jackson on March 23, 1982. Casey was always jealous of Amelia. She was more attractive, smarter, had more friends. Her family had money, and she was in a loving relationship with Maxwell Williams. When Casey and Jesus got home that day, Amelia and Casey got into a fight. Amelia and Casey also argued a lot, just like Amelia and Maxwell. Amelia was still upset from the night before and her fight with Maxwell. She took that anger out on Casey. They fought, and Casey snapped. They were yelling at each other. Amelia ended up walking into her room. Casey followed her in there."

Even though Rachel didn't agree 100 percent with this argument, it was the only one she could make based on the evidence that actually came in during the trial. She continued, "When they got into Amelia's room, Casey hit Amelia in the head, and she fell on her bed. Jesus walked into the bedroom to see what was going on, and he saw Amelia lying on the bed. She was unconscious. The two of them didn't know what to do. They were panicking. They came up with a plan to pin it on Maxwell."

Jeff finally stood up. "Your Honor, there is nothing in the facts to support this notion. This is all just something that Ms. Nix is coming up with to distract attention from her client. I know I am not supposed to object to a closing, but this has gotten out of hand. I ask that any mention of this story about a fight between Casey and Amelia be stricken from the record."

The judge thought for a moment and finally decided. "Sustained. The jury will disregard everything that has been said about a fight between Ms. Jackson and Mrs. Cabrera, as well as any interaction between Ms. Jackson and Mr. Cabrera."

He then looked to Rachel. "Ms. Nix. You cannot discuss facts that are not in evidence."

Rachel nodded. She knew this was going to happen. They had been counting on Jesus Cabrera testifying, and getting the raw materials of this theory in during his cross-examination. As this had not happened, she had been hoping that she could get some of the information in before Jeff objected. He had allowed her to get further than she had expected. Even though the jurors were instructed to disregard her ideas, hopefully her words had done enough to convince them that Casey and Jesus had something to do with the crime.

Rachel continued, "The version of the facts that the State would like you to believe is just one of many scenarios that could have happened. There are so many different scenarios that are more plausible—one of them is the truth. We will never know what the truth is because Amelia's father used his influence and power to direct the investigation to look only at Maxwell Williams. Little did Mr. Jackson know that in pointing the officers to Mr. Williams, he was letting his daughter's real attacker or attackers go free. Mr. Jackson's disapproval of my client clouded not only his judgment, but his ability to see the real truth behind Amelia's death.

"Mr. Jackson hated my client. There is no doubt about that. You could clearly see the hatred during his testimony. He took that hatred and disgust and did everything he could to make sure that Maxwell Williams went to prison for a crime that he didn't commit." Rachel had been hoping to add that his influence had also led the prosecutor to keep evidence from the defense attorney in the first case. Unfortunately, the judge had ruled that information inadmissible during a motion in limine. A motion in limine is a request heard by the judge prior to the trial whereby the attorneys argue about what evidence can and cannot come in at the trial. Rachel was prevented from mentioning this particular fact to the jury.

"A few hours into the investigation, the police were handed a suspect. The suspect was the victim's boyfriend. It is common that when someone is murdered, their significant other is the suspect. They are often the first ones questioned. Despite having other suspects who were more likely to have done it, the officers were directed to look only at Mr. Williams. From that point on, they made sure that the evidence fit the predetermined narrative that Maxwell Williams had committed the crimes.

"In 1982, there was no reason to bring DNA into the trial since such evidence would not be admissible. But they collected the DNA evidence anyway, and it is a great thing that they did. That evidence sat in the police evidence room for forty years. Luckily, science has advanced by leaps and bounds, and now we can test it. The DNA in this case was tested. You heard the testimony. The DNA on Amelia Jackson did not belong to Maxwell Williams.

"What does that tell us? That tells us that Maxwell Williams was not the one who assaulted and killed Amelia Jackson. If he had been, his DNA would have matched. There has been no other testimony about who the DNA could belong to. Amelia Jackson had other males in her life. Jesus Cabrera was one of those men. Would the DNA on Amelia match his?" Rachel kept her wording broad enough that there was nothing for Jeff to object to. "All we know for a fact is that the DNA does not match Maxwell Williams 's, and therefore Maxwell Williams did not do this."

Rachel paused to take a breath. She was getting toward the end of her closing. "It is simple. The State has not gotten anywhere close to proving their burden. They have not proved beyond a reasonable doubt that Maxwell Williams committed the crimes he is accused of. They cannot prove it, because he did not do it.

"Maxwell Williams is here today asking that you find him not guilty of the charges against him, and set him free from this nightmare that he has been living these past forty years. Correct the wrong decision that the jury made so long ago. Give Maxwell Williams his life back. We owe him that much." Rachel paused to let that last part sink in, trying to make eye contact with each juror individually. "Thank you," she said. She walked back to her seat and sat down next to Maxwell. Jason put an arm on Maxwell's arm in a supportive manner, and Rachel put her hand on Jason's.

Jeff made his final argument, and the judge spent an hour going through the elements of the crimes and the final jury instructions. Once that was completed, the jury was officially sent to deliberate. They were charged with the task of determining whether Maxwell Williams would be sent back to prison, or would go home a free man.

CHAPTER THIRTY-FIVE

Three days later, the jury was finally back—three long days of waiting, pacing, worrying, and thinking of every single thing that could have been done differently. They were all back in the courtroom waiting to hear the results.

"In the matter of *State of Minnesota v. Maxwell James Williams*, Count I, burglary in the first degree, we, the jury, find the defendant not guilty."

There was a big sigh of relief from everyone at the defense table. They thought this was a good sign. If Maxwell had been found innocent of this charge, that made it more likely he would be found innocent of the others as well.

Rachel grabbed Maxwell's hand and squeezed it. She gave Jason a hopeful look.

The court reporter went on, "In the matter of *State of Minnesota v. Maxwell James Williams*, Count II, sexual assault in the first degree, we, the jury, find the defendant not guilty."

Another big sigh of relief from the defense table. It was as though each and every not guilty verdict would take more of the pressure off their shoulders. Maxwell was finally feeling hopeful for the first time in forty years. He couldn't believe it; had they actually done it? Had they convinced the jury that Maxwell had not done the horrible things that he was accused of, that he didn't kill the love of his life? He had spent forty years sitting in a prison cell, eating food that was barely edible, sleeping on a cot that was thinner than a sleeping bag, and only being allowed outside for a few hours each day. Was his nightmare finally coming to an end?

"In the matter of *State of Minnesota v. Maxwell James Williams*, Count III, murder in the first degree, we, the jury, find the defendant not guilty." The three people at the defense table had to keep themselves from celebrating. They had won on the first three charges, the original charges that had been brought against Maxwell. Rachel was already starting to think about all that Maxwell would do when he went home that day. All that was left was to get a not guilty verdict on the amended charge, for murder in the second degree. The jury had found him not guilty of the higher-level crimes already; there was no doubt that it was going to be a not guilty verdict across the board.

Jeff must have been thinking the same thing, as he started to gather his things together. He had a grim look on his face. There were already murmurs in the gallery after the first two verdicts were read. After the third not guilty verdict was read, there was a commotion behind the prosecution's table. Cordwell Jackson and his wife were yelling and getting up out of their seats.

"This is outrageous! That man killed our daughter. How can you be so blind?" Mr. Jackson said. He attempted to come through the swinging doors, looking as though he intended to attack Maxwell. The bailiff went running to the swinging doors to grab him before he could come any farther.

"Order! Order in the court!" the judge bellowed, his voice echoing through the courtroom pandemonium. There were photographers from a few of the newspapers taking pictures of what was happening. "Get him out of here," the judge directed the bailiff, who was now holding Mr. Jackson by the arms. He led him out of the courtroom, which made his wife cry even louder.

"Mrs. Jackson, you are welcome to stay for the remainder of the verdict reading, but you must control your emotions. If there is another outburst, you will be taken out of the courtroom like your husband. Do you understand?" the judge said.

Mrs. Jackson sat back down in her seat and nodded solemnly. She had to be in the courtroom for the reading of the last verdict, even if she thought it was going to be another not guilty verdict. She owed that to her daughter. She needed to be there for the last part of this unbearable tragedy.

The disbelieving jurors had all reacted to the Jacksons' outburst in different ways. Some of them had stood and headed toward the jury door out of the courtroom, looking for safety. Some of them had sat still, watching everything play out. There were a few who had crouched on the ground as if there were going to be gunshots. It was like something that normally only happened on television. Outbursts like this didn't usually happen in real life. Jason knew that much. It was like a real-life version of *Law & Order* playing out in front of him. This was the kind of drama that originally drew Jason to criminal law. He couldn't believe what was going on around him. He was in a sort of haze as it all happened.

Rachel was just as shocked. She was used to criminal trials and the drama that came along with them. She had never seen anything like this happen. Sure, the victims' families were always upset when there was a not guilty verdict, but she had never had a family member try and come right through the swinging doors. Her heart was racing. This had started when the not guilty verdicts were being read, and had intensified when the commotion broke out behind her. After Mr. Jackson was taken from the courtroom, she started to calm herself, and her heart rate slowly went back to normal.

After everything settled down and the courtroom was quiet again, the judge said, "Can the defendant and the attorneys please rise again?" They all complied. Then he asked the court reporter, "Will you please read the last verdict?"

It seemed like just a formality at this point. Everyone expected the last verdict to follow the pattern set by the first three and come back as not guilty. Most people in the courtroom weren't even listening anymore; as the reporters were finishing up making notes and packing up. The other spectators in the gallery were starting to grab bags and purses to leave the courtroom.

The jurors, on the other hand, were all seated quietly, waiting for the last verdict to be read. The court reporter said, "In the case *State of Minnesota v. Maxwell James Williams*, Count IV, murder in the second degree, we, the jury, find the defendant guilty."

The courtroom was in a collective state of shock. Nobody was sure that they had heard right. Had she really just said "guilty?" There had to be some mistake. Mrs. Jackson began to sob loudly in the gallery. She could be heard saying, "Thank God," over and over again as she sobbed. The reporters were taking their notepads back out and scribbling more notes. The photographers were taking pictures of the jury, the defendant, his attorneys, and the prosecutor.

Maxwell Williams fell back into his seat and his head fell into his hands. Just minutes ago, he thought he was going to get his life back. He thought the nightmare was over. There was finally hope that people would see the truth and let him go home. He couldn't comprehend what had just happened. There were so many questions running through his mind. Rachel and Jason had assured him that if the first verdict said not guilty, that likely meant the rest of the verdicts would follow suit. They were the professionals. How could they have been so wrong?

Rachel heard the guilty verdict, and all of the air left her lungs. She had to put her hand on the defense table to catch herself from falling. She was weak in the knees and suddenly felt dizzy. None of this made any sense. Legally, it didn't make any sense. How could they find him not guilty of the burglary, sexual assault, and murder in the first degree, and then find him guilty of murder in the second degree? They hadn't presented a defense to account for murder in the second degree. The only reason that had even been added as a charge was because of the mistake that Jeff had made in his opening statement. The facts that the jury had determined made Maxwell not guilty of the first three crimes were the same facts that somehow got them to a guilty verdict for the fourth. It didn't make sense. How could this happen?

Jason knew enough about criminal law to know that the verdict wasn't right. He couldn't fully understand what was going on or how the jury could have reached such a conclusion. Jason knew that jurors didn't always know the ins and outs of the law or how their verdicts should work. But he had thought that in this case the jury would at least know that the facts didn't support Maxwell's guilt. What was going on?

Everyone's thoughts were running through their heads at a million miles a minute. The judge finally said, "Would the attorneys like to poll the jury?" He was asking if the attorneys wanted each juror polled to make sure that this was their decision and that they all agreed unanimously. All Rachel could do was nod her head. The judge went through the jurors and asked each if this was their verdict. They all answered in the affirmative.

He went on, "The court thanks you all for your service. Our justice system would not work without each and every one of you and the work that you have done here. We thank you for your sacrifice in taking time away from your families and jobs to be here. We thank you for your hard work and determination in coming to a unanimous decision on this matter. You are now free to talk to your families and friends about the case and what you have heard. You can also do your own research on things; all the previous restrictions on you are now removed.

"I told you before that the attorneys could not talk to you. At this stage, the attorneys, their staff, the press, and any other person can ask you about the decision that was made, and how you got to that decision. You are not required to talk with anyone or answer any questions, but if you wish to do so, you may. Again, the court thanks you for your service, and you are free to go."

The jurors started to get up to leave. The judge waited until they were all gone, then said, "I would like the attorneys back in here in a half hour to set a sentencing date."

Jason and Rachel collected themselves and went to see if any of the jurors would talk to them. They told Maxwell to stay where he was, which wasn't hard, since he was still in a state of shock and confusion.

CHAPTER THIRTY-SIX

Jason and Rachel caught a few of the jurors as they were leaving. Most of them declined to talk with them but gave them a sad shrug as they walked by. They finally found one juror who was willing to talk. The only explanation he could give was that they had no other person to point to definitively, and the first jury had found Maxwell guilty. He said that it made sense that Jesus or Casey could have done it, but they hadn't heard any reason why that would be the case. If only they could have found Jesus Cabrera to testify, Rachel would have been able to ask him her questions to get the information out of him. Or, if she had known Jesus wasn't going to testify, she could have tried to get more information from Casey.

Rachel and Jason thanked the juror for his time, and he apologized as he left. Rachel looked like she was about to cry. She had lost trials before, but nothing like this had ever happened. Not only was her client innocent, but they had convicted him without the evidence being there. Worse, they had convicted him of something that was only in the jury instructions because of her. What the juror had just described didn't come close to the State's having proved their case beyond a reasonable doubt. They were still holding Maxwell's prior wrongful conviction against him. This system was so unjust. She couldn't believe it. How could she have devoted her life to something that was so unfair? Was this her fault? Had she put too much emphasis on the fact that her client was wrongfully convicted in the past? So many things were running through her mind.

Jason hugged her and said, "We should go back in there. Maxwell needs us right now." They returned to the courtroom and went over to Maxwell, who was still sitting at the defense table with his head in his hands. They all headed into a conference room. Maxwell was clearly upset and had been crying. His eyes were puffy and red.

Jason shut the door behind them, and they all sat down at the conference table. "How?" was all that Maxwell could say, as he fell into a chair.

Rachel took a deep breath. "I honestly don't know, Maxwell. I don't understand what happened."

Jason took the lead when Rachel paused. "We talked to a juror, and he basically said that because the first jury convicted you, and there was no solid proof that another person did it, they had to convict you of something. It doesn't make any sense, and legally that is not how it is supposed to work. Like we talked about, if it was not guilty for the burglary, it should have been not guilty for the rest of the crimes."

"How could they do this to me again?" Maxwell asked. "I didn't do this," he said with conviction. "I didn't kill Amelia."

"We know you didn't," Jason said. "The jury messed up . . . again."

Rachel had gotten over the shock now, and said, "Maxwell, what they did is appealable. The fact that they found you guilty of the defense to the highest charged crime, when we didn't even bring that defense, is an appealable factor."

Maxwell sighed and his shoulders slumped. "My fate is left up to the court of appeals again? I have been down this road many times. Don't you know how many times I got my hopes up that other judges would see the truth and do the right thing?" He paused and wiped a tear off his face. "I don't know if I can do that again. I can't keep getting my hopes up for them to just be shattered again."

Rachel felt the tears welling up in her own eyes. She choked them back and tried to say something, but her voice was shaky. She waited a minute more to calm down. She had seen clients upset when they lost, but this feeling was new.

Maxwell finally asked, "So what's next? We get the sentencing date, and I go back and sit in a damn cell again?"

Jason looked to Rachel, not wanting to be the one to answer that question. All Rachel could do was nod. Just then, the bailiff came and knocked on the door. Jason thought he looked a little grim now as well. The three of them made their way back into the courtroom and sat at the defense table.

"We are back on the record," the judge stated. "Madam Court Clerk, can we please get a sentencing date as soon as possible?" he asked.

There were a few minutes of silence as the clerk looked for an available date. "I have moved a few things around, Your Honor. We can do it in ten days at 8:00 a.m."

"Very well. I will see everyone back here in ten days at 8:00 a.m. sharp. I want the attorneys to hold off on filing any motions before then. I have some things to think about and research to do, and I want to do all of that before reading any motions."

Rachel looked confused. She wasn't sure what the judge was getting at. She pushed that thought aside and continued listening.

"Does anyone have anything else to put on the record at this time?" the judge asked.

"No, Your Honor," Rachel said, almost whispering.

"No, judge," Jeff said.

"Then we are adjourned for today. Bailiff, can you please take Mr. Williams back into custody? But keep him in the jail until sentencing. There is no reason to send him back to prison and then have him brought back in a few days."

The bailiff looked surprised, but nodded. This was something else that normally didn't happen, but the judge's reasoning seemed to make sense.

The bailiff came to take Maxwell away, and Rachel said, "We will come visit you once you are settled back in the jail."

Maxwell looked at her with sadness in his eyes. "Don't bother for tonight. I need some time to be alone. You can come in a few days if you like."

Rachel felt like a knife was just plunged into her heart. She had failed Maxwell, and he knew it. It was all over his face, in his voice, and in his request that she not come for a few days. How could this happen? "I understand," she finally said as they were taking him away. Rachel fell back into her seat, and Jason put a hand on her shoulder, not sure what else to do or say.

The judge and his staff left the courtroom, and Jeff and Mia packed up their things. Jeff walked over and tried to shake Jason's hand, saying, "Better luck next time."

Jason just looked at his hand and didn't say anything. Jeff shrugged and walked out, with Mia in tow behind him. Rachel continued to sit there, her mind racing. Jason just stood there and let her have a minute. The bailiff finally came over and told them that they had to get going because he needed to lock the courtroom. They packed their things and walked out to the car in silence. The silence continued the whole way to Rachel's apartment.

Once they pulled in, Jason decided he was going up with her even if she protested. To his surprise, she didn't. They walked into the apartment, and Rachel broke down. It was like the floodgates had opened and there was nothing that she could do to stop them. Jason just hugged her and let her get it all out for the next ten minutes. He knew there was nothing to say. He still didn't understand the ins and outs of what had just happened. He hated to admit it, but he found himself asking himself if this was Rachel's fault for arguing to get the jury instruction added, or for not subpoenaing Jesus Cabrera herself. He hadn't known better himself; it would never have occurred to him to advise Rachel to subpoena Jesus or leave the jury instruction out. Not that Rachel had talked it over with him before making the instruction argument.

Jason hated questioning Rachel and her abilities as a defense attorney, but he was concerned that she might have made some mistakes. Despite his thoughts on it, he still needed to be there to comfort and reassure her. Rachel finally stopped crying. She wiped her nose on the sleeve of her suit jacket. "This is all my fault," she said.

"No. No, it isn't. You did the best you could. You heard that juror. It wasn't anything we did; it wasn't even the evidence in the case. It was solely because of the first conviction. We couldn't change that fact."

"I shouldn't have argued to get the jury instruction put in for the crime of passion. It was just a quick, on-my-feet decision. It quite possibly is what led to this conviction. If I hadn't asked for that to be included, would they have convicted him at all?"

"Well, let's think about it. Based on what the juror said, it seems like they were going to convict him of something, no matter what. Look at it this way—maybe you saved him from being convicted of a higher-level crime."

Rachel thought about this for a minute. That did make sense. They would never know now, though. If the jurors didn't see the evidence there for the burglary and sexual assault, it didn't make any logical sense that they would find Maxwell guilty of murder. She felt awful. Rachel had never felt this defeated before. When she had lost cases in the past, there had been some type of evidence or connection that gave the jurors a reason to convict. That wasn't the case here. There was literally zero evidence that pointed to Maxwell Williams committing the crime.

"I think you should go home," Rachel finally said. "I need to be alone."

"No. I am not leaving you like this. We can talk this through and figure out what to do next," Jason said reassuringly.

"No!" Rachel almost yelled, and it caught Jason off guard. "Just get out!"

"What? Why are you acting like this toward me?" Jason asked, feeling himself get angry.

"I don't want to talk about it, and I don't want you here."

"I am not the enemy here," Jason shot back, his confusion, anger, and sadness for Maxwell getting the best of him. He finally couldn't hold it in any longer and said, "This is not my fault. If anything, it is yours." The moment that came out, he regretted it. This wasn't going to help the situation.

Rachel looked at him in disbelief. She stormed off to her room and slammed the door. Jason thought about going after her to apologize, but thought better of it. They both needed some time to cool down. He walked out the door and went home. Rachel sat in her room sobbing, telling herself that what Jason said was true and that that was what he thought of her now. Was this case going to end things for them? Was their relationship going to be collateral damage of the verdict?

That night, Jason sent Rachel a text apologizing for what he said. He explained that he hadn't meant it and had just been upset and confused about events and her reaction to them. She didn't respond until the next day. All she said was that she understood. The two of them didn't talk at all the next few days, outside of a few "good morning" and "goodnight" texts. Jason could feel the relationship dwindling. He didn't want that to happen. No matter what the outcome of the trial, it wasn't supposed to affect their relationship.

A few days after the verdict, Jason went to visit Maxwell alone.

He walked into the attorney meeting room and waited for the guard to bring him in. Once Maxwell was seated and handcuffed to the table, he looked up at Jason. "Did she make a mistake by getting the jury instructions added?" His eyes locked onto Jason.

Jason couldn't pull his gaze away from Maxwell's as he honestly said, "I don't know."

Maxwell's head fell. "I really believed in you guys. I still appreciate everything. I really do. It is just..." He paused, collecting his thoughts. "It is just so damn hard to be happy with the outcome, or hopeful about the next steps to come."

"I get it," was all that Jason could say. "I am disappointed too. Disappointed isn't even a strong enough word to describe what I am feeling. It truly doesn't make sense. I don't think it even makes sense procedurally."

"What do you mean, procedurally?" Maxwell asked.

"Well, I don't know for sure, because Rachel won't talk to me or answer my questions about it," Jason admitted.

"What? What do you mean? The two of you haven't talked about it? Is she just giving up on me now?" Maxwell asked, his voice rising with anger.

"No. We are not giving up on you. I am not giving up on you. Like we talked about, I am just a volunteer. I don't practice this kind of law, so I don't know the ins and outs of it all. But I think that there may be some way to argue that the conviction can't stand as it is now."

"Well, where is Rachel? Why isn't she answering your questions?" Maxwell asked.

Jason looked down. "We were both upset after the verdict, and she reacted in a way that I wasn't expecting. I sort of said something that I shouldn't have, and she hasn't really talked to me since then."

"I am sorry, man," was all Maxwell could say, but honestly, he didn't know if he was sorry. He had just had all his hopes of getting out of this godforsaken place ripped away from him, and he wasn't sure if it was because of something Rachel did. He had bigger problems to worry about than the lawyers' relationship.

"Don't be. This is not on you," Jason said. "It's okay that she isn't here right now. We can't bring any motions until after the sentencing hearing anyway, so we can talk about that stuff later. I think it may be best if we all just take time to cool off and then meet up again in a few days to talk it all over."

"Yeah. I think you are right. I might say something that I don't want to if we talk too soon. I am just so upset, man. I don't know what to do with all of this anger. I know it shouldn't be directed at you or Rachel, but I just don't know."

Jason nodded. "I understand. This whole thing is messed up. It doesn't make any sense. I don't blame you for being mad, or blaming me and Rachel." It seemed like everything had been said at that point, and it was time for Jason to leave. "How about Rachel and I come in three days, and we can all talk then? Maybe we can both get our questions answered and come up with a game plan?"

"That sounds good," Maxwell said. "I will be here." His face fell.

Jason left the jail and tried to call Rachel. There was no answer on her cell. He tried to call her work phone, and again there was no answer. He finally called Dylan Franks, who informed Jason that Rachel hadn't been into the office yet. He was a little concerned about her. Jason decided that Rachel wasn't ready to talk to him yet, so he went back to work and let her reach out to him. He sent her a text saying he had just met with Maxwell and told him that they would both be seeing him again in three days.

Rachel didn't respond until later that night, and all she sent was a thumbs-up emoji. Jason felt himself getting hot when he looked at the message. He felt like this reaction from her was unfair. She wasn't the one who was sitting in a jail cell because of the verdict. Maxwell had questions, Jason had questions, and she was the one who could answer them. It didn't seem fair to him that she was throwing a pity party for herself and shutting out the world. He pushed those feelings aside and tried to focus on work.

CHAPTER THIRTY-SEVEN

Jason and Rachel sat waiting for Maxwell to be brought into the meeting room. Rachel was fidgeting with her hands and couldn't control her nerves. She was dreading this meeting, not wanting to face Maxwell and the anger she expected him to be carrying toward her. She couldn't blame him. Maxwell came in and sat down. He didn't have the same anger on his face that he'd had days earlier, when Jason had visited. He looked almost numb to the world around him.

Maxwell didn't say anything, and Rachel finally said, "I am so sorry, Maxwell. I am replaying every second, every decision that I made during the trial. I feel responsible."

"I have thought a lot about it in the last few days, since meeting with Jason. I still think you did an amazing job. I think the real blame lies with the jury, the prosecutor, and the police who screwed this thing up in the first place. You did the best you could with the hand you were dealt." He paused. "I don't blame you. Either of you."

Rachel lost it. The tears streaming down her face, she said, "But it is my fault. I shouldn't have brought up the defense; I should have made sure we subpoenaed Jesus ourselves. It is my fault."

Maxwell said, "Hey. Look at me." Rachel looked up at him, her mascara running down her face. Her eyes were already swollen and red from the crying that must have occurred over the last few days. Maxwell continued, "This is not your fault. I don't blame you. It was always a long shot that I would be found not guilty. The system is against guys that look like me. It is what it is. I have accepted it and want to move on to what we do next." He gestured toward Jason. "He thought maybe there was something procedurally wrong that we could challenge?"

Rachel nodded her head. "Yes. Procedurally, it doesn't make sense that they convicted you based on the defense to first-degree murder. They would have had to convict you of first-degree murder, but state that they believed that it was a crime of passion. At that point, the defense would kick in and the verdict would be downgraded to a second-degree murder conviction. Maybe they were just confused, or the jury instructions didn't read as clearly as they should have. Regardless, I think we have a good chance of getting a reconsideration."

"What's that mean?" Maxwell asked.

"We can ask the judge to reconsider the verdict based on the fact that the outcome of the trial doesn't make sense, legally or procedurally," Rachel explained.

"And we do that when?" Maxwell asked.

"We would do that after the sentencing hearing."

"Okay. Well, in the meantime, what is the worst-case scenario at sentencing?"

"I honestly don't know," Rachel admitted. "I have been thinking through it and rereading the sentencing guidelines. I don't know what the judge will do with sentencing, since the verdict doesn't make sense."

Maxwell sighed. "Well, I guess we just have to wait and see."

They were all back in the courtroom preparing for sentencing. They all stood, and the judge came back into the courtroom. He sat down and put his glasses on. "We are back on the record in *State of Minnesota v. Maxwell James Williams*. The jury has come back with a verdict of not guilty for counts I through III, and a verdict of guilty on Count IV, murder in the second degree. Count IV was added as an amended charge, as well as a defense to the charge of first-degree murder, after a decision by the court that the State's opening statement opened up an argument for a heat of passion defense.

"If we are being honest, I was unsure whether to allow the jury instruction for the defense and amendment. At no point was the defense making a heat of passion argument, and if the prosecutor had not made what I would categorize as a misstatement in his opening statement, we might not have arrived where we are right now. I have been wondering if we may have confused the jurors in our presentation of the jury instructions and questionnaire. Unfortunately, we cannot go back and fix that now. The jury has the ultimate decision-making power, and they have made their decision.

"The problem I have with that decision is that I do not believe it can be supported by legal analysis. Frankly, I believe that the defense would win on any appeals that they might bring. I may even grant a motion to reconsider, if one is brought. After proceeding with sentencing today, I will allow any additional motions to be filed for consideration, if there be any. Before we start sentencing, are there any questions?"

"No," both attorneys said in unison.

"Okay. Ms. Nix, do you have anything to put on the record in regard to sentencing?"

"Yes, Your Honor. I agree with you that the jury instructions may not have been clear. It does not make sense that the jurors came to the conclusion that they did, and my intention would be to bring a motion to reconsider after the sentencing today. The evidence does not add up to proof beyond a reasonable doubt. In fact, it heavily suggests that the crime was committed by another person or persons.

"Maxwell Williams has already been sitting in prison for the last forty years for a crime that he didn't commit. I know that is not lost on the court, but it does need to be mentioned. I am asking the court to be cognizant of that fact as they make their ruling on sentencing." Rachel paused, and then finished with, "Thank you, Your Honor." She sat back down.

"Mr. Williams. Do you have anything you would like to say to the court?"

"Yes, Your Honor." He stood. "Your Honor, I didn't do this, sir. I did not kill Amelia. I loved her so much. I am still in shock that this nightmare is continuing. I don't necessarily understand it all, and I am not sure I get what these motions you are talking about mean. I know I can talk with Ms. Nix about that more when the time comes. I guess, sir, I'm really just asking for you to have mercy on me. I have already sat in prison for more than half of my life for something that I didn't do. This system has not been fair to me, and I just hope that you can see that and make the right decision today, Your Honor. Thank you." He sat back down.

"Mr. Malone?" the judge asked.

"I have no comments, Your Honor."

"Very well," the judge said. "Mr. Williams, will you please rise?" Maxwell and his two attorneys stood up. "Mr. Williams, the jury has found you guilty of second-degree murder of Amelia Jackson. As I stated before, I do not believe that they can legally make that determination based on their other verdicts. However, I must abide by their verdict. The crime you are convicted of carries a maximum sentence of twenty years in jail."

He looked down at his notes. "Mr. Williams, you have spent more than 480 months in prison. You are hereby sentenced to 240 months in prison. You will receive credit for good time, making your actual sentence 160 months. You are given credit for time served of 480 months, which will leave you with no additional time to serve. Based on your additional time served, I am not requiring you to serve any probation on this matter."

The judge paused and looked at the people in front of him in turn. Jeff Malone was still seated and taking notes feverishly. Jason Michelson and Rachel Nix were looking at him with their mouths wide open. They were clearly following what the judge had just done. Maxwell Williams stood there, a confused look on his face. He was clearly not following what was going on.

The judge smiled at him. "Mr. Williams, do you understand what that means?"

Maxwell shook his head. "I don't think so, sir, no."

The judge's smile grew wider. "Well, sir, that means you are free to go. I am finding that the time you have already served is more than enough, based on the facts and the evidence that has been presented here."

"What?" Maxwell said, as tears started to fill his eyes again. "I am free to go? Like I don't have to go back to prison?"

"You will need to be processed out of the county jail, which will take a few hours, but after that you are a free man." Maxwell lost it and began to sob. Jason had to hold him up so he didn't fall. He turned and hugged his mom, who had been in the gallery every second since day two of the trial.

The judge continued, "I believe that there are ample grounds for your attorneys to bring a motion to get this conviction reconsidered. If the court grants the motion, there is a chance that the verdict may be overturned altogether. I cannot guarantee that, but it is a possibility. I can guarantee you, though, Mr. Williams, that you will not serve any additional time for the charges in this case. I wish you the best of luck."

With that, the judge adjourned the court, got up and left. Jason,

Rachel, and Maxwell all sat down and tried to process everything. Jeff and Mia gathered their things and went to exit the courtroom. Jeff stopped. "Congratulations, Mr. Williams," he said. Then, to Rachel, "Let me know if you are proceeding with post-trial motions." Rachel just nodded, and Jeff left.

Maxwell, Rachel, and Jason went to a conference room to talk for a few minutes. Rachel explained to Maxwell how being processed out of the county jail would work. Jason and Rachel would be there to meet him once he was out. They would go and talk about everything at the office after that. Maxwell left with the bailiff.

Three hours later, Maxwell Williams was processed out of the jail, and he met Jason and Rachel outside in the lobby. They all shared long hugs and made their way out to the parking lot. Maxwell stopped and took it all in. This was the first time he had been outside of the prison in more than forty years. There was no chance of him going back. He took a deep breath of the fresh air and looked all around him. A big smile came across his face. It was the first real smile that Rachel and Jason had seen from him. It made them both smile too. The two of them had talked out their issues and made up while they were waiting for Maxwell to be released. They were back on good terms, and it seemed like their relationship was going to be just fine.

They walked to Jason's car, and they all got in. The Exoneration Project had programs to assist people when they got out of prison and needed help getting back on their feet. The three of them went out to dinner at Red Robin and had a mini celebration. It didn't seem like they should be celebrating because the jury had still found him guilty erroneously, but Maxwell was out of jail and that was something to celebrate. They were driving to the hotel where Maxwell was going to be staying when he said, "I don't want you to do any motions or appeals."

Rachel was surprised and looked at him. "What do you mean?

You could have the verdict overturned completely. They could expunge your record."

"I understand that," Maxwell said. "I just want this case to be over. I am out free now. I don't want to spend any more time fighting. This case has taken forty years from me. I don't want to let it take any more. I want to move on with my life." Maxwell was calm and it seemed like he had made up his mind.

"Don't you want to prove that you didn't do it? If it's still on your record, it could cause you other issues. Like if you get arrested for something, or it might prevent you from getting a job," Jason said, concern in his voice.

"I understand all of that. I have made my decision. I don't want to pursue it any further. Nothing we do is going to make a difference. The system is unjust, and I am just one person. I have come to the conclusion that I cannot change that. You are not going to change my mind on this."

Rachel and Jason decided to stop pushing. It was up to Maxwell, and if he didn't want to do anything further, that was his choice. They needed his cooperation and permission to bring any motions or appeals. Rachel finally said, "I understand, Maxwell. Please let me know if you change your mind." She planned on trying to convince him again later on. She wanted this conviction overturned.

"I won't," was all Maxwell said. The three drove in silence the last few miles to the hotel. Maxwell said his thanks and hugged the others once more before he walked into the hotel. He would be going in to meet with Rachel the next day to go over the next steps on how the Exoneration Project programs could help him.

Jason drove back to Rachel's apartment, and they both went inside. They talked through everything again to make sure that they were both on the same page with things. Rachel told Jason that she was going to push and see if she could get Maxwell to agree to let her bring the motion for reconsideration. Jason agreed that it was a good idea. They talked again about how messy this all was and how they couldn't believe what had happened. They finally decided to go to bed, both of them reflecting on the deep flaws that cases like this exposed in the American judicial system.

CHAPTER THIRTY-EIGHT

The next few days were a blur as Rachel helped Maxwell get through the next steps of his reintegration into society. Jason was pulling all-nighters at the office to try to catch up on the work that he had missed. In the week following Maxwell's release, Rachel and Jason only managed one dinner together and didn't see each other otherwise. They still both felt like they had failed Maxwell, and could have done more. They were still talking, though, they were still together, and their relationship was going to survive this mess.

Maxwell finally agreed to let Rachel bring the motion for reconsideration. She had explained in detail what it would mean if the judge overturned the verdict. It would be like he was never convicted in the first place in the eyes of the law. Part of what swayed Maxwell was that if the judge denied the motion, there would be no appeal. Rachel could understand where he was coming from, and agreed that she would let it go after that. She was feeling good about their chances, though.

It was Friday now, and Emily Cruze's company was finally going public. It was a huge day for Emily and her company, but also a big day for Jason as her attorney. This was going to make the firm a lot of money and solidify Jason's position as the newest junior partner.

Jason and Amy were at Emily's corporate office at 7:45 that morning so they could be there as the company went public. They had a countdown, and once it was time and the company was public, there was confetti shot and a balloon drop. They all celebrated and there were hugs all around. This was a big day and Jason should have felt excited, not only for Emily, but for his future at the firm. But he was finding it hard to shake the fog that he had been in since the verdict was read in the Maxwell Williams case. There was just so much that he couldn't wrap his head around. He was replaying everything that he had done in the case and thinking how he could have messed something up. He had to find a way to let it all go.

Emily was hosting a party that night to celebrate, and Jason promised that he and Rachel would make an appearance. He made sure at every possible opportunity to mention that he was seeing Rachel. This was intended to be a constant reminder to Emily that nothing could ever happen between them. Emily had been respecting the boundaries that had been set regarding the two of them, and Jason was thankful for that.

Overall, things between Rachel and Jason were going well. They had spent a lot of time together leading up to the trial. The verdict had taken a toll on them, and they hadn't talked much since then, but they were both busy catching up on work. They had talked through the things that had happened right after the verdict and had both moved on from the things that were said. They were going to be together that night to go to Emily's party. Then, they had a weekend getaway planned. They had rented an Airbnb a few hours away. They just needed some time away from work, from the Twin Cities, and from the long few weeks they had just endured.

The rest of Friday flew by and before Jason knew it, it was 5:45 p.m. Amy came into his office. "What time are you heading to Emily's party? I think I am going to stop by for a little while."

Jason looked up at his clock. "I think Rachel and I were planning on heading over that way around 7 p.m. I have a few things to finish up here, and she is finishing organizing some files from the trial."

"Okay. I will plan on getting there at the same time, then. Do you need anything else from me before I go?"

"No, I think I am good. Thanks, Amy. We will see you in a bit."

Jason went back to what he was working on. He could feel that Amy was still there. He looked up, and she was staring back at him. "What?" he asked.

"You know you guys did everything that you could, right? Sometimes people just make the wrong decision. The most important thing is that Maxwell is free and can move on with his life."

Jason sighed. "I know. I just wish it would have been a different outcome. It should have been. It just isn't fair."

"Don't beat yourself up. There will be plenty more cases and people to help. It could have been a much worse outcome for Maxwell, and he could have spent the rest of his life in prison. He is out, thanks to you and Rachel. That is a win," Amy said, and she gave him a smile. "You did good, Jason."

He smiled back at her. "Thanks, Amy. What would I do without you?"

"You would be screwed. So don't ever think about getting rid of me," she joked.

"I would never imagine it," Jason said with a laugh.

"All right. I will see you there. Don't work too hard." Amy walked out of his office and then called back, "Don't forget to finish up your pro bono hours sheet."

"I will do it tonight. Thanks!" he called after her.

Jason worked for another hour and then his phone rang. He looked, and it was Rachel. "Hey. I am just finishing up. Are you here?"

"Yeah. I am just pulling in. How much do you have left? Do you want me to come up?"

"No. I just have one thing to finish and then I will be right down. Just park in my spot, and I will meet you there." Jason had Ubered in to work that day so that they only had one car to bring to Emily's party. It also allowed Jason a little more time to get work done before they went.

He put down what he was working on and opened his pro bono tracking Word document on his desktop. He put in the last few days of trial and totaled up the hours. He had spent 104 hours in 2022 working on the Maxwell Williams case. That, in addition to his 116 hours in 2021, made a total of 220 hours that Jason had put into the case, from the beginning research through the jury verdict. He reflected on that time and all the things he had learned.

There were sections in the document for how many hours were worked on the project each month, what the project was, and a brief description, and then there was a section for comments. Having put in the total number of hours, Jason put "*State v. Williams*" as the project name. For the brief description, he wrote, "New Trial." After he typed that description, his phone pinged. Rachel was wondering where he was. He packed up his things to go. He was considering what to put in the comments section. It came to him. He turned off everything else in his office and got ready to go. He sat down to type his notes before he left. He decided on three words to sum up his work on the Williams case. It was something Maxwell had said during the trial.

Under the comments heading he typed, "The Unjust System." He saved the document and shut down his computer for the weekend. He smiled to himself, finally coming to terms with the outcome of the case. Jason had helped make a difference in Maxwell's life, and that was something to celebrate. Rachel had convinced him to bring a motion for reconsideration, and the judge could overturn the new verdict completely and expunge the charges from Maxwell's record. It was going to be okay. He turned off his last light and rode the elevators down to meet Rachel in his parking spot.

He got in the car and gave her a big smile. He leaned over and kissed her. "I love you, Rachel Nix."

Rachel looked back at him and smiled. "I love you too. What's gotten into you?"

"I just realized that even though we didn't get everything we wanted, we got Maxwell out of prison, and his life is forever changed. *We* did that." He smiled again.

Rachel smiled back at him, seeing it the way that he did. They both were going to be able to move on from this. They had to. There was always more work to do. Rachel already had five other cases on her desk for consideration. There was always another wrongfully convicted person sitting in prison who could use help from the Exoneration Project.

"You think you could help me on another case some time? You have a knack for criminal law," Rachel teased.

"I think I will need a little break. I do need at least 100 pro bono hours each year, though. Do you think you could pencil me in for one case a year?" he asked.

"I think I can do that. I could use all the help I can get." Rachel reached over and grabbed Jason's hand. He squeezed it and pulled it up to his lips. He kissed Rachel's hand softly and then rested it back on top of the center console. They listened to the radio as they drove over to Emily's office. When they got there, they parked and walked into the party, holding hands. There was a lot to celebrate that night.

ACKNOWLEDGMENTS

I would like to start by thanking The Innocence Project for all of the amazing work that they do for those wrongly incarcerated. Their work is what inspired the topic in this book, and I hope to shed light on them as an organization. I want to thank my criminal justice professors from St. Cloud State University that first introduced me to The Innocence Project and their mission.

I want to thank Nicole Reger for offering to be my first beta reader and giving me such helpful feedback and changes. The book would not have been the same without her assistance and edits.

I owe a huge gratitude to my publishing team at Wise Ink especially Amy Quale for believing in my book before I even knew if I wanted to publish it. Thank you to my coach Crown Shepherd, my marketing director Hanna Kjeldbjerg, my manuscript editor Ariana Benson, and my cover designer Emily Mahon. The end result of *Unjust* would not have been the same without each and every one of you and I appreciate you all more than I can explain.

Thank you to my husband, Dylan Holmes, for supporting me through this process and giving me the time to work on writing and publishing the book. Your patience and support have been greatly appreciated and I am so lucky to have such a great man to go through life with.

Thank you to my mom, Laurie Bednarczyk, for instilling in me at such a young age the importance of reading. Thank you to both her and my dad, Tom Bednarczyk, for their love and support and for always pushing me to accomplish more in my life. Thank you both for teaching me a great work ethic and that I can do anything that I set my mind to.

Lastly, I want to thank Allen Eskens for being my literary inspiration and being the reason that I decided to pursue my dream of writing a book in the first place. After reading all your books and hearing how your background in the legal field was similar to mine, it gave me the courage to start this project. I aspire to be even a fraction as successful as you have become.

ABOUT THE AUTHOR

Brooke Holmes, J.D., a Minnesota litigation attorney, brings realistic true crime aspects to her debut legal thriller. She was born and raised in Forest Lake, Minnesota, and currently lives in New Prague with her growing family. She is a Partner Attorney practicing in criminal defense and family law, who was awarded Minnesota Attorney of the Year for 2021. She received her Bachelor of Science degree in Criminal Justice where her love for criminal law blossomed and led to her to the legal career that she enjoys now. Brooke hopes that *Unjust* and the rest of the series to come will educate people about realities and shortcomings of the American Judicial System.

Made in the USA
Monee, IL
22 August 2023

41444920R00184